**Also available from Anna Richland
and Carina Press**

HIS ROAD HOME

Coming in January 2015

THE SECOND LIE

FIRST TO BURN

ANNA RICHLAND

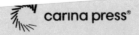

carina press®

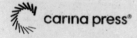

carina press®

ISBN-13: 978-0-373-00254-2

First to Burn

Copyright © 2014 by Anna Richland

www.AnnaRichland.com

Recycling programs
for this product may
not exist in your area.

www.CarinaPress.com

Printed in U.S.A.

Dear Reader,

Inspiration comes for all of us from unexpected places, whether it's a quilt inspired by trees in a yard or a new recipe inspired by leftover turkey. I discovered Wulf, the hero of *First to Burn*, while reading an illustrated version of the *Beowulf* epic. That picture book took hold of my imagination and grew into the Immortal Vikings series.

As a reader, I don't usually think of paranormals when I think of family stories. However, as I wrote Wulf and Theresa's story, I realized family was at the root of almost every element: Theresa's need to build a life independent from her family; Wulf's anger at his brother, but his love, too, for the only person in the world who shares the memory of their mother; and Wulf's devotion to his special operations teammates, men who make another family.

Wulf is especially close to the other bachelor on the team, his friend Cruz. After I finished writing *First to Burn*, Cruz insisted he was ready to find a love as special as Wulf and Theresa's. If you want to know how he finally stops chasing the wrong type of woman, his novella will be published by Carina Press in October 2014.

I hope you enjoy the mix of paranormal, military and suspense I've conceived for my Vikings in *First to Burn*. For more information about my books, please visit my website (www.annarichland.com), where I have photos from several of the locations in my stories and peeks at upcoming releases.

Thank you,

Anna Richland

Acknowledgments

I became a writer on my own. I became a published writer because of Greater Seattle Romance Writers of America and its annual Emerald City Writers' Conference.

I could not possibly name everyone in my chapter who has helped me, but any list would start with Anna Alexander, Julie Brannagh, Eilis (and Mike) Flynn, Josie Malone and Shelli Stevens. Thank you also to the Starcatchers cheering section of the 2011 Romance Writers of America Golden Heart Finalists, especially Julie Brannagh, Amy Raby and Rachel Grant. Thank you!

I relied upon the website Beowulf on Steorarume (Beowulf in Cyberspace) by Dr. Benjamin Slade at www.heorot.dk for the Old English in Chapter 24. I also read *Beowulf: An Illustrated Edition*, translated by Seamus Heaney, edited and illustrated by John D. Niles (W.W. Norton and Company, 2007) until the binding died. All correct references to the epic are possible because of these experts. Errors are possible because of me. For other research, I went straight to the internet's Viking Answer Lady.

Several doctors provided invaluable help: Dr. Naomi Sullivan, who shared poster slogans and was never the weak link in any chain, army or otherwise; Dr. Stephen Buetow, the first Afghanistan veteran to read this; Dr. Crista McHugh, fellow romance writer and explainer of fainting; Dr. Elizabeth Moynihan, fellow college romance reader and explainer of symbiotic microbes; and Dr. Josh LaBaer, who figured out why my Vikings need Grendel's bones. Thank you all!

FIRST
TO BURN

Dedication

The cast of characters who help an author with a first novel is immense, but three people have been so important to this journey that I dedicate *First to Burn* to them.

First, my husband. He has supported my pursuit of publication for the last eight years. Once upon a time I shared one of my deepest fantasies with him. I told him that when both children entered school full-time, I intended to reorganize every closet, drawer and cupboard in our house. The obvious disbelief on his face annoyed me, until he explained, "I know you can be very organized, but you'll have a three-book deal by then and life will be crazier than it is now."

Second, Brenda Novak. As part of her *Annual Online Auction for Diabetes Research*, she selected *First to Burn*—and me—to mentor in 2010. She invested her time, energy and enthusiasm in a complete stranger, merely because she made a commitment. Brenda taught me to place my characters in their settings, to slow down where necessary and to really look at what my characters saw. As an unpublished writer, I struggled to be as consistent as Brenda, but she never failed. It will require a long career to live up to the example Brenda set.

Third, nothing I have written would be readable without my friend Mary. She's read *First to Burn* almost as many times as I have, told me straight-out when characters whined or when scenes had no point except cute. I can call her anytime and talk through writing quandaries, or I can say "I have to write" and she's not insulted. Mary, there should be a commemorative plaque at the housing office where we met!

Chapter One

WULF CLAWED A path to consciousness, embracing the grinding pain in his left leg as a sign that he'd emerged from oblivion, until the engine whine and floor vibrations warned him of a problem worse than his injury. He was trapped in the second most dangerous place in Afghanistan for a man like him: a U.S. Army medevac helicopter.

"Easy, Sergeant." The flight medic who leaned into view squeezed a bag connected to the mask covering Wulf's mouth. "You're safe."

While oxygen inflated Wulf's lungs, a functioning corner of his brain demanded answers. His commander would never call an evacuation chopper for him, so who else had been hurt? Struggling against the painkillers, he tried to remember everyone's last positions. Kahananui had been on his right. *He has two little girls.* Five meters ahead, Cruz had taken point. Was it Cruz? *He pays for his mother's diabetes drugs.*

Wulf tried to turn his head and search for his teammates, but he couldn't move. He tensed his abs and lower back and jerked to lift his shoulders, but again he couldn't move. The certainty that one of his men needed him struck like a spear between his ribs, but no matter how he strained his arms and chest, he could not move. Not his arms, not his body, and by the gods, not his legs, despite the agony that intensified in his left one as the painkillers faded.

"Stop fighting, Sarge." The medic was young, mid-twenties at most, but his voice carried over the chopper racket with the confidence shared by those who served in aviation.

Free of morphine fog, Wulf understood he wasn't paralyzed, only slapped into a neck collar and strapped to a stretcher, complications that, like his injuries, weren't insurmountable. But his teammates couldn't conquer wounds so easily. "Whoshhurt?"

"I know it hurts, man. We're eighteen minutes out from Camp Caddie, so hang on."

Dammit, the medic didn't understand him through the oxygen mask. He needed to see *who* was in this helicopter. Not knowing compressed his chest until he groaned.

"This will help the pain." One of the man's hands reached for something outside Wulf's circle of vision.

Skīta. He didn't want the guy to up the intravenous dope before he could discover who'd been hurt. The last thing he remembered was freezing in place when the team's German shepherd had hunkered in a bomb-alert position in the middle of an apricot orchard.

Like their dog Garbo, they'd stopped. All, that is, except an Afghan training with them who'd been distracted by lighting a cigarette and had moved forward two more paces. The blast had thrown Garbo against a stone wall. Rocks, dirt clods and metal packed around the improvised explosive device had pounded Wulf's helmet and body armor, mangling his leg. *Fucking smoker. Could've killed us.*

This time Wulf spaced his words as carefully as sniper shots. "Who. Else. Hurt."

The medic's eyes flickered to the port side of the Black Hawk helicopter. "Two Afghans. At least one's not going to make it. And your dog."

Relief that he'd been swept up with an evacuation of Afghan National Army soldiers, not one of his own men, crested with the newest wave of meds. Temporarily woozy, he slurred his next question, *howshGarbo*, but this time the medic understood.

"Ear and head lacerations, possible broken leg, but the pooch armor did its job."

His system processed this smaller dose faster than the earlier morphine, providing only minutes of peace before the torment of growing fresh bone, a torture he imagined to be comparable to a drill bit tunneling through his shin, crested.

Locking his jaw stifled his groan, but barely. He hadn't endured a lost leg since Antietam. He'd forgotten. "Hurts."

"More?" The medic calculated with his fingers. "Sergeant, you have more pure in you than Keith Richards." Eyebrows lost in the top of his helmet, he shook his head. "Can't believe you're lucid."

This agony blended with memories of a September afternoon in high corn, moaning next to other Union volunteers as blood-frenzied flies circled. His pain had been caused by healing. Theirs, by dying. When he'd recovered enough to carry his unit's drummer off the field, the ten-year-old's eyes had no longer blinked at the sun. Some hurts were worse than regrowing bones, took longer to mend. At least today he didn't face such a loss.

Instead, he gritted his teeth, concentrated on the pain of his nails digging into his fisted palms and planned. Without being able to test his strength or see his leg, he wouldn't know the extent of his progress until the itching started. Didn't matter. The moment the flight medic transferred him to someone who hadn't seen his original injury and the straps were unbuckled, he'd walk away. He'd done it other times. He had to be ready because under no circumstances could he end up in the most dangerous place for an immortal soldier: a hospital.

"A TRANSTIBIAL WITH HEMORRHAGING!" The rage in her chief surgeon's voice as he yelled at someone on the other side of the camouflage netting froze Captain Theresa Chiesa. Past the curtain was Camp Cadwalader's emergency receiving. On this side, three surgical pods showed no signs of recent patients, and definitely not evidence of a soldier with a below-the-knee amputation and a big bleed. "Are you the one who called that shit in? What were—"

"Yessir, I reported the sergeant's injuries."

Whoever the other voice belonged to, he had balls to interrupt Colonel Loughrey. Nobody on the fifty-person combat hospital staff interrupted the boss. Not if they wanted to leave Afghanistan with their army careers intact.

"Well, Tinker Bell, lay off the fucking morphine. Your call mixed up the dead Afghan and a soldier with a two-inch incision on his fucking calf! Our guy didn't even have a fucking concussion!" Something metallic banged, then crashed to the floor. It wouldn't be the first time her colonel had kicked a folding chair or a rolling cart. "Wardsen put on his own butterfly strips before he waltzed out."

Wardsen. That name was familiar. She flicked through the papers in her hand, orphans she'd gathered from random shelves and desks in the medical office. Filing wasn't an officer's job, and other doctors actively shirked administrative tasks, but she hated messy documentation. In a place as isolated as Camp Cadwalader, filing and labeling medical records as directed by Army Regulation 40-66 beat watching dust dry. Despite searching for half an hour, she hadn't found any intake forms, charts, discharge records or follow-up notes to match the two inbound medevac calls about Staff Sergeant Wulf Wardsen, Operational Detachment Alpha-5131, 5th Special Forces Group. It was as if he'd walked off the helicopter into the sunset both times.

"Sir, I assessed him in-flight—" The voice contradicting Colonel Loughrey belonged to a flight medic. She'd wager her silver captain's bars that the new total of incoming without follow-up was three. What was going on?

"Assessment! Piece of shit. Shitty as a latrine. Shitty as this whole fucking war! Sh-iii-t." Her commander worked the word. Six months into the hospital team's yearlong deployment, some doctors had begun smoking to relieve stress. Others had succumbed to profanity, none more than the colonel.

"Sir, I don't understand." The medic's rising voice sounded confused, and she stepped closer to the curtain to listen. "Wardsen's leg was fully opened. I held the bone—"

"What you held was your own dick."

Theresa respected the pilots and medics who brought out the wounded—a riskier job than hers. Whatever problem had the boss worked up, she doubted the fault was medevac's. Three bad calls could only be Special Forces covering for something, or for someone. They might be the toughest guys on the planet, but they shouldn't be allowed to mess up hardworking troops like this medic.

"I won't have my staff pulled off other soldiers—ones with real fucking injuries—or the night shift woken up from sleep—for your piece-of-shit calls."

She evaluated the loose papers in her hand. Her commander was a surgeon, and that meant his picture popped up when someone searched for the word *perfectionist*. At the best of times, he detested incomplete data and vague conclusions. Right now she suspected he wouldn't like anything less than a ticket home.

"Fuck up again and I will personally see you grounded." Colonel Loughrey would, but not out of vindictiveness. Out of concern that incompetence would kill someone. He printed the name of every soldier they hadn't saved on an index card he carried inside his helmet. Last week she'd seen him write the first name on the back. He was a good man, and a good leader, but he was wrong to blame the flight medic. Something bigger was going on, something that seemed to have happened before, although she didn't know what. The name Wardsen was her first clue.

As silently as combat boots allowed, she retreated. She'd meet with the big guy when she had more answers. This afternoon she had only questions.

Chapter Two

THERESA HATED TREADMILLS, gym rats and clanging weights. She hated to stretch in front of half the American soldiers in Paktia Province, their eyes all over her, but this was Tuesday, when she didn't have the luxury of a solitary four miles at dawn around the airfield's dirt track. On Tuesdays, she warmed the doctor seat at the 0600 briefing before her clinic shift. If she ran outside now, the eighty-plus-degree May afternoon would drop her like an aneurysm. At her normal duty station in Fort Hood, she could endure the Texas swelter, but Camp Cadwalader's elevation seemed to add an insurmountable layer to the heat. Preferring to survive the second half of her deployment, on Tuesdays she thumped the treadmill in the air-conditioned gym.

"Hey." Her roommate stepped on the next machine. "Finally finished the M and M." Responsibility for the weekly morbidity and mortality report rotated among the four captains in the medical unit.

Theresa punched the button to decrease her speed enough to talk. Since the acoustics sucked in the converted Soviet warehouse, she also raised her voice. "Tough?"

"More missing paperwork."

"The same?" After eavesdropping on Colonel Loughrey's blowup last week, she'd told Jennifer about the pattern with Staff Sergeant Wardsen. Only four hundred twenty permanent parties crammed into this camp, but neither of them could find Wardsen.

"Yeah." The second treadmill reached speed and they matched strides. "Inbound medevac call. Projectile penetration, a by-the-book gunshot wound, but nobody showed. Nada."

"Think he exists?" Maybe Wardsen was a fictitious name Special Ops used for cover-ups or to treat anonymous CIA spooks. No one could have wounds like medevac had reported for Sergeant Wardsen and keep walking away.

"Uh-huh." Jennifer entered a faster workout phase. "I think…SF guys…take paperwork…away." She panted up the incline. "Secrecy…freaks."

In her cooldown, Theresa could breathe and talk easier than her roommate could. "They're not allowed to do that." Her duties included coordinating patient care for soldiers moving between camps or leaving theater. If people removed their paperwork, follow-up care would disintegrate, an outcome she wouldn't accept.

"*You* tell them…what they can…can't do."

"If I can find them." Theresa stepped off her machine, plucked her towel from the safety rail and wiped her face to unstick strands of hair from her forehead and neck. Turning, she froze halfway through retrieving her water bottle from the floor.

Isn't that ironic. She and Jennifer had been griping about how hard it was to find men who were right behind them. Across the gym Captain Chris Deavers, commander of Special Forces Operational Detachment Alpha-5131, crunched out sit-ups on an inclined bench.

Jennifer punched a button to override the hill function and twisted to look. "Hellooo, girlfriend, now what are you cooking up?"

"I'm going to ask Chris about his sergeant." Straightening out this mess would take three or four simple questions. She aligned the corners of her towel.

"Chris?" Her friend's eyebrows arched.

"We're both captains. It's perfectly acceptable to use his name." She folded the towel into thirds lengthwise and draped it over her forearm.

Her roommate looked at the white fabric, then at her face. "So why are you stalling?"

"I know Chris, but the others…" Faded Cyrillic graffiti climbed the walls above the cheap mirrors that multiplied the dozen men lifting in the corner. Her first week at Caddie, a nurse had told her the Russian translated to "Trust your mother, shoot the rest," which fit the men surrounding Chris. Despite superficial differences in skin color and hair, they shared identically serious expressions. These men didn't trash-talk while they cranked out push-ups and pull-ups, and they were the only men who didn't stare when the Wonder Twins—two postal clerks from a Florida reserve unit rumored to be professional football cheerleaders in civilian life—did lunges. Their focus insulated them from the gym cacophony.

"Forget it." Jennifer broke into her thoughts. "Their super secret special ops voodoo isn't going to crack for you. What's a little missing paperwork?"

"They can't flout the rules any more than anyone else." Regardless of her stepfamily's choices, she'd always believed rules, like laws, should be obeyed. Entering the army had reinforced and rewarded that belief. She squared her shoulders and tossed her towel at Jen.

Her workout partner caught and twirled it. "Sure you won't need a white flag?"

"Not a chance." White flags were for bandages, not her. She wasn't a quitter, and she hadn't given up on anything since the day she'd joined Army ROTC and paid for Princeton without one cent of her stepfather's dirty money. After two years of her returning the envelopes of cash Carl and her mother left in her dorm, her family had accepted that she was going to make it on her own, completely legit. She could do this, easy as taking blood pressure.

Jennifer touched two fingers to her eyebrow in a mock salute. "I'll be here when you scurry home."

Interrupting their training might be a faux pas, like pushing aside a curtain before a patient fully disrobed, but it wasn't wrong. As she drew closer, she recognized a soldier she'd examined for concussion and temporary hearing loss after an explosion. *He* hadn't sneaked away with *his* paperwork. One man stood out, although she couldn't pinpoint the reason. Leaner than the others but well-muscled, he wasn't the shortest or the tallest. His dark blond hair almost curled on his neck, but the SF guys always pushed the army's grooming standards, often growing beards to blend with the Afghans.

When he returned her scrutiny across fifteen feet of empty mat, she understood why she'd noticed him. His eyes. Their blue depths carried burdens she could see from here. He appeared to be younger than her, but his stare spoke of losses no one should bear. She thought of the faces she'd seen during her residency ICU rotation, the expressions in the eyes of parents holding a dying child or the man kissing his wife as her ventilator was removed.

She bit her lip against the need to offer him a comforting touch. She had another purpose.

"Hey, Doc." Chris recovered from his sit-ups and jumped to his feet, wiping his palms on a towel. "What's up?" The captain's smile shined with Midwestern sun.

"I want to locate some forms for a soldier on your team." She took a deep breath and focused on Chris, ignoring the man with the devastated eyes and the others who crowded the mats. "A sergeant who was injured."

"Sergeant Jackson? He's great. Your people treated him well."

"Not Sergeant Jackson." She shook her head without looking away.

Although his smile barely shifted, Chris's welcome face closed with a nearly audible slam. None of his men moved. The packed mass didn't even seem to breathe.

"Nobody else was hurt this week." He lifted his towel to wipe his forehead as if nothing mattered, but veins popped in his neck. He wasn't as relaxed as he pretended.

"Look, today an inbound medevac radioed an incoming with penetration wounds, Staff Sergeant Wardsen." Her words hung between them. The wait seared her lungs, as if the air-conditioning had stopped, until she felt compelled to fill the silence. "We're missing his file." She could smell her own sweat despite the fully saturated tang of the gym. "Was he treated?"

"No."

The men beside Chris loomed larger as she turned to search each face. Their physical training uniforms didn't have name tapes, so she couldn't determine who among them was Wardsen. The dark blond with the tortured eyes shifted his weight, but a Polynesian-looking soldier shouldered into him.

She wanted to ask Chris for the real story, but the testosterone and stench clogged her throat. "Can we talk about this somewhere else?"

"No."

"What?" She struggled to keep her eyebrows from meeting over the bridge of her nose. She needed to project friendly and professional, and she didn't want to come off like a badgering fobbit, the stereotype of a forward-operating-base paper pusher. She worked up a smile. "Well?"

Chris shrugged. "Nothing to talk about." He bent to a barbell for a set of arm curls. "Dust-off made a mistake."

"Four times with the same soldier? And only *that* soldier? I don't believe it." Chris was concealing either who had been injured or how. But why? "I want to meet Sergeant Wardsen."

The dozen men blended into a pool of silence so thick, so viscous with disapproval and rejection, that she struggled to move. The answer hit like a fifty-pound weight— *friendly fire.* The other captain didn't make eye contact. "If that's all, Doc, we have our workout."

"Fine." A fellow officer had dismissed her in front of a pack of staring enlisted guys. Her cheeks burned and she could barely pry her lips far enough apart to speak, but if Chris wanted a pissing contest, she'd give him one. "You'll receive a written request from me tomorrow for the sergeant's treatment records."

"Classified." He grunted over another rep without facing her.

"Really? We'll see what Colonel Loughrey and I can do about that." She spun on her heel and stomped to Jennifer.

Her friend slowed the treadmill. "How'd it go?"

"Don't ask." Theresa grabbed a five-pound barbell and curled with gusto. The weight bounced off her upper arm. *Whoa, too hard.* She'd have a bruise.

"Didn't I tell you not to bug those guys? They don't talk to lesser mortals."

"You were right."

Jennifer tucked her chin and stared, eyebrows raised. "You *never* say that."

"To quote the boss, they're shitheads." She thunked the weight on the ground. She needed to get out of the gym. Now. "You can write that in stone."

THIRTY MINUTES LATER, draft memorandums requesting medical files danced in Theresa's head as she left the women's shower for the dining facility. After six months in-country, Theresa ranked the lavish mess hall food provided by Black and Swan contractors on par with cold med school pizza. Crispy shrimp, loaded burgers, and surf and turf were better than the chicken breasts she cooked, but she missed her empty apartment fridge in Texas. At least when she opened it after a night on call, the half-and-half carton and jar of olives were hers.

While she stopped at the dining hall entrance for the mandatory weapon safety check, a soldier exited and the cold burst of air-conditioning brought the promise of dinner. Tuesday's meal rotation included the one item she still desired: deep-fried chicken cordon bleu. She usually substituted salad for fries, but no monthly weigh-in could make her give up cordon bleu.

Inside the metal building, she headed for the hot line as the server slipped the last golden mound to the private in front of her. She hadn't run four miles on a treadmill for iceberg lettuce. "Excuse me, are there more?"

"Two minutes, ma'am."

A green tray slid behind hers on the line. "Are they bringing another pan?"

Theresa glanced at the speaker and froze. This close his eyes were as compelling as they had been across the gym, but now she could see brown-and-amber flecks around the iris—a rare combination that gave depth to the blue—and a star-shaped scar on his left temple that she hadn't cataloged earlier. She imagined he'd hit a corner of a board or rock and left it unstitched.

She broke the stare and read his name tape. *Wardsen.*

"You!" She studied his body. Feet planted firmly on the floor, weight distributed evenly without favoring a leg. His uniform pants stretched across his thighs and tapered down his calves to tuck into tan boots. Nothing in his posture hinted at a concealed injury. She raised her eyes to his chest, and he obligingly took a deep breath. The line of his shirt across his shoulders didn't appear to hide evidence of bandaging. When he'd been wearing less clothing in the gym, she hadn't seen bulky wrappings, but then she hadn't known he was the elusive Staff Sergeant Wulf Wardsen.

"Would you like to check my teeth?"

She snapped her gaze to his face and collided with his smile. It transformed him from a carving of a thunder god into a heartthrob.

"You give a thorough exam, Doc."

"You weren't shot!" Her heart rate notched up as she prepared for a second confrontation.

"Good to know." He lifted an eyebrow, its toffee color darker than his hair.

Her eyes narrowed. "Why did medevac report you?"

"I didn't realize they had."

"Then what are you hiding?" He must have overheard her exchange with Chris, but he wasn't making it easy to argue with him.

"Nothing." His smile didn't budge, his eyes didn't shift, his expression didn't flicker.

"I will find out what's going on." She focused on the small, steady beat at his neck. His skin didn't have the ruddy tone of most fair-colored people, as if the stones of Afghanistan had scoured away any hint of pink long ago. Blond hairs showed above the neck of his T-shirt. Unlike the rest of him, they looked silky soft. "The flight medic got reamed by my commander. Whatever you're up to, other people are paying for it, so knock it off."

"Understood." He nudged his tray until it touched hers. "Are you going to keep holding up the line?"

She turned her shoulder to cover her embarrassment. First she'd stared at him like he was a particularly succulent entrée, then she'd chewed him out. "I'm waiting for cordon bleu."

"That one?" He nodded at a plate sitting on the serving hood.

Grabbing it, she turned to the salad bar. As she piled lettuce and cherry tomatoes on her plate, the hair on her arms stood up, letting her know he'd lingered.

"Captain Chiesa." He put the correct Italian spin on her name, pronouncing the first sound like "key" instead of "chee."

She concentrated to avoid spilling salad dressing. Having him watch her made her hands not work the way she intended.

"About that misunderstanding in the gym."

"What misunderstanding?" She set the vinaigrette next to the other bottles. Her palms were slippery, but she didn't want to wipe her hands on her pants in front of him, so she gripped her tray and hoped it wouldn't drop.

"Captain Deavers came down a little hard." He looked at the floor as if struggling with how much to say. "I'm sorry. The team's sorry."

It sounded like a genuine *I'm sorry*, and her stomach muscles unclenched, the tension replaced by a feeling almost like the euphoria that came from eating dinner after having missed lunch. Sergeant Wardsen had apologized for the humiliation she'd felt talking to a bunch of men's rears.

"He's receiving rough email from his wife. She's not coping well alone with their new baby. He's worried she has…postpartum depression?" He said the words as if using a foreign language guidebook.

"Thank you for telling me." The awareness that Chris had bigger problems, and yet she'd hounded him about medical records, embarrassed her enough that she wanted to slink into a hole darker than Tora Bora. To be successful in private medical practice next year, she'd have to clue in better to patients' unspoken needs. "Maybe I can help?"

"Please. That would take a worry off the team's minds." Wulf suspected the doctor fulfilled her promises. The way she'd barreled across the gym for his paperwork told him she was determined, and the glare when she'd ordered him to stop involving flight medics in his team's escapades had rivaled desert heat. "Maybe you could be subtle?"

"You don't want your commander to know you talked to me?" Captain Chiesa spoke over her shoulder as she carried her tray to the beverage dispensers.

If he didn't want to shout loud enough for the guys

to hear, he had to follow the damp ponytail bouncing in front of him. She'd tucked her dark hair under and up in one of those styles used by female soldiers. It made some look like bobbed horses, but on her it highlighted her cheekbones and eyebrows. "The captain's a private guy."

Captain Chiesa rolled her eyes. "And I had the impression you were all over-sharers." Humor added cinnamon and cloves to her brown eyes, and the dimple that flashed in her cheek turned the steamroller into somebody's girl-next-door. But not his. He couldn't afford a soft spot for a woman.

"His wife's in charge of the family support group." If he prolonged the conversation, he might catch a whiff of her shampoo. Women's hair had mesmerized him since he had watched his mother plait her braids. "Might reflect badly with higher-ups if she can't hold it together."

"Can your wife help her?"

Centuries had blunted the ache of losing Zenobia enough that he didn't clench his fists or lock his jaw or betray with his eyes what that word had once meant. Instead he lifted his mouth in a half-assed smile. "If the army wanted me to have a wife, they'd issue one."

"I wasn't asking…" Her olive skin darkened at her cheekbones, broadcasting embarrassment with a color lighter than the angry flush she'd shown in the gym. "So, what post are you guys from? Maybe I know someone who—"

"Fort Campbell." He handed her a bottle of water to cut her off. She wouldn't like to be caught babbling. Bits of frizz softened the sharp widow's peak of her hairline, and he wanted to trace the heart-shape with his finger. Better to grip his tray. "The lieutenant's wife should be able to reach the captain's wife. Shall I get their emails from the LT?" He bit his tongue as she nodded. Now he was the babbler, because of some straying hair and the fact that she cared enough about people to jump in and help a flight medic. Damn. Even if army rules didn't prohibit touching to find out if those curls felt as soft as he suspected, he could never get close to a doctor. Faster than other women, she'd notice he was different.

"I'll remember your assistance." He withdrew two steps, a strategic retreat, but his stomach flipped as the distance between them stretched greater than his reach. "Thanks."

"Don't get shot for real." Her wish sounded so damn sincere. Her smile seemed so damn wholesome. Her tilted head revealed the curve of her neck and a smooth expanse of skin so damn *vulnerable* that he couldn't help sucking air between his teeth.

"If I do, I'll make sure my paperwork's complete." He laid a hand over his heart.

Her eyes followed the gesture. When she looked up, her gaze didn't rise past his lips.

He could almost feel her fingers brush across his mouth. A woman's touch was a rare treasure in this hole.

No. He shook his head and broke whatever linked him to Captain Chiesa. He didn't know her first name, but already he'd built a fantasy that risked the life he'd constructed.

She blinked twice and muttered something that sounded like, "My food's getting cold," before she walked away.

He nearly sagged against the counter as he filled two glasses with milk, but her reflection on the stainless-steel dispenser kept him standing tall. She crossed the room to her friend, probably another doctor. They stuck together as much as his A-team did. The army was a big gathering of small clans who spent their days working and eating and bunking together, which made it easy to hide in plain sight. Like the doctors, his team stayed apart from most others except the Night Stalker aviators. His men's silence, their separateness, protected him.

His tribe had gathered midway from the flat-screen television. Tonight the commander and lieutenant had chosen to eat with other officers, so nine pairs of eyes stared as he sat in the last-man seat closest to the door, with his back to the room. Nine brothers, each as concerned as his blood kin at the chance he'd be exposed, but he couldn't rewind ten minutes to skip his conversation with Captain Chiesa. Even if he could, he wouldn't. He liked the spark he'd felt when he looked at her hair and eyes, and he'd liked it especially when she told him off.

"Took you long enough." Sergeant Kahananui broke the silence. "Cruz volunteered for recon patrol."

Ignoring the big Hawaiian, he bit into his corn on the cob. Chewy, no crunch. Frozen too long between an American field and this dining facility fifty klicks from the Pakistani border.

"That doc jacking you?" Sergeant Cruz started to rise, but Wulf shook his head.

"Don't think our high-speed leader is getting jacked. Yet." Kahananui had usurped Wulf's usual spot, from which he could observe the whole mess. "Need us to run interference?"

"I'm fine." He hadn't told the doc anything that was an actual lie. With luck, he'd deflected her questions. He chomped another bite. Spray-on butter instead of corn flavor, but it was still good fuel.

"Mmm-hmm." Kahananui raised both black eyebrows and curled his lips, like he'd pulled the pin on a grin and was about to let it rip. "Had a funny view from this seat."

Men's stares ping-ponged across the silent table between him and Kahananui, but he wouldn't talk with his mouth full.

Cruz took the bait in his place. "What?"

"Saw a wolf separate a doe from the herd," Kahananui said.

The guys always joked that Caddie's three dozen women traveled in packs and never gave a lonely soldier a fighting chance. Most of his team had stable marriages, wives and kids waiting stateside, so they loved to flip shit at guys who didn't, like him and Cruz.

"Didn't know he was on the prowl, did we?" the Hawaiian added.

The three men closest to the Big Kahuna snorted. Another one fluttered his eyelashes and murmured a falsetto, "Oh, Wulf, want to taste my Italian dessert? It's a tir-a-*miss-you.*"

"Knock it off," Wulf said. Another mistake, but no stupider than trying to catch a whiff of Captain Chiesa's shampoo.

The rest hooted while Kahananui whooped like a pickup backfiring in subzero. "Got a live one, boys."

"Look, I convinced her to drop the medical records request."

"Hardship duty, huh?" Kahananui flashed a shaka hand sign at Wulf, thumb and little finger sticking out from his fist. "Capital H-A-R-D—"

"Enough already. She's an officer. And a doctor." Noise buried his last words as the engineering NCO lifted his palms across the table for high fives. Wulf sank his face in his second glass of milk. Fine. Better they think he was flirting with the doctor, which he wasn't, than that he'd asked her to help the commander.

GLAD THAT HER legs had brought her to the table without buckling, Theresa slipped into the seat across from her roommate.

Jennifer looked up from her phone. "What took you so long?"

"You didn't see?" How could Miss Nosy have missed this? Sergeant Wardsen had stalked her through the chow line in full view of the entire room.

"Text from my sister." Her friend leaned across the table. "What'd I miss?"

"One of the special ops guys." For the rest of this deployment, she'd savor the way that phrase froze the other doctor in her chair.

"What?" Jennifer's eyes bugged as if she needed a Heimlich.

"Sergeant Wardsen, he of the missing papers, wanted to talk."

"One of those ginormous mystery men spoke to you? Actual words? Wait—he exists?" She pointed her empty fork at Theresa. "You're shamming me."

"Am not." As she cut into her chicken, a rivulet of melted cheese pooled on the plastic plate, the way she liked it. A damn fine Tuesday. "He stopped me in line to apologize for his commander's rudeness in the gym. He said, and I'm quoting, 'I'm sorry. The team's sorry.'"

Jennifer's mouth dropped open for a long moment until she put a fork full of pasta in it and chewed. "So, was he cute?" She started to turn in her seat.

"Stop!" Theresa pinned her friend with a glare. Talking about men in the abstract, in the what-will-I-look-for-after-I-leave-the-army way, passed the time. But she drew the line at staring at *real* men. "Don't you dare look."

"Why not? A guy chatted with you. You're blushing. I want to check him out."

Theresa rolled her eyes. "He's a sergeant, Jen."

"That's not an answer."

"It is for me. It is for the army." They both knew the fraternization rules.

"And you're a short-timer, so why not? Human catnip, huh?"

"I'm not answering that." His pants had fit noticeably well, and when he smiled his bottom lip had curved with invitation, but she couldn't RSVP *yes*. Men were off-limits out here, and once she was back in civilization, she'd be so close to her final separation date, she wouldn't have time to think about dating until she was settled in the next stage of her life.

"And he speaks in full sentences?"

"Please, thank you, the works." Sergeant Wardsen's eyes had warmed as they talked, as if she'd thawed something inside him. She speared a tomato to stop the flutter in her stomach.

Jennifer sighed. "A sensitive warrior."

"Skip the melodrama." She'd never admit that Sergeant Wardsen's struggle to describe his commander's problem made her agree, so she ignored her roommate and ate another bite.

"You exchanged what? Three sentences?"

"More like…" Theresa replayed the conversation while she crunched the chicken's thyme-seasoned crust. "At least a dozen."

"With that much chitchat I'm surprised you don't know his Social Security number."

"I asked if he was—" A crumb stuck in her throat, and she had to gulp water to stop coughing. "Married."

"I couldn't possibly have heard that correctly."

She covered her forehead and eyes with one hand. "You did."

"No effing way." Through her fingers, she saw Jennifer's shirt front droop into leftover red sauce as her friend leaned halfway across the table. "Is he?"

"Nooo." The single stretched sound might have been an answer to the question or a plea to drop the subject or even good advice to herself. She couldn't decode her emotions.

Jen whistled without a sound and shook her head. "When you go for it, you don't mess around. And a *sergeant*."

How did her friend know exactly the tone her grandmother had used when good Italian girls dated outside the faith? "That's why we forget it." Her gaze drifted to the special ops table where guys were high-fiving each other while Sergeant Wardsen sat with a stiff spine at the end of the row. "He'll never talk to me again."

"Oh, I don't think those dudes give up easily." Jennifer gulped her cola. "If you won't let me stare from here then I need a refill."

"Please be subtle. *Please*." That was like asking a surgeon to thank you when you provided a clamp, so she slipped lower in her seat as Jennifer marched to the drink bar.

CLAIMING A SEAT by the door usually improved John
Draycott's odds of a pleasant dinner, since none of the
thugs currently working for Black and Swan wanted
their backs exposed with every entrance or exit. A decade of Afghan operations had weeded the decent guys
out of the organization, leaving men who increasingly
resembled the manager of Bagram Airfield. Efficient and
ruthless, to be sure, but not men with whom Draycott
wanted to dine, so in addition to choosing a bad seat, he
always read a book as a barrier to company.

Tonight the printed page didn't hold his gaze. Only
forty years of clandestine training kept him from blatantly studying the soldier who sat across the mess hall
with the Special Forces. He was the spitting image of another man, one Draycott had met in Mogadishu in 1968.

Despite Draycott's attention, America's finest didn't
show a flicker of return interest. Soldiers barely glanced
at civilians unless they were the Dallas Cowboy cheerleaders or surrounded by a security detail. Since he had
neither tits nor an entourage, merely extra chins and a
comb-over, he chewed—and occasionally glanced at a
certain table—unnoticed.

Although his vision had degenerated along with his
waistline, it didn't matter that he couldn't make out a
name on the staff sergeant's shirt. A professional never
forgot the face responsible for a failure, and certainly
not the face responsible for his *first* failure.

While he cut his meat, he remembered Somalia.
Beautiful place in '68, when the station chief had sent
him into the capital's slums to find a Belgian gun for
hire. His agency boss had wanted a photo that allegedly
linked a local mercenary and a World Bank official. *The
days of simple photos and film negatives.* He'd assumed

he was on a haze-the-new-guy snipe hunt to acquire an envelope full of Asian porn or Monopoly money. Assumed, that is, until he'd returned from the jakes to find his Belgian and a stone-faced blond stranger pointing guns at each other. One breath later, all assumptions had died as his contact choked on a knife.

The assassin had retrieved the blade, picked a bloody envelope from the dead man's shirt pocket—indeed, there'd been a picture—and stalked out of the shack that doubled as a bar. And so on the first day of his first job, Draycott had vomited next to his first body. Four decades later, he appreciated the killer's polite half salute as he'd exited. Opponents who understood limits had become less common over the years, and those with flair had evaporated with the Cold War. The man in Mogadishu had left him alive, and thus able to sit in a chow hall in Afghanistan, one donkey ride past the end of the earth, and stare at the assassin's identical twin.

Except that was absurd. The soldier sitting across the mess had the same profile, but the sergeant couldn't be a twin, or the same mercenary. Every joint in Draycott's body attested to the years since 1968. Although Draycott knew three men who seemed eerily unaging, this soldier couldn't be like them. He might be the son of the man from Mogadishu, but not the same man.

With his steak finally cut to a width matching the oven fries, he set the knife across the top of his plate. His shoulders itched to fill in the blanks and connect this sergeant to the Mogadishu hit, but gathering information about a member of Special Forces could boomerang and impact cargo ops. The company pulled in two-point-five million euros per week, nicely north of three-point-three million dollars, tax-free. He earned one percent of

gross as a combination secret shopper, help desk, quality
control and security hotline. His thumbs-up or thumbs-
down went to the Director. Therefore his decisions had
to align as perfectly as the food on his plate. Because
operations in Eastern Afghanistan were as orderly as
the stacks gracing his dish at the three, six, nine and
twelve positions, he would not check into this sergeant.

Personal curiosity about an episode from his past
couldn't be allowed to jeopardize his current job. If it
did, the Director would fire him. With extreme irrevo-
cability.

Chapter Three

ANOTHER SATURDAY AFTERNOON in her plywood office. While the nurses were in staff training, Theresa anticipated tomorrow's break. Most of Camp Cadwalader worked seven-day weeks, but Colonel Loughrey ran the clinic half staffed on Sunday afternoons. Barring mass casualties, she had four hours off every fourteen days. Four hours to lounge on her bunk, ponder her leave itinerary and maybe paint her toenails.

"Busy?" The deep voice pulled Theresa out of her reports and to her feet.

"No, sir. Paperwork." She blinked to merge her memory with the ruffian on the other side of the intake counter. "Sergeant Wardsen? You're here?"

He stuffed his boonie hat in a cargo pocket. His hair, definitely shaggy, showed the imprint as he rubbed his neck. "We were on patrol with the Afghan National Army for ten days."

"You look like you returned in the last five minutes." Dirt blurred the pixelated camo patterns on his pants and shirt, and his smell rivaled the dining facility Dumpster.

"Fifteen." One corner of his mouth turned up as he indicated his uniform. "Guess I should've waited to come. The others draw lower pay, so they get first shower."

"No privileges for rank?" She'd learned that Staff Sergeant Wulf Wardsen was the A-team's noncommissioned officer in charge.

"None I've noticed." He slid a folded paper across the particleboard counter. "Still get yelled at by officers."

Her face heated as she recalled telling him to knock it off. "I didn't mean—" When the wicked teasing in his eyes registered in her brain, she closed her mouth.

"The email I promised. I told the team we were chipping in for a baby gift, so they don't know about this."

"You should do that. In fact, buy a baby jogger. I read about postpartum depression, and sometimes exercise helps. Wait." She hunted on her desk, then joined him at the counter. "These are details on the new-parent-support program at Campbell. They're trained to recognize depression, make medical referrals and facilitate infant bonding." He didn't smell much worse than the gym, and the trade-off for standing this close was that she could see the cleft in his chin. "And they do home visits. I emailed the coordinator last week, and she has openings for Tuesday afternoon and Thursday morning—"

The crinkles around his eyes deepened as his lips twitched and *ohmigod* she'd turned into an uncapped gusher *again*. She shut up, but couldn't look away. Above his stubble, his cheekbones beckoned her fingers to explore, so she locked her elbows at her sides.

"You don't mess around, do you, Captain?" His voice had dropped to a register that vibrated the air trapped between her skin and her loose shirt. His compliment sounded like an open-door invite straight to trouble.

"I wanted to be ready in case you came the next day." She bit her lower lip. In a softer voice she added, "I hadn't realized you were in the field."

He stared at her so long she stifled the need to touch her hair and check for strands that had escaped today's bun. Amber flecks swirled in his blue eyes like a whirlpool, but she needed to avoid being sucked under, no matter how much she wanted to lean close to count each speck and learn their different colors.

"Would you like an adventure?" No one had ever asked her something so ambiguous or seemingly forbidden. "We need a female doctor to examine a village leader's third wife. She's pregnant. You'd fly in with us and do what you can."

Her chest inflated and she bit her lip to keep from cheering at the thought of going beyond the sandbags and blast wall. Aching to do anything that wasn't paperwork for her four-hundredth respiratory complaint, she must've nodded her agreement because he smiled.

"Monday. Be at the flight line in battle rattle at 0600. Doctors do have combat gear?"

"Of course. We even have to qualify with our weapons." *Crap.* Her mouth had sped past her brain again, but at least he was too polite to roll his eyes at a doctor who talked weapons.

"Until then." When he removed his palms from the top of the counter and left as silently as he'd arrived, legs and arms flowing as smoothly as his namesake, she realized her forearms were also on the counter. They'd been leaning far too close to each other.

She'd see him again in two days. Then the enormity of his request hit: pregnancy, real Afghans, outside the wire. After six months of staring at the mountains that ringed this plateau, she'd set foot on one. *With him.*

On the counter he'd left a playing-card-size patch of dark fabric embroidered with a poppy. She opened her mouth to call him, but then she understood. *For her.*

The silk's miniscule irregularities caught her dry skin as she traced the stitches of the blood-tinted petals. In her brown-toned world, the red blossom popped with promise. Verdant leaves reached for her as she lifted the fabric to her face. The scrap retained his body heat and caressed her cheek like skin on skin.

She squashed those thoughts. A sergeant was off-limits. If Colonel Loughrey authorized the medical mission, she could see Sergeant Wardsen again, but she could never consider more.

MONDAY MORNING ARRIVED before Theresa felt ready.

"I am so freaking jealous." Jennifer leaned against the metal bunk post, watching her quintuple-check the tactical vest spread on her bed. "I haven't escaped Caddie since we got here. You're going out on a mission and in two weeks you're on midtour leave."

"Sixteen days." Theresa tried to ignore her stomach flutters. She was due on the flight line in twenty minutes.

"Glad you're not counting."

She clutched a sealed bag of surgical gloves and another with antibiotics. "Where should I stuff these?" Four loaded magazines for her Beretta M9 pistol filled the vest's ammo pouches, her most serious pocketknife and a strap cutter graced chest loops, and her personal first-aid kit and tourniquet attached on the shoulders.

Her roommate studied the bulletproof vest. "Cargo pocket."

She squeezed her left thigh, where she'd stuffed a meal-ready-to-eat. No space. In her right she had a waterproof notebook—as if it might rain this year—and pens, but the bags fit. Even her gear was cooperating to send her packing.

"You fiddled with this load for two days." Jennifer crossed her arms. "Time to put it on."

Filled with her stethoscope, blood pressure cuff, a portable heart monitor she hoped could detect a fetal heartbeat and every other drug or relevant equipment she could snag from the clinic storeroom, her ruck weighed a thousand pounds. The weight of it and her vest probably compressed her spine a half inch.

"Here." Jennifer held out a Tic Tac mints box. "Stick these somewhere handy."

"What for?" She leaned forward to create enough slack to snap the pack's waist belt.

Her friend shoved the gift closer. "Fresh breath."

She must have looked blank because Jennifer continued. "You are single. You are almost thirty. You'll be spending a day with several manly men, one of whom watches you at meals like you're an ice cream cone he wants to lick."

"He does not." She didn't have to ask who Jennifer meant.

"He does so. Take them."

"Fine." The tiny mints rattled a warning from inside their plastic box. *Chhk-chhk-chhk-don't-think-it.*

"Adios." Jennifer followed her to the prefab's door. "And be safe!"

"Bye, *Mom*." She escaped through the dawn and headed for the flight line.

The normal eight- or nine-minute walk stretched to twelve, then fifteen, as she struggled. Her feet wanted to shuffle, and her shoulders tipped forward despite constant effort to lift her legs and straighten her back. She'd almost prefer a kidney stone to this gear. Almost.

Trying not to resemble a tent with legs prevented her from absorbing the activity at the flight line until she was seated aboard the Black Hawk helicopter for the crew chief's safety brief. As she inserted a pair of squishy foam earplugs, Sergeant Wardsen—she couldn't allow herself to think of him as Wulf no matter how much Jennifer teased—buckled into the next spot. A prudent professional would nod politely, then ignore him.

Wh-wh-wh-whump-whump. The Black Hawk lifted off, shifting her into his upper arm, the one body part he didn't have sheathed in a protective plate. Her vest and gear refused to obey her spine's signal to sit tall; each lurch of the helicopter bounced her against his shoulder.

Forget polite. She needed to get *off* him.

She braced on his solid thigh, another part decidedly without armor, and pushed. The contact lasted a second or less, a blink, but his quad jumped under her hand. It left a brand of hard male muscle that seared her palm even after she'd planted her boots on the vibrating floor and pinned herself to the side of the helicopter.

Then he spread his legs for stability too and crowded a finger width from her space.

Maybe her flush could pass as a heat reaction. If she unclenched her fist, could she let go of how strong he'd felt? She had a better chance of the metal decking opening up and swallowing her *right now* while she counted rivets on the walls, read the yellow warning stencils, searched for a distraction that didn't include his thigh.

A soldier clipped to a safety line manned a .60 caliber gun in the open side door. Past him, the land streamed below. She'd flown into Caddie at night. For six months her workday glimpses of summits beyond the camp walls had seemed more like theater scenery than reality, but this morning her flat, orderly world disappeared, replaced by carved and eroded mountains, valleys and gullies. Below the helicopter any green, anything alive or made by humans except this machine and themselves, had vanished. They could be flying through time instead of air, heading for Genghis Khan or an ancient myth instead of a pregnant village girl.

Her watch said they'd been in flight forty-five minutes when the ceaseless unfolding of mountains was interrupted by a narrow green line where water enabled valley farming. *Toto, I have a feeling we're not in Caddie anymore.* The Black Hawk's wheels settled on a plateau of packed dirt and rocks above the irrigation canal. At the dusty edge of the rotor wash, a half dozen boys wearing traditional baggy trousers and dress-length shirts jumped from foot to foot.

She followed the team out of the bird and found herself in the middle of their line formation. At the front, boys clustered around the tank-size sergeant from Hawaii, who doled out oranges and bananas from his cargo pockets. A mud-walled compound hung so precariously from the cliff above that she worried anything dropped from a window would hit her. The walls had turned the exact color of the earth and stones, nearly white with reflected glare if she looked over her sunglasses, pale brown when she looked through the tinted lenses.

The hike up a winding, rocky track dragged on until the ground shimmied with each step. She blinked to keep sweat out of her eyes, because lifting a hand to wipe her forehead required extra effort. Not even breathing through her open mouth banished this dizziness and nausea. Maybe helicopters didn't agree with her.

Sergeant Wardsen came alongside and matched her pace. "You'll be on your own with the girl. Okay with that?"

She nodded while trying to conceal her gasps. If she

didn't pull herself together, she'd fail before she had a chance to start examining the patient.

He grabbed her hand and pressed his thumb to the inside of her wrist. For a moment she stopped her plodding to concentrate on breathing.

"Damn." He thrust a blue-and-white canister with a cup-shaped lid at her. "Take a hit."

She let her eyebrows ask *What is it?* because she couldn't speak.

"Canned Oh-Two. We're over seven thousand feet and you're humping at least forty pounds. You need oxygen." Mercifully, he flipped the lid over and held it to her face. "Steady, Doc. You're not acclimatized to this elevation."

Ahhh. Her vision cleared and the flutters in her chest calmed with each suck.

"Better?" His question anchored her in the here and now.

Hypoxia. She'd succumbed to altitude sickness so quickly she hadn't recognized her own symptoms. She pulled the face mask off. "Thank you. I—"

"Move out." He waved a hand over his head to indicate the others should continue forward. They rose from defensive positions in the rocks. Only she and Sergeant Wardsen had been standing like sandwich boards, and his body had been positioned between her and the edge.

She couldn't let that happen again. She'd keep up or puke trying, and she damn well better remember her soldier skills.

After circling a boulder, the path ended at a mudcrete wall bisected by a wood-and-iron gate. How long ago trees that size had grown where now she only saw scrubby orchards, she couldn't imagine. The gate led to an open-air courtyard. More than a dozen men sat on carpets under a cloth shade. One of them, his weathered skin contrasting with his white beard and eyebrows, had a sunken atrophic scar instead of a left eye. When he smiled and rose to welcome them, she noticed he had proportionally fewer teeth. Sergeant Wardsen and Captain Deavers spent enough time greeting this man that she assumed he was the leader whose wife needed medical care.

"Captain Chiesa, please join us." Hearing Sergeant Wardsen speak English startled her. She'd been so absorbed in studying the clothing and architecture, she hadn't consciously processed the fact that he didn't use an interpreter.

While they sat on elaborate rugs, the next half hour stretched through introductions to the elderly leader—Dostum—and tea-drinking formalities. The other Afghans studied her freely during the old man's deep conversation with Wulf and Captain Deavers. She didn't see any women or girls. Finally Dostum seemed to be satisfied, and everyone, including her, stood.

"Mir will take you to the women's quarters," Sergeant Wardsen said.

A boy wearing a blue-and-gold vest led her through a door with a labyrinthine pattern of inlaid wood and across a small room, then pushed aside a heavy curtain. She had time for one breath to steel herself—she didn't know what she'd be able to accomplish alone after she crossed that threshold—before she ducked into a concealed world.

As if bricks had been left out during construction, square openings well over six feet up the wall allowed in dashes of white sunlight. No windows at person height meant no ventilation. The odors of kerosene, pungent

food and stale bodies were strong. Amid the glittery dust
motes a dozen women surrounded a young girl curled
on a woven carpet. A shawl had been draped across the
girl's belly mound. Her patient.

The women turned to stare. Their clothing ranged
from embroidered and bespangled fabric on the older
women to threadbare tunics and dark scarves hanging
loosely on the girls. If elaborate clothing denoted house-
hold status, her plainly clad patient ranked at the bottom. Her stomach heaved at the idea that this child—was
she even thirteen?—was that old man's wife. Kneeling
within reach of the girl, she murmured an introduction
she knew no one understood.

"Ma'am, Dostum requested I translate instead of
the interpreter. His youngest wife's name is Nazdana."
Wulf's voice penetrated the curtain; she could see his
brown socks under its edge. "Dostum would rather an
American than an Afghan terp from a different tribe
speak to his wife. If you work close to the curtain we
won't need to shout."

"Fine." She readied for the exam while women chattered. Her patient's topaz eyes barely moved. Dark circles and bloodshot whites indicated exhaustion and pain.

"You must be doing something very interesting."
Wulf's voice had the background rumble of a man stifling laughter.

"Changing from my gear to a sterile jacket." She
slipped the pale blue coat over her standard tan T-shirt.

"That explains it." His voice conjured the memory
of his smile in her office, the smile that had closed the
space between them and made the air take weight.

"Explains wha-at?" *Darn girly lilt.* She spread hand
sanitizer up her forearms.

"Not repeatable, ma'am."

She glared at the curtain. He had to be sitting, because now she could see pants fabric in the gap between the cloth and the floor. "If you want to interpret for me, you can't edit."

"Your call." The rising drawl on the end of his statement baited the hook. She knew that, but couldn't resist.

"Go on."

"They said it's no wonder American babies grow so tall if their mothers have such admirably big—"

"Enough." She'd invited these burning ears. He couldn't see her chopping gesture through the curtain, but his snort meant he knew he'd scored a point. "Can you ask the women to back away from my instruments?" She'd spread her diagnostic equipment in a row on a sterile sheet, but it was in danger of being contaminated.

The women shifted to give her space after Wulf spoke. She couldn't understand his words, but his tone matched the reliability of everything else about him.

"Please tell Nazdana this black band will go on her arm. It will tighten but it won't hurt."

"Ma'am, use an interpreter by speaking directly to the other person as if I'm not here. I translate what you say to her, then her replies. You don't talk *to* me, just *through* me."

"Oh. Thanks." Nazdana's blood pressure, 160 over 100, displaced her thoughts about the sergeant. The exam result wasn't good. In fact, it was very bad. To help her patient relax, she slipped the end of the stethoscope under her own shirt and let the girl listen to the steady thumps of her heart. The childlike eyes widened, and Nazdana's eyebrows rose into her pain-lined forehead.

"Now I need to check your body and the baby with this," she said. "Does he kick much?"

Wulf translated her question and Nazdana's reply. "He kicks at night and now I am not sleeping. He is taking all the space inside me and I cannot eat."

Dark eye circles and rapid heartbeat hinted at anemia, but she couldn't diagnose that without a blood test. "How often do you eat meat?"

The girl hadn't seen Wulf and probably couldn't imagine the warrior and weapons behind the gentle voice. "I am permitted to eat meat the first wife declines. Two days ago she left a piece of goat, but when devils came in my body she would not feed them."

"Please ask what she means by devils in her body." Theresa pulled a blue exam robe and a cotton sheet, both sealed in sterile plastic, from her pack. "We can put this robe on you, but I have to see and feel the baby, so your heavy clothing must come off." Theresa had no idea if women disrobed in front of other women, foreign women, or if that was considered immodest. "I'll give you privacy." She turned her back and heard giggles and a quick exchange with Wulf.

"What'd you say that made them laugh?" she asked.

"I told her the robe is what Americans wear in the hospital. She thinks Americans aren't as rich as she believed if they can't buy a full robe to visit someone as important as a doctor."

Within minutes Theresa knew the worst would happen to Nazdana. Wulf's translation of devils in her body sounded like convulsions. Her hands and lower legs showed distinct edema from fluid retention. Life-threatening eclampsia alone justified treatment at an American hospital, but Theresa pressed again on the hard round part presenting far too high on the girl's abdomen. "Nazdana, I believe your baby's bottom and feet are coming first instead of his head."

Her patient nodded to Wulf's soothing voice, as if he held her hand through the curtain.

"I would like to take you to the American hospital to have your baby. We might have to do surgery," she continued. Wulf hadn't finished interpreting before the girl's eyes widened and her mouth formed an O. "We would take good care of you and your baby."

Wulf said, "I think we can convince Dostum because he's desperate for a living son, but a woman can't go alone." Conversation flurried between him, Nazdana and the older women. "They want to send the first wife's youngest—a daughter named Meena—no, he's a son— ahh."

She could *hear* Wulf's understanding nod. "Maybe you can share the revelation?"

"Meena is Dostum's favorite daughter and attended school two years ago. When his last son died fighting Taliban last summer, they changed Meena into a boy. Now he's Mir."

"What?"

"Many patriarchal cultures do it. Cut their hair, dress them like a boy, change their name. Then Dostum has a son for prestige and the women have someone to run errands. Win-win, as long as no one outside the clan knows."

"Is it a win for her?"

"Which would you rather be? Meena, married at eleven, or Mir, outside playing soccer?"

"Point made." As a kid she would've traded her dolls for a soccer ball, but thankfully in New Jersey she hadn't had to. She bit her lip. "I need to call for permission to transport." She'd urge Colonel Loughrey to push the request, but air evacuations of civilians had strict eligibility rules. The army didn't have the resources to become every Afghan's ambulance.

"Negative. The team will take her down in a stretcher and boogie out."

"Sergeant, you *know* the regulations." Air evacuations didn't happen as easily as a buzz cut. They had to follow protocols. "We can't fly a local civilian without preapproval."

"Captain, you *don't* know Special Forces."

She pictured him shaking his head.

"We never ask permission."

Chapter Four

KNOWING THAT THE addition of a patient and a kid would completely change the Black Hawk seating, Wulf hadn't expected to be close to Theresa on this trip. Shortsighted, because of course she'd sit on the deck next to Nazdana's stretcher, and he'd have to be ready to interpret. He held out a spare communication headset. Its cord dangled inches short of brushing Nazdana, who lay between them.

As soon as Theresa replaced her helmet with the noise-canceling headphones, she twisted the plug in the air. *Where's it go?* her eyes asked. The brown depths revealed her thoughts to him as clearly as if she'd spoken. He could tell when she focused exclusively on her patient because her eyes turned sharp and narrow, the same expression Cruz had during emergency ordnance disposal. Other times, like on the ride here, he'd catch her with her eyelids lowered and her lips parted, and he knew she shared his thoughts about more personal activities. Being able to read her eyes was dangerous enough; if she read his, he was finished.

He pointed at a commo jack on the side of the bird above Nazdana's legs. Between them, the girl was strapped to a stretcher, which in turn was latched into tie-downs recessed in the floor. Theresa had fitted Nazdana with an oxygen mask connected to an inboard tank.

It decreased the girl's wheezing, but she remained pale and sweaty.

"Nice." Theresa's voice came through the headphones clearly. "Think the gear's interfering with the portable EKG monitor? It was reading the fetal heartbeat fine when I attached the belt in the women's quarters, but now the readings are wacked." She tapped the instrument in her hand. Wires from it went under the neck of Nazdana's robes. "Maybe the belt I used slipped while the guys carried her." She laid her free hand on the girl's stomach, patting lightly, as if feeling for something.

Her fingers looked small and slender compared to his, or to the hands of the men he worked with. Even her touch looked lighter, gentler. He wished...he crushed that thought faster than a tick. With his teammates, he'd made a family, the closest he'd had in centuries. They welcomed him into their homes, trusted him and never asked questions he couldn't answer. Pulling his weight as part of the team gave him a purpose every morning. Eventually, inevitably, he'd have to start over, but he wanted to hold on to this band of brothers for as long as possible. Although Theresa's hand might look delicate, experience told him that a woman's fingers had the strength to rip apart his security.

"The belt's in place," she said, "so what could—"

He'd never seen her eyebrows drawn so hard together over her nose.

"Holy crap." Her eyes widened and her mouth dropped open. "I get it. Two fetal heartbeats. That's why the readings keep changing."

It took a moment, but then he understood. *Twins.* Nazdana's face blended with his memories of Zenobia's dark hair and pain-hollowed eyes when she'd fought to deliver her twins, the babies he'd vowed to raise as his own. Despite the years, fear gored his gut as sharp and deep as a bull's horn. He didn't know this pregnant girl, but he couldn't watch anyone suffer like that. Hand shaking at the edge of his vision, he thumbed on his mike.

Theresa bent closer to her patient, as if trying to hear over the rotors and engines.

"Captain," he spoke into his mouthpiece. "Request you pick up the pace ASAP. Uhh—"

Nazdana's eyes rolled until only the whites showed. One side of her mouth twitched repeatedly.

"Seizure." Theresa scrambled in her ruck and pulled out a sealed bag of intravenous tubing and syringes. "Get her sleeve off." Her command was loud enough to carry to him.

The girl's body went rigid as Theresa ripped open an alcohol pad.

He sliced the bunched fabric away from Nazdana's arm, but she didn't move.

"Repeat request?" The pilot's voice spoke in his earphones.

"Her mouth—put something in—next stage's biting—" Theresa had the needle against Nazdana's inner elbow.

"Twins," he told the cockpit. Nothing except metal and useless plastic bags in reach. No wood or leather. "Hit some stick!" He stuck his left first finger in Nazdana's mouth.

"Will comply," the pilot replied.

Immediately the engine roared and the Black Hawk's nose pitched forward, the massive power surge echoing the adrenaline and panic rising from his stomach as he watched Nazdana's left arm flail. Theresa dodged, and the girl's hand only clipped her shoulder, but she didn't have the IV started yet. With his free hand, Wulf reached over Nazdana's thrashing torso and pinned her upper arm. She had the strength of a writhing cobra, but Theresa was able to seize her forearm and insert a needle parallel to the girl's skin. In his peripheral vision, he saw Kahananui kneel beside him to restrain Nazdana's legs. He focused on the flash of red blood flowing backward into the catheter. *Almost there.* In seconds Theresa had the needle removed and tubing attached, as smoothly as if the girl wasn't having an inflight seizure.

Then Nazdana clenched her teeth so hard on his finger, he closed his eyes to conceal the pain while he braced her tongue flat to keep her airway open. He couldn't let Theresa notice, but damn, the girl could bite like Odin's wolves.

He counted past one hundred before her jaw loosened and she collapsed into a semblance of regular body tension. Through slitted eyes he saw Theresa sag as if she'd let out a long-held breath, but if he released his, he might groan. His finger fucking *hurt.*

"Can someone radio to Caddie for operating room prep?" Theresa spoke into her mike. "Tell them we have an emergency C-section with possible eclampsia complications and potential multiple births en route. We need a full receiving team at the landing zone."

After Theresa's request went out over the air, Kahananui elbowed Wulf's right side and slipped a clean degreasing rag under the edge of the stretcher. Now Wulf had to figure out how to retrieve his finger.

"What miracle drug was that?" The Hawaiian leaned toward Theresa, plopping his massive shoulder in front of Wulf and jostling him closer to Nazdana's head. "I like to know about the good stuff in case we have to treat Afghans in the field."

"Magnesium sulfate and hydralazine." Voice strong and calm over the headset, Theresa sounded like she did this every day, not like delivering babies midflight was the scariest shit in the world. "The combo is a safe anticonvulsant and muscle relaxant for pregnant women. I found them in supply because they're also hypertension drugs."

They discussed side effects and dosages as if Kahananui played a television doctor, which allowed Wulf to slip his finger out of Nazdana's mouth and wipe the pink froth off her chin. A flap of skin hung from his finger like a bloody lip, exposing nubs of bone where the girl's teeth had dug the deepest. Blood dripped into his palm and between his fingers. It looked worse than it felt. Barely. He stuck his rag-wrapped hand into his pocket and prayed Theresa wouldn't notice.

"She's breathing on her own, good sign, but we need a CT scan to figure out if she's in a coma or just knocked out by the drugs."

Coma. Zenobia had slipped into that dark world after three days of bleeding and never emerged. Never opened her eyes or spoke to him or held the tiny boys during their brief hours. Theresa wouldn't let that happen to Nazdana. She wouldn't.

Theresa adjusted her patient's oxygen mask and then carefully opened the girl's mouth.

Wulf stiffened at the sight of Nazdana's bloody teeth.

She used a tongue depressor to separate Nazdana's jaws and examine her tongue. "She didn't bite herself, so…" She pointed the red-stained stick at him. "Show me your finger."

He shook his head. "She didn't bite through." Despite his finger itching like a dozen hairy caterpillars all circled the same spot, he couldn't be sure the healing had finished.

The helicopter's forward motion stopped. Over his headphones, the pilot and air traffic control rushed through landing protocols. A minute or two of obfuscation and he'd be clear.

"If she broke the skin, you could get an infection. You might need stitches."

"She didn't break the skin." *Please let that be the truth by now.*

"Let me be the judge." Theresa dropped the stick and reached for him. "Your left hand."

If he satisfied her that nothing was the matter, this could end and she wouldn't chase him down or demand follow-up. He had to show her, had to hope he'd given himself enough time.

With the bloody rag abandoned in his pocket, two red half-moons, one on top of his finger, one underneath, were the only signs of Nazdana's bite. As he watched, the marks faded to pink and then disappeared.

Theresa raised her hand to grab his, but left the connection incomplete. She stared between his fingers and the blood-speckled tongue depressor lying on Nazdana. Her expression revealed confusion, but their wheels touched ground before she could shape a question.

Thank Thor, her patient came first.

In the week since the hospital interpreter had rushed between him and Theresa at the flight line, Wulf had deliberately avoided the doctor. Kahananui had waited outside the operating room to report to the team about Nazdana's successful delivery. Other team members popped in to visit the patients during the day, but Wulf timed his visits for after Theresa left. At nearly six pounds each, the twin boys could already wrap their walnut-size fists around his fingers. Last night, when he'd stroked one's spiky black hair, identical to the downy heads of the babies he carried in his heart, envy had almost driven him from the room. He'd abandoned his mercenary life, surrounded himself with honorable men, made the right choices, but even an illiterate opium grower had something he never would. In the centuries since his brother and he had realized what their healing abilities had taken away and he'd lost Zenobia, he'd avoided children. Now the curiosity of Mir, the kid who was into everything, and the near-adoption of the twins by his team had snuck past his walls and knocked, no, pounded, on a hollow space under his ribs.

Part of him had a crazy urge to fill the void with more than memories. The rest of him panicked and gulped dinner if Theresa entered the chow hall. Left the gym if he saw her ponytail on the treadmill. Did an about-face if he heard her laugh. Ran from the opportunity to screw up his life. Because he *was* the lonely horndog that Kahananui often accused him of being, vigilance was becoming a full-time occupation.

Today he made it to the team's ready room without seeing Theresa, with space to wonder why Deavers had beeped him during lunch. His commander had a guest Wulf recognized, a Night Stalker named Morgan from the 160th Special Operations Aviation Regiment. He must have been visiting from Bagram Airfield in Kabul, because Wulf didn't recall an air-mobile mission on tap.

The helicopter pilot's mouth bisected his face like

a slash. "Chief flew two medevac tours in Vietnam."
The aviator continued speaking as if he hadn't noticed
Wulf. "Thirty years flying the governor for State Patrol,
wildfires with the Guard, two tours in Iraq, before he
volunteered for this sandbox. He taught me more about
flying in two days than I got in six weeks at Rucker."
He thrust his head and shoulders forward. "Chief John
Mitchell did *not* shoot his own leg cleaning his weapon!"

Wulf had met Chief Mitchell enough times to agree
with the captain's assessment. Chief had been the guy
you put in charge of loading the lifeboats, the guy played
by Clint Eastwood. Not a Snuffy who made a mistake
like shooting himself in the femoral.

After introducing Wulf to the pilot, Deavers launched
into an explanation. "This month Morgan and Chief
Mitchell returned shipping containers to Bagram
from outposts here—" Deavers tapped their wall map,
"—here and here. Should've been empties swapped for
resupply, but they registered six hundred kilos over listed
empty weight." His commander's coiled stillness broadcast clearly. Higher headquarters assigned ninety-five
percent of the team's missions: hostage extraction, training ops with the Afghans, target surveillance or neu-
tralization. Five percent of the time the team set its own
agenda, unrecorded missions of their choosing. Deavers
especially liked to make the world right when he had the
chance to go off the record.

Now Morgan had brought them a five-percenter.

"Chief didn't like jerks screwing with our loads. He
wanted to *know*." Eyes red-rimmed, the pilot stared at
Wulf. "That last day, we landed the conex hard. Busted a
corner. On purpose." He covered his face with his hands
and rocked forward, elbows on his knees. "I walked

off—my son was suspended and my wife needed to talk—God, I should've stayed."

Deavers looked from the other captain to Wulf. "Chief Mitchell was checking the container the last time he was seen alive. Morgan noticed the flight-line manager running over."

The hairs on Wulf's neck turned into bristles. "What'd the guy say happened?"

"Never did." The pilot spoke to the floor. "He left that night. Black and Swan charter. Hour after I found Chief in his hut. By the time I went hunting for him, he was wheels up. B & S claimed he had a family emergency."

"Bag of Shit." One of many names for the contractors who pretended to be above the law.

Deavers nodded. "Morgan wants us to ride shotgun on container deliveries and pickups to figure out what's inside. Nothing written. No records."

Ride-alongs sounded like a perfect excuse to get out of Caddie and away from the soft-skinned, sweet-smelling problem that had him running laps every night at oh-dark-thirty, hunting for exhaustion.

"The team will open the can, get our answers and close it up, good as new," Deavers promised the pilot.

"Or we could open it and blow it." Wulf made his own suggestion. Cruz and Kahananui enjoyed testing explosives. "Fake an RPG hit."

"Whoa—" The pilot's voice cracked, and he swallowed. "Not my definition of fun. No rocket-propelled grenades near my Black Hawk. No exploding sling loads."

"The Big Kahuna's the best. He'd direct the blast away from your bird. You probably wouldn't even notice."

"Negative." Morgan's forehead rested on one fist with

his elbow braced on his leg, but Wulf could see that he was blinking rapidly.

"We could be jack-in-the-box and pop out to surprise whoever takes delivery," Deavers offered. His voice sounded slow, like he was planning, but his slightly tilted head and his single raised eyebrow flashed a different message to Wulf, a plea to fill the room with talk until Morgan had recovered. Let the man get himself together, Deavers seemed to signal.

"Negative on that idea, sir." Wulf nodded once to acknowledge his understanding. "You ever spent time locked in a shipping container? Hotter than peppers on a Punjabi grill. Your Minnesota roots can't take it."

They traded meaningless barbs until Captain Morgan finally spoke through hard-pressed lips. "Thanks. I knew you'd come through for me. For Chief. Thanks."

"Give us the call, and we're ready to go." Wulf put a hand on the pilot's shoulder and offered him a bottle of water. "We've got your back. We'll find out whatever Chief knew."

Ten minutes with barely a thought of Theresa. This mission would be good for him.

Chapter Five

THERESA CLOSED THE postal trailer's door with her hip, the sun-parched afternoon making her squint after the dim interior. The two packages in her arms were the first good omens since she'd realized Sergeant Wardsen must be avoiding her.

"Captain Chiesa!"

She couldn't mistake that voice after listening to it through the curtain and on the ride where they'd struggled to help Nazdana. Before she turned, she knew Sergeant Wardsen would be there, his warm melody of words able to comfort in any language. He could probably soothe the damn dust if he spoke to it.

Three feet away, he stood like a granite monument, one hand on the pull door that covered the letter slot. Her exit had caught him in the middle of depositing a handful of letters.

If she hadn't been holding the boxes, she could've touched his cheek. Clean-shaven, he was as delicious as a recruiting ad.

"How are Nazdana and the little guys?" Below his reflective sunglasses, he grinned like everyone in camp did when they asked about Caddie's favorite guests.

"Great. Eating lots." She wanted to keep him there, talking, even if only about this safe topic. "Someone made two cradles and the nurses are stitching quilts out of the camouflage patterns of all the NATO uniforms."

Refusing to obey her brain's warning to keep her distance, her feet carried her down the steps. "They'll be ready to go home after this weekend."

"We'll be on a mission. Can they stay until Tuesday?"

"Sure." *Then we'll have to see each other again.* "Extra days can't hurt." Her goal wasn't to stand here and stare at him, especially when she couldn't see his eyes through the lenses, so she asked, "Does your team know any other women who need maternity care?"

"Planning to open a women's clinic?" His lips twitched at one corner of his mouth. "What's the regulation authorizing that, ma'am?"

"No idea." She squeezed her packages tighter, unsure how to present her half-formed plan to Colonel Loughrey. The sixteen hours it had taken her to track down a supply of vitamins with extra folate deliverable to Caddie hadn't left much time to refine her idea of mobile prenatal visits.

"Kidding." He caught the smaller box as it slipped across the larger one's top. "It's a great idea, and we'll find you someone." He gestured to the bigger package she held. "I'll trade you."

Her mother could fit an entire vacation wardrobe and dozens of cookies into a box the size of a file drawer, but it was heavy enough to make her arms ache. Asking him to carry it would be wimpy, but he'd offered. She wouldn't lose her *atta-girl* credentials if she accepted his help as far as her hut.

He palmed the carton as if it were a basketball and handed her the smaller one to tuck at her hip. "So, what exciting contraband am I hauling? It's not heavy enough to be beer."

"Shoes." She looked at her tan suede boots. "I need civvies for leave next week."

"I'm carrying women's shoes? Spiky things?" He shortened his stride to stay next to her.

"Probably." She had no idea what her mother had sent, but smart money would be on black kitten heels. Refusing her stepfather's dubious cash was one thing, but Theresa had long ago resigned herself to her mother's extravagance. Buying clothes for her only child was an expression of love, as well as an attempt to make up for the losses of Theresa's early years. Despite Carl's jokes about his wife's skill at money laundering whenever she went to the mall, Theresa knew everything in the box had been selected and mailed with her mother's love.

"This is cause for despair?" He pulled his sunglasses halfway down his nose so she couldn't miss his raised eyebrows.

"I asked for something comfortable for walking. I doubt that describes anything here." A strong mother-daughter bond didn't guarantee the same taste.

"Next you're going to tell me there are clothes in this."

Part of her knew she shouldn't follow the conversation away from safe medical subjects and into the risks of personal details so easily, but that part had lost its voice.

He stopped moving and his eyes skimmed her body all the way to the ground. "Silk."

His single word conjured a lush image that brought her to a standstill, an image of a man's hand sliding a swath of fabric over her throat and chest to caress her skin. Her eyes locked on his fingers, tanned and strong, spread wide on her carton. They weren't too thick, and his nails were clean. At his wrist, blond hairs touched his watchband. *The hand would be just like Wulf's.*

"Or lace?" His voice had slipped to a depth that she rarely heard, because men didn't describe medical symptoms in that slowly melting tone or present slides at battle update briefings with that husky vibration deep in their chest.

"I hope not." Her voice barely squeezed out of her paralyzed throat, but she had to answer. Why was he flirting with her? She wanted to ask about helping Afghan women—she couldn't allow anything more—but why did he want to talk to her? They both knew army rules; a relationship between them was off-limits. Special ops soldiers calibrated risk and quantified outcomes as finely as neurosurgeons, or they didn't stay alive, yet he wrapped his voice around her like a net. She swallowed the knowledge that he wanted to take his chances.

"Dare I imagine a dress?"

A dress. She focused on her gray-and-brown pants fabric. This close, the blocks in the design were right angles, orderly and regular, like her life. To keep it that way, she had to stay far away from this man. A semi-secret maternal clinic was enough professional risk. To pile on more by—*no*—they could be nothing to each other but people who nodded and exchanged half smiles across the dining facility.

"Imagine a dress if you want." She started to shrug, but the move would lift her chest, so she turned and spoke over her shoulder as she moved away. "I'll imagine practical pants." Whatever her mother had sent, she doubted it would be practical, unless it was a nail file. "I hope being that close to something the army didn't issue won't cause you problems."

"If I have a heart attack, I'm confident I'm in good hands." He came even with her in three strides.

The image of leaning across his body to press his chest flashed in her mind, so real that her arm spasmed on the smaller box until its corner dug into her waist. She'd almost reached the end of temp city, rows of tents for soldiers taking breaks from more remote outposts. By comparison, the plywood hut she and Jennifer shared with four other females seemed posh.

"Where you headed?" he asked as they approached the rows of prefabricated housing that marked the main area of Camp Caddie.

"Bravo 8." Revealing her hut location felt like giving out a phone number at a bar, but this afternoon she couldn't blame alcohol.

His glasses re-covered his eyes. "For leave."

"Oh." She'd misinterpreted his question. Maybe she had read too much into all his conversation. "Rome."

"Ahhh." His sigh reminded Theresa of someone sinking into a hot tub. "Lucky you."

"I know." She lifted the smaller box. "Guidebooks."

"Meeting someone?" A casual, polite question. He wasn't fishing for her dating status.

"No. Planned it myself. The books should be enough, although I might join a Vatican tour. I've read that—" His sideways smile made her want to slap a hand over her inner babbler.

"So." He stopped walking. The banter, and his smile, faded. "Someone sent the clothes and shoes?" His attention fixed her to the gravel.

"My mother." Her throat clogged and breathing took effort. *Too much dust.*

He leaned closer. "Did she include anything else…"

Two tiny Theresa reflections stared at her, brown butterflies pinned to his lenses.

"…tempting?" he finished.

"Umm." *Flirting.* Not her strength. His mouth came closer. She couldn't think and watch his lips at the same time. "I mean—not unless you lose, oh, fifty pounds. Even then I doubt the clothes would match your, ah, active lifestyle."

Lame, lame. She wanted to slap her forehead, but he laughed obligingly. "A mother who doesn't send cookies?"

"Cookies? Oh." Her shoulders fell away from their tight bunch by her neck. "Yeah, of course. She knows I have sergeants to bribe." Grabbing the subject change would remind him of their different ranks.

"This particular sergeant is very bribable. And carrying your incredibly heavy box." He sagged as if the contents had turned into concrete.

"Fine." They were close to her quarters. Time to retrieve her box before someone saw. "Lend me a knife?" She'd pay him off and send him on his way.

He shifted the box to his other hand and pulled a serrated blade from his thigh sheath. The blade stretched from her fingertip to the base of her palm.

"Nothing small about you, is there?" *Crap.* Her cheeks flamed when his shoulders shook with laughter. She closed her eyes but couldn't erase his white-toothed grin from inside her eyelids. "I didn't mean—" She swallowed. "I give up. Go ahead."

Holding the box between his forearm and shirt, he slit the tape and sheathed the blade with an economy of movement a surgeon would envy. At this distance she could see the pulse beat in his throat, but the thump-thump in her ears had to be her heart. If she placed her hand where his fingers hovered, above his thigh, she'd feel his quadriceps. Last night in her bunk, she'd squeezed her leg to recall the living steel that she'd accidentally gripped on the Black Hawk flight, but her own muscle had nothing in common with his. Today he stood next to her, a simple box separating them.

No. She grabbed for the cardboard flaps to end this folly.

"Oww." A line of blood welled from a slice across the pad of her second finger.

He touched her wrist, then tugged her palm closer to examine the cut. A sensation not unlike hypoxia, complete with vertigo and shortness of breath, spun from her stomach to her head and knees. She wouldn't, couldn't, faint over a simple paper cut.

"I apologize." He bent over her hand.

He wouldn't kiss her finger; she couldn't allow that. "It's not your fault." She tried to retrieve her hand, but his thumb pressed into her palm and he cradled her knuckles. Tugging harder didn't help.

"My knife cut the box edge, not the tape."

"I'll be fine." Her high-pitched tone must have reached him, because he released her. She immediately wished he hadn't, then stifled the thought. "What were... oh, cookies." This time she used care to open the flaps.

"Delicious." His slow, deep voice returned, cueing her to look down.

Her mother hadn't put cookies on top. Black lace peeked out of pink packing tissue. Jet beads caught the sun and winked at her from ribbon trim that connected two scalloped bra cups. She shoved the offending object deeper. Her jaw hurt from the pressure of gritting her teeth, but nothing she could say, nothing, would make this go away. She should shut up. *Right now.*

"If you decide to take her advice…" His smile lifted one side of his mouth.

What was he talking about? She followed his gaze to a sticky note that'd transferred from the tissue paper to her forearm. *Not for your roommates! Share these with a nice boy.* Written in her mother's distinctive slanted loops.

She needed to escape before she surpassed her record for embarrassment, set the day she broke her holster in pre-deployment training at Fort Benning, and her Beretta slipped down inside her pant leg. Two more minutes and she'd blurt out that story. That would impress a Special Forces stud.

"Here." She reached deep, felt plastic and tugged out a bag of chocolate espresso swirls. After he caught them, her free hand snatched the carton he held, and she jammed the small box into the top. She was out of here like crap in a case of salmonella.

"Would you like to see a movie?"

Her mouth opened a second before her thoughts gelled into speech. "What did you say?" She suspected her mother's cooking had led high school boyfriends to date her longer than they might have, but never had the effect occurred from merely seeing the food.

"Friday night movie at our ready room. Maybe cookies would cheer Captain Deavers." The eyebrows arched over his shades ruined his sincerity. "Team's worried."

"Laying it on thick, aren't you? I know his wife's been to three parenting meetings already."

"We're showing *Cinderella*."

"Tell me that's not spelled with an *S*."

"Disney, I swear." He raised a palm like a Boy Scout. "Kahananui's pick. His girls are into the princess lifestyle. He wants to share it with them." Lines at the corners of his mouth betrayed his struggle to hold a straight face. "You could bring Meena."

"She still insists on being Mir." She shouldn't say yes, but how could she deny Nazdana's helper the chance to see a cartoon?

"The rest of the team might know a new patient for you."

This felt like high school, when guys had three idiotic ways to explain why getting a burger wasn't a date, but finding women who needed medical care would involve Wulf and his team. "Okay, what time?"

"We start at twenty hundred. You know where our ready room is?"

"Yes." If he knocked on her hut, gossip would explode like a rocket-propelled grenade.

"Until tonight." He leaned in until her face filled his reflective lenses.

Did her eyes really look half-closed? Her lips half-open? Her sports bra compressed her chest as she struggled for air, waiting for him to close the last inch between their bodies even though *he must not*.

He swung a second bag of cookies in the air as he pulled away and gave her the free-form salute perfected by Special Forces.

She squeezed the big box until its seams creaked. The shameless bastard had grabbed her butteroons.

WULF'S INTERNAL CLOCK passed nineteen hours fifty-five minutes. He didn't lurk next to the ready room door, but his team sensed not to get between him and the knob. *He* would answer when she knocked. At three minutes before eight, he heard two taps. He snapped the waistband of his army running shorts and counted to five before opening the door.

He hadn't been this close to Captain Chiesa in a workout uniform since the first day in the gym. A benevolent deity had issued her the smaller size T-shirt, and she hadn't swapped it for the gray garbage sack most females wore.

She cleared her throat.

Remembering his manners, he looked at her face. Fuck. She was frowning. He beckoned her and Mir into the room. "Welcome to our humble abode."

Inside the door, Mir slipped off her sandals and barreled across the room to throw herself on a stack of embroidered pillows, but Theresa paused. "This is your ready room?"

"Expecting camo netting?" Rugs on the plywood surfaces showcased the colors and textures of the Silk Road. On the walls, birds with black-and-gold tails cavorted with deer in shades of brown, while geometric red-and-black designs softened the floor.

"Wondering what it keeps you ready for."

Before he could reply, Kahananui dimmed half the lights and announced, "Aloha, ma'am. Thanks for bringing our buddy. And now *Cinderella* is about to begin."

As Theresa bent to untie her running shoes, her black nylon shorts stretched across her ass like plastic wrap on cherry pie.

Fuck good manners. He stared.

Quiet, stifling as a sandpit, descended on the room until she shifted position to tuck her butt to her heels. She lowered her head, too, but not before he spotted the red color spread across her cheeks. Shit. She'd realized where every last eye had been plastered. His frown whipped the circle. Immediate conversations about the Yankees, whether frozen fish retained its texture in the mess and Cruz's daily hypothetical—*would you rather wake up as the Terminator or Linda Hamilton*—where did he get those?—filled the dead air.

Her eyes and posture had the awkward, blinking innocence of a colt, as if she might leap to her feet and stagger away, so he'd let her come to him. Instead of pointing to the pillows and low table he'd chosen, he summarized the movie plot in Pashto and told Mir where to sit. The nine-year-old grinned and grabbed Theresa by the hand as Wulf brought over the coffee tray.

Good girl, he wanted to say, but the other guys understood enough of the language to catch him out, and they'd had his number since the cafeteria weeks ago. "Your beverage service, ma'am." He said Theresa's title as if it were an endearment, not a barrier. To a man who'd stolen Ottoman princesses, higher rank was not an obstacle.

She laid three bags of cookies on the table before she lowered herself to the pillows, but her spine didn't bend until Mir hugged her. He'd send the kid home with reams of paper and every government Skilcraft pen in camp to start her own school if she remained on his side.

When he lifted the silver coffeepot, someone with a death wish snickered, but the modern custom of flashing a middle finger solved that.

The opening credits hadn't finished before someone called, "Sarge, pass a cookie?"

Reaching across Mir to the bags in front of Theresa, he slipped a slice of nut and raisin roll onto a napkin and handed it away.

"Wulfie, dude, me too." This request came from the other side of the room.

This time he handed a cranberry chocolate chip concoction past her. Inches from his forearm, her breasts rose as she inhaled and held her breath, but he mustered his self-control. If he brushed them, even with the outside of his arm, he suspected she'd flee.

"Over here, Sarge." The team was having too much fun.

"Don't make me teach you manners tomorrow." Although he didn't mind being the butt of a joke—he'd pin them on a gym mat until they whimpered—Theresa had sunk lower and hunched her shoulders as the needling continued.

"Yeah, knock it off, you puky wahines." Kahananui jumped to his rescue. "You're worse than my six-year-old. I want to hear the frigging mice."

Immersing herself in the story despite the language barrier, Mir flipped to her stomach and slid under the low table until her head came out the other side. And when she did, the feeble obstacle her presence had provided between Theresa and him disappeared.

He knew how to hunt. How to stalk. How to capture. He could cover the space to Theresa in one move, but it was smarter to bide his time. He shifted his hip, placed his coffee on the table and shifted again to recline. Here the carpet radiated warmth, as if she'd withdrawn only a moment before. They were close enough now that although their bare legs didn't touch, his skin vibrated with awareness.

When the stepsisters attacked Cinderella and shredded the mouse-made gown, Theresa tensed.

He took the opening and slipped his hand over hers.

Her hand turned and squeezed as, on-screen, pearls flew and the frenzied sisters continued the mugging.

Closing his eyes, he blocked out the princess-erella so he could absorb the feel of a real woman's fingers. His thumb traced her knuckles. Like a miracle, her thumb returned the circle on his palm. He opened his senses to her, but the syrupy blonde and squeaky rodents intruded. At least tonight Kahananui hadn't picked *Sleeping Beauty.* Last week that dragon had given him a nightmare. Even after he woke, he'd had sulfur and charred horse meat in his nose and Jurik's name caught in his throat. He'd tried to joke about his thrashing by blaming Kahananui's socks on the end of the bunk, but it had been the fire breather. Jurik had burned while the girl ran the wrong way, ran *at* the beast, too fast to catch when he was hampered by chain mail.

Theresa tugged her hand. His memories had caused him to squeeze too hard.

When he loosened his grip, the next step came easily in the dark. He trailed her shaking fingers across his lips, a light brush as he inhaled. Chocolate cookies and coffee perfumed her palm, better than harem attar. Her scent replaced the vile smoke of his memory. The rustle of her nylon running shorts replaced the screams. Then the skin above her socks branded his knee, a brand that howled *my woman touched here.* His imagination soared with the movie waltz.

Behind him someone coughed, a throat-clearing hack that sounded like his name.

"Hah-chh-out," someone else sneezed. *Watch out,* they meant.

Touching Theresa was boneheaded for at least fifty reasons. He dropped her hand.

As Cinderella dashed down the steps to escape being unmasked, the music's shift to desolation mirrored his feelings. He didn't want to leave these brother warriors, and whenever he chased a woman, discovery followed. Women never let details pass unnoticed. No matter how much he yearned to whisper her name and feel its shape on his tongue, he couldn't. If he pursued Theresa, he'd end up alone on the side of the road like this cartoon girl. Doctors asked questions and collected data, yet he'd touched one willingly, as eager as a dog to feel her fingers ruffle his hair, as needy as that round mouse.

No. Pushing to his feet, he staggered to the fridge. He'd found a home with the best men he'd ever fought alongside. They'd have to be enough. A few men turned at the white glow as he grabbed a bottle, but most stayed engrossed in the movie as the mice stole a key.

The cold water froze his frontal lobe and unlocked his sanity. Real life never worked out cartoon perfect, but Wyrd offered men choices for a reason. Fate allowed him to shape his destiny. Tonight Kahananui or Deavers could escort Theresa home.

Tonight, like a thousand nights before, and ten thousand upon ten thousand before that, he would be alone.

Chapter Six

WULF PAUSED BEFORE he ducked into the dust cloud created by the UH-60 Black Hawk's rotors. The orange sun rising between two eastern mountain peaks sparked his memory, and he smelled citrus again, like the scent of Theresa's hair when he'd sat close to her during the movie. A day and a half, two showers, and Black and Swan's version of spicy Italian sausage pizza filled the interim, but her scent still came and went at the shittiest times.

Captain Deavers slapped the side of Wulf's helmet as he passed and gestured toward their ride. This was the team's second airborne hunt for an overloaded shipping container. Yesterday's resupply run had proceeded by the book, and Alpha squad had returned disappointed, without intel or leads about what the chief had discovered before his death. Today Alpha squad would make a visible presence around Caddie while Wulf, Deavers and Bravo squad road shotgun with the pilot, Morgan.

Hunching lower to avoid decapitation from the rotor blades—once per thousand years was once too often—Wulf followed his captain. The four blades overpowered other sounds, but he knew what his commander would say if they could hear each other. *Time to move out on this be-yoo-ti-ful Sunday morning. Time to find some shit to fry in a pan.* Last night Kahananui had taunted the guys on this trip about missing the Sunday omelet bar, so Deavers had found a dozen eggs and stuffed the Hawaiian's running shoes. Shit *was* going to fry, but he'd be a hundred miles away and three thousand feet off the ground.

Inside, he tuned to the helicopter crew's communications.

"Green on fuel. Green light from the flight line." Captain Morgan finished his preflight checks. "Your team's a go?"

"Ready." Deavers's voice crackled as he handed Wulf one of two metal cases the size of a quart of milk. "Got our toys."

"No fireworks?" The pilot waited for Deavers to say no, then continued. "Right then, let's pick up our delivery and boogie."

Despite swinging a loaded twenty-foot shipping container, the tactical flight over the barely lit land was fast and stomach-dropping. Wulf rehearsed what-if scenarios, but the stretch of Theresa's T-shirt when she leaned on her elbows intruded. He'd been surrounded too long by Afghan women swathed head to toe, or army women dressed to resemble chunks of concrete, because her gray cotton tee had seemed revealing. Thirty-two hours later, he could conjure her next to him, her legs stretched alongside his, butter-rich cookies and Turkish-style coffee mingling with that damn citrus scent that clung to her. He'd eaten an orange with every meal since *Cinderella*, proof of his stupidity.

Focus. Bringing his rifle stock to his nose, he sucked in dark oil and metal. His weapon. His mission. His team.

In the twenty minutes before they reached Firebase Rushmore on a ridge commanding a valley bend, he

managed not to think of her six more times. The Black
Hawk never touched ground while the firebase grunts
worked with the crew chief to swap the supply container
for its empty twin. Eight and a half minutes, and then
Morgan lifted their new load off the packed dirt rectangle next to the sandbagged compound and soared away.
The poor bastards at the firebase wouldn't see another
friendly for fifteen days.

With Rushmore three ridges and two valley twists
behind, the pilot called Wulf and his commander forward. "See the weight?" Morgan pointed to a dial. "Six
bucks heavy, when all it's supposed to have is outgoing
mail and unburnable plastics."

"Jackpot." Wulf's arms and chest tingled with anticipation. They had over six hundred kilos of secrets hanging below. "Pick your spot. We'll execute." Distractions
fell away as he became one with his squad. They had
separate arms and legs and beating hearts, but one mission: the box. Find out what it held and why Chief was
dead, then balance the books.

"Studied topos," the pilot said. "There's a partially
concealed saddle fifty klicks west."

"We saw it. Drop our snipers on the overlooking
ridges." His commander nodded as Wulf continued,
"Our commo will stay on board to coordinate. The captain and I go in the can."

"Roger that." The pilots would hover, prepared to
haul the container off with Wulf and Captain D inside
at hostile contact.

Before the dust boiled from the ground, Wulf had
an instant to gauge the distance to the corrugated roof
of the half-size twenty-footer. Reassembled, his welds

would be easier to conceal on the rippled metal than on flat steel, where they would look exactly like a trapdoor.

He fast-roped to the top, the zip a rush that was always over too soon. Next to him, Deavers was nearly invisible through the brownout. Wulf's blowtorch had to be roaring, but the massive rotor blades overhead left no air for other noises. Dirt scoured his goggles until it was impossible to see past his arms. No way could his commander spot an elephant next to them, let alone a Taliban fighter with a rifle a half klick away. For the other man's sake, he hoped the team snipers had clearer views.

The steel square of roof fell into the void. Odd to see it disappear, to know it clanged metal on metal as it landed, when he could only hear the overhead thwacks.

He dangled on the edge and dropped, followed by his commander. The dusty light that filtered through their entrance point revealed four shrink-wrapped pallets of white bricks fixed to tie-downs on the floor. An instant after he registered the incongruity of commercial packaging in the wilds of Clusterfuckistan, the pickle-barrel smell walloped him. It wasn't the lethargic dream-scent of raw poppy resin, so Deavers wouldn't fail his next piss test just by breathing. This was the stink of hundreds of bricks of processed base.

His flashlight played over the cargo and lit his commander, who tried yelling loud enough to be heard. Even inside the can, the Black Hawk obliterated every noise, but his lips were easy to read. "O-pi-um?"

"Morphine," Wulf mouthed back. He unstrapped the metal case from his chest. Flat transmitter chips, the size of match heads, nestled inside in packing foam eggcups. While he peeled protective paper from a wood-patterned chip and fixed it to a pallet, he calculated the requirements to prep and pack this much junk. Water. Fuel.

Lime. Ammonium chloride. Space. Multiplied by the number of containers Morgan had noted, the processors would need more square feet than a hilltop firebase like Rushmore offered. The lab had to be somewhere else.

At the other end, Deavers slit a tiny hole in the plastic and inserted his last tag between paper-wrapped blocks. In two minutes, they'd marked the whole load for satellite tracking, but the bigger problem sliced through Wulf's gut like a seax.

How were drugs getting inside containers at different firebases?

Not via American soldiers, please. Let it be someone else. The kids out there couldn't be responsible for loading this shit. The army and marines had enough to do being policemen and border patrol for places the Afghan government didn't reach. If soldiers tried to tackle poppy production, they'd also end up being the chamber of commerce, the farm bureau and social workers, so they usually stuck their heads in the sand and left drug policy to the State Department and politicians.

Now that would change. Because someone had killed Chief, someone inside the wire who was neck-deep in the opium trade, that fucking ostrich was about to raise its head and come up locked and loaded. His team would find the truth.

He hoped the truth didn't suck as badly as he suspected it might.

Chapter Seven

"WILL YOU STOP that already?" Jennifer's annoyance caught Theresa off guard.

She jerked her eyes away from the dining hall door to her roommate's frown. "What?"

"Stop jiggling. You're moving the table. You haven't sat still since Friday." Jennifer's eyebrows merged over her nose. "I can guess, but what the heck's going on?"

"Nothing." Theresa stared at her barely touched Greek omelet. When had she eaten the hash browns?

Her friend muttered a profanity at the same time that part of Wulf's team entered the mess. Theresa's lips and cheeks automatically stretched into a wide smile as she fixed her gaze on Jennifer. "So, what are you doing today?"

"Working. Like you. You know, at the hospital?" She leaned across the table. "Relax, my partner in crime. He's not with them."

"I don't know who you're talking about." So she and Wulf were playing that never-crossing-paths game again. Her spine drooped into a curve.

"You're full of shit, Ms. Captain Promotable, but I'm the only person who knows."

"There's nothing to know." She picked olives and feta out of her eggs. The situation had escalated too far during the movie. Damn if she'd think about touching that overconfident piece of man again, not after he'd left her sitting on the floor like a sack of trash. If her near-mistake with a sergeant had demonstrated anything, it was that her next job had to be a place where the vast majority of eligible men weren't off-limits, somewhere like a big university hospital. "Last night I read about another position in New York."

The change of subject wasn't blatant enough for Jen. "Look, I made a mistake."

At her roommate's unusually serious tone, Theresa lifted her gaze from her dish.

"I shouldn't have joked about him or pushed you." She turned her paper coffee cup around and around. "Everything you said about fraternization, your career—I acted like it was no big deal—but you'll be a field-grade officer in six weeks. And you need perfect references for your job search." She took a deep breath. "Being downrange is making me crazy and bored. Teasing you seemed…" She hunched her shoulders. "Funny, I guess. But it's not. You're going to be a major."

"I suppose when I get that gold oak leaf cluster, our fun has to stop." Theresa waved at the gray-painted dining hall. "I'll send the reality television crew home and cancel the hot tub. Sayonara Spring Break Afghanistan, hello eighty-hour workweek."

"I sooo cannot picture you in a hot tub." Jen wrapped her arms around her waist and snorted. "You'd check if the chlorine levels met health code, or swab for bacteria on the deck."

She wasn't that joyless, was she? "Thank you for making me feel like a total loser."

Jennifer stopped laughing. "I didn't mean—"

"I'm not hungry." Theresa stood and piled her cup and napkin on her tray.

"Sorry I—"

"See you at the office, okay?" Everything inside her twisted as she crossed the plywood floor toward the service window, but the plastic tray in her hands was indestructible. She could squeeze it as hard as she wanted.

"Aloha, Doc."

It wasn't Wulf's voice, but it was familiar. She turned and saw the linebacker-size Hawaiian from Wulf's team, the one with the daughters who liked princesses. "Sergeant K."

"On for Tuesday?"

"For what?" They didn't have an appointment.

"To return Nazdana, Mir and the twins. We're free and a Black Hawk's available."

"Whenever." She dropped her paper plate of food in the can. "They're fine to travel."

"How's your schedule?"

"Me?" Silverware in the gray bin. Tray to the civilian contractor in the window. "Why?"

"You'll be the guest of honor." His teeth were blinding white in his tan face. "Boy twins are like winning the lottery to a dude like Dostum."

"I'm too busy. My midtour leave starts Wednesday."

"Dostum's going to want to thank someone."

"Colonel Loughrey did the caesarean. Invite him." No way could she sit next to Wulf. The truth rolled around her stomach and threatened to boil up her throat. Remembering the way he'd caressed her hand still woke her some nights in a sweat. She couldn't spend more time with him, not if she wanted to stick to the rules. "I assisted a little and cut the cords. That's it."

"Whoa." Kahananui held up plate-size hands. "Our team doesn't know that, and neither does the proud papa.

He thinks Nazdana had a female doctor. She was unconscious and Mir was in the hall with me, so you'll leave everybody sharing that happy belief, right?" He loomed closer to Theresa.

She retreated until the garbage can bumped her thighs.

"You'll come? For her safety?" he pressed.

The photo she'd seen of a Pakistani girl with her nose cut off flashed in her mind. Similar honor crap happened in Afghanistan too. She'd have to go along to protect Nazdana from the risk of punishment for having been alone with unrelated men. Special Forces were expert at boxing people into corners, weren't they? "What time?"

"A nice civilized oh-six-thirty Tuesday at the flight line."

She'd have to find someone to cover her seat at the battle-update brief, which meant she'd probably have to do Monday's brief in return. Clear her patient charts a day early. Pack for Italy. Check her battle rattle gear. Restock her rucksack with bandages, antibacterial ointment, prenatal vitamins and immunizations.

She'd also have to immunize herself against a certain Special Forces staff sergeant.

FLYING FROM CAMP CADDIE to Nazdana and Meena's home, Theresa had wedged herself between the two Afghan girls and avoided contact with Wulf. Returning, other soldiers had positioned themselves between her and Wulf so deliberately that for a second she wondered if they guarded him, but that was dumb. He wasn't at risk from her.

Her head bobbed as she reviewed the day. She'd spent the first hour on the ground exchanging formal phrases and presents with the babies' male relatives, and the next three in the women's quarters giving physicals to Nazdana's extended family. Then the serious eating had begun. Mir had guided her through the array of foods using English words and phrases she'd learned during her weeks at Camp Caddie, but Theresa hadn't needed the girl to translate the women's fingers-to-mouth gestures as they piled her plate with garlicky lamb kabobs and spinach-filled dough pockets. The party had been like Christmas at Nonna's, down to the armed guards outside, but with spicy tea substituted for wine.

Each rotor turn bounced her helmet on the Black Hawk's vibrating side. The silk-wrapped bundle in her lap contained presents from Dostum: a silver cuff bracelet, waterfall necklace and chandelier earrings. According to Wulf, the azure stones were lapis, a perfect souvenir of her deployment. Federal ethics rules required her to report gifts this valuable to Colonel Loughrey, but maybe she could keep the scarf tied around the set.

Thoughts of Meena burbled through her food coma as they blew past kilometers of dirt and rock. At goodbye the girl had reached deep into her English. *Doctors help mothers.* Her hands, skinny and chapped from labor, had cupped Theresa's cheeks to say farewell. *Doctor!* Meena had pointed at her own chest. *Mir and Captain Key-sa!* She still refused to wear girl clothes or answer to her feminine name. *Doctor and doctor!*

Against the brutal odds of Paktia Province, Meena aspired to be a doctor. Like *her*.

Could she establish a fund for a girls' school? Perhaps her old high school could become a sister school. If she could establish links to enough local women through maternity visits—

K'BOOOOM. Her body jerked against the safety harness, then slammed into the metal side of the helicopter. Black smoke erupted from the rear, choking her, and men started firing out the open side doors as the flight rerouted to hell. *We're hit.*

"Brace yourself!" Wulf shouted as the helicopter lurched and dropped.

She covered her mouth to hold in her scream or her lunch or *Holy Mary, Mother of God* as her butt left the jump seat. Only the harness kept her from hitting the ceiling. Then the helicopter's landing wheels smashed hard and her world filled with the sound of metal shrieking against its maximum stress. The rotors kept spinning and the whole machine *bounced.* Her stomach freestyled away as they rose for an instant like a tethered falcon and the heaving floor jacked her legs into her chest, but then they crashed down a second time. If metal could give a death rattle, she heard it.

Men fired and moved in a blur while the crew chief sprayed an extinguisher on flames snapping from the tail section. Black smoke set her coughing, but she swept her legs out of the way of the bodies launching out both doors. Her gut screamed commands—run, hide, shout, jump, shoot, dodge—but first she had to click the fast-release buckle on her harness.

"Out, out, out!" Wulf grabbed her shoulder and flung her past the sixty gunner in the port side door. His hand never let go as he crashed on top of her.

Beneath his weight, she felt as flat as her vest's armor plates. The *ta-ta-ta-ta* of automatic rounds merged into one roar as the door gunner swept the terraced fields ascending the hillside. Dirt geysered where his rounds hit, earthbound fireworks.

"On *go* run for the rocks and *get down.* I'll be on your nine!" Wulf yelled.

She couldn't nod with her cheek jammed into the dirt.

"Go!" He came off her to her left, already firing. *"Go! Go!"*

She launched to her feet and raced for the goal he'd identified.

He ran alongside, rifle blasting as they bolted for the rocks.

Leaning forward past full tilt, mouth open for air, she pumped her arms to force every drop of speed that she had from her legs.

He paced her, long after the point when her legs and lungs burned for relief.

She *knew* he ran *faster.* He was *waiting* for *her.* So *stupid.* They'd *make* those *rocks,* make *them,* make *them.*

As they did, a soldier grabbed her forearm and jerked her to the ground faster than she could dive. Her shoulder scraped stone as she toppled into cover, safe, and even the searing air trapped with them between the car-size boulders was a gift. Rolling to her side, she sucked in enough oxygen to cheer. "We made it!" She turned to share her exultation with Wulf.

He was sprawled on his stomach next to her, fingers spread in the dirt—slack.

"No!" She scrambled to roll him. Underneath, dust had blackened and clumped on the blood-soaked ground. "Wulf!"

His gear wouldn't open, so she yanked the strap cutter off her vest. His chest rose, but not on both sides. Pneumothorax.

"Medic! Medic!" Screw his name. "I need a chest tube!" Dammit, she'd donated everything from her ruck to the Afghans.

Wulf's blood covered her hands as she cut through his shirt to a palm-size exit wound on his right pectoral. A slippery red mess obscured her visual of the shredded flesh, but she knew he wouldn't need a chest tube if air escaped the cavity on its own. The left side of his chest rose, so he had one working lung, but she heard a Darth Vader suck.

"Medic!" She tore Wulf's hemostat bandage off his gear. Her hands couldn't shake or the bandage would stick uselessly to itself. "Where the *fuck* is the *medic?*" Clotting adhesive would help control hemorrhaging at this spot, but she needed another for the entry point.

Chris Deavers yelled coordinates into his radio handset. Everyone ignored her and Wulf, as if they were too busy shooting to care that their sergeant was dying.

Whump-boooom. A wave of air solidified and hammered into the back of her vest. Spinning fragments impacted above her head. Visions of shrapnel injuries terrified her, but she kept pressure on the wound.

"Deep breaths, Doc." A young sergeant dropped to his haunches at Wulf's feet.

"He can't—"

"Meant you." His Deep South accent radiated calm as he screwed a metal launch tube into tripod legs. "Don't you worry, ma'am. Those fuckers suck with mortars."

"Who's the medic?" She pressed harder on Wulf's chest.

He glanced at Wulf as he pulled a fin-tailed canister from his gear. "Wulfie don't need help." He spoke so slowly she wanted to punch him.

"He's not dead!" She wouldn't allow him to die, but he'd lost so much blood.

"Ain't that the truth." He slipped the rocket into the

tube's mouth. "Now you cover your ears and look away, ma'am, while I show how a Bama boy uses his ruck rocket."

She managed to turn her head as the young soldier yelled *shot out*, but the foam earplugs she'd worn on the helicopter were more wish than protection from the sound punch.

"Splash over," he called, saying *oh-vahr* like this was ordering up an egg. Well, screw him and this whole team.

"Inflate, dammit!" she yelled in Wulf's face, but he didn't move. "Keep breathing!" With the pressure bandage sealing the exit wound maybe he did need a chest tube to let the air out of the cavity between his lungs and chest wall. She wasn't a surgeon. She treated diarrhea and flu, pulled muscles and common shit. She'd never handled a wound like this by herself.

He could die.

Where was the entry wound? So much blood, she couldn't find the point of entry.

"Shot out!" *Boom.* Another mortar. "Splash *oh-vahr.*"

Left armpit, entry wound. She stuffed it with the bandage from her own gear but blood soaked through.

"Apaches ETA three minutes!" Chris relayed news of the attack helicopters coming to support them. "Blue Deuce and friends."

Lives could be lost, saved and lost again in three minutes. *But not this one.*

Automatic weapons, men yelling, radio static, incoming mortars landing obscenely close, others launching back from closer—the noise crushed her. She wanted to curl her arms over her head, but she kept pressure on the makeshift bandage and—*Yes!*—both sides of his chest rose. That wasn't enough. His bleed had soaked his dressing. The bullet must've nicked something. He'd need a transfusion soon, and the ability to give one was another thing she didn't have.

A second soldier crawled over. "Looks bad this time. I've got saline." He pulled out a pouch of fluid and yanked Wulf's arm from the remainder of his sleeve. He had to be the medic.

Instead of swearing, "*Took your fucking time*," she managed to say, "Give me another hemorrhage dressing, and he needs blood or plasma. What have you got?" She jockeyed to keep her hands on the bandages, but the medic's armor-plated torso squeezed her farther down Wulf's body until her arms extended past where she could apply adequate force.

Shrugging, the medic glanced at the saturated dressings. "No point wasting another." He slipped the needle in Wulf's vein on the first try. "Might need it."

She bumped against him to reposition herself closer to Wulf's wounds. "Wulf needs it!"

"Don't think so." He nodded his head at Wulf's chest. "Bleed stopped."

"Don't tell me my job!" As she argued, she realized that blood no longer seeped through her fingers.

"He's my team, so I will." The medic squeezed the intravenous bag to move it faster. "Pump saline, nothing else. No drugs, nada." He shoved the bag at her, and she released one dressing to grab it. "*You* don't do anything for him." He crowded close. "Understand?"

She did. Anything could happen—it already had happened—and she had no one to trust. These men were willing to let Wulf die, and she was in their way.

WITHIN TEN MINUTES, the Apache attack helicopters had completed their lethal work and circled like sharks scenting chum, but after the rain of Hellfire missiles, the attackers in the hills surrounding the boulder fortress couldn't be more than ash piles.

Theresa bent to Wulf. "Medevac's coming. We'll get you out."

His eyelids fluttered.

"Wulf!" Her throat clogged as he stared at nothing. "Hang on!"

"Dust-off's here, Doc." The Southerner sounded like he'd answered a doorbell. When her cramped legs wouldn't unfold, he hauled her to her feet. "Captain D, you willing to take the doc while we load Sergeant Roadkill?"

"Watch out for him!" She staggered on numb legs and strained to reach Wulf, but Chris's left hand manacled her upper arm.

"Bravo Squad, pull security for the aircraft recovery team." While Chris ordered half the men to stay on-site, he marched her to the rescue helicopter.

"He needs a litter!" she yelled at the two men carting a sagging Wulf.

Instead of listening, they dumped him on a seat and handed him a peanut butter packet from a meal pouch.

"He can't have that!" He'd hit surgery as soon as they landed at Caddie, and most likely be pushed forward to the main hospital at Bagram, so he was nothing-by-mouth.

When Chris dropped her arm to give the pilot a thumbs-up, she lunged for her patient.

The helicopter's surge flung her sideways and the landscape dropped away through the open doors. She tried to find a handhold or a safety line to grab, but a track embedded in the floor caught the toe of her boot. Skidding, she slapped air when the Black Hawk banked. Rocks blurred behind the door gunner. As the helicopter gained height and speed, the opening pulled her like a drain sucking water. She leaned away, but her soles couldn't grip.

Everything seemed to stop except the ground rushing past at the bottom of the slope that, seconds before, had been level.

She was falling.

Chapter Eight

THE HELICOPTER BANKED the opposite direction at the instant the back of Theresa's bulletproof vest jerked. Airborne, she felt, for a millisecond, what an astronaut must experience without gravity, before her landing jarred every vertebra between her tailbone and neck. Someone's hard-shelled knee pad slammed her chest armor and another bracketed her spine.

Her lungs expanded with a breath she hadn't expected to own. Almost unbelievably, she hadn't cartwheeled out the door. Who'd yanked her from the brink? She shoved her helmet higher on her forehead and twisted from her huddle to identify her savior.

All colors except blue had vanished from Wulf's eyes, and his cheeks conformed to his skull. He looked cold and drained as he slurped the traces of peanut butter from the packet. Next to her jaw, his other wrist trembled where he gripped a loop on the shoulder of her gear. He'd saved her again, but his heroism might have cost blood he couldn't afford to lose.

She stretched for the sliced flaps of his shirt.

"Stop." His lips were easy to read over the noise of the engines.

"Wound check," she yelled back.

"Don't." He shook his head from side to side as he reached for her wrist. "No."

"I have to." She blocked him with one hand and laid

her other palm over the bandage. His body was feverishly hot, oddly so when chill and shock were the common responses after a serious injury.

He slumped, eyelids lowered and chin tucked to his chest as if he was ashamed. He shouldn't have been, because she was the one who'd run too slowly, not him. Her fingernails caught the edge of the gauze. She meant to check for fresh bleeding, but the bandage peeled into her hand like wet paper and revealed his chest, whole and white. It wasn't bloodless white, but a healthy breadcrust color with traces of veins and dark blond hair.

"Wulf!" She couldn't pull her eyes from the textbook perfection. Minutes ago she'd pressed her fingers into a three-inch hole right there, where her blood-streaked hand stood out dark and filthy against his unbroken skin. Prepared to celebrate, she stretched toward him from her spot between his knees. "You're—"

She shut up when she saw the despair etched on his face. The main rotor's *thw-thw-thw* pounded a question into her brain: *how-how-how?* The blood on his sliced-up clothes didn't lie. He had been shot through a lung, a killer shot, but he'd healed in minutes.

Then the pieces connected. The medevac calls, the missing paperwork, even the blood in Nazdana's mouth after her seizure—he'd been injured, but, like today, he'd walked away whole. This was the secret the team had tried to conceal in the gym.

The rhythm of the helicopter rocked her against his legs, but she was too numb and shaky to push herself from the metal deck. They stared at each other in a parody of an embrace, his arm cradling her shoulder, one of her hands on his leg, the other spread across his bare chest, while liquid pooled in his eyes.

Finally the Black Hawk surged forward, and the changed motion broke their stalemate. He signaled to someone past her shoulder. Big hands hoisted her into a seat.

"Don't move." Sergeant Kahananui's broad face resembled an unsmiling idol as he buckled her harness. "Don't talk."

Demanding answers from the wall of silent men would be pointless. In addition to Wulf, slumped in his seat, the two door gunners and Deavers stared out of the helicopter. The Hispanic medic watched Wulf, and the young Southerner closed his eyes. Beside her, Kahananui read the label on a bottle of water as if it was a skin magazine. No one looked at her or met her eyes. Everything appeared to be normal, yet nothing was. No one so much as twitched until Wulf removed the intravenous needle and folded the empty saline bag into his cargo pocket. Then the medic tossed him a roll of duct tape to secure the sides of his shirt and vest where she'd sliced the Velcro. The efficiency seemed frighteningly routine from a man who should have been dead.

She had so many questions, but the rules her mother had established about her stepfather's garbage business flooded back as the rescue flight stretched. *Even Miss Smarty-Pants doesn't need to know everything.* She understood that the team's secret wasn't her affair, but whatever had given Wulf this healing ability could save hundreds or thousands of soldiers. It would advance trauma care and possibly end combat deaths.

The end of death.

Her hands shook. Clutching the fabric of her cargo pants didn't stop the trembling, so she jammed her fists into her armpits. Was Wulf part of an experiment? Now that she knew, what would happen to her? The air was cooler at this altitude, but the bumps up and down her arms had nothing to do with temperature. How far would Wulf's team go to keep his secret?

One step at a time. First she had to get away and pull herself together.

Deavers and the other men wouldn't look at her, but she reminded herself they were American soldiers like her. They'd saved her today. *Wulf* had saved her twice. The man who'd eaten her mother's cookies, who'd held her hand in the dark and cared enough to translate for a desperately ill Afghan girl, that man wouldn't hurt her. She clung to her faith in him, despite a whisper of doubt that asked, *Wouldn't he? Is he who you think he is?*

The forward motion ceased as they hovered over the airfield at Caddie. Less than one minute to landing, and suddenly every pair of eyes focused on her. She felt pinned.

Were *any* of them who she thought they were?

No sticking around to find out. Her thumb slipped under the buckle's release mechanism, and she pushed the soles of her boots against the metal deck, ready to bolt.

THERESA LOCKED THE female shower unit's door and stowed a clean uniform on the bench with the relief of a homecoming. Between her years in college and med school dormitories, her residency apartment and cheap off-base housing, she'd spent a dozen years behind plastic shower curtains whose speckled bottom seams didn't bear inspection. Worse, she'd stored shampoo and soap in her indestructible caddy longer than she'd been able to buy a drink.

Hot water sluiced over her body and created a cloud of steam that separated her from the day's events. She attacked her fingers with a nail brush until her hands pinkened. Not an iota of Wulf's blood remained in the creases or under her nails, but even with the evidence of his injury washed down the drain faster than the wounds had disappeared from his chest, she knew his healing hadn't been a dream.

With everything she understood about the human body threatening to change, how could the face looking back from the mirror while she combed her hair be the same? The head tilted when she needed to reach to pin her bun, and the fingers in the reflection obligingly buttoned a clean shirt, but she felt removed from that person.

Dressed, she rolled her stained shirt carefully into a zip-closing bag and concealed it with her towel. The blood smears were the only evidence to support what she planned to tell Jennifer.

On her black sport watch, the day flashed: TU. Tuesday. Today was Tuesday and—*oh shit, tomorrow*—Wednesday she had to report at 0400 to the helipad for an 0500 lift to Bagram Airfield in Kabul. She had a seat on an air force flight to Kuwait City, where she'd switch out of her uniform and catch a commercial flight to Rome. The black civilian carry-on her roommates took turns using on leave waited, packed, at the foot of her bunk. She'd loaded it yesterday, expecting today to be hectic.

Hectic described today like *stomach bug* described *Vibrio cholerae* bacterium.

A reverberating knock on the bath unit's aluminum door spun her around.

BRACED ON THE wall across from his commander's desk, Wulf acknowledged his miscalculation. Forty minutes ago when Theresa tore out of the helicopter, he should've followed her and untangled this clusterfuck, instead of trailing after Deavers to coordinate the downed aircraft recovery team. His captain and Kahananui had that situation handled. With the last man inbound, the disabled Black Hawk sling-loaded under a heavy-lift CH-47 Chinook and the incident report delegated to Cruz, he could no longer ignore his woman problem.

Letting go of his support made his head wobble, but before he could find chow he had to shower off the blood. If the stars favored him, maybe Theresa hadn't yet talked to anyone about what she'd seen.

"Hold on." Deavers spoke around the tobacco in his cheek. "The drugs in the container we found with Morgan are moving."

"Damn." He didn't need this now, not when he felt like the walking dead. "Where?"

"The marked load's part of a Black and Swan convoy to Peshawar. Presumably to a ship in Karachi." The squint lines around his commander's eyes announced that he wasn't finished.

"And?" Wulf's lips were too stiff from his effort to stay upright to say more. He needed ten times his normal calories after the amount of collagen his cells had burned regenerating his muscles and skin. Peanut butter and sports drinks kept him conscious, but he needed more carbs and fats, a lot more, to feel human.

"Someone ought to eyeball the load. Collect HUMINT and determine the destination."

Human intelligence gathering in Karachi, Pakistan, required a fluent speaker of Urdu, Pashto, Punjabi and Sindhi. Wulf knew only one screwed soul who fit the bill.

"*Someone* means me?" Didn't the captain understand what was on the line if Theresa poked deeper into his life? She'd searched for his medical files once, and now she had a reason to dig. "You realize I've got to find the doc—"

"Out of it, aren't you?" Deavers spit in his cup. "Bama Boy's keeping an eye on her."

"What if she talks?" He scratched his chest. Until his body pushed out the fabric shreds and other debris trapped between the new cells, his skin would itch worse than a week-old jockstrap.

"He'll keep her roommates away. Doesn't she head out ASAP for midtour leave?" Deavers riffled papers on his desk. "Sure I can forge a Red Cross message requiring you out of theater for an emergency too."

"Ahh." Wulf sagged against the wall. He should've had faith, but that commodity was scant when his tank was this empty. "Where would my emergency be?"

"Karachi first, then wherever our mystery cargo goes. Find out who takes delivery." Deavers handed him a blurry photo of a brown-haired man whose full mustache didn't conceal his jowls. "Morgan's disappearing flight-line manager. Cruz couldn't dig up a better shot because he's been wiped from the B & S database. And this—" he added a business card to the photo, "—is the best CIA guy in Karachi, if you need backup."

Wulf pocketed both. "Who's the worst one?"

"That'd be the new guy, name of John Smith. Seriously." Chris rolled his eyes and grinned past the wad in his lip. "Going to play dumb?"

"Crossed my mind." In a clueless nasal tone, he asked, "Uhh, can you tell me where the docks are? Is that the ocean?" before reverting to himself. "My coloring stands out in Karachi. Everyone's so suspicious after the bin Laden job, I might as well go for laughs."

"Your choice, but hurry and pack your cling things. Morgan's on night ops so he can drop you on the convoy before it hits the border at 2330 tonight."

Fast-roping onto moving targets was usually Wulf's favorite part of a mission, but riding spider style was French for shitty sleep. He'd have to stay suctioned or magnetically attached to a container roof until they stopped somewhere he could disembark unnoticed.

"While you're gone, we'll hunt the lab." Deavers pulled a map with red dots marching down a valley like a line of fire ants. "Firebases where Morgan picked up overweight loads."

"Sorry to miss hide-and-seek." Wulf's stomach rumbled like Kahananui's coffee grinder.

"You look like a dead trout." He picked up his spit cup and tilted on two chair legs. "Better get to chow."

"Love to. Some paper pusher with unauthorized side business kept me late."

"Well, frag the son of a bitch next time." Deavers tossed him a can of foul-n-fizzy energy drink. "Oh, wait, you mean me. Scratch that."

Wulf popped the top. "Come on, any leads on my destination? Europe? North America?"

"No clue, but that much of Afghanistan's best doesn't fly special delivery. You'll have time to kill before the boat unloads down the line." The captain's humor disappeared as his eyes locked with Wulf's. "I hear Rome is nice this time of year. You might check it out."

Wulf's breath caught. Had his commander ordered him to follow Theresa? His expression must've communicated his question, because Deavers nodded.

"The team can't lose you." His captain left the instruction unspoken, but not unclear. *Handle the problem with the doctor.*

Wulf acknowledged by lifting his can in the informal salute Special Forces used among themselves. No need to let on he didn't have the energy for a full hand to brow.

WHEN THERESA PEERED out the narrow opening of the bathroom trailer's door, she saw a woman with her fist raised to knock. Relief, as warm as the shower she'd finished, flooded her.

"Ma'am? Everything okay?" The private, who might turn twenty on her next birthday, frowned. "The sergeant asked me to check." Her voice rose as if she wondered why, but then she answered her own question. "He said he heard a noise and thought maybe someone slipped?"

Theresa's gaze followed the private's thumb. Wulf's teammate with the Southern accent stood in the shadow of a building kitty-corner to the shower unit. He held a phone, the picture of a guy looking for privacy to call home, but she knew better. He was watching.

"Ma'am? You okay?"

"I—I—" Her mind churned. She couldn't stay trapped here, and she didn't want to leave alone in case he followed.

"You need some water or something?" The private raised her hands as if to catch her.

"I skipped lunch to make weight." Totally the opposite—she'd had a massive feast—but she needed a plausible excuse to ask for help. "I'm feeling shaky."

The enlisted woman's forehead wrinkled. "Can I walk you to sick call? Or your hut?"

Both would be empty at dinner. She wanted people, a lot of them. "I should eat. Maybe the dining facility..."

"I'm headed to the DFAC myself, ma'am."

Theresa glanced at the bundled uniform left behind on the bench as she locked the door. For now, the women's shower was probably the safest place for the stained shirt. As she descended the three steps to ground level, the other woman's hand hovered next to Theresa's elbow. From the corner of her eye, Theresa saw the watcher sidle away between two prefabs.

"Thanks for your help." She meant those words more than the other woman could imagine.

WULF'S FIRST TWO servings of ravioli had disappeared by the time Theresa entered the chow hall with a female private. Not likely she'd confide in someone that junior, so he let himself absorb her while she paused in front of the tray rack. Her hair was darker and smoother. Wet, from a shower. They'd been doing the same thing in different places. Maybe they'd been thinking about the same thing too.

Of course they had. He'd been thinking about her, and no doubt she'd been freaking out about him and what she'd seen.

"Going to talk to her?" Cruz asked from his left.

"Here?" He watched her hands hover over the silverware baskets. Those hands hadn't hesitated when she'd worked on Nazdana or him.

"No way, dude," Kahananui interrupted from his other side.

"He's good to go," Cruz argued. "I can tell he puts the salsa in Doc's tacos."

"My life, fucked up by committee." Craving more

fat and sugar, Wulf shoveled vanilla ice cream down his throat. "Got more brilliant advice?"

"Don't let her think too much," Cruz said. "Women get worked up real fast about shit."

She made her way to the hot chow line. Her hair probably smelled like oranges again. If he talked to her, the scent would carry him to Karachi. Part of him wanted that hit, like a rush of adrenaline to his soul instead of to his muscles, but part of him knew he should stay in his seat.

He was a trained killing machine afraid of smelling a woman's shampoo…

"I live with four women." The Big Kahuna held up a hand with the thumb folded down. "My wife, her mother—" He wiggled two hot-dog-size fingers.

"So that's why you volunteered for this unit," Cruz muttered.

"—and our girls. I'm saying, privacy's a big-f-deal. I told Jewel about that tenth-anniversary cruise in a take-out line, and I did not hear the end of it for two damn months. You got to find private space if you're serious about some please-be-quiet magic. The dining facility is not the spot to talk, I'm saying."

"Gentlemen, just because I'm not married and I won't help Cruz pick up twenty-five-year-old twins on the internet doesn't mean I lack a working knowledge of women." Wulf knew very well how to engage and entertain the softer gender. He also knew the cost of caring, something Cruz and Kahananui couldn't advise him how to avoid.

Theresa slid to the end of the line with her empty tray, past the cordon bleu the server had automatically held out to her.

"He could ask her to step outside." Cruz leaned across Wulf's chest to argue with Kahananui. "Parking lot's usually quiet during chow."

Wulf tilted his shoulders to see around Cruz. Theresa had paused before the salad bar.

"Earth to Cruz—that, booga, is why you haven't done a horizontal hula in nine months."

"We've been here seven!"

Soldiers behind Theresa stepped around her to reach the lettuce, but she didn't move.

"My point," Kahananui shot back. "You wasted two months at home because you don't know a parking lot from a—"

He didn't know what he'd say, but the way she seemed to vibrate with tension convinced him he had a chance to persuade her to remain quiet. He would beg, if that's what it took, because if he couldn't win her over, the ride to the border Deavers had arranged for him might have to pull double duty as his final exit.

THE SALAD BAR wouldn't answer her questions no matter how long Theresa stared. A jostle at her shoulder cued her to take a plate and pretend to the normal motions. No one freaked over cherry tomatoes, although she remembered a guy who'd lost it when the cooler ran out of his favorite sports drink. He'd kicked the metal sides and screamed while half the mess occupants worried he'd shoot the fridge. The other half had cheered him on until his platoon leader hauled him out. Stuck here, it wasn't nuts to imagine an out-of-stock beverage becoming the last straw.

Tonight nothing in the hot line or the salad bar appealed, so she turned to the ice-cream cooler. For the first time since she'd entered the building, she glanced at the room.

Wulf sat facing her at his team's usual table.

Her breath stuck in her chest, but her heart dropped the opposite direction to her stomach. She'd been so relieved that the special ops sergeant hadn't followed her, she hadn't bothered to wonder about his team, and the joke was on her. Plates and bowls littered Wulf's table like detritus from an Atlantic City eating contest. Even though barely more than two hours had passed since the killer shot through his vest armhole, the goat-cheese color of his skin had returned to a healthy flush, and he was as whole as any of the other soldiers. He was perfect.

Slow, deep breaths, that's what she told patients and reminded herself. She couldn't lose her shit. Not here, not publicly.

Two of his team argued across him, but they faded around the edges as he filled her vision. She felt as if a zip line linked them. If she didn't go to him, he'd careen over here to swoop her away and everything—her hold on that scream, her promotion, her references, her future, everything she wanted—would end.

Another bump, this one against her hip, encouraged her to stop blocking the drinks.

As soon as she moved, Wulf stood.

She whirled and shoved her empty tray at the return slot, but missed. While the clatter of the tray hitting the floor echoed behind her, her palms slammed the exit door hard enough to jar her teeth. For once the darkness offered more security than the light behind her.

Under her feet, gravel crunched loud enough to hear over the generators. Or maybe her hearing had sharpened from the adrenaline pumping through her system.

The door squeaked behind her. For an instant the clattering of pans and blur of voices increased as another person left dinner.

She sped around the corner and smacked into something. Correction, someone.

"Doc." The voice belonged to Chris Deavers, Wulf's commander. He gripped her left arm. Doors in the two long sides of the building had overhead lights, and the kitchen at the opposite end had a lit fire exit, but she and Chris stood in a dark pocket created by the windowless wall that supported the dining room's giant television.

"Let go." She pulled sideways, straining to hear whether whoever had left the mess was coming.

"Can't do that," the Special Forces captain said, his voice clipped.

She opened her mouth to argue, but he must've thought she intended to scream, because she suddenly found herself spun in a one-eighty, legs and feet twisted weird directions. His hand slammed over her mouth as he jerked her arm behind her back and up, and *fuck, that hurt.*

"Ease it, boss." Wulf's voice lashed out of the dark. "She's not the enemy."

Chris released her so abruptly she crashed into the end of the building.

Wulf stepped between his commander and her, hands held in front of him as if prepared to fight.

Oh please, God, no. She flattened herself to the wall. Having a married officer and an enlisted man brawling over her would be the hottest gossip in ten deployment cycles.

Chris retreated and dug the heels of his palms into

his eye sockets as if waking up. In front of her, Wulf's shoulders relaxed.

"You're toast, both of you." Her inadequate threat was further weakened by her croak. Their combined stares didn't help her recover, but after scrubbing her hand across her mouth where Chris had stifled her, she tried again. "Let me put it more clearly. You're fucked. You better kill me and clean it up extremely well, because in three minutes I'm calling a lawyer at JAG and reporting you." She glared while she massaged her shoulder. "For *assault*."

"Wulf hasn't done anything wrong. Just me. I'm sorry. I'm really—shit." Chris grabbed his head. "I don't know. Everything went red. Oh God, I'm sorry, Doc." He seemed as genuinely horrified as the surgical nurse Theresa had known during her residency who'd neglected to count used clamps until after the appendectomy had been closed.

The weight of his career hung between them.

"I know it's no excuse. I should never have grabbed you, never. But it feels like I haven't breathed since everything went down today. I'm sorry."

The fact that Chris was apologizing instead of threatening her went a long way toward making her decision. "Leave," she ordered. "Just leave me alone."

"I screwed up." He turned to Wulf. "Ninety minutes and ticking until your ride's here. Make it count." He stumbled around the corner.

Wulf remained. "Hey." The shadows were too dark to decipher his expression, but that single syllable, spoken low and slow, carried a familiar warmth. "You didn't eat before you ran out." He held out an orange wrapped in a paper napkin. "Here."

She ignored his offering. "What's wrong with you?"

"Nothing." The hand with the orange fell to his side. "I'm fine. Isn't that the problem?"

"I don't mean…that." She waved her hand in the air, uncertain how to describe what she'd seen in the helicopter. "I mean tonight. The sergeant watching me. You, following me. Chris, just now. What's going on?"

"The captain's handling a lot. I've never seen him flip like that, but he knows he made a huge mistake." He inhaled deeply and closed his eyes. "You do like oranges, don't you?"

"Chris was bad cop and now you're good cop?"

"Not at all." There was enough light to see him dig a thumb into the fruit and pull off a chunk of peel. "You have a secret clearance? Standard for officers?"

"Uh-huh." She licked her lips and tried not to watch his hands as he unveiled the orange's flesh. The pith glowed in the faint light at this end of the building.

"You know what level clearance we have?" He stowed a handful of peel in his pocket.

She shook her head. Her mouth felt drier as the citrus scent reached her, and she yearned for a taste, but asking would be tantamount to surrender.

"Top secret with sensitive compartmentalized information access," he said.

"What's that have to do with anything?"

"You need to understand there are things my team knows, things we do, that we legally cannot tell you. Things the president or secretary of defense tells our chain of command directly and that neither you nor anyone else, not even Congress, is allowed to know." He inserted his thumbs into the end of the orange and pulled. As it separated into two hemispheres, a mist of juice sprayed the air and landed on her cheeks and lips, as fine as dew. "We could go to jail for discussing those things. So could you."

"Today…" Was he trying to explain why no one had talked to her in the helicopter?

He nodded. "Now you know one of those things. Here." He held out a section to her.

The orange scent that enveloped her was already strong enough to taste, so she might as well accept. It burst with flavor in her mouth, sweetness after a day of hell, and strengthened her urge to push on. "That's not enough of an explanation."

"Ask away." He handed her a second slice of orange. "I can't promise to answer."

"You were shot today?" She continued even as he nodded. "And the other times?"

He nodded again.

"And your body repaired itself completely?"

Another silent affirmative.

"Is this…" While she considered her phrasing, she accepted two more orange sections. Their taste reminded her of sunshine. "Are you part of a medical experiment?"

He nodded a fourth time.

"The others?"

He shook his head. So it was only him.

"This is ridiculous. I suck at charades." Although she wanted to tell him to stuff his crapload of games and contradictions into the holding tank of a porta-john, the compulsion to unravel this mystery overwhelmed her frustration. "Is this a drug trial?"

He parried her question with one of his own. "Are you familiar with hemoglobin?"

"The iron-containing metalloprotein in red blood cells? A little." *More like a lot.* Curiosity built in her chest, threatening to bubble over as she leaned toward Wulf. After her hypoxia sickness on the first hike to Nazdana's village, she'd never admit that her thesis had focused on isolating a genetic mutation that allowed certain mammals to survive at extremely high altitudes. Hemoglobin, which assisted in carrying blood oxygen, had been a key factor in her research, but she didn't see how it could've caused Wulf's abnormally rapid healing. "If it's a research project, I'd love to help. Can I report on today to—"

"Whoa, Doc." He raised his hand, palm out, and shook his head. "You can't talk about what happened. It's above your clearance, way above. You shouldn't even think about it."

"You think I can forget?"

"You have to."

"A treatment that can repair injuries nearly instantly? Do you know how many lives could be—"

He leaned so close she could smell hints of Italian seasoning from his dinner, and she realized she was famished as well as excited.

"It's no longer available." The flat tone of his voice almost stopped her.

"But someone could—"

"The source is dead."

Four short words, spoken so slowly they carried enough weight to crush her excitement, her hunger and maybe even her breathing.

"Go pack. You're out of here, remember. Don't think about me again."

As if she could control her thoughts. Tonight she'd honor his request and let it go, because tomorrow she was scheduled to boogie out of Caddie, but like hell would she drop it.

AFTER THE CRUNCH of Theresa's footsteps had faded in the direction of the housing area, leaving Wulf with nothing but sticky citrus-scented hands and the memory of her distracted goodbye, his commander stepped around the corner.

"Think that's the end of it?" Deavers asked.

Wulf snorted. "I figure it'll take her half an hour of internet research, tops, to blow that story. Hemoglobin was the only big word I could scrounge. Remember that immune booster shot they stuck in us?" Hopefully it would stop her talking to other people tonight.

"So she'll ask more questions." His boss sounded tired.

"She's not a quitter. On the other hand, I didn't get the sense she's going to call JAG."

"Thanks for that." The pause was heavier than a combat load. "Don't know what happened with me."

"Thought about visiting the chaplain? Seems like a squared-away guy." There were times Wulf wanted to talk about the fog that enveloped him when his brain mixed the voices and faces of people who'd died alongside him in previous centuries with the people around him now. While he couldn't take his problem to the chaplain, his boss could try.

"I'll be fine." Chris raised his fist, and a moment later Wulf connected his in a familiar bump.

"I think you will." He must have sounded authentic, because his friend's shoulders relaxed.

"I better scrounge up that emergency leave paperwork." His boss snorted. "Enjoy Rome, but don't forget *force protection.* I hear Cruz has an unopened box in his footlocker."

"Sir." Since Special Forces never used their commander's title privately, maybe saying it would shut Deavers up before he followed that thought too far for Wulf's comfort. "Sir, it's inappropriate—"

"Right, she's an officer, you're not. Still—" Chris broke into laughter, the normal kind that sounded like something a person would hear at the unit picnic at home station.

Good *he* could see the humor in the situation. With his future on the line, Wulf couldn't. "Sir, I've been ordered to pack." As he left his grinning commander, he tossed over his shoulder, "And, sir? Fuck off."

Chapter Nine

WULF REPLACED THE porcelain cup in its saucer. Without the CIA agent across the table, the croissants and hot coffee would be ideal after two days transiting between Caddie and Karachi. Although he hated coordinating with the CIA even more than drawing a crapfest burrito from patrol rations, he was too damn blond to recon Karachi's docks without drawing attention from Pakistan's secret intelligence service. The U.S. consulate was the place to acquire a CIA beard.

J. T. Smith, pseudo public-affairs assistant, had the bleary eyes of a college student killing time between frat parties and a ruddy complexion that broadcast permanent discomfort in the tropical sun. He'd been in Pakistan three months but, according to taxi drivers who loitered down the block, hadn't mastered the exchange rate between dollars and rupees. Because he overpaid for every ride or scrap of information, he'd become excessively popular among those seeking to simultaneously mislead American intelligence and make a buck. Sticking to J.T.'s rising star was perfect cover for playing dumb American.

"The rules of engagement don't permit us to operate on this side of the border." He stifled his urge to add, *So we can't claim expenses when we do.* "We need your help to find out when we'll have space to move a surveillance antenna."

"An antenna? How's that getting here?"

Look out the window. How do you think, super spook? "By ship. We have to know when the containers in the way move and we have space to land a stealth-technology CH-47." In case Smith didn't know his helicopters, Wulf whispered, "An invisible Chinook. Bigger than the sneaky bird we flew in the Abbottabad op against OBL."

"Wow." Smith's eyebrows jumped so high on his forehead Wulf wondered for an instant if the guy was conning him back. "How many of those do you have in theater?"

"Classified. But I can say less than a baker's dozen." If Smith passed that canard to his superiors, he'd find out how hard they could mock a guy who believed what he heard from the army. Interagency feuds were bitter; intra-agency ones, brutal. "What's the wharf situation?"

"Want to head over and see? I'm free this morning." The agent grinned like a puppy.

"My captain hoped you'd show me around." *Deavers knows the CIA can't resist meddling in Special Ops business.* "Do you have a terp on call?" He'd no intention of letting Smith know he understood the lingua franca.

"My local interpreter's the best." Smith pulled out a cell phone.

"Keep this off the airwaves." Wulf wrapped his hand around the number pad. "Ask him to show up, but don't say why."

The new American consulate occupied twenty acres next to the Port of Karachi, so it took less than a half hour for Wulf and his escort to leave security and be driven to a corrugated metal shack at the Western Wharf. Afghanistan was far from the sea for a man raised at an oar bench, and normally Wulf would revel in the briny wind off Baba Channel. Today all he wanted was intel.

Although it wasn't yet ten-thirty, the wharf's chief guard invited them to share a hookah. A clipboard hanging behind the Pakistani's head noted vessels and destinations, and Wulf expected to know the shipping details by the end of the smoke break. With the right cabbie, he'd make his flight to Dubai and be in Rome for dinner. He was due for a break, if only because he had to endure this CIA kid's chatter for another hour.

SWEAT STUCK DRAYCOTT'S stained *salwar* pants to the creases of his groin while he crouched near a stack of concrete blocks. Despite his racing heart, he forced himself to breathe with the wheezing rattle of a near-dead beggar. When he'd donned this stinking outfit, he'd anticipated nothing more exciting than counting rusty containers as they loaded onto the equally rusty *Horizon Kaptan*, not the arrival of a Special Forces sergeant from Camp Caddie. A month ago he'd noticed the Green Beret and put a name on the eerily familiar face: Wulf Wardsen. He should've trusted his intuition and probed deeper after that hair-trigger manager had screwed up and killed an aviation warrant officer, but instead he'd ignored his doubts and recertified the supply line. His mistake might roll up the network.

He knew who the Director would blame.

"This is an efficient facility for its age." Wardsen and his companions lounged by the hookah, close enough for Draycott to hear the interpretation of the sergeant's next question. "But surely the new wharf will better meet modern standards?"

"The Western Wharf exceeds world standards." The

guard defended his fiefdom. "We accommodate Pana-max ships. What ports along the Indian Ocean do that, I ask you? Name one."

"That rust bucket loading out is no Panamax. I doubt it can carry more than a hundred, hundred-fifty con-tainers."

As soon as the sergeant's challenge was interpreted, the security officer burst into praise of the ship in ques-tion, the one that would load ten particular Black and Swan containers.

In contrast to the guard's volubility, Draycott doubted his own powers of speech, because at this angle he could see the other side of Wardsen's face. His temple had a star-shaped scar of pale skin. It was the same scar at the same spot where the man in the Mogadishu bar had lifted his fingers to mockingly salute a green CIA agent on his first day. That mark was branded as per-manently in Draycott's memory as it was on the skin of the man smoking the hookah and asking about ship-ping schedules.

This soldier *was* that man, not a son of, not a relative, and the knowledge froze Draycott as surely as if he'd been dipped in liquid nitrogen. It wasn't the impossibility of a man not aging for forty years that chilled him, since he'd stolen a photo from CIA archives of arms deals dur-ing the Iran/Iraq war. He already knew the Director and his two partners hadn't gained a wrinkle or lost a hair since the day in the eighties when they'd shaken Sad-dam Hussein's hand in front of a secret camera. No, it wasn't this soldier's eternal youth as much as the logi-cal next question: if the sergeant shared the Director's extraordinary ability, had he been sent by the Director?

Had his position become redundant?

He saw two choices. He could update the Director and gamble that the intelligence protected him. If it didn't, he'd have to run. His wife had mentioned retiring from Northern Virginia traffic to Florida, her Plan B. Everyone had a Plan B. He had C, D and X, one of which might hide him from the Director, but he couldn't be sure Jane would accept a fugitive life. She'd never break contact with her daughter.

The beggar he played shuffled to the end of the wharf, not waiting to hear the soldier ascertain that the Turkish vessel and its load were bound for Durres, Albania. The fetid air inside a public outhouse that dumped into the bay choked him, but behind its door no one would see a beggar use an encrypted smartphone.

"You have an emergency?" The Director never used names.

"Yes, sir." Because the Director revered formality, Draycott spoke as if his boss was the crown prince of a repressive oil state. He never let himself mock the Director, not even silently, since the coworker who'd once performed an unflattering impersonation had found his dog's head in a sink. "I apologize, but Charlie network's turned red. A Special Forces soldier from a camp near the Paktia facility showed up in Karachi this morning to observe cargo loading."

"Can he be neutralized?"

"Unclear, sir." He had to convey the soldier's extended youthfulness without betraying his own knowledge of the Director's past.

"Explain."

"The soldier seems familiar from my previous career." As he brushed away flies attracted to the salt in his sweat, he waited, but no prompt came from the

Director's end. "He strongly resembles a mercenary I encountered in 1968. If it weren't impossible, he could be the same man." He needed more air. The stench pressed on his chest until all he could manage was a croaked, "He hasn't changed a bit." While he parsed his superior's silence, the faint warble of a call to morning prayer emerged from the phone. Automatically, he calculated the Director's location as an Islamic country approximately five hours behind Pakistan time. That equaled West Africa: Morocco, Senegal, or Mauritania. Mali was too chaotic.

"Describe this soldier." The tone of the order brought to mind the one time he'd seen his boss personally execute a man. A Hong Kong syndicate leader had cheated the opium scales, so the Director had sliced fat from the man's buttocks and weighed it, announcing the total until the man died. Chinese operations had been fully compliant for the seven years since, and Draycott's own ass still tightened with fear at that hollow pitch.

"Blond. Blue eyes. He's a staff sergeant."

"Not an officer?"

Relief rolled through Draycott, so sharp and hard he almost staggered against the feces-encrusted wall. The soldier wasn't part of the organization and hadn't been sent to take over. "No. Goes by Wardsen. Wulf Wardsen."

Although Draycott didn't recognize the language, the Director clearly swore. Draycott also heard shattering, as if glass or china had hit the floor.

"That bastard. Sends his brother to—" The Director stopped.

His boss had a personal rival, and that equaled a lever.

Perhaps the Director didn't yet realize, but a tiny shift in the power balance had occurred.

"Sir, Wardsen knows this week's cargo is en route to Albania. Shall I divert the ship? Or prepare a welcome in Durres?"

"We can't wait two weeks for Durres. I want him neutralized sooner."

"Yes, sir." The memory of the speed at which Wardsen had thrown the knife at the Belgian's throat forty years ago filled Draycott's mind. He suspected he'd agreed to the largest challenge of his career.

"Until I send a takedown team, watch him. I want to know everything he does, everyone he talks to, every bite he eats and every thought he thinks." A sound like a fist pounding metal, perhaps a steel file cabinet or table, filled Draycott's ear. "Everything!"

"As you wish, sir." Ankle-deep in shit, Draycott suppressed the joy of living another day from his voice. From here on out, each day could be his last.

Chapter Ten

THERESA LEANED AGAINST a stone balustrade midway up the Spanish Steps. A mix of Romans and tourists filled the piazza below the widest staircase in Europe, everyone chatting, strolling, waiting, smoking—the things city dwellers do outside on a warm evening. For the next eleven days, instead of being a soldier stuck inside barbed-wire barricades, she was one of these free people. Free to eat and drink, free to roam and, most of all, free to roll her eyes while listening to her mother nag.

"No, Mom, I'm not phoning Uncle Sal. He's not really my uncle and I haven't seen him in twenty years." Like a good daughter, her first call from her disposable cell phone was to let her mother know she'd arrived in Rome. She was a day and a half late to her destination, but after a nap and a shower, she felt ready to tackle the city. If she could get off the phone.

"I told him you were coming and now your cousins want to meet you!" Her mother's voice rose with joy knowing unattached Italian men inhabited her daughter's time zone.

"So he has a bunch of loser sons who want to meet a green card." She had no illusions about how her mother presented her unmarried offspring.

"No, darling, some are nephews."

"You're incorrigible." Half her brain listened to her mother describe the Silvios and Tonios in her first step-

father's family tree while a quarter of her mind worried
about pickpockets and the last quarter watched couples
wander through the June twilight.

"What did you think of the clothes I sent?"

"Everything's beautiful. Thank you." She would
not-not-not remember Wulf finding the lace bra. That
piece of clothing had stayed in her footlocker at Caddie.
"I'm wearing the poppy-print skirt." Left to herself, she
would've paired khakis and polos with running shoes
and a black nylon daypack and wandered around resem-
bling a retired teacher.

"Look inside the purse. I sent a list of how to wear
the outfits."

"You didn't." Theresa shook her head while she watched
the crowd at the bottom of the steps.

"Of course I did. You wore sweatpants eleven days
in a row. I will never forget that."

"Ma, it was the state play-offs. It was my uniform.
And I was in high school."

"Well, you're not in high school anymore, and you're
not getting any younger, so wear the clothes the way I
listed them."

She sighed. At the border between casual and fancy,
the wide belts, retro dresses, cropped pants and ballet
flats made her feel dressed to go out, never mind that
she knew no one here.

Her mother was still talking. "When you told me
you were going to Rome I had to watch *Roman Holiday*
again, and of course that led to *Breakfast at Tiffany's*
and *Charade*."

A bigger-than-medium blond man stood in front of
the glove store across the piazza. In the dusky light, the
angle of his shoulders made her abs clench.

"Impossible," she whispered. *He* was in Afghanistan. He had to be.

"Not at all. Carl watched the movies with me. I knew the belts and dresses would work because you do have my figure."

She lost the man's shape in the throng loitering around the sinking-boat fountain. Her hand tightened on the phone as she stretched to look over the potted azaleas. He hadn't walked. He'd glided like a predator. *Hunting.* Her shoulder blades prickled, suddenly chilly under her thin top, and she glanced up and behind, but the man didn't appear above her on the steps. Damn, she'd taken her eyes off the piazza, even though he couldn't come down from above if he'd been below her. She swung back to scan the crowd.

"Sweetheart? Is everything all right?" Her mother's voice had slowed.

She'd gone too long without speaking. "Sure. Everything's fine, Mom."

The couples mounted the steps, connected by hands or entwined arms, focused on each other. The singles talked fast into phones or stared at tiny screens. No one made eye contact with her. If she vanished, none of these people could describe her. None of them had seen her, except for the man who'd disappeared. The tight skin on the back of her neck told her that he'd looked at her. Carefully.

"I put Uncle Sal's phone number in the black purse for emergencies. Call him."

Tourists parted around the man, who appeared from the crowd at the bottom of the steps.

"Ohmigod, it *is* him. What's he—"

"Who? Who?"

"Nobody." Theresa answered her mother without taking her eyes off Wulf. He'd come for her. She couldn't remember if she'd told him where she was staying, but maybe Jennifer had. She forced herself to sound casual as her mother pressed for more. "Just a guy."

"A man? You met a MAN already? Is he Italian?"

He started up. In contrast to the men lounging with cigarettes or using mobile phones, he looked at her without distractions chiseling bits of his attention. As they locked gazes, his undivided regard made her aware of her mouth.

"Gotta go." She licked her lips. "Call you later."

"Wait! Be care—"

"Love you, Mom." She disconnected as her tongue moistened her lips again. They hadn't been chapped after her flights, but right now they'd become too dry.

Wulf reached the landing below her and kept coming. She could spot a fellow soldier halfway across a concourse at Newark by relying on posture and haircut and a dozen other cues, but in the violet evening light Wulf looked nothing like an American. His thighs pressed the seams of his linen pants until she might have believed he was a German soccer player or an Austrian skier during the off-season. The flat front of the pants emphasized that his stomach and abs were as carved as the marble statue in the fountain. She knew how those muscles looked and how they felt under her hand. They felt *whole* and *healthy*.

"Why are you here?" She held out a stiff palm to stop his advance, although she recognized his presence as inevitable. If the powers that be needed to keep tabs on her now that she knew about the hush-hush experiment, who better to send?

"Theresa." His voice rumbled up the six steps that separated them.

She shouldn't allow him to use her first name but—*sayonara*, self-preservation—she wanted to hear it again. "After our last discussion, I won't believe you need a checkup."

ALTHOUGH HE WAS close enough to touch Theresa, Wulf suspected he'd have better luck if he stayed two steps lower to reduce his threat profile. He paused, eyes level with the hollow of her throat. Perhaps her swallow indicated nerves that matched his. "I had leave. Recalled you didn't have a tour guide."

"You already have a job. Three thousand miles away." She crossed her arms, unbending.

"My boss thinks I need a break." His voice came out as even as he intended, no hint of his racing heart.

She countered with a raised eyebrow. "I don't buy it."

"Can I convince you across a plate of pasta?" He touched his right hand to his chest, then held it out, palm open as if making an offering.

"No, thank you."

"There's a wonderful restaurant on Via Margutta." Let her agree, let her take his hand, because if she turned him down, he didn't see how he'd persuade her to ignore what she'd seen on the helicopter. "Join me."

Shaking her head, she refused, and he dropped his hand to his side. He hadn't prepared for the way her white shirt molded her waist and outlined her breasts. Maybe Cruz would have expected the visuals to be this much fuller than her uniform had let on, but he was struggling to focus facing her pair of high and tights.

He'd been silent too long, staring, and her eyebrows

had drawn together. Being civilized meant conversation, even if the Viking part of him wanted to throw her over his shoulder and run for a longboat, even if the red flowers printed on her silk skirt made him yearn to inhale her heady opium, even if she was sure to intoxicate more than any other contraband. "Poppies?"

"My mother's unintentional homage to Afghanistan's cash crop. At least, I hope it was unintentional. Sometimes hard to tell with her." The slight warming in her voice nourished hope that if he kept her talking about clothes or her mother, she'd change her mind about dinner.

"Beautiful flowers." She wore that skirt without knowing where he'd come from or where he had to go next week.

"And a useful painkiller for injuries." The edge returned to her voice.

He'd come to Rome to win her trust, misdirect her if he could, mislead her if he had to, but not to argue. That wouldn't help his cause. "Don't."

"Don't what?" She might imagine her crossed arms posed a barricade, but they also deepened the shadowy cleft between her breasts. "Don't think about what I saw on the helicopter? I was stuck in Kuwait for twenty-two hours. The airport had free wireless."

She'd done the research he'd warned Deavers about. If he couldn't convince her to stay silent, he'd lose his team. Loki had dangled her in front of his eyes to mock him, because no gods allowed men like him to have everything they wanted.

"Did you know I was an undergrad molecular biology major?"

That phrase, *molecular biology major*, carried a ring of doom.

"My thesis was a study of oxygen-carrying capacity in the blood of certain mammals. Specifically, I researched hemoglobin."

"Ouch." He let her see his wince. "You caught me."

"Somehow I don't think it was the only lie you've told."

"I'll concede one or two others." He hoped his smile appropriately blended charm and contrition. "But I trusted you with the important stuff, remember? Helping Deavers with his wife, saving Nazdana and the twins. I never lied about them."

"You're not playing fair."

Exploiting the softening of her mouth, he said, "Don't forget Mir-Meena. If not dinner, what about a gelato?" He willed her to stop fiddling with her purse strap and agree, so he'd have a chance to salvage the life he'd built in Special Forces. "Have you tasted every flavor yet?"

While she studied him, he wondered whether desperation worked for him or against him.

"My favorite is *nocciola*, although I could be persuaded to try anything you want." He gambled on her being too kind to kick him while he was down, literally, on a lower step.

Her eyes answered before her mouth did. The brown warmed like rocks kissed by the sun and the tiniest lines gathered at the corners. "You think that will make up for the complete line you fed me about hemoglobin?" A smile flitted across her lips, then disappeared, but he recognized opportunity.

"Come for one scoop, then let me know if you forgive me."

"If I agree—and that's an if—" She inhaled as if preparing to dive. "Does the dinner invitation stand?"

"It does." He had his wish. He only needed one, but if granted a second, she could take another deep breath while he watched her shirt buttons stretch. A man in his position shouldn't wish for too much, but maybe he'd be lucky.

"You'll stop the bullshit? First lie, and I'm gone."

"Promise." He put his hand on his heart. Even to himself, his latest lie sounded sincere.

THE THREE BLOCKS to the vine-shrouded osteria left the hubbub of the Spanish Steps so far behind that Theresa pictured a Tuscan village. The restaurant's interior was decorated in reds, blues and golds. Fringed lamps hanging between the ceiling beams cast light on a mix of paintings and gilt-framed mirrors. While she admired the decor, which felt more than slightly like a high-end speakeasy, Wulf requested a table, his Italian flawless.

"How many languages do you speak?" she asked after they were seated. The phrases she'd learned from Nonna—mostly *mangia, mangia*—were as useful here as junior-high Latin.

"Italian's the most beautiful." With his straight face undermined by the deepening smile lines at the corners of his eyes, he continued, "The language matches the women."

She rolled her eyes. "Don't tell me—the number of languages is classified information."

"You said it, not me." His full smile highlighted how ridiculous continuing to interrogate him across a vase of peonies was, but didn't provide answers. "May I recommend the risotto?"

After six months with pans of food on a steam table as a visual aid and two and a half days of airport food, using a menu, even the English one the hostess provided, overwhelmed her. She followed Wulf's suggestions and chose risotto made with vodka and pistachios as a first course, and veal *saltimbocca alla romana* for her main dish.

With the basics of ordering food and tasting the wine accomplished, they circled back to looking at each other and hunting for things to say that weren't weirdly awkward. Every question she wanted to blurt out sounded crazy across a pressed tablecloth, but what she knew about him *was* crazy. They had to start somewhere.

Her lips parted, but he jumped first. "Your name's Italian, isn't it?"

If he wanted to exchange background tidbits as a warm-up, she'd play along. "My grandparents emigrated after World War II. One of my grandmothers came to America on the *Andrea Doria*, before it sank." In college she'd crafted a version of her family story that she could share to appear normal when others inquired. "And you? What type of name is Wardsen?"

"A Danish patronym. The ending *sen* means son of." His shoulders twitched as if he'd startled himself.

"Son of Ward?"

"Ward's a modern version of Wonred." His eyebrows drew together in thought. "My...ancestor...was named Wonred."

"Your parents really chose Wulf? Or is it a nickname you adopted when you joined—"

His brief head shake reminded her not to name his unit.

"Wulf's better than Wonred." He shrugged. "That

means lackwit or sloppy drunk. I'm officially a son of a drunk." As he enunciated the last word, his eyes darted first to one edge of the table, then back to the flowers on the other edge, as if he'd become suddenly wary of an unexpected attack. She had the impression this anecdote might be one of the more truthful things he'd told her. "Don't know why I still use it."

"Chiesa means church. Nothing like extra pressure in Catholic school."

They sipped wine until the shadows receded from his eyes. Drinking alcohol with enlisted personnel at unit functions wasn't fraternization, but this restaurant, with its dim lighting and tiny tables, wasn't a hail and farewell at Club Hood.

Stay focused on questions, she chided herself. *That's the purpose of this dinner.*

"Your mother's a wonderful baker." Again, he changed the subject. "And an excellent judge of clothing. Do you have other family?"

"Some." She reached for her wineglass to cover her pause. She didn't talk about her stepfather Carl or her stepbrother. Twenty years ago, when her mother had married her third husband, she'd drilled her daughter never to talk about her new family. *Never tell our name to people who don't know it. Never tell anyone where we're going or where we went or who we went with. Not ever.* As an adult the dictum had been easy to follow, because she'd tired of boyfriends who either dropped her when they suspected the nature of Carl's business or made constant clichéd jokes about the mob. "You?"

"About the same."

"Be careful. We shouldn't get too personal. Anything you tell me might be a security breach." She started laughing and had to set the blue cut-glass goblet down abruptly to avoid spilling wine. This was June in a lovely restaurant in Rome, and she'd already reminded him they were thousands of miles from everyone who knew them. Perhaps tonight she should enjoy a sample of what life for women outside the army was like. No deployments, no rank, no archaic rules—only dinner. Dress rehearsal for next year in the civilian dating scene.

"Can you say all that again, slowly? I like watching the way your lips move."

"Then watch closely." She leaned forward until the tabletop pressed into the space under her ribs. It brought her very near to him. "You're. A. Big. Liar."

"Once more? I didn't quite hear—"

"Gladly. Biii—"

He popped a tiny pickled gherkin into her mouth.

She chewed. "Ohh, that's good. Vinegary and salty and sweet."

"Thought you'd like it." After the waiter refilled their wineglasses, he continued. "So why'd you decide to be a doctor?"

"I drew a quartermaster assignment graduating from ROTC." Her turn to shrug. "With my luck, I'd have ended up commanding a laundry, so I opted for med school. Fewer suds."

"Now who's not being honest?" Their first course arrived, interrupting him, but he kept his gaze fixed on her face. "I thought I asked a fair question."

She looked down first, and studied her spoon and fork as if it mattered which she used for risotto. Talking about her father wasn't like talking about Carl. It wasn't betrayal. It was just…personal.

"When I was five, my father died. He had stom-

ach cancer, but no one knew until the end. Everyone
thought he had ulcers, and some people said he drank
too much, but he barely touched alcohol. He was a big
Italian guy who delivered vegetables, you know. Strong.
So he couldn't be sick. And then he was gone. My first
stepfather died after only a few years too." What had
made her share that? She tried not to revisit her past, but
Wulf's story about his name had seemed so personal.
"Guess I want other kids to have their dads longer."

"Then you're in the right job." His voice was very
soft.

He didn't know she was a short-timer with less than
a year to go, so he couldn't have intended to make her
squirm, but she drew a furrow in the saffron-colored rice
and stared at her food instead of him anyway.

"Why not an E.R. somewhere? Why the army?"

The emotions bottled in her chest shattered, leaving
one: anger. "People ask women that all the time. They
ever ask you?" Dammit, they'd been doing so well. "Who
says, 'Hey, badass guy, why are you in the army?'" Part
of her registered his head shake, but she couldn't stop.
"Nobody gives your career choice a second thought unless you're a woman, then they're always asking why,
why, as if it's a mystery why a woman would want to
serve her country. Well, I do. I'm an officer in the army.
They paid every penny of my Princeton tuition and now
I'm giving back. And I love it." Her speech hung over the
table, a sharp and angry contrast to the soft pink peonies, as she dropped her hands to her lap. Nothing short
of traction could stop Italian hand-talking. And nothing,
not even how much she believed in her mission for the
army, was going to keep her from achieving her dream
of a nine-to-five life.

"Wow," he said, staring at her with raised brows.

"Oh, geez." She wanted to slip under the table, but all she could do was cover her eyes with her palm. "You didn't deserve that rant. I'm sorry."

"Don't be. I'm more sorry. I never realized how… sexist?…that question sounded. You're right that no one ever asks me why I'm in the army. I deserved to be set straight."

Had he said she was right? She lowered her hand and looked into his face. She had heard him correctly. Instead of thinking she was a nutcase, he'd apologized for making chauvinist assumptions. Why was this paragon of a man still single?

Jazz began at the piano across the room. Candlelight flickered in the wineglass facets and reflected off the silverware as they ate, and talked, and laughed about music and travel and food. When she imagined dancing with him, his gaze connected with hers, and he stared like he too imagined where they might go next. Just as well that the music stopped and after-dinner espressos appeared alongside their empty bottle. It was their second, wasn't it?

A tendril of sobriety returned, enough to prod her into one more try for answers. "You promised—promised—if I came to dinner, you'd tell me the truth."

"I promised I wouldn't lie."

"That's—"

"Different." He softened his refusal with a smile.

She rolled her eyes. Semantics. But a night of wine and music made it impossible to be annoyed about anything except how little the two bottles affected him.

"While the hemoglobin comment was a juvenile effort, and I deserved to be caught out, the rest of what I said about security breaches stands."

"You're so…" Next to her empty glass, her fingers clenched into a fist. "Frustrating."

"I know." He ran a finger down her knuckles, the first touch since she'd locked eyes with him at the Spanish Steps. He took his time circling each bump and into the dips, back and forth in an intricate tracery on her hand.

Her fist unfurled as her fingers sought his. While he limited his touch to her hand, she wanted to stretch like a cat, even wiggled her spine in her chair.

"You're afflicted with a powerful case of curiosity, aren't you?"

With her voice trapped in her throat, she answered by nodding. She couldn't look away from where his hand stroked hers against the white tablecloth. Darkness had shrouded their connection at Caddie during the movie, but tonight she could see every caress as his fingers entwined with hers and his thumb circled on her palm.

"Are you curious about…" His voice deepened as if he too were affected. "Us?"

She nodded, speechless with the desire that flowed from the brush of his hands. She imagined his hands moving over her body, looking as strong and golden while unbuttoning her shirt as they did against the candlelit tablecloth. Her chest swelled with each breath as if he were already touching her breasts.

He stood and helped her to her feet. "I look forward to satisfying that curiosity."

Her daze continued as they walked to her hotel with her hand tucked between his elbow and side, close enough to bump hips or shoulders every third or fourth step. She drifted across the lobby to the elevator. She hadn't needed to tell him which hotel; he'd admitted his captain had asked her roommate for details under pretext of an anniversary vacation. As if that would've fooled Jennifer. It only guaranteed a bucket of questions she'd have to answer back at Caddie.

"Which floor?" he asked.

"Three." Reality intruded with the ding of the elevator's antique bell. Reality bit. "I can find my room." She stepped over the threshold into the old-fashioned metal cage. "Alone."

"Nevertheless, as a gentleman I shall escort you." The metal grille rattled closed, locking them in the tiny space.

"Nevertheless?" The elevator jolted to a start, knocking her into his shoulder. "Who replaced Sergeant Wardsen with an English major?" At dinner she'd avoided using his name, but as each ding marked another floor, she had a deadline to remind him of their different ranks.

"What time shall I come tomorrow?" His arm circled her shoulders while his other hand slid the cage door open.

"You're coming back? What are you, a con-she-, I mean, con-see-erge?" The plastic key card flexed in her grip.

"Your mood for the last five minutes hasn't changed my mind." As he steered her along the hall, his grip was firm but not grabby. He wouldn't *be* grabby. "I like smart mouths even more than beautiful women who can't hold their wine."

His meaning temporarily eluded her, but he'd said beautiful and he'd smiled, so it must have been fine.

Although she didn't care if he liked her. He couldn't

like her. She was a superior officer. She couldn't like him. Not *that* way.

She tried to slip the key card in the slot but couldn't make the pieces connect. Sounding remarkably like her roommate, a voice in her head buzzed that he'd be able to connect the right parts. When his hand wrapped around her fingers, her knees wobbled from the urge to rest against him, but instead she jerked to the side.

"Whoa, gotcha." His forearm supported her as he eased the card out of her fingers.

The electronic lock clicked and flashed green. *Enter.* He couldn't. She couldn't.

"Shall we say oh-nine-hundred?" Pushing the door open, he shepherded her past his body. His hand, above the rise of her butt, seared through her clothes like an electrocauterization.

"I'll bring aspirin," he said. "Sleep well."

She turned too slowly to see him before the door shut, but she thought he'd murmured *domani ci baciare.* What the...he didn't want to...*why not?*

She glared, but the closed door didn't offer an explanation.

And didn't that Italian bit mean something about tomorrow and kissing?

Chapter Eleven

THERESA PERCHED ON the edge of the blue-velvet fainting couch and leafed through her guidebook for the third time. Two glasses of water and twenty push-ups had tied off the slight hangover threading through her head, so she could decline any aspirin Wulf might bring.

If he showed up.

Her book extolled restaurants, nighttime strolls and ideas for *la dolce vita*, as if every tourist had a partner. So what if these photos of the Roman Forum at night made it harder to turn Wulf away and go forth unaccompanied? To follow the rules, she had to. She'd thank him for last night's dinner and then politely refuse today's invitation. No waffling, no sinking in his eyes.

The knock jolted her to her feet. She settled the wide belt of her safari dress, then crossed to the door.

"Good morning." The standard greeting covered her awkwardness as she drank in the contrast of his square shoulders against the hallway's cream-patterned wallpaper.

"Good morning to you too." His deep voice, not the simple words, sent tingles racing from her chest to her fingertips.

She retreated, but he mistook it as an invitation and followed. Knowing he'd pass too close, she abandoned the dim entry for safety in the middle of the well-lit room.

"You picked a good hotel." His gaze traveled her curves.

"How can you tell?" Until he'd invaded, her room had felt spacious. Now it felt as tight as the littlest two-seat cars that roamed the city. "You haven't looked at *the room*."

He glanced past her to the bed. She'd smoothed the duvet and fluffed all six pillows, but his eyelids lowered as if he could see through her effort to the sheets where she slept.

"It has everything that matters." His nostrils flared and he closed his eyes. When he opened them, it was as if he'd forced himself away from a ledge. "Ready?"

"Um, no." Somehow she had to ask him to leave. At the bureau, she fiddled with a lip gloss tube and caught a glimpse of her face in the mirror. *You need color*, her mother would chide. "You don't really want to sightsee."

"No." He stalked closer as she unscrewed the plastic cap. "But I'll sacrifice for you."

Sounding like a bigger promise than a few hours of his day, his words recalled the helicopter crash aftermath. Her hand trembled as she brought the squeeze tube to her lips without looking away from his reflection. Automatically, she stroked the shimmering wine color across the bottom curve while she watched him. The nerves and muscles connected to her quivering thighs urged her to pivot into his arms, but her brain rejected risking her career. "Don't—"

Outside, metal grated on metal, as if a car scraped a steel post.

Wulf spun in a blur, hands up and forward of his body, to face the window.

The metallic rasping stopped.

The speed and intensity of his startle reflex reminded her that he was a Special Forces soldier, trained to be fast and alert. He was also a mystery, and the only way to find answers was to spend time together.

In a few seconds the low hum of the room's electronics and muted street noises released him from his defensive position. He stared into her eyes, his gaze heated by what she guessed was a mix of adrenaline and embarrassment spiking his system like a potent drug.

Her hands braced on the vanity behind her hips. The starched edges of her dress sleeves rubbed the underside of her arms where she supported herself. He was six feet away, but it was almost as if he stroked her body, because she could feel every seam of her clothing where it touched her skin. She swallowed, at a loss for her next words as he continued to stare. She wanted to ask if he was fine. She wanted to tell him to stop staring. She wanted to lay her palm on his cheek and whisper that he was allowed to relax because this was a vacation. But his gaze pinned her into unmoving, unthinking, unbreathing silence.

Then he turned away. By the time she exhaled, a chasm separated them.

"Unless you put out a Do Not Disturb sign, we're leaving." He spoke from the entry, his back to her. His head hung low, and his hands gripped the door frame above his shoulders, as if he waited for a whip to descend.

She, the good girl, the smart jock, the girl picked first in intramurals but not for house parties, had reduced him to a penitent. Gathering her self-control along with her purse, she decided they both needed fresh air.

He must've heard her footfalls on the carpet, because he opened the door and held it. Without exchanging a word, they let the elevator deliver them from temptation.

Each ding as they passed a floor unwound her tension another notch. In the populated safety of the lobby, she found her voice. "You've visited Rome before, haven't you?"

"I lived here for a while."

"Lucky you. When?"

"Before I joined the army."

He couldn't have been more than thirty, and to be a staff sergeant he would have been in the army at least eight years. "An exchange program? Or with your family?" She preceded him through the outside door.

"Exactly. Last night you mentioned the double-decker bus tour, so I bought tickets."

"That sure of me, were you?" She turned and caught him staring at her butt.

"Hopeful." The oversized paper stubs in his hand and the crinkles around his eyes mollified her into a smile. "Rome's the Eternal City. I'm eternally hopeful."

"Well, I'm hopeful about some espresso, if you pick up the pace back there." She whipped forward, her take-charge voice damping her desire to let her hips sway.

"Yes, ma'am."

"OUR NEXT STOP is Bocca della Verità," Theresa read from the guidebook as the bus rolled through narrow streets. "After we visit the Mouth of Truth we can lunch across the river." The past three hours with Wulf had been perfect. Following breakfast, they'd strolled to the Ara Pacis Museum, where he'd touched her back to alert her to stairs or ramps while she immersed herself in the audio tour. He didn't roll his eyes or interrupt while she absorbed the art. As they left, he'd plucked a straw hat from a street vendor and settled it on her head. He'd been right about the sun on the uncovered top deck.

"Shall we de-bus?" she asked, the part of her that struggled to maintain an appropriate distance restraining her hand from touching his shoulder.

"You're in charge." He folded the tourist map with a soldier's ease.

Perhaps he didn't notice when his trousers brushed the bare skin between her knee and her hem, but she did, because she wanted to stroke her palm across the fabric. She imagined it would be warm from his leg, and smooth under her fingers, but she ordered herself to sit like the frieze of Octavia until the shuffling of other tourists released them to exit.

In the shade of the front portico at the Basilica of Santa Maria in Cosmedin, they waited their turn to approach the giant stone face. The parents of a boy, four or five years old, urged him to poke his fingers in the carving's mouth while they took a picture, but he crossed his arms and tucked both hands securely in his armpits.

"He has the right idea," Wulf whispered. "Don't reach in farther than you can see." Then his body tightened like a tourniquet, and he dropped his sunglasses from the top of his head to his nose while he slid behind her.

"Surely you don't believe in the Mouth of Truth?" She twisted to see him.

"Do you?" His stance altered, as if he poised on the balls of his feet, while he tugged her hat across her forehead until it tipped awkwardly toward the floor. The line inched forward as the family left, replaced by Japanese tourists.

"It wouldn't matter if I did. I don't lie so it won't bite." She pushed the brim out of her eyes. His stance and his face reminded her of his reaction to the noise this morning.

"I don't intend to stick my hand in." On the way up, his palm passed hers coming down and again he jammed the hat to her eyebrows. "Leave it." His voice sounded lower and uninflected, like a command instead of a request.

"You don't lie that much, do you?" She'd intended to pat his arm and reassure him that for right now she wasn't dwelling on his lies, but he must have thought she wanted to remove her hat because he intercepted her hand. His clenched fingers revealed his tension, although he knew how to check his strength so his grip didn't crush her. If she could've seen behind his mirrored lenses, she suspected she'd have recognized his on guard squint. Was it the crowd that had tightened his screws? Being in Rome, in civvies, and away from their duty station didn't sanction holding his hand, but he seemed to need reassurance—justification enough to twine her fingers with his. "The story about liars is only a legend."

"I lie to everyone. To you, to the army." The corner of his mouth drooped, and his voice grated across his vocal cords, its smooth cadences replaced with sandpaper. "Even to my team." Her fingers fluttered in empty air as he abandoned her and made a fist against his thigh. "My whole life is a lie."

She didn't know how to respond, so she rested her hand on his upper arm. His muscles quivered, tense and on guard like his fist and jaw. "We can go."

"No, you want to do this." He gestured her forward. "Be quick."

The blank eyes and raised brows carved on the ancient stone resembled a face frozen by fear more than a truth-seeking river spirit. She cradled her right arm across her torso. He had a point about sticking hands into dark holes.

"You don't have to do it either," he whispered in her ear. His shoulders walled off the sunlight. "But the line is waiting."

She couldn't recall the last time she'd told a lie. This was a silly myth, so she closed her eyes and shoved her hand in the opening.

Nothing happened. She started to turn, but he gripped her upper arms and kept her facing the stone.

"I'll snap a picture of both y'all," an American voice offered.

"No, thanks." Wulf's voice sounded muffled, as if he'd tucked his chin to his chest. He lifted her nearly to her tiptoes and shifted her along the wall so fast she had to crab step to keep her feet in line with her hips.

"What are you—"

Without turning their bodies from the wall, Wulf hauled her over Santa Maria's threshold and kicked the door closed.

"Hey—" She wiggled and tried to peer at the door behind them, but his shoulders and chest blocked her sightlines, as if he'd doubled in size. "Why—"

"Move." Locking her wrist in an iron grip, he dropped her flat-footed and hustled her across the sanctuary.

Chapter Twelve

"WHAT'S WRONG?" THERESA demanded as her leather-soled ballet flats skidded across the church's marble floor.

"Guy was too nosy." Despite Wulf's size, his feet skimmed noiselessly through the interior as he dragged her between columns.

"Nosy? What do you mean?" Behind them the door to the courtyard opened. Outside light penetrated as far as the first aisle, but didn't illuminate the entire nave.

"Had his phone out." Wulf pushed her through an almost unnoticeable door into a short hall. Each wall canted differently, and none of the corners formed right angles, as if the room enclosed a void where separate buildings failed to join. "He was taking pictures."

"It's a tourist spot." She rolled her eyes. "That's what people do."

"Of us. Only us. Not the Mouth." He shoved something from the floor—a wedge—under the door behind them and drove it deeper with the heel of his shoe. Clearly he wasn't joking. "Didn't you notice?"

She'd noticed his behavior change, nothing else, but she wasn't the trained threat sensor that he was. "Are you sure?" Even asking that made her tense, as if she stood at the top of a stadium, looking down a hundred rows.

"Yes." He opened one of the two other doors to reveal an ascending flight of steps, and then he whipped the new hat from her head and tossed it to the point where the stairs vanished at a turn. The soft swish as it toppled one step lower was followed by the whine of ancient hinges as he partially closed the stairway door.

And then followed by a squeak next to her.

The brass knob on the door between her and the sanctuary rotated first one way, then slowly back. Someone wanted to come in. Part of her brain inventoried her systemic reactions like she would a patient's responses. *Respiration speeding to produce more oxygen? Check. Muscles from neck tendons to foot arches tensing for flight? Check.* The rest of her watched as faster spins rattled the knob mechanism, and then she heard a thunk as something heavy, heavy like a man's fist, hit the wood.

Someone really wanted in.

She smothered a gasp as the person pounded again, but the metal-bound door held square in its frame and the wedge didn't shift. When she would have stared, transfixed by the shaking knob, Wulf grabbed her wrist and pulled her through the third opening and into a hall. A carpet runner with a grayed path down the center led to a massive door. Thrusting it wide, he revealed sunlight, and then they were out, away from the pounding that beat alongside her heart.

She followed him around a corner and faltered in front of Santa Maria's arches. A line of oblivious tourists stretched from the portico to the sidewalk. "Why back here?"

"There." He pointed to another double-decker bus and ran, still holding her wrist.

To stay connected to her arm, she sprinted with him to the end of the block, and he hauled her on board a moment before the doors snapped at their heels. They'd made it. Eyes closed, she panted against his shoulder while relief turned her knees to overcooked linguine. She clutched his waist to stay upright. His scent, evergreen and soap, wrapped her in safety as the bus lurched from the curb. A man hadn't held her like this, with his arm looped around her shoulder and his hip bumping her hip, in too long. She'd missed that connection of curves and planes, the feeling of two different-size bodies filling one space.

"People on the bus go up and down." Under her cheek, his chest vibrated like a big cat, a very big cat, whose paw kneaded her spine in time with his words. "Up and down, up—"

"Stop that." Her order, drawn out and trembling, held no authority. "This isn't the place." Her cotton dress left no doubts about every corded muscle and bulging *whatever* that Wulf pressed against her hip. Jammed next to him in the doorway, she could feel that he was hot and, she strongly suspected, half-hard.

"Stop," she whispered again, despite the stupid-crazy part of her that wanted to arch closer in a *bus vestibule.*

"Negative on that request." His fingers snuck past her intentions and circled into the small of her back. "After a successful E-and-E is the perfect place for—" he nestled her deeper into his body, "—this."

"You'll be escaping and evading without that hand if you don't move it." Women at Caddie joked about guys with boners after successful missions, so she knew his post-adrenaline reaction had jack to do with her. Just like her trembling and wide-open senses had nothing whatsoever to do with him. Nothing. She inserted a forearm between them and pushed, almost as hard as a chest compression, but he only let her reclaim six inches of space.

"Let go, Ser—" She broke off before she spit out his rank. *Don't draw attention to military affiliation in public*, security briefings emphasized before anyone could take leave.

A man coughed loudly into the pause, drawing her attention past Wulf's shoulder. The bus driver leered back. They had an audience.

"Biglietti?" He honked with one hand and gestured for tickets with the other.

"Sì, sì," she said. *"Un minuto per favore."* Fumbling with her purse, she caught the eye of the motorbike driver stopped outside the glass doors. He was grinning too. Crap. Every Roman on the road had witnessed their clutch.

Wulf didn't drop his arms, which meant she had to stay contorted while she hunted through sunglasses, tissues and the map. Damn, she could *not* focus with her entire side plastered against him.

His hand skimmed her hip from belt to thigh.

She clenched her teeth. "I told you. Stop it."

"Don't want you to stumble at a sudden stop." His whisper ruffled the hair at her neck, an emergency-code-level distraction that did not help her to find the tickets. She'd used the bag for a day and a half and it was already a Dumpster.

The driver made a sound like *puh-tou.*

Kicking Wulf's shin with her flats would only hurt her. Finally, she extracted two slips of paper. Her left elbow connected briefly but satisfyingly with Wulf's solar plexus as she liberated herself and flourished the tickets. She marched past the circular stairs that led to

the crowded sightseeing deck and aimed for a bench seat
at the rear of the inside compartment.

No surprise, he followed. At least he didn't sit, so she
had space to breathe.

After she straightened her dress hem and crossed her
ankles, she felt composed enough to speak. "What happened at the church?"

The bus turned a corner while she watched him cling
to an overhead strap and peer out the rear window. Then
he answered. "I don't like having my picture taken."

"That was a bit much to avoid an online photo album."
Her boss had circulated mandatory reading about soldiers with complex post-traumatic stress as a result of
ongoing battle exposure rather than an isolated, acute
trauma. She'd spent her deployment huddled in relative
safety at Camp Caddie, but Wulf encountered real ene-
mies with every mission. He was trained to anticipate a
gun or a bomb under any jacket, in any package or car.
Shifting gears to enjoy a vacation probably challenged
him to his core. "How many tours have you had?"

She swayed as the driver took a corner too fast.

Whatever Wulf saw, or didn't see, through the glass
must have satisfied him, because he let his weight shift
from his feet to the wrist and hand looped on the strap.
"Six in the 'Stan."

"Iraq?"

"Four."

"Ten?" She gasped at the impact of his answer. One
trip to Afghanistan had left her feeling jangly in crowds.
Of course he expected threats everywhere. "You've had
ten combat tours since 9/11?"

He shrugged. "Give or take."

"I'll confess that I almost freaked out on the Spanish

Steps before you found me." She tapped the seat next to her. "People, noise, everybody drives like crazy—but this isn't a combat zone. It's Rome." Someone had turned that doorknob, but it wasn't rational to think that the man from the line had chased them. Wulf had secrets, and so did she, but no one would chase them through Rome.

Would they?

He sank to the leather-covered bench less than a hand's distance from her leg.

"I'll help you remember this isn't Afghanistan if you'll help me," she said.

They sat together. They didn't move or touch, but the longer they sat with the bus vibrating around them, the higher the energy ratcheted, until the air felt super-charged. One touch from him and she feared sparks would shoot out of her skin like she was an overhead power line.

"What next?" His question shocked her into twitching against the window.

Did he mean the next bus stop, or what would happen between them? She answered the easy question. "St. Peter's." She tried to smile. "Two thousand people with cameras."

He managed a sound that might have been a chuckle. "Lunch instead? That exercise made me hungry."

"Sure, you can laugh, but that *exercise* made me *scared*." She couldn't forget standing in that odd-shaped room while the doorknob turned. "And I liked that hat."

"I'll find you another." His hand reached for the hair clip at her nape.

She batted him away. "No touching. And we really shouldn't—"

"Do I need to feed you again to have a civil conversation?"

"All we ever do is eat." He was right though; she was famished.

"I'd happily pursue other activities." Desire flared in his eyes and crossed the space between their bodies, so hot and sudden she raised a hand to her throat. "Say the word."

She couldn't speak, couldn't tighten her lips enough to swallow, couldn't count fast enough to measure her own pulse, but none of that mattered when he stared at her with such hunger.

"That's all you have to do—*say yes*—and you won't think about food for days."

She tried not to imagine spending days wrapped around him. She knew how good he smelled, the sound of his voice and the feel of his hands. The only sensation left to her imagination was his taste, and that answer could be hers right now. And it would cost her integrity at a minimum; maybe her career. "You said…lunch?"

In the silence, he searched her eyes and must have seen how she clung to her responsibilities.

"Coward." He leaned away, and the taut skin around his eyes loosened with a smile.

Her pulse slowed enough to permit coherent speech. "I prefer to be called cautious."

"Trying to convince yourself, or me?" His grin broadened.

Dammit, eyes that beautiful shouldn't have been issued eyebrows that mischievous.

They both stood when the bus eased into the next stop. She wanted a meal, but the narrow-eyed scan Wulf gave out the back windows before he let her proceed between the seats made her wonder if food wasn't his main motivation.

"Signorina e Signore." As the Hotel d'Inghilterra bartender spoke, he placed a tray carrying after-dinner espresso, the saucers adorned with sugar cubes and spirals of lemon zest, on the ottoman in front of Theresa and Wulf. She'd agreed to a last coffee in a private alcove off the lobby in order to delay the moment when Wulf would suggest he escort her to her room. She didn't want to banish him into the night, not after a day and evening exploring Rome together, but she couldn't change the rules both of them had sworn oaths to obey.

Opposite their couch, a tilted mirror showed their side-by-side reflections. Folding doors divided this secluded nook, with its wine-red upholstery and discreet lighting, from the lobby. *Be honest. Today was a date,* her conscience said, *with a sergeant.* If called to task, she had no other explanation. *And it's no fun to pay for the ride,* the proverbial bad angel on her shoulder continued in a voice that sounded like her ranch-born roommate's, *but never get to pet the pony.*

Wulf's cup rattled against its saucer when he returned his espresso to the tray. "You don't want this coffee, do you?"

His question ignited tremors for reasons she knew she shouldn't explore. Maybe it was his tone, as dark and rich as the tiny chocolates they'd shared after dinner, or maybe it was the unbidden thought of what she wanted. Him, pinning her to the couch and kissing her the way his eyes promised whenever their gazes locked. Her espresso sloshed over the demitasse rim, so he curled his fingers around her hand and removed the drink to rest safely beside his.

"Relax." Warm and gentle, those same fingers tilted her chin.

She closed her eyes as he neared. Her skin heated until his breath felt almost cool as it brushed the corner of her mouth and along her cheek.

"We saw everything you wanted today." After stroking her bare arm, he eased his hand between her spine and the couch as if worried she'd spook and bolt.

Far from it. She wanted to slide closer.

"I followed your directions." He arched her body the fraction of an inch that brought her breasts against the wall of his chest.

Her hands drifted to his shoulders, then down his back to the groove where his shoulder muscles overlapped. They were hard and distinct, and the pleasure of touching him sizzled from her fingers to the rest of her body.

"I went everywhere you wanted to go."

The empty ache inside her needed to be filled, yet he was taking his sweet time.

"But we didn't do everything you wanted, did we?" Then his mouth covered hers.

She'd been kissed before. What Jersey girl hadn't? But she'd never known a man who kissed like this. His lips were perfect, firm but not overwhelming as they molded to hers. His hands cradled her head and rubbed her scalp and neck at spots that made her gasp with pleasure. His kisses submerged the methodical doctor into a woman who'd sit entwined with a man on a hotel couch. The doctor wouldn't let her hands wander across his shoulders to seek the hair above his collar. *Noooo*, that woman would never lose her self-control. Only a wanton would pull him closer and let her fingers trace the muscles wrapping his spine. The doctor would never move her chest in tiny circles to create delicious pressure against a male chest. Only a wanton would offer her neck and encourage his kisses to drift lower.

She opened her eyes. In the mirror over Wulf's shoulder, her tanned hands contrasted with his white shirt. Her fingers shifted to his hair. It was multicolored from the sun, like gold and sand and honey gliding over her skin.

"You're watching us, aren't you?" His lips hummed over the nerves on her clavicle. Her neck begged for the magic of his mouth, while his hand slipped from her waist upward along her ribs, toward breasts that swelled to invite him. His reflection claimed her reflection, consumed her with his kisses.

A phone rang somewhere far away.

What was she doing? Even with the folding doors latched, they were in a lobby. Strangers could open those doors, see them, post a picture on the internet. One careless keystroke could ruin their careers. Her shoulders stiffened.

Wulf's breath slipped across her neck like a noose. During the day he'd seemed like other men, but he had secrets. She couldn't forget what had happened on the helicopter ride, the lies and half-truths he'd told since, and under no circumstances could she fall deeper into his web.

In the mirror, he blotted out every bit of her except a blur of dark hair and one of her eyes. Her sclera completely circled her iris, like a horse she remembered from a trip to the Meadowlands with her stepfather. Right before the mare had tried to jump the wall in front of her seat, its eye had been a giant white-rimmed spot of fear, like hers now. The horse had broken a leg and men had dragged out screens and downed it right there, on the track. She rolled her head and saw the lobby lights through the slats of the louvered doors. Her stomach spun.

"Stop." She pushed his shoulder. "Stop!" Anxiety quivered in her tone.

His deltoid jumped under her palm. Then, one long heartbeat later, he pulled away. "You're right."

Immobilized, they locked stares while their pulses slowed. She shouldn't have regretted the right decision this much.

He stood and offered his hand. "I'll say good-night at the elevator." As soon as she reached her feet, he let her go. "Share tomorrow with me." His request was quiet. "Please."

She thought she saw need in his expression, not merely desire, and his ten combat tours weighed on her conscience. "You're willing to do more sightseeing after today's fiasco?"

"Fiasco?" He glanced at the imprint they'd left on the couch, and his mouth slowly turned up and into another wicked promise. "I think not."

She fingered her collar and hoped he wouldn't ask about her itinerary. She'd probably blurt *you*. "Get one thing straight. We're not going to—" She couldn't say it. A doctor, and she couldn't spit out *have sex*.

"We will. And soon." His outstretched arm indicated she should precede him into the lobby. "But you'll have to ask very nicely."

"Not a chance. I won't—" She spun to contradict him. He raised an eyebrow as if daring her to issue a challenge or an ultimatum, either of which would have been an absurdly bad idea, so she gave up and strode toward the elevator.

"Tomorrow it's my turn to choose where we go." Following, he opened the elevator cage without guidance from his eyes, which were occupied staring at her legs.

"You could lose a finger that way." She pointed at his hands.

"Not worried. Much as I appreciate you in a skirt, wear pants for my plans."

"What plans?" She stepped into the space, but he didn't follow.

"I'll be here again at nine." He shut the doors. He really wasn't going up.

"What plans?" If she rattled the folding metal *she* might lose that finger, but he was toying with her.

"A ride you won't forget."

The image of herself straddling his hips and looking down at him weakened her knees to the point that she reached a steadying hand for the control panel. She knew how his eyes would look half-closed with his face taut below her, because that was how he watched her, but the fantasy couldn't become reality. Not unless she traded her career for it.

Then the outer doors closed, removing temptation for at least nine hours.

THE UNDER EYE concealer from her mother didn't match Theresa's soldier tan, so dark circles advertised her sleepless night. She'd rejected her travel-stained jeans for cropped black pants—"pedal pushers" on her mother's list of outfits—and a black-and-white plaid shirt that tied at her waist like a fifties cliché. Thankfully her mother hadn't been in a Bond girl phase.

This morning's double-thump knock caused her heart to pick up speed even though she wasn't startled. She'd brushed her teeth twice, just in case Wulf tried to pick up where they'd stopped. Before she reached for the knob, she wiped her palms on her pants.

Wulf's faded jeans outlined every bulge of his thighs, and the stand-up collar of his black leather jacket emphasized the cords of his neck. Complete with finger-tousled hair and a half grin, the man leaning on her door frame looked like a very bad boy.

"Will this work with your mysterious plans?" She held out her arms, then dropped them. It was silly to worry about her clothes, and worse to invite him to stare.

He stared.

If she crossed her arms over her chest, she'd appear defensive. If she didn't, he'd notice her nipples through the cotton.

His smile deepened. He'd noticed.

She stuck her fingers in her pockets, thrust her elbows out and hunched her shoulders forward, which lifted the starched shirtfront away from her chest.

"Do you have different footgear?" he asked after his gaze reached the floor.

"What's wrong with these?" She pointed the toe of her ballet flat at him.

"No protection against the road."

"Why would I—"

He pulled his arm from behind the door frame and showed her two motorcycle helmets.

"Not a chance." Becoming that personally acquainted with Roman traffic was not on her to-do list. "Absolutely not."

"Absolutely yes." His boots crushed the carpet pile while he swung the helmets as if to hypnotize her. "You really, really want to go for a ride with me."

Of course, as medical personnel she had a responsibility to monitor Wulf to ensure he didn't freak out again like he had at the Mouth of Truth.

Her rationalization almost sounded legitimate.

"Yesterday I shared you with thousands of strangers." He headed for her closet. "Today's for the two of us."

"I intend to survive this trip." She followed him, eyes on the helmets. "That means no motorcycles."

He hunted on the floor. "These—" a running shoe dangled between his thumb and first finger, "—are the sturdiest shoes you have?"

Three pairs of boots at Caddie, useless at this moment. "Nothing's wrong with my shoes. They're perfect for visiting the Borghese Gallery."

"It'll be another four hundred years before I—" He snapped his mouth shut and picked up her purse, which looked so ridiculous in his grip that her last resistance melted. "Come with me."

DRAYCOTT SETTLED ONCE more into his chair after his foray to the street next to the Hotel d'Inghilterra. In less than the time it took his Earl Grey to steep, he'd popped a button-size tracking device on the frame of Wardsen's motorcycle. With no need to hurry when his target and the brunette doctor emerged from the elevator, he rather hoped they became busy upstairs.

Two days ago Wardsen's bread crumb trail—airfare in Karachi, clothes and shaving gear in Dubai—had led to Rome. One phone call, and Draycott had possessed the name of the only traveler the Bagram Air Field office of Black and Swan had processed during the last ten days who'd had a similar destination: Captain Theresa Chiesa, M.D. Unsurprisingly, she also hailed from Cadwalader. Aviation flight manifests also listed the doctor on two recent Special Forces missions, and her credit card had been swiped at the terminal thirty feet across the lobby.

He enjoyed a slow sip of his favorite tea blend. After yesterday's debacle at the Basilica of Santa Maria— only the worst novice asked to photograph a target like Wardsen—he'd assumed lobby surveillance until experienced professionals arrived. This pathetic crew was only authorized to follow at a distance via the global positioning system.

Thirteen minutes after Wardsen had ascended to the doctor's room, the couple exited the elevator. Sad what seven months in-country did to a man's stamina.

Camouflaged by his *Continental Daily News*, Draycott assumed they wouldn't register his presence. If they remained as absorbed as they'd been in each other yesterday, the smartphone concealed beneath the trilby on his knee could sing "God Save the Queen" and they wouldn't turn.

"Sorry to break your heart," the woman said. "But I don't like shopping."

"Humor me." Wardsen passed within fifteen feet of his seat, the doctor on his far side. "You need better footwear first."

So they weren't headed directly for the motorcycle.

WULF'S CHEEKBONES AND tight denim achieved what Theresa knew she never could have: two Prada salespeople reduced to kittens lapping milk. She should have been mortified that he insisted on kneeling in front of her rather than allowing the assistants to do their jobs, but as his fingers wrapped around her calf and he eased the second black knee-high boot on to her leg, she liquefied.

When he traced the open V of the leather upper, a line of fire tattooed her skin. The tiny grind of zipper teeth rent the charged silence as the smooth calfskin closed.

"How's the fit?" Behind the inner bend of her knee, his hand provoked tremors while his expanded pupils drew her into swirling blue and amber until she felt nearly dizzy.

Guaranteed she'd collapse if he asked her to stand or walk; answering seemed to be nearly as difficult.

"The *signorina* will wear the boots." He held her ballet flats in the air for the male clerk. "Please deliver these to Signorina Chiesa at the Hotel d'Inghilterra."

"Yes, I'll take them, *grazie*." Theresa swallowed and opened her purse. The boots passed perfection, transforming her from Audrey Hepburn in a classic screwball comedy to a femme fatale, an international assassin, a woman men *noticed*. She offered her credit card.

"Signorina, it has been done." The female employee's eyes flicked to Wulf.

"You can choose these." He hadn't stood, so his eyes remained level with her glare. "But you can't pay. It's completely inappropriate and I can afford—"

"My day." He pressed his finger over her lips. An impish smile dared her to contradict him, as if he wanted to misbehave in front of the clerks. "My gift."

His cockiness punched her last button. He couldn't tease her and then expect her to mold herself to his dictates. "No." She bit his fingertip.

The salesman squeaked.

Wulf sucked in his breath and stood, towering over her as he picked her up by her elbows and set her on her feet. "We'll go *now*."

"Yes, master." Arms crossed, she glared. "Shall I walk three steps behind?"

He hustled her out of the store and around the corner. Before she could ask about the red-and-chrome motorcycle, he thrust her against the stone wall and covered her lips. This embrace resembled last night's as much as molten chocolate lava cake resembled office Halloween candy. He didn't play or coax. He demanded that she open for him, and she did. As his tongue traced her lips, she tried to bring him into her mouth, but he controlled the kiss. His body pressed hers at every point, legs and hips pushing into the cradle of her thighs in a way they hadn't while sitting on the couch. His hands shielded her head, but the roughness scraped her shoulder blades through her shirt. If the building disintegrated, she'd spiral into the depths of space with him, uncaring and unaware.

"You bit me." He slid his mouth along her cheek to her ear. His teeth closed on her lobe, making her shiver. "Did you think I'd let that pass?"

"No." She clutched his shoulders, the jacket leather too slick, not what she yearned to touch, not his skin, the heat and suppleness that made even the best leather seem monotonous.

"You want this as much as I do."

"Yes." Tilting her hips matched the bulge under his fly to the part of her that most wanted to be pressed. She slipped her hands under his coat and up his chest, then around to his—

Gun. She froze, her hand on a hard shape strapped over his upper ribs. Although she could barely move her lips, she managed to ask, "What's that?"

"You know what." He shuddered and separated their bodies.

"Why?" Chilled without his embrace, she waited for his answer. He took so long she wondered if he hadn't heard the question.

"I'm not entirely convinced yesterday's adventure was my imagination."

The sun seemed to disappear, leaving the cobblestone alley merely gray and musty. "But a gun is more dangerous to—"

"I've carried one nearly every day since before you were ali—allowed to drink." His expression told her nothing. "You carry one everywhere at Caddie too, Doc."

The reminder made her wince.

"Haven't shot an unlucky patient, have you?" He cocked his chin as she slowly shook her head. "Not your foot? Well, I'm going out on a limb, but I bet my weapons training is a bit more intensive than what you get in the Medical Corps."

That she couldn't dispute.

"And before you ask, I have an Italian gun permit in my back pocket." He twisted to show her the area in question. "Want to fish it out and check?"

"In your dreams, bud." Her cheeks heated at her predictability. Certainly not at the view.

"Then let's get moving." He jerked his thumb toward the motorcycle. Triple exhausts, chromed to a precious-metal shine, swooped along each side like an orchestral horn section. On the gas tank and body panel, the bike proclaimed itself a Benelli 750. No way could he rent such a spectacular ride.

"Where'd you get that?" Her stepbrother would pant with excitement over a Benelli.

"Friend." His answer didn't even attempt subterfuge.

"Another top secret pal?" While he lowered the helmet over her head, she recalled the accidental-death statistics Colonel Loughrey had brought up at a staff meeting. "You know vets are five times more likely to die on a motorcycle than a civilian?"

"I have no interest in dying on a civilian." His visor obscured his expression, but his voice gave away his smile. "Can you offer me odds of expiring on a captain?"

"Zero." Now that she'd fulfilled her professional responsibility to address the safety issues, they could go.

He snapped her chin strap without catching her skin. "You've ridden a motorcycle?"

"I'm from New Jersey. What do you think we do in the summer?"

"With a man?" His hands lingered under her chin, not tickling, but heightening her awareness of him.

"No, with a space alien." Filled with energy, she rocked from her heels to the balls of her feet, an urge to move brought on by his nearness. "I can walk and chew gum too."

"Then you'll remember how." He tapped the side of her helmet to turn on radio speakers. "Follow my lead, hmm?"

They roared away, and she closed her eyes only once, when he cut across four lanes of traffic at the Victor Emmanuel Monument. She didn't want to enjoy the ride, but wrapping her arms around him while unleashed power vibrated between her thighs was an undeniable thrill.

"Theresa," he said as the gritty urban outskirts blurred past. "Did you talk about our plans?"

"No. Why?"

"Idle curiosity." The voice coming through the helmet speaker sounded too clipped for that to be true. "Who knows about your trip?"

"Jennifer and my other roommates. Colonel Loughrey approved my leave." The trickle of anxiety down her spine reminded her that the only absolute truth she knew about Wulf was his rank and unit. He admitted he lied to everyone, including the army.

"Outside the army." His words were curt, but she didn't know why.

"My mother. She sent the clothes." God was punishing her for not returning her mother's calls. The woman who gave birth to her had probably petitioned the patron saint for mothers with ungrateful daughters. *Please, Saint Gina the Miracle Worker of Newark, make my little girl call. Scare her if you have to. It's for a good cause.* "I talked with her this morning," she consciously lowered her voice to keep it from cracking as she lied, "and said I was meeting you."

"Who would she have told?"

"Half of New Jersey." That wasn't a complete fabrication. Her mother would've talked about the Rome trip to everyone, as in, *Theresa's not coming home for leave like the Gianni and Marotta boys did. What, her mother's pasta isn't fancy enough?* "The Italian half. Why?"

"Nothing." His tone resurrected the sensation of watching the church doorknob turn.

The crowded sidewalks of the city center had vanished, replaced by cinder block buildings squatting behind chain-link fences topped with razor wire.

Wulf snorted. "You'll crack my ribs if you squeeze harder."

"Sorry." She loosened her grip and forced herself to keep talking. "You didn't answer my question. Why do you want to know who I told?"

"Because we're being followed."

Chapter Thirteen

WULF WISHED HE'D chosen the ring expressway, where he could've opened up the throttle, but on Via Ostiense potholes and traffic limited his speed. "Black Fiat four cars behind us."

"Remember, this is Italy, not Afghanistan. Don't over-react." Her knees clenched the outside of his thighs as he pulled around a car. "Besides, they're all black." Her decisiveness contrasted with the pincer grip on his waist.

The pressure doubled the dread in his gut. "I've watched the same one since Saint Paul's Outside the Walls. No left headlight. Missing front plate." In his mirror the car slipped closer. No question, this date had a party crasher, but was it a stranger from Rome, someone from Karachi or someone from Afghanistan?

For several seconds his helmet radio delivered nothing but Theresa's breathing, loud enough to distinguish from road noise. He tried to peer around the vehicle immediately in front, a battered red mini-truck with a wooden canopy enclosing the cargo bed. To call that canopy "custom" was an exaggeration. The slatted lumber cage was as jerry-rigged as the hillbilly armor troops had scavenged and welded onto their vehicles for the first years of the Iraq war. Some entrepreneurial Italian had built his truck addition so wide Wulf couldn't see if he had passing room.

The Fiat passed a white sedan. Now it rode the bumper of a tan two-door.

He shouldn't have come to Rome from Karachi, but it was too late to undo the arrogance of mixing Theresa into his mission to gather intel on the smugglers. All he could do was try to keep her safe.

The tan car slowed and turned into a driveway, leaving only a one-vehicle buffer between his motorcycle and their tail. This close, he could pick out the driver's silhouette through the tinted windshield. There were no passengers.

The red truck in front belched exhaust and rocked faster until its cargo, crates of fruits and vegetables, swayed in their stacks. This straightaway offered the best chance to maneuver. As the now-or-never decision surged through his arms and legs, his right hand twisted and his wrist dropped the fraction that would notch up the speed. Revving the Benelli, he pulled around the vegetable truck.

A boxy Mercedes G-Wagen rocketed toward them from a hundred twenty yards away. As soon as Wulf passed the truck's rear bumper, there wouldn't be a chance to change his mind or debate their chances. Leaning forward, he committed Theresa's life with the decision to pass.

Theresa screamed and the oncoming four-wheel drive blared its horn.

As his motorcycle overtook the vegetable truck's rear wheels, a taste like spoiled milk filled Wulf's mouth. In maybe six seconds they'd meet the G-Wagen's front grille.

The driver tried to stop, but Wulf couldn't brake without skidding. Unable to return to the right lane and unable to veer left without hitting the steel barrier and catapulting over the handlebars, he accelerated. At fifty miles an hour, wrestling the handlebars on the rutted road felt like waterskiing behind a helicopter.

The curve of Theresa's helmet dug into his back, while wind jammed his elbows to his sides and compressed his chest until he could barely inhale. Still, he pushed with every cell, as if the force of his will could hurl them through space. With thirty yards to collision, he could see the wide-stretched mouths of the G-Wagen's driver and the woman next to him.

The motorcycle roared past the red truck's rusty bumper.

He turned the bike handlebars. There was a sermon of horns and shrieks as disc brakes locked, but nothing hit them except the backblast. They'd made it; the empty lane ahead proved it.

His heartbeat felt like an M249 blasting a thousand rounds a minute. He had to swallow before he could speak. "Lost him."

"Ohmigod." Theresa's breath shuddered over the helmet radio, a drawn-out sound nearly drowned by the rev of his bike. "Ohmigod."

"Don't freak out, Doc. We lived." He didn't mean to sound cavalier, but they weren't clear until he'd put enough distance between them and the Fiat to confirm they'd lost the tail.

They rode in silence. His mirrors stayed empty through several turns and evasive maneuvers. With the immediate threat over, his adrenaline-heightened senses absorbed the way her inner thighs cradled his hips and her grip curled around his waistband.

"We have to talk."

Ominous words, but he ignored them to concentrate on the feel of her body behind his. Hell, they could ride to Kyrgyzstan like this. He'd be happy.

"Risk taking's a common post-combat response." The fear and edginess had left her voice, as if she liked leaning against him, but the damn leather jacket was thick enough to blunt the feel of her rack. "We will talk about this," she repeated.

"Sure." Their date could still happen. Plan A, the ruins would drive unpleasant conversation out of her mind. If not, he'd implement Plan B: kiss her until she forgot about the psych eval.

Because Theresa's left hand had relaxed open to spread across his thigh, he almost missed the sign for Ostia Antica. No one could expect him to read when each bump jolted her fingers closer to the bad boys, but he didn't miss the billboard advertising a new airport hotel.

Chill. He wanted her, but not in a generic room shaken by jets every four minutes. He turned into the gravel lot and parked in the shade of the umbrella pines. A single tour bus close to the entrance didn't interfere with the solitude promised by the acres of ruins. Without the engine throb or his helmet, he heard birds from the banks of the Tiber. Yesterday she'd made clear she liked history as much as some women liked chocolate, so today he'd play personal audio guide until she marveled over him like she'd stared at those marble effigies.

"Where are we?" She swung her leg to dismount. Her knotted shirt hitched up on one side and showed the smooth tan of her bare waist, a shade darker than his.

"Ostia Antica." If he licked that patch of skin, he imagined it would taste sweet and salty, like caramel gelato. "The Roman Empire's version of the ports of Long Beach or Houston."

While he spoke, she laid her helmet on the seat and shook her sweat-flattened hair.

He wanted to lift that dark fall, but she beat him to it. Did she know that finger combing her hair, with her arms raised, also jacked up her killer round parts? And some of his parts too? "After the river silted—" he swallowed, trying to create enough saliva to continue, "—the shoreline moved, shipping stopped and the city emptied." His words felt as dry as his mouth, but maybe conversation would consign his hard-on to history. Otherwise, given the way his jeans had tightened, he'd be challenged to get off his bike without busting a rivet.

"We can't ignore what happened on the way here." Her eyes were so deep brown and all-encompassing that it seemed as if he'd plunged into a pool. Her mouth moved, but he couldn't look away from her gaze even as he absorbed how her eyebrows drew together and a crease formed over her nose. "You can't let strangers spook you into losing control."

Before he could reply, she bent at the waist to flip her hair upside-down.

"I wasn't spooked." Now he could stand and adjust without her seeing his condition. "And I was in full control of the bike." Right, that sounded defensive.

"I know that." Her voice sounded muffled. "I meant control of *yourself.*"

If he had control, he wouldn't be staring at the whorls of hair that edged the nape of her neck. He surrendered. Careful not to pull the cashmere strands between his fingers, he cupped her head and nudged her upright. Loose strands clung to his fingers when he traced her jaw. Her chin was strong. Stubborn. Her lips parted, making him think—

A car engine downshifted and tires crunched gravel.

By reflex, he flicked his eyes to the driveway. Years of training primed his muscles to react before what he saw fully registered. His hand grabbed her arm, anchoring her to the far side of his body where his bulk offered a barrier, while his legs sped into motion. "Move!"

The black Fiat had caught up. With the river to their right and access to the road on the left fenced off, only one route remained—into the ruins.

"Whaaat?" She glanced over her shoulder as they sprinted around the tour bus. The moment comprehension hit, her arm spasmed in his grip. "Is it—"

"Yeah." He shoved a handful of euros through the ticket window and, in Italian, told the disinterested guard to keep the change. "Her husband hired the man in the car, you understand? Perhaps you could assist with a delay?" Neither the best lie Wulf could manufacture in seconds nor the extra cash distracted the man from his text messages.

"How'd they follow—" Theresa stumbled on the cobblestones and swore.

"Probably a GPS bug." Wulf yanked her forward while he inventoried his assets: a Heckler and Koch Mark 23 automatic pistol, ten rounds and a Benchmade 3300 knife. More than enough to protect himself, but inadequate as piss with her safety at stake. "Move faster."

Ahead, where a clump of pines and ornamental shrubs opened into a sunny clearing by the remains of the warehouse district, two dozen Scandinavian-looking tourists milled with a guide. He decelerated to a speed walk. "See the tall guy in jeans and a black windbreaker?" At enough distance the tail might not realize the guy was in his fifties. "Next to the grandma Valkyrie with the blue sun hat?"

"Uh-huh." Theresa panted.

"Stick to him as if he's me, no matter what." Numbers would insulate her while he took his questions directly to a man with answers. "Do not leave this group." Over his shoulder, he noted their follower was hung up at the admission window. By Frejya's necklace, Italians did enjoy a love triangle. "If I don't meet you, get on their bus. Pay, faint, twist your ankle, whatever you have to do, but do not go off alone."

She had those tight-pressed lips he already associated with challenges, so he pinned her with the look he used to test fresh team members. "Understand?"

"No, I don't." She lowered her voice as they reached the fringes of the group. "Shouldn't we call the police?"

"Not if it's about Afghan heroin."

Her mouth dropped open, and she pulled away before he realized how that had sounded.

"My team's *investigating.* It's army business, got it?" Shifting his grip, he brought her hand to his lips. "Don't worry. You'll be fine."

Letting go of her felt ominous, worse than any first step into a hostile building, but he had to work alone. Screened by the mass of Scandinavians, he slipped through the remains of an arch. Beyond the tumbled blocks in the rear of the building, a former alley paralleled the main road, and he doubled back through half-crumbled columns and piles of sun-bleached bricks, their marble veneers long ago looted for Renaissance palaces. Occasionally a higher-pitched laugh carried to him, indistinct on the breeze, but it didn't disturb his hunt.

At the next corner he spotted his prey scurrying to catch the tour group. The beefy man with a sun visor, baggy khakis and fanny pack was the eager photographer from the Mouth of Truth. Following them once might be nosiness; twice was surveillance. Wulf melted behind the stones and changed course to match his quarry, but the other man never turned, never looked over his shoulder, never noticed that he'd acquired a stalker.

Ahead, Theresa's guide stopped and directed the group to consider the Baths of Neptune.

The follower slowed as if unwilling to overtake them.

Wulf's alley ended in a T intersection at the multistory remains of the baths. He broke right, heading north, and sprinted to circle the rear of the large structure. Taking his eyes off the target felt risky, but without a partner he had to gamble and use his knowledge of Ostia to set an ambush. As he dashed down the lane that separated the baths from the barracks of the Vigili guards, the sun beat on his head. Perspiration stuck his jeans to his legs.

He stopped at the last corner, concealed by the wall, and watched Theresa and the tour group drift toward the restored amphitheater at the center of Ostia Antica. He'd wanted to saunter through the ruins beside Theresa, not hunt some fat, slow prey like his namesake taking a sheep. Some days it felt as if everything he wanted for himself, everything he tried to build in his life, ended up as jumbled and empty as the roofless two-thousand-year-old apartments that stood between him and the spot where he intended to act.

He trotted in the shadow of the buildings, scanning for one of the slaves' passages that would bisect this faded street. Halfway to the main road, a slip of alley barely wider than his shoulders cut west to the plaza where the others had gathered. At the end of the passage, he dropped behind a stack of bricks high enough to conceal a prone man.

Theresa, still in the midst of the Scandinavians, craned her neck and studied the ruins. Her arms crossed above her waist as if her stomach hurt, but she hunched her shoulders and traipsed with the others into the amphitheater's entrance tunnel.

He'd attended enough summer concerts here to know the dark ramp sloped below street level, then emerged into sunlight in the middle of a half circle of two thousand seats. In seconds, the group would be facing the stage and the remnants of the guild halls. With that spectacular sight in front of them, no one ever looked behind. There'd be no better strike opportunity.

The target slunk into the tunnel without checking over his shoulder. Dude wouldn't last one hour in Special Forces Q-Course; he probably wouldn't make it on a playground. He didn't hear Wulf until after Wulf's elbow hooked his throat. Wulf jacked the man's arm between his shoulder blades and slammed him face-first into a wall niche. "Shut up, or I'll pop your shoulder." He twisted the arm high enough to trigger groans while he frisked him one-handed.

Zipped into his fanny pack the guy had a nine-mil Beretta semiautomatic. That was an immediate game changer. Anger erupted in Wulf's chest as hot and lethal as the volcanic ash that had doomed a different ancient city. This man had come after Theresa with a weapon. It would be so easy to break his arm, and he deserved it. Deserved worse.

He only rubbed his captive's face into the stone until he whimpered.

"FYI, buddy, zipped up your ass is a stupid place to keep a weapon." He pushed his prisoner up the ramp toward the road. "Someone might jump you from behind."

The afternoon was not going to include gelato from the café at the other end of the ruins.

He shoved the guy through the first gap in the rubble across the street.

Today was not going to involve a pleasant blend of beer, sun and a frisky woman.

Shoving hard, they zigged and zagged deeper into the unkempt section of the ruins.

This outing was not going to end in Theresa's hotel room. To the ever-sucking contrary, it was going to be soldier shit, him and this fucker hidden deep in seared grass past rows of mausoleums, while the woman he wanted until he ached—who also controlled his future if she talked to the wrong people—boarded a bus and rode away, like he'd told her.

He'd had more successful dates after sacking a convent.

The stacked stone arch in front of Theresa framed more stone blocks and sun-dried weeds, the opposite of the dampness where her shirt clung at her armpits.

After the amphitheater and guild mosaics, she'd realized the tail had vanished. The tour guide had called the boulevard that divided the ruins the Decumanus Maximus. The unmowed area south of it, away from the tourists and gift shop, was the logical place to find Wulf and, by extension, the man who'd pursued them.

Now that she had no doubts they'd been followed,

she'd realized an unfortunate truth: Wulf might not be who the man was keeping an eye on.

Another plane roared overhead for Fiumicino Airport as she rubbed her palms on her pants and reminded herself that there were dozens of people in the park who could hear her. She wasn't alone. She stepped into the open space through the arch, expecting to find nothing.

Something—someone—spun her and smashed her body against a wall. The iron tang of blood mixed with chalky dust to become a foul paste that glued her lips to her teeth. Crumbling bricks dug through her clothes to chafe her thighs and chest. Next to her ear, a man's breath hissed in and expelled like an espresso machine.

"Why aren't you with the tour?" The anger in Wulf's whisper flayed her skin. His mass pressed her against the stone, but without the care he'd shown during their kisses.

She couldn't suck enough air to reply.

"I mistook you for an accomplice." He moved an arm's length away. "I could have hurt you, dammit."

After she peeled herself from the wall, she scrubbed the back of her wrist across her lips and tried to swallow.

"Why'd you disobey me?"

"I'm not under your command." She'd done nothing wrong, but she gave in to the urge to slide along the wall before she continued. "The guy in the car—"

"What about him?" Wulf stalked her. His head and shoulders loomed in her space.

"He could be…" She took a deep breath. "One of my sort of stepcousins."

No rocks fell on her. No lightning bolts. The ground did not open.

"Why do you say that?" His alert stance didn't change.

"I need to see him." Don't let the guy be a misguided emissary of Her Nosiness.

"First answer me." His face matched their surroundings, hard and dry. "Why do you think he's a relative?"

"I told you my family's Italian." She brushed her pants, but her sweaty hands smeared the dust that had transferred from the wall. "My last name, Chiesa, it's from the Piedmont region. Maybe my mother called some—local relatives. Asked them to look me up." *They* were from Naples, not part of the Chiesas or her mother's side, but she was sticking close to the truth.

His look changed to disbelief. "What kind of family do you have?"

That she really didn't want to answer.

"Anyway, he's not Italian."

Thank you, thank you, thank you. No need to explain her family to Wulf, or anything about Wulf to her family.

"See for yourself." He gestured behind a collapsed pillar.

She shuffled around rubble that had once stood vertically. On his side among smaller stones, eyes closed, lay the American who'd offered to take their picture at the Mouth of Truth. Wulf's belt bound the man's elbows behind his body, shoelaces crisscrossed his wrists and it looked as if he had a sock stuffed in his mouth.

Wulf had captured a prisoner, but they weren't in Afghanistan.

Only one thing could be worse. "Is he dead?"

"I wouldn't have wasted time on restraints. Carotid artery sleeper hold."

Not dead was good. "Have you checked his circulation?" If she focused on the man's well-being, maybe she'd fool herself into thinking they had a prayer of getting out of whatever mess tying him up was going to cause. "Those bindings look painful."

"Not compared to this." Out of his waistband, Wulf pulled a Beretta identical to the one she'd locked in the arms room before catching her flight. "I took it from his fanny pack."

Her neck and shoulders prickled to think that this man had followed them yesterday, even into the church, with a weapon.

Wulf rested the Beretta near his torso, pointed at the ground like an extension of his hand. Eyes narrowed, he stared at her. "Have you seen him in the sandbox?"

"What?" If their stalker wasn't a member of her extended family, she had no clue what was going on. "Other than yesterday at the Mouth of Truth, I've never seen him. You're the one who said this was army business."

"It is. Look at his feet."

The tan suede boots, minus the laces employed on his arms, were common to everyone with the army in Afghanistan, from general officers to privates, including most civilian contractors. Looking closer, she realized his receding hairline showed a white strip where he usually wore a hat, but the rest of his face and neck were tanned. "Is he a soldier?"

"Age, gut, shiny watch. I'd guess contractor." He slipped the Beretta into his waistband and untucked his shirt, its bottom creased by sweat. From a row of items on another rock, he chose an unfamiliar cell phone. "Have anything in your purse to copy his call history?"

The only paper inside the leather bag hanging diagonally across her body was a postcard she'd bought at the Ara Pacis, a reminder of the morning before the world had shifted at the Mouth of Truth. The tourist who had reveled in the beauty of the altar celebrating Roman peace was gone, replaced by a dry-mouthed woman whose mind raced past branching consequences faster than she could search her purse.

Hunting for a pen, her fingers wrapped around a plastic rectangle that made a familiar tick-tick sound. The mints from Jennifer, weeks old but brought along for the trip because she'd wanted to be prepared for any hot guys who thought she was like ice cream. Simple problems.

Today absolutely called for two of the white mints, which hit her tongue like a shot of epinephrine.

Wulf fanned the man's wallet contents in one hand and silently held out the other to her.

She shook two into his palm, but he kept his hand open. "I'm rationing." Like hell she was giving him another. "For the next happy surprise."

"Fair enough." He nodded and examined the plastic cards in his hands. "Texas driver's license says our buddy is Jack Spencer."

Sitting on a chunk of rock, she studied the phone. A simple disposable like hers, it didn't seem to have fancy locking functions. Finding the call history wouldn't be hard.

"Better photo on the Indiana license for Mr. Jim Schroeder," Wulf said. "Before he ate too many fries chez Black and Swan."

Her stomach growled, but she forgot about it when beautiful columns of numbers appeared on the screen and one of the tentacles squeezing her chest unwrapped.

While she wrote, her eyes darted from the phone to her notes to Wulf.

"Here's a credit card for John Sullivan. Guess he doesn't like to redo those J-S laundry tags." Wulf dropped to his haunches next to the bound man. "If you're coming round, Jack, let me reassure you. I'm a law-abiding type of guy." He spoke barely above a whisper.

She strained to hear his next words while scribbling numbers.

"Ask people who know me. I'm easygoing. Fun-loving. Except for one thing."

He was no longer the gentleman who'd wined and dined her. He had the same hair, same shoulders and same clothes, but this Wulf came from the part of the army that ended lives with precision. She came from the part that saved them, and the difference had never been so stark.

"One thing pisses me off." He spoke to the prisoner. "People who spy on me."

Suddenly she was very glad she hadn't requested his personnel records after their first meeting in the cafeteria. "Finished." The postcard covered with numbers trembled in her hand.

As Wulf left the bound man and returned to her, he switched to a smile. "Do you have a phone too?"

She nodded, then stopped, but it was too late.

"A disposable?" He held out his hand. "I need it."

His stare compelled her to pull it from her purse.

"Yours should be clean. At least until Jack's missed and someone starts checking where his phone last registered its location, and then finds other phones on at the same place and time."

"How can someone—"

"Hack phone company records? Easily, but these people probably won't have to." As he spoke, he tapped keys and waited for someone to answer. "I'd call the billing department with a story about my daughter losing my phone and say it has the number for my boss's vacation house. I have to find it because I'll lose my job if I don't tell the boss his wife is coming up a day early. Maybe drop a reference to his young blonde assistant, and how much I need to keep this job because my wife's been laid off." The worry in his voice made her want to give him whatever he asked, even though she knew he was fabricating the story.

On the phone, he greeted someone named Lorenzo. Their Italian conversation flew too fast for her to catch more than Ostia and Roma and *ciao* before he hung up.

"Everything's squared." He popped the SIM cards from both phones. "Of course, Black and Swan's so connected, they can probably tell the U.S. embassy to send the Italians a terrorism investigation letter of interest."

She froze, hands in midair reaching for her phone, but Wulf stuffed it in his pocket. Whatever a terrorism investigation letter was, she didn't want to be named in one. She was an American and an army officer. Things like extraordinary rendition or secret CIA prisons couldn't happen to her…could they?

"If we're named to the Italian government," Wulf continued while he gathered the man's papers, "we're playing high stakes poker."

Chilled in her short-sleeve shirt, she stared from the bound man to Wulf. The fear she'd battled all morning became much closer to panic. She didn't want to spend another minute with the mystery man and the threat he represented. "Let's go. Leave him and call the police later. Anonymously."

"I made arrangements to dump him until we figure out the who, what and why."

"That's kidnapping. Won't it make this even harder to explain?" She had to draw a line. "We can't do that."

"Who do you think will report our buddy Jim missing?" His eyes flicked over to the prisoner. "I doubt he brought family on this trip."

Chapter Fourteen

"THIS GUY HAD three identities and a semiautomatic. He's no tourist." Wulf's voice was steady, his tone as rational as if they were discussing the probabilities of medical outcomes, but it wasn't enough to convince her to abduct a man.

"It feels like *we're* committing the crime." She couldn't ignore her roiling stomach. "I don't understand what—or why—"

"Fine." He threw his hands in the air. "My team's investigating Afghan heroin shipments. Black and Swan is moving the junk in empty cargo containers. Before flying to Rome, I tracked a load to a ship in Karachi that's due next week in Albania." His eyes didn't break contact with hers. "We think the smugglers killed a warrant officer who discovered an earlier cargo."

"Then this is absolutely a police matter. We have to—"

"You think the army wants this publicized? That army resources, even inadvertently, are smuggling drugs? A soldier here or there with a duffel bag of hash, that's one thing, but tons of heroin sent around the world on cargo ships courtesy of American taxpayers?"

Despite growing up reading Nancy Drew, she'd never had an urge to become a crime fighter. She was a doctor, and that made her job crystal clear.

He wasn't finished. "We haven't figured out how high

up the corporate chain this goes. Black and Swan's too politically savvy to take on lightly. So no police."

Her head throbbed with the scale of what Wulf had revealed. The crazy-afraid part of her argued against his story, but her eyes couldn't erase the man, the identifications and the gun.

"If we stick together, we'll get out of this." He pulled several bills from his pocket. "First, I want you to buy a couple beers at the snack bar."

"Beer?" What was he thinking?

"I intend to haul our man to his car without being seen, but if someone stops us, we'll pretend he's drunk. For that, he needs to stink of beer."

So he didn't have a black helicopter on speed dial. But she didn't have a better plan, so she might as well do her part.

By the time she reached the snack bar's patio and dozen café tables, her doubts about Wulf's plan had increased. With the Scandinavians departed for the next stop on their itinerary, this was arguably the busiest part of Ostia Antica, and the only place she could find a telephone.

A family eating gelato sat at the only occupied table. The father and the older child, a boy of eight or nine, seemed to be competing to blow paper drinking straw wrappers into an empty cup. The mother scooped a blob of berry pink off the front of her daughter's sparkly T-shirt. Speaking to them was completely, utterly off-limits to a person with problems that included guns and drug smugglers.

Inside the café, a grandmotherly cashier sat by the register reading a magazine. If Theresa had gone to New Jersey for leave, she'd be shopping with her mother instead of staring into a refrigerator while mentally rehearsing how to ask for the *polizia*.

Between the crook of her elbow and her chest, she stacked two waters and two brown bottles of Italian beer. If she called the police, Wulf would undoubtedly vanish into the air, leaving her to be questioned while the authorities sorted out the facts.

The U.S. embassy would assist a captain in the United States Army, wouldn't they?

When she thumped her purchases on the counter, the cashier barely looked up. The magazine cover showed a scantily clad woman and a glaring headline about the *ministro della giustizia*, the Minister of Justice. If she was arrested, would reporters from magazines like that camp out at her mother's house? Would they discover her stepfather's business connections? News scrutiny would ruin her life, and her mother's. Carl, who, despite how he made a living, loved her, would go down too.

The request for the police died in her throat.

She left the snack bar with the bottles weighing on her forearms like shackles chaining her to Wulf. Holy Mary, Mother of God, she was *in*. This was how boys started with Carl.

Fifteen minutes later, their odd trinity paused at the edge of the ruins close to the parking lot. Jack-Jim-John lolled unconscious over Wulf's shoulder, beer splashed on his shirt and shoes, while she carried the empties.

Wulf indicated the recycling bin thirty feet from the exit. "Drop the glass in. Loudly."

"Now you're a model citizen?" She rolled her eyes at him across the unconscious man.

"Diversion." With his free hand, he slipped two buttons on her black-and-white shirt free of their holes.

"Keep the ticket guy's eyes on you while I stick Jack in his car."

Each stride across the open space was harder than the one before. Her back felt exposed without Wulf next to her, and she expected to hear a shout or a siren, but she kept walking. At the kiosk, the ricochet of glass dropping into the metal cans jangled her nerves, but it caught the stare of the park attendant.

Keep his attention. Bending, she fiddled with her boot zipper and stuck her ass in the air in the pose that had once riveted Wulf's team at movie night. This guy wasn't any more stalwart. When she stood, she braced one hand on the bin, took her boot off and shook it upside-down as if it had a rock in it. The guy leaned over his desk, so she shook the boot and everything else that would jiggle right at him.

Wulf was halfway across the lot heading for the black Fiat. She had to fill more time. Sliding her foot into the boot, she lifted her water to her mouth and let liquid drip onto her shirt. After plucking the cotton away from her chest, she blotted an imaginary wet spot over her nipple.

Come on, Wulf, I'm running low on ideas.

He slammed the Fiat's trunk closed and waved an all clear.

By the time she reached the car, both phones rested in the gravel next to the front tire.

"What are you doing?" She gripped the side-view mirror to keep from scrabbling for her plastic salvation.

"You copied the call history, so I'm destroying the hardware." He pried her hands loose and brought them to his face, forcing her to look at him instead of the phones. "Even crap disposables can have internal GPS, and they triangulate location from towers."

"We could turn it off."

"Some can be turned on remotely by the service provider. I'm done taking chances." He started the car and forced her to step away to avoid being bumped by the open driver's door as he rolled forward and back. The phones became bits of black plastic and broken electronics. Finished, he flicked pieces of the SIM cards into the weeds.

"Come on." He circled to the passenger side and held open the door. "We're out of here."

Minutes ago he'd tipped an unconscious prisoner into the trunk of a car they were about to steal, and now he was holding the door for her. It was absurd. But not funny.

"Theresa."

She had a credit card and cash. A road arrow next to the parking lot pointed to a train station.

He read her mind. "I can't guarantee you'll be safe if you walk away. That's all I want right now—to get rid of this guy and get you somewhere safe. Please let me."

Carl always wanted to keep her mother safe. That's what her childhood had been about. And her mother— every time they video-chatted, her mother always ended with *stay safe*. Usually it annoyed her, but right now it sounded pretty damn good.

She slipped into the passenger seat.

As Wulf started the car, she managed a steady voice despite the scratch in her throat. "Where are we going?"

"We're taking our passenger to a cleaner."

She doubted he meant a place that did shirts.

SHORTLY AFTER THEY left the express highway that circled Rome, their prisoner started thumping the rear seat, so

Wulf turned up the radio volume. The front-seat conversation, already limited, fizzled while Theresa sipped water and considered where exactly she should have walked away to avoid ending up in a stolen car with a drug smuggler stowed in the trunk.

The neighborhood outside was the type where dense trees clustered behind brick walls and gatehouses fortified the entrances to unseen homes. She broke the silence with a question she'd chewed over for miles. "What if there's a GPS hidden on this car too?"

"It's a risk." Wulf turned between two stone lions and rolled down the car window to type on a security pad. "Most people aren't paranoid enough to track themselves."

The iron gates swung open. Two lines of poplars led to a white stucco mansion. The grand effect of a three-tiered fountain, complete with Neptune and cavorting naiads, inside the circular drive was lessened by a lack of water. The place felt vacant. "Where are we?"

Instead of answering, Wulf followed a spur of the driveway to a garage tucked behind the house. Its keypad required a palm-print verification to activate a steel roll-up door.

"Do you know these people? Is this some Special Operations safe house?" She stood in the garage bay and slammed the car door.

"Yes to the first, no to the second." He left the prisoner's identifications, the gun and the list of numbers on a shelf. "In about an hour, a man should arrive who'll take care of Jack for us and trace the phone records. You—we—need to be gone."

"That's it?" She ducked under the descending garage door. "We're leaving?"

"Yep." He double-timed up the driveway.

"Where are we going?" Her frustration rose as she followed. She wanted many things, starting with real answers and proceeding directly to a shower, clean clothes and a meal. Bashing her head against his solid wall of super secret nonanswers was not on the list.

"Planning that now."

He truly didn't have a backup plan? His squared shoulders exuded authority she wanted to rely upon, but he was apparently as clueless as she was. Well, shit.

"We can't talk here. You wouldn't enjoy meeting the owner." He had to use a third security system to open a person-size exit door concealed among the dense laurels.

"Then I'm going to my hotel." Her room had pressed sheets and hot water, and the management left biscotti and fruit on a side table near the elevator.

"Negative." Without pause, he strode downhill, away from the walled compound.

"Since you knocked this morning, I've been chased, stalked, bashed around and scared." She trotted to stay up with him. The direction seemed likely to lead toward the Tiber River and thus to familiar scenery. "I'm filthy and I want a nap. Ergo, my hotel."

"Where do you think they tagged my motorcycle?" Like he was making a double-tap execution, he fired the question at her and then answered it. "Your hotel."

She stopped dead. She hadn't connected the dots until he said it.

"Down!" Hands out, Wulf sprang and shoved her sideways to the ground.

Her hip and shoulder slammed the pavement at the base of a stucco wall. Wincing, she blinked her eyes clear. A white sedan wove along the curb with Wulf hanging from the passenger door, both his arms thrust into the open window while he grappled with a man inside.

Pop-pop. The passenger held a gun fitted with a long black cylinder that she belatedly recognized as a silencer. And he'd fired. At them.

Wulf smashed the man's forearm against the window frame, bending it backward from a point on the lower arm that no ulna bone could withstand. Three things happened in an instant, but she saw each one flicker separately, as if she were channel surfing. The pistol fell in the road. The man screamed, high and screechy like a zoo peacock, as his arm flopped at an angle that equaled compound fracture. The driver floored the gas.

As the car hurtled forward, Wulf released the man's broken arm and dropped off the vehicle, rolling harmlessly as the sedan squealed around a corner.

She reached her feet a second after Wulf found his. Perhaps ninety seconds had passed since she'd asked about going to her hotel. Silence wrapped around them.

"You said—" Her chest heaved as she struggled to control her breathing and repress a scream. "You said people don't track their own cars."

"To quote a former boss, I misunderestimated." Handling the abandoned pistol with his shirttail, he tossed it over a wall into dense shrubs, then towed her across the street. Ahead, several businesses and cafés lined an intersection.

As she moved faster than a walk, but not at a flat-out run, her senses sharpened. Her hearing became especially acute, until even a vehicle honking blocks away caused her to jump.

"Lots of cars in Rome," Wulf muttered. "Don't panic."

"I'm not." She slowed to match his pace as they reached the first shop. "I'm not panicked." No, that would be *calmer* than the churning stomach and puppet-on-a-string jerkiness she felt in her shoulders and arms. She'd welcome mere panic.

Up the block, two men stared into a convenience store's plate-glass window.

"Italians don't wear loose jeans." Wulf pulled her through the closest entrance and into a men's clothing store. The middle-aged proprietor stared while Wulf spoke in rapid Italian.

As they followed the man's gesture toward the rear, she glimpsed herself in a wall mirror. Her jaunty shirt had come untied, her hair had morphed from flowing to unkempt and her pants had turned splotchy with whitish-gray dust.

"We're disappearing. Somewhere no one will follow." Wulf dropped a ten-euro bill on a shelf next to the exit and grabbed a broom and a can of cleaning spray. In an alley too narrow for American garbage trucks, he stopped over a manhole cover, shoved the broom handle into an opening on the edge of the iron circle and pushed on the lever.

Understanding dawned, then disbelief. "A sewer?"

Wulf wondered exactly what would cause Theresa to stop arguing. Clearly he wasn't going to find out today. "Yes." Thor's hammer, this drain needed to open *right now*, but in the last sixty years it had rusted shut tighter than his brother's smile. "Find something. Help me."

He heard scrabbling by a garbage bin, and within seconds she returned and shoved a second piece of wood, tapered as if it had been a chair leg, into another notch on the cover's rim. Force and levers. Simple physics.

Veins popped in his forearms as they raised the iron circle an inch. He couldn't break his promise to keep Theresa safe. His tongue pushed the back of his teeth, pushed with the rest of him, until he tasted blood.

With a noise like an armored vehicle scraping cement bollards, the lid popped free and skittered half off the hole, leaving him on his hands and knees next to a sickle-shaped opening.

"Hey!" a man shouted from the end of the alley. "I found them!" He spoke in English.

Uninvited guests had arrived for this shit barbecue.

Wulf jammed Theresa's legs through the opening, trying to be more gentle than he was when he shoved a door ram home during an entry. But it was the same concept: Get in. Fast.

"Aiiyy—" She flailed, torso sliding after her legs, but he caught her arm and slowed her in time to keep her chin from bouncing on the edge of the hole. Her eyes, so wide with fear he could see the full circle of white, held on to him although the rest of her had sunk into the dark.

There was no bang, merely a thup, as a round hit and sent stone chips to shred his cheek and neck. These men also had suppressors.

"Now." He loosened his grip and let her elbow, her wrist and finally her hand slip through his fingers, but he reminded himself that she wasn't gone. She was safer.

Another round hit the cobblestones near his body, driving him headfirst into the sewer without time to be sure she'd stumbled clear.

"Are you okay?" She crouched between him and the crescent of light above, and one hand stroked his cheek.

The illumination gilded her nose and cheeks with a halo as ethereal as a painted Madonna. "Wulf?"

"I'm…" The landing had knocked the wind out of him. Moving was a bitch, as if he'd dislocated his left shoulder, but he hadn't crashed on top of her. "Good to go." He couldn't remember the last time a woman had cared about his injuries. Theresa's fuss beat Cruz's all to hell, and he wanted to let her coddle him, but they had to put distance between them and the men above. "I'll take rear. Head downstream, left hand on the wall."

He heard men above, indistinct but excited. "Don't dawdle."

"No chance of that." Judging by the splashing, she was already moving.

"Cover your ears." He reached under his jacket.

The face that popped into the opening above his head disintegrated with a direct round from his Mark 23. A hollow point at ten feet does that. After seeing their buddy pulped, it'd be a while before someone else dropped in, so he followed Theresa.

About seven feet high, the walls were close enough to touch without pulling his elbows off his sides and as solid as everything else the Roman Empire had built. While counting paces, he tried to recall subterranean diagrams of the neighborhood. Even though it was near his brother's house, he hadn't worked the tunnels in this area much after the fascists seized Ivar's mansion. His brother had expected to lose their Italian properties once he committed to structuring sales of England's war bonds, so the return of the house and castle in 1946 had been a bonus. Ivar had always possessed a knack for turning a profit while doing the right thing.

Wulf's talent was fighting.

"Is it okay to talk?" Theresa's question interrupted his memories.

"Sure. What's the weather forecast up in front?"

"Partly damp with a chance of rats."

Listening to her voice was like having a light even in the dark.

"So why doesn't it stink down here?"

"This is a storm sewer, not a sanitary one." The tunnel smelled no worse than a leaky basement—a fresh Christmas tree compared to Fort Bragg's portable toilets in July.

"Then I'm glad it's been dry."

So was he. The puddles of water accumulated in the bottom were far better than the knee-deep torrents of the winter of 1942, when he'd lost two Allied agents to pneumonia.

Under another manhole, pencils of light poked through ventilation spots. Theresa paused, looking up. "How do we get out?"

Seeing her scan the dark for him, he moved into another thread of light, within arm's reach. "With proper tools, it's not hard to find a cover in a quiet alley or courtyard, hook into a rim hole and crank."

"Tools?" Her voice rose.

"That's our problem. Most lids are too high to exert sufficient force pushing from below with our bare hands, even if they weren't rusted shut. There are places where street regrading has exposed the system." Not that he knew if they'd been covered in the last seventy years. "Or we could revisit the Mouth of Truth. It might even bite you now."

"What?" Her question echoed off the stones.

"The side sewers eventually connect to the main

sewer, the Cloaca Maxima, which empties into the Tiber River near Ponte Palatino and the Mouth."

"Wonderful." Her laugh rose and fractured as it bounced off the walls and doubled to echo in his ears. "Exactly what I was hoping for. A do-over."

"A do-over?" He wrapped his arms around her and realized her thin shirt was useless in the damp. Like shivering, laughter was one of the body's ways to generate heat. She needed more, so he shrugged out of his leather jacket and maneuvered her into the sleeves. "You're not having fun?"

She snuggled into his coat with a sound that reminded him of guys breathing steam off coffee post-night patrol, and her laughter subsided into full-body hiccups. That type hurt like hell.

"I must not be a very good guide." He buried his face in her hair and inhaled the lingering echo of her citrus shampoo, a hint of normal.

"Don't expect—" another hiccup, but weaker this time, "—a tip."

"I'll make it up to you with the best dinner of your life tonight." He remembered his last meal at Cesare's, the tiny restaurant that guarded an entrance to his secret apartment. "You, me and *pappardelle al cinghiale.* Pasta and simmered wild boar sauce." Maybe she'd have a drop on her chin he could rub with his thumb. In the dark he recalled how, when she drank the last sip from a wineglass, she tilted her head until the line of her throat invited him to taste her. Hell yes, he'd take her to Cesare's, and then to his concealed rooms. The thought of her naked and wet in his private pool threatened to weaken his knees; he couldn't allow himself to imagine more until they made it out of this. "Ready to drive on?"

"Army ready."

She could handle anything. Maybe even the truth about who and what he was.

"MY STAY WAS most pleasant." Deep in his English persona, Draycott spoke to the clerk like an old chum while he signed the charge slip for his room at the Hotel D'Inghilterra. "I regret that an emergency with my elderly aunt—a broken hip, and she's my late mum's sister—calls me to Lancashire." He sighed. The emergency requiring that he vacate the hotel was more dire than a broken hip. "There was one place I intended to see…"

"Yes, sir?"

"I've visited the Paris sewers and intended to poke around for a similar tour here in Rome but didn't have time. By chance, do you know of one?"

"I'm sorry, I don't."

"I must have been mistaken that Rome had historic sewers. Perhaps I'm thinking of Vienna." He folded his reading glasses into his tweed jacket. Someone on this amateur team he'd been forced to use had countermanded his directive to observe at a distance, with ugly results. One man was missing, one required arm surgery and one had been rendered faceless when Wardsen and the doctor disappeared like alligators down a sewer.

"We also have such sewers, but in Rome tourists may only view the exit."

"Where might that be?" Ten minutes ago, the Director had clarified that the men should be removed from the worsening situation. Not pulled out. Not relocated. With the pending arrival of a better team, they'd become loose ends.

"The Cloaca Maxima is opposite the island in the river near the Bocca della Verità."

"Ahh." Draycott beamed and nodded like a satisfied elderly tourist. "Quite near." Close enough for Wardsen to handle the unpleasant parts of Draycott's next task, if he pointed the remaining men that way.

THERESA'S LEATHER BOOTS had soaked through, and her feet had passed cold en route to dead numb as they trudged the sewers. She'd stopped counting paces, ceased trying to measure time or distance, and now she merely worked to keep her feet moving on the slightly sloped stones.

Her face registered a breeze and she lifted a hand, but Wulf snatched her backward.

"Our tunnel's reached the main one. Let's not fall in." He gripped her tightly. "The Cloaca Maxima's deeper and faster, but the catwalk's on our side, so we don't have to cross."

The jacket he'd given her didn't cover below her hips, but pressing close to his body warmed her butt and thighs as efficiently as leaning against a radiator.

"We're going downstream," he continued. "We'll use noise discipline. If I squeeze your shoulder, it means halt. Two taps means move out."

Downstream. Closer to the main exit that everyone in Rome knows. "Isn't that where these men could enter the sewers to find us? Why not the other direction?" She pushed out of his arms, one of her hands on the wall to orient herself away from the open drop. "We could bang on a courtyard entrance until someone lets us out."

"Not my way."

"None of this, absolutely none, is my way." Frustration expanded her chest until her bra started to bind. "It's not my way to kidnap people, steal cars, fire guns on busy streets." Maybe that wasn't fair, because he hadn't done that, the bad guys had, but the point was basically the same. "I want this to end. If that means running away, then let's do it!"

"Listen, *Captain*, you outrank me but you don't know close-quarters battle." His face was so near his breath seared her skin, hot like the sun at Ostia. "The sewers are my turf. Up there, explanations are a total bitch. Down here, I have nothing to hide, nothing to clean up, got it? We have the advantage, so I say we take it." ·

"*You* say—"

"Stop telling me how to do my job!"

"You're right. This isn't *my* job." Stuffing her hands in the jacket pockets was the only way to stop herself from jabbing randomly in the dark until she poked something, preferably *him*. "My job is saving people. I've been too flexible on that today, but I took an oath to do no harm."

"Count on it, these guys want to put the harm on us."

"I've gathered that. So why are we headed right for them?" She paused for a breath, but this time he didn't interrupt. "If you want me to go that direction, you'll have to knock me out and carry me like the guy at Ostia."

"Fine." The gritty clack of his teeth gnashing, amplified by the dark and her imagination, sounded as loud as grinding gears. "You stay here, I'll head downstream and make sure it's clear, then come back for you. Waste of time, but will that make you happy?"

"I'm not a suitcase. I won't be here. I'm going upstream." She hoped he couldn't tell that the thought of striking out alone almost paralyzed her.

"You are the most frustrating…" He sucked air through his teeth. "Exasperating…"

"Keep digging, Roget," she said.

"Irritating…woman!"

"Then you shouldn't have followed me to Rome!" The tension emanating from him was so palpable she could nearly taste it. It drove her darkness-enhanced senses into a matching frenzy and vanquished the cold and fear, replacing them with heat that pulsed through her veins and required deep breaths to slake her need for air.

"I couldn't help it." Given his growl, he had to be speaking through a clenched jaw.

"I'm some mythical siren you can't resist? Forgive me if I don't buy that."

"You should."

The air between them changed as if lightning had struck, shocking her into silence when he found her shoulders and drew her so close that their legs entangled.

"Sometimes you're so clinical." His voice, lowered in tone and volume, wrapped around her as deftly as his hands. "You act arrow straight, all by the book with your questions."

When he brushed her hair from her forehead, her body no longer felt stiff. The heat of his thighs relaxed her frozen muscles. On their own, her hands sought his body and wrapped around his back. He was definitely a weakness of hers.

"When you get fired up about postpartum depression, or the wasteland of women's health care in Afghanistan, or the symbolism in a Renaissance fresco, or I piss you off—"

His quiet laughter sent riffles of air across her neck and made her smile in the dark. He liked to bait her, but she supposed she made it easy.

"That, my good doctor, is when you speak very fast and your eyes turn the color of exotic spices. Like treasures from the Silk Road, worth a ransom of gold and pearls."

When he talked about her with the voice of temptation, the one she thought of as his prelude-to-a-kiss voice, and he showed that he listened to everything she said and cared enough to remember...he had her.

"That's what I can't resist."

Even without light she knew his lips were only inches from hers, so she did what she'd wanted to for so long that she marveled at the self-control it had taken to wait until this moment, and *she* kissed *him*. Her lips found his, and they shared the hunger and intensity of two people who wanted to become part of each other as much as they wanted to live. Her mouth, her heart, her whole being seemed to melt into him as he crushed her body to his.

He must've leaned against the wall, because he easily slid her up and down the hard planes of his chest and abs. It wasn't enough. With her hands locked around his neck, she stretched, her toes barely on the ground, until he squeezed her buttocks and lifted her, raising and lowering her body again and again past the length of his need. Nearly dizzy with greed for his touch, she tried to fit herself against his thrusts, and still they kissed.

And then his mouth was gone and his hands left her standing on her own, between his spread legs, but without his support.

"Ahh." He shuddered and she thought she heard his head thunk into the stone tunnel wall. "This is...this is the worst possible..."

"I know." Her body clamored for more of his heat,

but intellectually she accepted the ludicrous, crazy absurdity of their position and timing. They had to stop.

"We can't. We have to go."

"I know," she whispered a second time.

Connected as they were, he ought to understand she didn't want to walk away from him, but she wouldn't head into a fight they could avoid. "Let's back off."

"Okay." His words vibrated along her skin. "We'll try it your way."

His answer didn't feel like she'd scored a victory. She couldn't feel triumphant when the thought that drummed in her head was, *Please, don't let my way be a mistake.*

IF WULF HAD kept his pistol instead of arming Theresa with it when they'd started upstream a quarter-hour ago, maybe its textured grip would have been his lifeline to the twenty-first century. Without that anchor, the watery rush below sucked him back to the beginning, to that Danish swamp, and the day his world changed.

Pushing after his brother Iovor, he told himself 'twas only the swamp's foul air wet his tunic under his iron-ringed byrnie, but the evil of this fen touched fear to his back until he sweated. He was no boy to believe himself safe from death, nor yet a hero assured of Valhalla.

Ahead Iovor followed their liege Beowulf in the place of honor, and a score of warriors trailed behind. In the Kingdom of the Spear-Danes their leader had become the great man Iovor had foreseen when they cast their lots with this adventure. Now they, the two sons of a drunken lackwit, offspring of a man who had traded his shield and

*honor for a horn of barley ale, walked as the right
and left hands of a hero. When telling of these
deeds, every hall's skald would recite the names
Iovor and Wulf alongside the name of their great
lord.*

*Vines dripped from trees like a net to catch the
unwary. Water as dark as moss seeped in their
tracks, and broken branches, their tips painted
with black blood, showed the path. He knew himself to be a tall man compared to most, but these
jagged sticks stabbed air above his head. They
marked the height of the creature's shoulder,
where Beowulf had split its arm from the sinews
and left a gaping death wound.*

*Two nights ago Grendel had rampaged this
route to find doom in their lord's grasp and returned bloody to die in the fen. Last night the
beast's hell-mother had beaten this way carrying
a thane of King Hrothgar. This day Beowulf led
his line of Geats-men to seek Grendel's corpse
and make a second death mound from its dam.
Or die trying.*

*Iovor halted. From habit Wulf closed on his
brother and turned, back to back, spear and shield
held before him to guard his brother as his brother
guarded him. Despite seven suns at the oar bench
with the others, rowing to reach the Kingdom of the
Spear-Danes, he did not know how the men about
him fought in a forest. He wouldn't risk his man-
wick on a gamble that this crew of misfits could
stand against evil that came in the night.*

*He had faith only in Lord Beowulf, in his
brother and in the spear in his own right hand.*

Wulf's hand flexed with the need to hold something to keep him in the present and far away from the ancient swamp that stalked his memories. His front pockets yielded his compass, a coil of wire and a lighter, which reminded him of the aerosol spray he'd grabbed at the shop and jammed in his back pocket. The cool metal of the can in his palm was completely modern and, paired with the lighter in his other hand, a damn fine weapon.

Minutes later an out-of-place scent, like soap or deodorant, wafted from a side tunnel. Whirling, he brought the aerosol and the lighter together, thumbs on both buttons, at the same time stinging pain punctured his shoulder.

Whoosh. A salvo of flame erupted from his can.

Bang-Bang-Bang. In between the punch of shots—Theresa's, he prayed—Wulf saw a man beat at a fiery halo and knew he'd fried his target. The pain-filled scream moved with the burning man as he staggered into the catwalk's railing. Brittle iron gave fast, and the attacker plunged to the rushing water, but a different fire, something that felt cold and hot simultaneously, rippled and spread from Wulf's shoulder. They'd jabbed something in him.

Before the afterimage faded from Wulf's corneas, he heard another burst. *Bang-Bang-Bang.* His pistol had held nine rounds. How many did Theresa still have? He couldn't add. His left arm hung like a wrung-out dick. Only muscle memory took his right hand to his ankle sheath. His eye twitched and he jerked to dislodge a hairy, leggy thing that had dropped onto his cheek. No—wait—nothing crawled on his face. That was the poison.

Bang-Bang-Bang.

A weight leaped onto his back, but Wulf dipped his

shoulder and allowed momentum to carry the attacker forward while slashing his knife into the man's inner thigh.

More screams. Farther away. Why had he moved so far from the fight? Had to get back.

Cold pressed on his cheek. Hard. Metal?

He was a puny thirteen-summer lad pulling a bench oar for the first time. The weight wouldn't shift. Over his head red-and-white sails soared. The whale road through the sea welcomed him home. A woman, his mother, her arms whitecaps raised to embrace him.

His mother was dead. Cold.

Salt tears pulled at him. *Please. Theresa. Please. Pull me back. Pull.*

Chapter Fifteen

TERROR AND SWEAT cemented Theresa's palms to the pebbled grip of Wulf's pistol. She opened her eyes, or maybe she closed them; in the absolute dark she couldn't tell.

"Wulf?" After the gunshots in the confined tunnel, she had no idea how loudly she'd spoken, because the only thing she could hear was a roar like an earthmover in her head. "Wulf?"

Temporary hearing loss. If he answered, she wouldn't know. Shit. She crouched, spine jammed to the wall, butt crushed to her heels, shoulders hunched, curled inward to become the smallest target she could manage. Everything was pulled in except the gun. The gun pointed out.

A hand could grab her. In the dark she wouldn't see it, only feel it.

New smells mixed with the familiar sewer dank: cordite, singed hair and blood. Without hearing, she'd have to find Wulf by crawling in the direction where he should have been. On hands and knees, she dragged the gun across the catwalk and trailed her empty hand side-to-side like a spider until she brushed…softness. She recoiled, but immediately forced herself back to the obstruction. It was a leg covered in smooth fabric, not Wulf's denim. It was one of *them*. Her fingers skimmed past the spot where the fabric changed to shirt cotton. Sticky blood pooled on a chest. She found a neck, but

despite pressing, she couldn't locate a pulse. This was
a dead man.

More than likely, she'd shot him.

Willing the hot ball in her throat to dissolve, she
vowed not to freak out. Wulf was somewhere on the el-
evated walkway, perhaps calling her name, perhaps too
injured to speak. She had to search. But, oh God, this
body blocked the catwalk.

She stretched until her knuckles grazed the metal
grillwork on the far side of the man's bulk, arching over
his torso like a cat to avoid touching him. With both
hands across, she started to swing her leg over, but her
foot slipped and her knee squished into his abdominal
cavity. Then her other foot and the hand holding the gun
skidded in opposite directions, leaving her sprawled on
the dead man's gut. Her whole being recoiled from the
contact, and she pushed her knee into soft organs, scram-
bling for traction she couldn't find. *Ugh.*

One of his ribs caved in like a crushed milk container,
but she couldn't get away. He was dead, dead, dead, but
he wouldn't let her pass. Her fingers clawed at the metal
walk until they latched on to the perforations. With a
terrified strength she hadn't known she possessed, she
pulled her whole body slithering across to the far side
of the dead man.

Finally, chest heaving, she lay on her back sucking
air. A new fear hit.

In the lightless void, unable to hear past the drill-
ing sound between her ears, she'd lost the wall. Was
safety at her head or her feet? If she chose incorrectly,
she could end up like the flaming man who'd crashed
through the railing.

Her hands retreated inside Wulf's jacket sleeves until

the pistol snagged the cuff. Darkness couldn't hurt her unless she panicked. Cold was the killer. It would sap her will. If she didn't pick a direction, she'd be sitting here next week, so she forced her arms to uncurl. With the fingers of her left hand locked on the catwalk, she shoved the gun ahead of her until it bumped into something that vibrated her arm from wrist to shoulder. *The wall.*

She pressed her forehead against brick that smelled of wet and age, vaguely reminding her of the inside of her great-uncle's garage. Not unfamiliar, and not the odor of blood, so she inhaled deeply and let the wall guide her progress until she touched fur. *A rat.*

Flattened to the bricks with her fist jammed below her clavicle until it hurt to breathe, she willed her heart to slow. The fur hadn't moved under her hand, so no, it wasn't a rat.

It was human hair, short and bristly, not Wulf's. No pulse here, either, but the torso angled away and up as if it covered a second person. Like a nurse changing sheets, she flipped the body to expose another underneath. The blood-matted hair couldn't be identified by feel, but the nose and cheekbone contours, open collar and shoulder holster matched her memory. *Wulf.*

Her heartbeat hung suspended too until she found a flutter of life in his neck. While she searched for a wound, hope rose from her chest to her throat and she wanted to sing, *He's alive, he's alive!* His clothes were sticky, as if he was drenched with blood, but she couldn't feel an obvious injury on his chest, abdomen or thighs. Under one pant leg she found an empty sheath. Under the other, a tiny flashlight.

Thank you, Wulf. Her finger on the circular button, she took a deep breath.

And heard rushing water. The background wail that had filled her ears since the blast of gunshots was silenced; she could hear. When she pushed the flashlight button, she could also see, and that made her believe they'd both make it safely out of this sewer.

A clear, round tube stuck out from Wulf's shoulder. Despite having seen thousands of identical tubes, it took her a moment to recognize it was a syringe.

"Wulf? Can you hear me?" Her voice sounded as if she'd exhausted it at a concert. She shined the light in his eyes. Fixed and dilated pupils indicated brain stem impairment or coma, but thankfully his breathing and pulse were steady. Slow, but steady. The syringe had been jabbed so deep his deltoid had clenched around it, and she needed both hands to yank the barrel free. As she watched, his breathing normalized and his blue lips regained a flush. This time, when she played the light over his face, his pupils contracted evenly. Like in Afghanistan, he was healing before her eyes. She leaned close enough to his face to see his cheek stubble. "Can you blink?"

His eyelids twitched frantically as his eyes rolled in his head.

"Stay calm." She pressed her hand to his cheek.

"Nnnn." His lips parted but he couldn't form a word.

"Don't try to talk." She stuck the flashlight under her chin and used both hands to steady his head. "I'll find help."

"Nooo!" Jerking like she'd zapped him with a crash cart, his wrist whacked the side of her head. The impact knocked the flashlight loose. As she tried to catch it, it hit her thigh, then clattered on the metal catwalk before rolling to the edge. It hung, mocking her clumsy hands, for a fraction of a heartbeat. Then the light disappeared.

"Fuck!" She peered through gaps no longer distinguishable from darkness. She could almost see a glow through the black water. Almost. But not really.

"No...help." His words sounded like they came from under a mountain.

"That was our light!" This blackness was worse because it was so unnecessary.

He breathed heavier and somehow shifted his body.

"What are you doing?" She groped for his wrist. "Stay still."

"Need...eat."

"Absolutely not." His pulse was stronger. Part of her wanted to squeeze too hard—she was that mad at him—but she didn't. "Not until we figure out what was in the syringe."

"In...purse." He panted after each syllable. "Eat. Mints."

"Not a chance. Candy won't help you flush whatever drugs those were out of your system."

"Please."

The word weakened her, and she found his hand. A connection in the darkness was almost like having a candle. Then her purse strap tugged across her shoulder and she heard a telltale rattling tick-tick. "What are you—" She dropped his hand and grabbed for her bag, but it was too late. The sneak had opened it and swiped the box. "I said you shouldn't—"

"Too late." The rising tone on the end of his statement—was he *laughing?*

She hunted through the air, but couldn't find his hand

to retake her mints, so she gave up and scooted against the wall. She was in a Roman sewer with two dead men, another man who was too weird to die, no light, no phone and no idea what had happened to Theresa Chiesa of Jersey City. At least the stones felt solid, and her knees pressed into her chest felt like the knobs of bone and cartilage she knew they were. This space and these two knees belonged to her and she could count on them, even when nothing else in her life was stable.

"Before I finish these, want one?" He sounded better.

She shook her head before she remembered he couldn't see her. "No, thanks."

Wulf had been drugged into a coma and then, *click*, he'd snapped to life, exactly like he'd done after the Black Hawk crash. What the hell could produce both a super kidney function to flush a systemic drug and super healing ability?

She heard crunching. "Those are loud mints when you chew thirty at once."

"I offered to share. I need calories."

It felt like an hour passed without either of them speaking, but it was probably only moments. The sound of tearing fabric was audible over the water.

"There are two dead men," she finally said.

"Two?"

She couldn't interpret his thoughts from his neutral tone. "I think I shot one." She'd been in Afghanistan more than six months, but the first time she'd fired a gun at an actual person had turned out to be while on leave in Rome.

"You okay?" His hand and forearm landed on her like a falling branch.

She winced. Should she be okay? "Yeah." Killing

probably wasn't a big thing to him. "I mean, he was try-ing to kill us, right?" Her hands felt dirty and crusty, as if splotched with dried blood, like Lady Macbeth. "What'd you do the first time?"

"First time I what?"

"Killed someone."

A lighter flame in his palms became, within seconds, a ball of light hanging from the catwalk railing. He'd crafted a lantern from the dead man's pants fabric and wire. The whole conglomerate hadn't yet caught fire, and he hadn't answered. "What did you do after?"

"It wasn't what you'd term politically correct." He scooted closer to the body, every movement an odd jerk, like his synapses had to fire individually to activate his muscles.

"By definition killing a person isn't politically cor-rect." Flickers of light reflected on the corpse's open eyes. She'd seen death, lost devastating battles in the hospital to it, but this wasn't remotely the same because she hadn't lost. She'd won. Here *winning* meant death.

Wulf stared down at the heavyset man. "Here's the solution to one of my problems."

"What?"

"My team's been looking for this guy." He turned out the dead man's pockets. "He was a flight-line manager at Bagram until last month." He removed the man's shoes, lifted the innersoles and tried to twist the heels. "Disap-peared after a pilot was shot," he added as he searched inside the man's belt, waistband, cuffs and collar.

"You're thorough." He didn't fumble over buttons or zippers. He'd regained his physical control, at least in this small way, and it soothed her.

"Ideas?" He handed her a leather case the size of a

long wallet. It held another hypodermic and two vials of liquid, one empty, one full.

By turning it toward the flames, she was able to read the label. "Ketamine. A sedative, mostly veterinary, off-label use as a rave drug." She calculated from the listed amount. "This would work on a Clydesdale. Maybe a whole team." Her throat closed and she stared at his face. The flaming cloth cast shadows that merged with the dark bloodstains until he resembled a ghoul from a Bosch painting. No miracle-science lab had created him. Her mind asked the question: *What are you?*

Her mouth opened, but surrounded by death, her lips refused to take the last step.

He reclaimed the drug case, put it and the dead men's identifications in a pouch fashioned from a jacket, zipped it closed and tied it around his body.

"What are we going to do about them?" Without asking, she knew the police wouldn't be one of his choices.

"Leave 'em. It's a time-honored tradition." After wiping his knife on a man's pant leg, he replaced it in his ankle sheath. "Emperor Elagabalus was tossed in the sewer at the end of his shelf life, so it's good enough for these scum." He hauled himself upright with help from the wall. "You're fabulous, you know that?"

"Not really." She shivered and hugged herself with hands as clammy as her wet pants, but she made it to her feet. "I lost it before you regained consciousness." His opinion shouldn't have made her feel better, but it warmed her at least as much as the coat she still wore.

He shrugged. "I've seen fresh Rangers not stay that cool."

"You don't have to be a guy to be…" Tough wasn't the right word. "Capable. Up to the job." Sure, she'd been

scared. She couldn't think about the crunch of the first
dead man's rib without her shoulders and neck hunching,
but that had nothing to do with being a woman. "I'm a
doctor. I deal with unexpected shit every day."

He untied the cloth ball and dangled it in front of him.
The smoldering light swung wildly close to his jeans as
he staggered. "Come on."

"You'll burn yourself." She scrambled after him.

"It'll heal."

That sounds like the truth, she thought. She followed
Wulf's light downstream. At the moment, she didn't see
another choice.

THERESA KNEW NO self-respecting Roman restaurant
opened before six, but Wulf had promised food if she
climbed this last hill. After leaving the sewer at the main
opening with barely a wave from tourists on the bridge,
they'd cleaned up in a church's dingy basement bathroom and walked backstreets to this spot. On one side
of the alley, ramshackle buildings backed into the rising
ground. On the other side a screen of trees, brambles and
ivy hid the cars honking below. Now that they'd stopped
walking, her legs felt odd.

"Fighting makes me hungry." Wulf knocked on a
black-painted door. "This was the meatpacking district
in the old days. My friend Cesare's father was a butcher."

The ground tilted. *Maybe I should sit.* The restaurant
stoop looked clean.

"Cesare learned to cook from his mother." Instead of
letting her sink to the step, Wulf put a hand under her
elbow and knocked again. "Butchers' wives cooked the
scraps. Good stuff."

Scraps. Behind her closed eyes, she saw the raw, burned face of the man who'd tumbled into the water.

"Hang with me, Theresa." He shifted her shoulders against his chest and reached around her to rattle the door. "This hill is a former Roman dump. Made of more than fifty million olive oil amphorae. Interesting, isn't it?"

She struggled to raise her eyelids, prepared to tell him *no* even as he tucked her deeper under his arm and pounded the wood with the bottom of his fist.

The old man who opened the door barely reached her collarbone. When he saw Wulf, his squint changed to a grin and wide-armed hug. They chattered in Italian, but she didn't care if they were twins separated at birth, because she'd detected the aromas of her mother's house—garlic and onions and meat, all simmering and roasting. If these two characters didn't move out of her path to that food, they might end up more crushed than Wulf's ancient amphorae.

"Cesare, mi scusi." Wulf drew her across the threshold. *"Permetto introdurre Signorina Theresa Chiesa."*

The cook kissed her cheeks, and Wulf guided her to a chair at the back of the room. He fiddled with a free-standing screen until she wanted to yell, *Get on with it!* She'd had a long day, no lunch and she'd freaking killed a man today and would do it again—*see if she didn't*—if they didn't bring out that marvelous-smelling food *pronto.*

Hot, damp towels arrived with the bread, shutting up the voice in her head. It stayed quiet while she savored antipasti, sliced meats, olives and a glass of Barolo.

"I'm ready," she finally said. "Let's start with the real medical story. No bull."

Wulf stared at his bread plate and shook his head. "This isn't the place."

"You've said that before." She popped an olive marinated with thyme and pepper in her mouth and worked the pit out with her teeth. "Ostia wasn't the place. The car, with Joe-Jim in the trunk, wasn't the place." The slice of *culatello* between her fingers folded and clung to itself as she draped it over a piece of melon. "But we had some time to ourselves in the sewer. That would've been a good place to explain how you do your nifty healing trick."

"I need more information."

"About yourself? I don't think so. Look, I followed you all day, broke several major laws." A statement so absurd she almost choked on her next olive. "And I haven't called the police because something makes me trust you." Maybe because she'd seen his kindness with Nazdana and Meena. Or maybe because the other guys were the ones firing first.

"Is it the food?" He nudged the bread basket closer to her plate.

"I'm serious." She used the look Sister Beatrice had bestowed on parents who skipped the Holy Names school auction. "I think the events of today have made security clearance issues irrelevant, don't you? I'm done following that rule."

"You have a crumb…" He touched a spot under his lower lip, where the skin made a dent above his chin. He didn't politely look away while she dabbed with her napkin. Instead, crammed in this intimate corner behind a screen, he stared at her like she was breakfast, lunch and dinner, even though she felt more like an olive—briny, bordering on bitter.

"I won't give up." She took a gulp of wine to reinforce her resolution.

With a sigh, he swirled bread through the plate of olive oil. "I told you my team's investigating heroin smugglers who use Black and Swan logistics." He smushed the piece harder into the dish, as if stamping a passport. "The guns didn't surprise me, but the tranquilizer was an unexpected move." Saturated blobs broke off the bread. "Maybe I was wrong and this is personal, not army business, but either way, they've linked you to me."

"But what is—" she curved her fingers to make air quotes, "—'this'? And why would 'they' be interested in you personally?"

"I thought the Ostia guy wanted to stop the drug investigation. Ditto the shooters. Clearly they're involved in the drugs, because one of them was a former Black and Swan manager." Abandoning the shredded bread in the olive oil, his hand covered his shoulder where she'd removed the syringe. "But that much ketamine. They have more information about me than they should. I need to know how they got it."

This was her answer, the big one. Her fingers clenched the edge of the table as she forced herself to stay seated. "So what do they know that I don't?"

"Coda alla vaccinara." Cesare set a dish family style between them. It held steaming chunks of oxtail in tomato sauce studded with pine nuts and raisins.

"Saved." The corner of Wulf's mouth tilted as he slipped a plate in front of her.

One bite, then she'd press him again. The sauce had an underpinning of bitter chocolate she associated with Mexican moles after living in Texas. Maybe another bite. He wasn't leaving.

"Did you have a laptop in your hotel room?" he asked.

"Unfortunately." She scooped a forkful of the disintegrating meat and lush sauce.

"Did you have information on it about me?"

Her mother had emphasized that it was rude to speak while chewing, so she nodded.

The lines between his nose and mouth deepened. "I hope you merely raved over my excellent tour-guide services."

She snorted and set down her fork. "Get real." While she considered an explanation that didn't sound *clinical*, she sipped her water. "I keep notes on medical situations and outcomes. Nothing scientific, no names." Nothing like real research. Because the army had sent her to Darnell Army Medical Center at Fort Hood, Texas, after her residency, she'd never had a chance to compete with her medical school peers for a research fellowship.

"These people, whoever they are, they may want to capture me. To know more."

So did she, but she wouldn't kill—or die—for the answer, although she might whack him with an olive oil bottle. Apparently it wouldn't hurt him for very long. "Look, I have a yes-or-no question. It's really…" *Dumb*.

He raised an eyebrow.

"Are you…" She stared at her cutlery. The question was crazy, influenced by her roommate's choice of escapist reading. If she looked at his face, she'd never spit it out. "A vampire?" She glanced through her lashes.

"There's no such thing." His nostrils spread and his lips twitched. "Or, if there is, I'm not aware."

Fine, he wasn't a sparkly bloodsucker, but his answer sure as hell didn't feel like the complete truth.

The restaurant's front door jingled.

Chapter Sixteen

IMMOBILIZED, THERESA WATCHED Wulf leap past the screen. He'd disappeared before his chair hit the floor. She half ducked under the table, expecting shots or crashing furniture, but then Wulf laughed and she recognized an Italian greeting.

In a moment he returned with a third chair and wineglass. Behind him, a dapper man in his early seventies wearing a subtle pin-striped suit and red-patterned tie paused to eyeball her. His mouth tightened until it looked unfortunately similar to a cat's butt.

She could guess what he saw. Her black pants, soaked and dried in place, itched. She'd scrubbed her hands and face in the church bathroom, but her clothes deserved a burn barrel. Ditto her hair. Wulf wasn't in much better shape. Dousing his hair in the sink and drying it with paper towels had only created cleaner snarls. He'd repossessed the leather jacket to cover his blood-soaked shirt, but the coat was unable to hide the dark splotches on his jeans.

"Theresa, this is a friend, Signor Lorenzo Rizzotti. Lorenzo, Captain Theresa Chiesa, a doctor with the United States Army."

After the mention of her profession, Wulf's friend's mouth fell open briefly. "I will return later, sir, when you are less occupied. And not with your...doctor." Despite his Italian name, Signor Rizzotti sounded like the BBC announcer on her hotel room's radio.

"Don't act bothered. I'm happy you received my second message about where to find us." Wulf indicated the third chair, placed between their seats. "Sit, Lorenzo, and tell us what you know."

"Sir!" As if shocked by the invitation, the other man stiffened.

Wulf grinned sideways at her. "This is how Deavers must feel when the team gives him the 'sir' treatment. Lorenzo, I'm not my brother."

Wulf had a brother? Chris Deavers talked about his family constantly, and most of Wulf's team had wives and kids, but she'd assumed Wulf didn't have close family. What other mistakes had she made?

"Nevertheless, your situation imparts certain responsibilities." Lorenzo emphasized the last word.

"Nevertheless?" Wulf's grin grew as he locked eyes with Theresa. "Who replaced my Italian butler with an English major?"

"I attended Cambridge, sir. When your brother was—"

Wulf waved his hand at the chair. "Inside joke, my friend." He leaned forward. "You dealt with everything I left in the garage?"

Lorenzo nodded, frowned and stared at the wall over their table, all at the same time.

"By the way, after we left the house, we were shot at, chased into the sewers and ambushed, so it's been a long day. Let's skip the formalities."

"You trust her." The flat intonation wasn't a question. It was more like an accusation.

"I do," Wulf said.

For Theresa, those two quietly spoken words rekindled the confidence that the older man's disapproval had begun to squelch.

"So be it." Lorenzo pulled reading glasses from a pocket inside his suit and laid several folded pieces of paper on the table. "The information you requested. Most of the numbers you gave me were easily traced, but for one I had to seek assistance from your brother." His glance cut to Theresa. "At the time I was not aware..." He appeared to lack a word to describe her.

Too bad. She had a couple for him. She dredged up the expression she reserved for preteen smokers loitering at convenience stores.

Lorenzo adjusted his cuffs, as if to indicate, *Your glare is a mere speck of dust*, before he continued. "All the telephone numbers, less one, are mobiles. The Italian ones are disposables activated in Rome within the past forty-eight hours and purchased with cash. Two are American satellite phones that appear to be owned by a business." His salt-and-pepper eyebrows raised to match the arches of an aqueduct lithograph on the wall. "Black and Swan."

"Can't say I'm surprised." Wulf remained impassive. "And the landline?"

The dapper man harrumphed into his fist before he continued. "Your brother traced it through Polish number forwards and two Caribbean exchanges. He was not amused."

"Is he ever?"

Theresa needed to hook a thumb under her bra strap and yank it into place, but the way the older man twiddled with his glasses, as if something as innocuous as a telephone number could disturb his world-class equilibrium, made her stifle the impulse.

"This number rings in an office in Langley, Virginia."

Langley? She ought to know why that sounded familiar, but her mind blanked.

"Your brother requests that you cease and desist activities that intersect with the American CIA. I transcribed his quote verbatim. Let me find it." He shuffled his papers. "Ah, yes. 'Tell the puny milk-sucking idiot not to involve me, my resources or you—' I believe he meant *me*, '—in this business again.'"

Wulf chuckled. "Tell my corporate-fat-licking big brother I salute his insult and would cheerfully exchange more over ale, if I weren't busy earning an honorable living."

"Of course." Lorenzo cleared his throat and stood. "Will that be all, sir?"

"The man in the car." Theresa's voice cracked, but she had to know before he walked away. "What did you do with him?"

Lorenzo looked startled that the wordless bump would speak. "He is locked in the wine cellar."

Laughing, Wulf tilted on his chair. "Hope you removed Ivar's cases of Château Pétrus."

"Sir, *I* am not a puny milk-sucking idiot."

In the silence after Lorenzo's departure, Theresa looked at the congealed chunks of gravy on her plate and realized her appetite had deserted her. Was the CIA on their side or not? What should they do? She still had her passport in her purse, but where could she go?

Again, Wulf read her mind. "We'll take the rear exit."

Because the restaurant had been dug out of the hillside, his plan made as much sense as dropping into the sewer, but she didn't have a better one. She followed him through a stainless-steel door and an industrial-plastic curtain.

"A refrigerator!" Her feet slid on the metal floor.

"Relax." His advice left a visible cloud in the freezing air.

She tried to ignore the red-and-white beef haunch he shouldered aside while he twisted an empty meat hook and immediately straight-armed a wall panel. It pivoted to reveal their path. Another. Damn. Tunnel. Every cell of her being balked. "Wasn't the sewer enough?"

"I promise there's a safe room and a bathtub at the end." He handed her a flashlight from a niche. "I delivered on dinner, didn't I?"

True, he had; more importantly, she wasn't ready to be left behind.

As they walked down a slight incline, pieces of something bigger and more slippery than gravel crunched under her feet. Although the tunnel smelled old, like Great Aunt Mary's living room, it was dry, which boded well for the room at the other end. She pictured cold beige tile and government-issue furniture, but it would be a secure space to clean up and rest.

Ninety percent of her believed Wulf could deliver hot water underground in an ancient landfill. The smarter ten percent focused on the key component of bathing: *getting naked.* Before she could decide which part to listen to, he stopped at a wooden door hung between massive beams and typed a numeric code on a keypad. A bolt snicked open. With the flick of a switch, he illuminated a large room. "Welcome to my parlor."

"Isn't that what the spider said to the—oh." This wasn't a sterile dormitory for American agents. As he beckoned her into a Renaissance fantasia, she understood why the fly had fallen for the fatal lure. A king-size four-poster anchored the right-hand wall, plum-colored velvet curtains trimmed in gold fringe matched tasseled pillows piled against the headboard and jewel-tone fabrics and polished wood filled the large room. The scene was the antithesis of the bland austerity she'd expected, and a manic need to giggle with relief expanded her lungs.

A few hours ago they'd been fighting to stay alive, and now...*those were gold tassels.*

Inappropriate reactions were natural after a release of tension, but she suspected that if she started to laugh, she wouldn't stop, so she looked away from the bed to the tapestries and gilt-framed landscapes that covered the walls. Above an empty pool in the floor, stacked semicircles of exposed pottery had been smoothed into undulating ochre waves.

Wulf turned knobs to make water cascade from a faucet shaped like a dolphin's head. "It takes time to fill deep enough for bathing."

The massive bath couldn't distract her from the bed. She knew exactly how far behind her it lurked.

As he shrugged out of his jacket and shoulder holster, Wulf stared at her face. One by one he undid the buttons of his ruined shirt. He intended to strip. In front of her.

"Who are you?" Grime glued her clothes to her back as she tried, and failed, to ignore the water thundering behind him. The steaming hot and clean water.

"You know who I am." He sat to unlace his boots. "Wulf Wardsen, staff sergeant, United States Army." He reached under his pant legs to unclip his knife sheath and the contraption that had once held a flashlight.

"How gullible do you think I am? You're no more

an E-6 than I'm a Swedish supermodel." Even with his head lower than hers and his body still in the chair, she couldn't feel at ease, so she put another chair between them. "Yesterday you said you lie to everyone. Right now that's all I believe."

"I am what I do." He offered her a neutral expression, neither threatening nor revealing.

"The fancy motorcycle, the dinners, that huge house." She waved her hand at his opulent cave, wanting to prod until he reacted. "And this place. Where'd you get the money?"

"My brother's an independent investor." To unbuckle his belt, he stood. "He handles my finances too."

Dinner soured in her stomach. She'd lived her whole life trying to distance herself from "independent investors" like her stepfather and his cronies. She'd tried to live by the ethics of her biological father, but one smoking-hot kiss and she wasn't so different from her mother. "I refuse to have anything to do with a criminal."

"So do I. I'm not one."

She yearned to believe him, to let him put his rock-solid arms around her so she could rest her head on his chest and stop worrying. She wanted to trust the man standing in front of her wearing only tattered jeans, but she still didn't know how to sort his lies from the truth.

"Take me to the airport." She couldn't look at him while she announced her decision or she'd waver. "I want to go back to Afghanistan."

"With Black and Swan looking for us, you're not safe there."

"I'm not safe *here*." *An understatement.* "So I might as well be there."

"I can protect you." He raised his voice louder than

the water pouring into the pool. He'd lost his detached look and instead coiled as if he might spring.

"What the fuck?" She felt like she'd been centrifuged. Everything she knew and believed about herself as a doctor and about the army and its people had been spun on its head today. "I've spent years taking care of myself, and I could do it a lot better without getting mixed up in your problems. I'm out of here!"

His nostrils flared. "No."

"Screw you!" He could keep his lies and mysteries. She flung herself at the door.

His hand shot past her shoulder to slap the wood as she grabbed for the handle. "You're safer here."

"Fuck off!" She jerked with both hands, and the door opened a few inches. But when her shoulder blades bumped his chest, his bare chest, she froze. The atmosphere was charged so high she feared any sound would ignite a conflagration. To her right, at eye level, nothing but his fingertips grazed the wood. Although she couldn't move without brushing his body, if she wanted to leave, all she had to do was pull again.

They both knew he wasn't to blame if she didn't.

"You keep using those words. Like screw." His voice had deepened and gone quieter. She only heard it because he stood close enough for his body to bracket hers. It was the voice he used before he kissed her. "And fuck."

She fixated on the ancient wood in front of her face. If she twisted, if she shifted one millimeter, her body would connect with his and then she'd be lost.

"You said that word more than once, didn't you?" He turned her around with hands that seemed to burn through the cotton of her shirt.

Pressing her temple into the wood, she closed her eyes

against the penetration of his gaze lest he read how easily he could change her mind. She didn't move, not when his fingers stroked the side of her neck. Not when she felt him lift her hair from one shoulder. She fought hard to suppress shivers, but she didn't tremble, not even when he spoke so close to the bare skin at her throat that his breath swept across every nerve.

"Do you like to say *fuck?* Do you want to say it again, right now? To me?"

Her glutes and inner thighs clenched.

"I think you were trying to give me an order, weren't you, ma'am?" He drawled the last word like he dared her to contradict him.

She pressed into the door, seeking something to grab that wasn't him. The croak she made was hardly a word, so she tried again. "This is against the rules."

"Wasn't it you who said we've broken too many to care?"

She lifted her hands to push him but stopped with her wrists against her own aching breasts. Inches from her fingers, his nipples showed through the golden hair that proclaimed him a man. She had nowhere to look that he didn't fill. And he was glorious.

"We have to stop," she whispered in a voice so soft she didn't recognize it as her own.

"Why?" He preempted her answer by wrapping his thumb and first finger around each wrist and raising her hands above her head.

Because if I don't leave now, I'll give in to you and I'll lose everything I've worked for. With her breasts higher and closer to danger, her breathing betrayed her excitement. She couldn't form the words *let go* because her mouth had rebelled to join her body.

"I'm only looking." He transferred both of her wrists to one hand.

"You're doing more than that." Each time he shifted, the bulges and ripples of his muscles worked seamlessly to do his bidding. The arm he raised had the contours and definition her imagination had supplied and more. Part of her wanted to pull against his grip so she could watch his body tense and uncoil, but a shred of common sense held her still.

"Order me to stop." His palm hovered over the spot where fabric stretched across her nipple.

She was the one who moved first, who pushed the pressure receptors in her nipple against the thousands of touch receptors in his palm, and they both knew it. Shock zinged from her breasts through her spine to her trembling knees while her body begged for more friction.

He brushed across her other nipple, the fabric of her shirt too flimsy to contain her breasts' pilomotor reflex, and she knew she wouldn't stop him.

"Tell me." His palm circled harder, drawing her tighter. "It's your decision."

"My questions…" She arched from the door deeper into his hand.

"Ask." His fingers changed the play and rolled her nipple tighter still. "Anything."

"Are you…" She wanted to touch him, but he kept her hands pinned. She twisted her head on the wood, trying to recall her questions. "Undead?"

"Exactly the opposite." His breath tickled her neck when he spoke. "I am very alive."

"Then what?" She wanted him to reach under her shirt as much as she wanted his answer. "What are you?"

"I am a barbarian." Saying it seemed to release his last restraint. The lust that burned in his eyes and hardened his face was a look her few, carefully chosen lovers had never showed. Something in him broke free, and she sensed it coming for her, stalking her.

She desperately wanted it to catch her.

"A scourge of peace-loving folk." He inserted his free hand in the neckline of her shirt and kept his gaze enmeshed with hers.

If he hadn't held her wrists, she might have slid to the floor. Past seductions had always followed the usual couch-and-grope routine, never words and walls and waiting, fully clothed and wobbling, for a touch larger than her imagination.

"A conqueror." He pulled until her neckline chafed her sensitized skin, then let go of her wrists to use two hands on her shirt fabric.

Leaving her arms extended over her head, she waited. The tearing sound blended with the moan she couldn't hold back.

"I am a berserker."

She envisioned him in battle, swift and brutal, as he'd been in the street. Would he drive into her here against the door? The thought called up an Amazon who wanted to fight free and conquer with him, conquer *him*. Maybe she'd take him here on the floor and damn everything. She squeezed her eyes shut and shook her head. "Nooo." Her hunger was too much.

Heat disappeared from her skin as even the rasp of his breath disappeared into silence.

She opened her eyes. His head was thrown back and he dug the heels of his palms into his eye sockets as if struggling. He'd misinterpreted her attempt to stop *herself*. Not him.

"Kiss me," she managed to whisper.

Shuddering, he dropped his hands and closed the gap between them until they shared one breath. "Don't ask me to stop unless you mean it."

His gaze called to cravings so intense that she shivered, echoing him. "I won't."

"Then I will pillage your mouth." With one finger, he touched her lips, then traced a line from her jaw to her throat. "I will claim your neck and your body."

She lowered her chin to watch his finger slip between the cups of her bra. Her torn shirt hung like draping on a statue of Venus while he trailed fire across her bare skin.

"I will plunder until my sword is exhausted." He wove a spell of words she never wanted to escape. "You will be my prize. But you must agree."

Closing her eyes, she moaned.

"Say it." His mouth returned to the pulse in her throat. "Say yes." His fingers covered her breastbone.

She wanted to abandon herself to his touch more than she wanted answers, more than she wanted to be a doctor, more than she wanted her next breath. *Yes.*

"Let me hear it." While his thumb drew a line along her collarbone, his voice pushed her to the end of her resistance.

"Yes." Dizzy, she swayed into his hand and spoke louder. "Yes."

Before she could help, he'd stripped the ruined boots and clothes from her body and carried her into the pool. Her skin prickled with the water's heat, but once he slid next to her on the submerged stone bench and ran his wet hands over every inch of her body, the hot steam cooled in comparison to the fire under her skin. He'd threatened to plunder, but instead he touched her as if she was as fragile as glass. Even his kisses had the tenderness of a first encounter, not the fierce need burning in her after days spent building to this point.

Where was her barbarian? While her hands stroked his shoulders and down his back to the tight rise of his ass, she poured her scorching feelings into their kiss. Her breasts dragged across his chest, seeking rougher stimulation than wet skin on wet skin provided, but no matter how hard she pressed, he didn't release his warrior.

"Wulf." She coaxed and ordered and begged all in one word as he lifted her hips from the bench, but his hands didn't speed or roughen on her body.

"Relax into the water." One hand glided along the length of her back, arching her body until her breasts jutted from the bath, while his other hand stretched her legs until her soles reached the far side of the tub. Heated water lapped at her calves, her ribs, her shoulders, all sensitized by his gaze and pleading to be touched, but his hands stayed fixed under her back and thighs. For interminable moments only his eyes moved from her lips and breasts to her uptilted hips and spread legs. "Grab the wall."

She obeyed. The stone was textured—not rough, but not as smooth or heated as his skin. She craved more. She craved touch. His.

He leaned down for a caress so brief she might have missed it if she hadn't been watching. His lower lip caught a droplet of water descending the curve of her breast, but he didn't press harder against her skin. His tongue never touched her. Instead it licked only his own lips, and took only that single drop before he straightened.

Torture, that's what making her wait amounted to. Her grip tightened on the wall behind her, giving her leverage to thrust upward and bring her aching breasts closer to him and his mouth, closer to the attention they needed, even as she floated.

At last his lips closed around her nipple, and she couldn't stay quiet as more need clamored in her body. Her moans mingled with the sound of his sucks. The louder she became, the harder he pulled, and she wanted it harder still. When her voice rose, he added his tongue. She felt her chest expand, heard air rasp from her throat, as he worked her.

Fire built where his teeth scraped, spread across her skin and burned despite the water. She squeezed her fists on the edge of the pool, squeezed her pelvic muscles, squeezed the pleasure from every touch, but she wasn't filled. She wanted to be, but his mouth only tightened her, it didn't finish the damn job.

Finally, his finger breached her triangle of need and she reached for his shoulders while she thrust her hips against his hand. Her unmoored body floundered, and his hand fell away.

"I told you not to let go." His voice sounded like an animal's growl. He rolled her nipple hard enough to make her shiver. Anticipation and need fought as she wondered whether obeying him or letting go would be the faster route to what she wanted.

This time she stayed where he put her, feet and hands anchored to opposite sides of the stone bath, her body floating in the hot water. For long moments he didn't touch her, as if testing her obedience, and then his reward sent a fresh surge of desire through her as he traced a line around the juncture of her thighs. Up and down, but not inside.

"More. Please. More." She'd tell him with words he seemed to like hearing. "Fuck me."

He gave her more, but it wasn't close enough to everything she wanted, even when he slid a finger past her entrance and sucked her nipple at the same time.

Her world compressed to her breasts and her core, and the sensations that sizzled from them to the tensed and vibrating muscles in her body. His mouth released her nipple, but he moved faster in her, with more fingers, and then his thumb touched a spot that ignited the water on her skin. She needed to shake, to writhe, to heave from the escalating tension.

"Hold still." His voice, gritty and barely audible, made her open her eyes.

The man who loomed over her, head flung back so far she couldn't see his eyes, wasn't in control. His lips curled back from his teeth, and his neck tendons stood out like wires. Even though he touched her so carefully, his chest heaved like he was racing for his life.

From her instep to her spine, she squeezed and sought leverage to thrust while his fingers drove into her faster and faster, sending her spiraling in a whirlpool of sensation until vibrations swept her body and matched the water that surged around them. She must have screamed then, because an echo hung in the air and her mouth was open.

He supported her as the ceiling came into focus. "Well?" Above her his eyes glittered like sapphires reflecting light. "How was that?"

"Terrible." Her feet drifted to the stones at the bottom of the deep tub as she sat. He deserved a little torture. "I can't think."

"Then don't." He laughed, his throat muscles sharp and enthralling. "You'll argue."

"Ha." She trailed her hand down his chest to where the evidence of his self-control stood hard and thick while he threw his arms along the pool wall and offered himself. His posture proclaimed, *It's your turn to explore.*

She loved how the male body contrasted with hers. Where her body was padded and curved, his had angles and separately identifiable muscles, like the crease between his torso and his hip. The dim light didn't penetrate the water, so she couldn't see the shape of his thighs, but they felt like logs, too hard for her fingers to probe or massage.

When she wrapped her hand around the part of him she wanted to possess completely, he shuddered. His shaft stood like a mortar set to launch, so she whispered, "Shot out," and slid her hand up and down his length. Her thumb barely touched her second finger. His thickness would fill her, fill every need she had and more.

Straddling his thighs, she guided his tip to her opening. They locked eyes and achieved the deeper union she'd yearned for each time their hands or bodies had brushed. This was the connection he'd started a month ago with his scrap of embroidered silk, the bond he'd built with his kisses, the link yesterday and today had forged.

His hands dug into her hips, yanked her down onto him again and again until waves collided and she braced on his shoulders and threw back her head while he thrust. Her body coiled tighter with each shove of his cock inside her, each impact of his pelvic bone on her inner thighs, each scrape of his teeth at her nipples. She came down faster and harder, striving for a second explosion, reaching for it with him, together.

With his neck tendons like ridges bisecting his shoulders, he looked like a man about to break, and then he bucked deeper yet and lifted her from the water with a last thrust. He yelled, a sound only, not the coherence of a word, and collapsed backward.

However long she straddled him, arms looped over his shoulders and face pressed to his neck while their breathing slowed, it wasn't long enough.

"Splash over, Doc." His hands framed her face. "Think that qualified as a hit?"

She groaned. She had no words, no thoughts, no plans. He could take charge.

He slipped to the other side of the pool. Water puddled everywhere, the aftermath a wet mess. Like her. Too sated to move, too awed at what they'd shared, she couldn't do more than watch as he opened a teak box and extracted shampoo.

The plastic bottle with its orange flip-top, so mundane, made her freeze. They'd forgotten one particular boring, dull, crucial, vital thing. *Shit.* "You've thought of…almost everything." The sarcasm didn't carry a sting, but she wanted to bawl, *Shampoo but not condoms?*

"So." She'd start normally before she opened *that* chat. "This is an amazing place. How often are you here?" *Okay, this is awkward.* She might as well have asked about the weather.

He glanced over his shoulder, almost as if he were equally uncertain about what to say or do. "Once or twice a year," he said, and then he returned to gathering soap and towels.

"All this—" she gestured around the room, "—for once a year?" Inside her head, she heard her mother say, *Enough questions, sweetie, or you'll end up single like Aunt Mary.* She shut up.

The shampoo cap snapped decisively. "It's been a lot of years."

"How many?" She watched his hands rub together until they were covered in bubbles, as ephemeral as this bond between them. If she pushed, would he shut her out even now? With the scent of oranges surrounding her, he massaged circles into her scalp, creating sensations so good she almost let her question drop. Almost. "I've noticed a pattern. You make a mysterious pronouncement, then when I ask you to explain, you distract me."

"I like distracting you." After he sluiced water on her hair without letting it drip into her eyes, his fingers followed the bubbles over her shoulder and across the swell of her breast.

Her body wanted to go all mushy a third time, but her brain issued a squelch command. She tugged his hand off her breast and frowned. "Not going to work."

He looked set to jump at the challenge she'd unintentionally issued, until he read her expression. Wise man.

"Rinse." He retreated to the other end of the stone ledge. "Then we'll talk."

She did as he said and pushed wet hair away from her face. "So, you never said how many years you've been coming here." This answer had become important out of all proportion.

Pulling his eyes off her chest, he looked at the ceiling, perhaps counting.

One question—how long he'd owned this secret

room—wouldn't tell her what she needed to understand, but she couldn't move on without knowing.

When he met her eyes, a single raised eyebrow defied her. "Six hundred years."

Her heart seized with the same chest-tightening confusion she'd felt struggling in the mountains to reach Nazdana's village. She couldn't have heard him correctly.

"I'm immortal."

Chapter Seventeen

THERESA'S DARK EYES were the sole color on her chalky face.

"At least I'm not a vampire." Wulf tried to smile. "I wouldn't know as many great restaurants." His joke bombed.

"What do you mean by…immortal?" Her voice revealed nothing of her thoughts.

"I can't die. I can't be killed." Sharing his secret directly was a step he'd never risked even with Deavers. "You've seen my injuries heal. They always do. And I don't age."

She studied him, her face as immobile as a Byzantine mosaic.

Seconds lengthened into a minute while he wondered for the ten-thousandth time what went on in a woman's mind. Although she relied on science, maybe she was one of the rare people who could believe and accept his story.

"I still don't understand. Are you…" Her inflections were choppy, with pauses where words ought to flow. "Like that movie. *Highlander?*"

"Not exactly." His jaw clenched at the comparison. Two deployments ago a new guy had thought it would make an entertaining movie night. After the captain snapped the DVD in half, he'd transferred the guy to a desk at Headquarters Company. It took a month of Judy Garland and Julie Andrews to expunge the swords, beheadings and stupid motto. "Fifteen hundred years ago I was a regular man. You would've called me a Viking. Then—" he forced himself to open his fists, "—I became this."

"How?"

No-nonsense Captain Chiesa, the straight-lipped woman who'd accosted his team in the gym, had returned. He couldn't complain, because he'd wanted someone who'd listen and believe and maybe even care. When she leaned forward to speak, her breasts jiggled, which sent tiny waves lapping over to his side of the pool with an invitation. Then she raised a hand, and water drops followed veins down the pale inside of her wrist. If he bent forward, he could—

"Stop it." She snapped her fingers. "You were finally talking. Keep talking. Tell me how you became immortal."

"Right." He chose a comb from the box by the pool's edge. It felt insubstantial, so he swapped it for the weightier shampoo. "Have you read *Beowulf?*"

"The English epic? With the monster?" Her eyebrows drew together, and she brushed his hands aside. "You've done my hair. Give me that bottle before you crush it."

Orders from her were a sign that his world might be intact, so he leaned back to let her touch him while he continued talking. "The *Beowulf* saga is true." When Galan had recorded their history in writing, he'd left out most of the men's names to protect them, but he'd included the songs and stories and even Hrothgar's queen's flirtation with Beowulf, all the parts that Wulf himself forgot whenever he remembered the monster.

She pressed on top of his head, circled and released. Her fingers must have deactivated most of his muscle groups, because his limbs flopped. "Are you saying you're Beowulf?"

"No, he was our liege lord."

"Our?"

"My brother and I." Ivar would knock out his teeth for talking openly, but he couldn't live in his brother's form of isolation. "We joined Beowulf's quest, looking for a bit of adventure, a bigger slice of reward. And of course we had our honor to prove. Common story. Ask any grunt today." They'd been desperate, the belly hunger of their childhood replaced by a thirst to restore their family name, but their father had gambled away their sea gear. Beowulf had gifted Ivar with a seal-fur cloak and outfitted Wulf with a boar's head helmet. From that moment they'd become more faithful than his hounds, willing to die for him.

Instead they'd been sentenced to live.

"Go on," she murmured.

"The first night at Heorot, we lost Handscio." Her doctor fingers moved to the nerves at the base of his skull and forced his eyes to shut. Never had the telling of this tale, nor even the thinking of it, come so easily, but with her hands digging into his muscles, he could recall the monster without shuddering. A half dozen arms had sprung from its body, enough arms to pin a man and claw him open and fight off other men all at once. When their swords hadn't cut the monster's hide, he and Ivar had been as helpless as newborns thrown in a fjord. All of them had been, except their leader.

"After Beowulf ripped the monster apart, we thought we'd earned our gold." He could keep talking if she kept touching him. Maybe he could even sleep afterward if she massaged his shoulders. "Hrothgar's men didn't

reminded him of her mortal body's limitations, so he helped her from the pool and toweled her dry. Although she raised her arms and turned at his prompts, she was close to asleep by the time he wrapped them both in robes and settled her on floor cushions.

"Relax. I'll take care of your hair." The comb drew dark, wet lines from the crown of her head past her shoulders as he carefully worked through each section. "I'll not mistreat you."

"Sometimes you sound—" her voice slurred as she started to doze, "—old-fashioned."

When he wanted to feel modern and energetic, he went to America. In Italy the past slowed him until he could appreciate beauty like the strands of her hair rippling from the comb. The lapels of her robe slid apart as she sagged onto his knee, asleep. His strokes slowed. How long could they stay in the moment, at peace like this?

Her sleeping profile, the shape of her lips and the sweep of eyelashes on her cheek, didn't change as he shifted her to the bed.

Trying to lie next to her was futile. His need to prowl and protect forced him to his feet. He cleaned and reloaded the HK semi, tidied the bath and inventoried breakfast supplies. Ivar would undoubtedly find some way to make him pay for compromising their security, but his brother's displeasure wasn't what kept him pacing after he'd finished his tasks.

The *Horizon Kaptan* would dock in Albania the next week. If he contacted police, he'd lose the opportunity to monitor the ship, because the operation would be gummed up by layers of law enforcement crossing the jurisdictions of Italy, Albania and America, plus European Union antinarcotics squads. He owed it to his team and the Night Stalker pilots to continue, but he couldn't leave Theresa alone while he went to Albania.

Montebelli was the solution. Besides being on the Adriatic and offering a boat or a plane for a quick trip to Albania, the fortress would be safe. Whatever the contractors had uncovered about him through the army, they couldn't know about Ivar's castle.

Tomorrow he'd take Theresa to Montebelli, Ivar or no Ivar.

THERESA'S EYES SHOT open, and her ears filled with the loaded silence that signals a failed alarm. She'd over-slept. Was it her morning at the battle update—no.

She wasn't in Afghanistan.

She was naked in Wulf's bed in an underground apartment. Last night she'd slept with him, which had been magnificent, except for the part where they'd skipped using protection, and the other part where it was a violation of the Uniform Code of Military Justice. *Shit.*

"You're awake." In fresh clothes, he smiled from the foot of the bed. Once again he resembled a European playboy. No matted hair, sandy eyes or fetid breath for him.

He must've sensed her unease, because his eyebrows gathered together. "What's wrong?"

"Nothing." She closed her mouth over her self-recrimination.

"Something is." Coming closer, he held out a small cup filled with espresso. A tiny rock of raw sugar and a spoon barely bigger than a toothpick sat on the saucer. "Will this help?"

She jammed the blankets into her armpits and inhaled

the coffee, which smelled fabulous but wouldn't change the facts. His life was all immortality, intrigue and excess income, but she lived in the real world where she needed to stay alive, employed and without kids. Yesterday hadn't increased her odds of continuing those states.

"Please don't decide anything until after your caffeine."

As she drained her cup, he leaned on the bedpost with his own espresso. The man didn't play fair. His morning offering beat army coffee with the same superlatives as last night compared to losing her virginity.

"I didn't know what you'd like." A faint red marked his cheeks as he nodded to a formation of three chairs sporting three outfits: a daisy-print sundress and white sweater, a black lace dress and khakis with a skinny pink polo.

"How did you—?" She stumbled into silence, aware that crossing to the new clothes would require loosening the security blanket tucked over her breasts.

"Checked your sizes." He pointed to her ruined clothes folded on an ottoman.

"And shopped in the middle of the night?"

He threw back his head and laughed, showing his corded throat muscles. "Not even in Italy. It's fourteen hundred."

"Whaaat?" Two o'clock in the afternoon? She glanced at the pool. "Do you have a regular shower? With a door?"

"The pool has a handheld nozzle." He unbuttoned a shirt cuff, grinning in a way that implied plans to use the shower nozzle for purposes not listed in the manufacturer's instructions. "You can use it while I cook."

She couldn't look away from his forearms. He took

his time rolling his sleeves, folding one cuff over itself twice before starting the other. She wanted to lay her arm next to his and stare at them, comparing the textures and shapes, the way his veins and bulges declared he was a man and her wrists could belong to no one but a woman. If she wanted to keep any backbone whatsoever, she would study the bed drapes or the walls instead of him, but he had the chiseled lines of a Michelangelo. She hoped she wasn't panting.

"If you hurry, I won't have time to peek." He pointed at the pool.

"You've admitted to being a habitual liar." She was no longer nervous, or not about the same things. These flutters stirred lower than her stomach and carried a deeper rhythm.

The moment he turned his back, she slipped from the covers. Sharing a shower unit with sixteen women had taught her speed, and she was toweling dry before he finished cracking eggs. The sundress and white sweater mimicked the Audrey Hepburn look her mother had chosen, which had proven its impracticality yesterday. If he thought she'd actually wear the black dress with the Versace label, last night in the pool must have been as boiling hot for him as it had been for her, because he'd purchased a complete man-fantasy outfit. Unfortunately she didn't know how to sit, walk or bend in a dress that stopped that close to her belly button. When she considered the third outfit, a pink polo and cropped pants, what he'd done clicked.

He'd purchased three costumes for her: a lady, a hot babe and a slightly fashionable nerd. Which way did he see her? Or as a bit of all three?

Then the realization that none of the outfits included underwear made her snort.

"On the table by the bed," he said without turning around.

"You should cook." She glared at his back. "Not eaves-look."

"Your huff was easy to interpret."

The table held a glossy black box tied with silver ribbon embossed with the name La Bellezza. She'd passed the flagship store on Via Condotti but hadn't needed to check prices to recognize a shop out of her league. Beneath tissue paper nestled two sets of lingerie, one fuchsia and the other black. Lace cups connected with a tiny bow and matching lace evoked orchids twining across the sides of the boy shorts. Only a tiny panel between the legs had any substance.

As she stared into the box, the desire to try on something so beautiful fought with the knowledge that she couldn't accept hundreds of dollars of lingerie from him.

"I pictured your skin under the lace." His silent appearance behind her made her jump. He pulled her into his embrace until his body cupped hers like a ball-and-socket joint.

If she shifted an inch, the ridge in his pants rubbed through her thin robe. Some traitorous part of her wanted to push and polish in the crudest way her Jersey-girl imagination could supply. Her skin had already warmed as heat crept up her body to her throat and cheeks. Now his scent, something manly and clean like trees after a rain, beckoned.

Move away, her brain cautioned her rebellious body, *don't repeat last night's screwup.*

"Did I tell you how beautiful you were asleep, with your hair spread across my pillow?" He lifted the strands trapped between their bodies.

Her brain gave up, shut down, rolled over and begged as her Viking locked her in his arms. They'd make love on the bed and in the pool and in the chair and he'd never let her go.

Never let her go.

"Stop!" She twisted her head and brought her arms up to break his hold. Sidestepping his embrace, she retreated until the backs of her thighs bumped the mattress.

"Finished with me after one night?" His white teeth flashed as he advanced.

Given that her body wouldn't listen to her rules, she had to cross her arms to hide the obvious points of her nipples under the silky robe. She couldn't force herself to say words to send him away, but they needed to discuss precautions before they collapsed onto that giant bed. Ruining her career was one thing—and she had no clue how to salvage this situation when they returned to Camp Caddie—but ruining her life was not debatable.

"Right." His smile fell away and he stepped back. "Maybe you are." He gestured at the table and chairs with one hand, a wave that dismissed his breakfast efforts as unimportant. "I came to tell you brunch is served. Ma'am." Her title sounded flat and hard.

"Don't..." Before she could complete her thought, he turned away and left her to dress. The lacy underwear barely concealed the parts worth covering, and now she couldn't enjoy them. Wearing the pink polo and khakis, which magically reshaped her butt more effectively than twelve months of power lunges, she crossed the room to where he'd assembled pastries, fresh coffee, individual pitchers of steaming milk and poached eggs.

He waited for her to sit before taking a chair, his manners as agonizingly perfect as everything else about him.

She hadn't thanked him for the clothes, which left her feeling like a jerk as she picked up her fork and knife. Setting them down next to her untouched food, she tackled her explanation.

"I'm sorry about—" she waved her hand in the direction of the bed, "—that. I wanted to, but I was…uncomfortable."

"Why'd you push me away?" He crunched his toast without looking at her.

This was the moment to discuss responsibility. "Last night we didn't use birth control."

Still avoiding eye contact, he reached for his coffee.

"I'm not—" She'd advised nineteen-year-old privates to have frank discussions about sex and Plan B, but couldn't spit the words out when it was her turn.

"Don't worry." He stared into the cup. "There won't—can't—be consequences."

The hollow tone of his voice warned her she was about to push on a bruise, but she had a right to ask after the previous night. "What do you mean?"

"Fifteen hundred years. I wasn't a monk, but I never fathered a child. Neither has my brother." One corner of his mouth twisted, but it wasn't a smile. No lines appeared around his eyes. "Ivar certainly tried during an Ottoman Vizier phase. He grew a bit obsessed."

Her hands felt frozen to her cup. Should she reach across the table to him?

"Modern science eventually let us look. It's extraordinary." He took a deep breath and blinked rapidly but never raised his gaze from his empty coffee. "Little guys have too many tails. Some have five or six." His words bumped into each other. "They don't swim well, not well at all, mostly circles. They get all tangled up. So you don't—" he swallowed, "—you don't need to worry."

In the silence, she knew her face must reflect her shock.

Wulf shoved to his feet. "Would you like more coffee? I'm—I'm getting some." He left before she could answer.

Nobody could be as alone as the man hunched over the sink. No wonder he sometimes had that devastated look in his eyes. Deavers and Kahananui and the rest of his team had families to send emails and packages and pictures. They had two lives, the army and home, but Wulf had only one. What was it like for him, back at Fort Campbell, when the other men went home? Where did he go?

He returned with fresh coffee.

I'm sorry felt completely inadequate, so she kept her mouth closed and tried to think of something else. *Hey, now that you've resolved my pregnancy fears, let's*— Uh, no. *What shall we do today*— After yesterday, she wasn't sure she wanted that answer.

"Last night Lorenzo gave you another paper." Her voice croaked, and she took a gulp of juice. "Have you read it?"

"I have." He reached for a croissant. "Our Ostia Antica friend's answers. We guessed right. He worked for Black and Swan." He took his time breaking the roll in half and brushing tiny flakes into a line with one finger. "He came in from the Iraqi Green Zone and met five guys—hopefully the broken arm, the face shot, and our sewer friends, not five others—at the airport."

She wanted to yank the croissant from his hand to make him hurry, but she knew he had to go at his own pace.

"They received text directions from someone they never met. Picked up our photos at a dead-letter drop in the Borghese gardens." He wiped his lips with a napkin. "All very Cold War."

"But I still don't understand *why*."

"According to Lorenzo, our prisoner assumed they were protecting drug operations. His mission was to follow us and report periodically. He claims he didn't know what the other men planned to do."

"Do you believe him?"

"Lorenzo gets results. Probably the hoity-toity accent. Or maybe the wine cellar."

"Is he—" She didn't understand why her tongue stalled over *immortal*. "Like you?"

"No, but close enough." Wulf shook his head. "His family's worked for my brother for seven generations."

When Wulf had decided to open up, she couldn't have imagined the explanations he'd give her, let alone that he'd answer everything she asked. It felt as if she'd been invited across a fence, leaping from outsider to insider status, privy to all his secrets.

He scraped yolk from his plate. "We'll leave after kitchen patrol."

"I suppose that's best." Her empty, streaky dish matched her emotions at the news their time was over. As soon as she'd decided to enjoy having an affair in Italy, he'd taken the decision from her hands. "We can report all this back in-country."

"But we're not going back to Caddie." His multicolored eyes showed a thread of his normal bad boy. "You're still on leave, so I'm taking you to the countryside. Emilia-Romagna, near Ravenna."

Her imagination supplied a tile-roofed farmhouse,

pasta in brightly patterned bowls and an olive grove outside a window. "We don't have reservations—" she began.

"Don't need them." Now he had a full-on grin. "My brother and I happen to own a castle there."

A castle? She shut her mouth to contain a squeak. Peeping sideways at the chairs with the two rejected outfits, she almost expected to see glass slippers, but the floor held only leather ballet flats. Yes, confirmation that even if Wulf did have a castle, she'd never be a princess.

Chapter Eighteen

LOSING THE FIRST team in the Roman sewers had improved Draycott's luck. Since that afternoon, he'd achieved every task the Director had demanded. He'd coordinated with the lab courier. He'd acquired mountaineering equipment, night vision gear and an anonymous van. Now he stood in baggage claim holding a welcome sign for a bogus Japanese tourist while he watched for the last member of the takedown squad. He'd already spotted the first four. If plans continued to proceed this smoothly, he had a good chance of leaving Italy alive.

The new men were South African and obviously paramilitary professionals instead of organization flacks. He had cautious confidence in their ability to capture Wardsen and a bad feeling about the brunette doctor's odds of avoiding the cross fire.

As soon as the fifth man emerged from security and proceeded to baggage claim, Draycott pulled a cigarette pack from his jacket and headed for the sidewalk. The foul things were ubiquitous with drivers and thus good cover. Well apart from the other cabbies, he dialed his boss. "Sir, they all arrived."

"Deliver them to Emilia-Romagna. A town called Montebelli off the E55 highway. It's not on most maps. Cliffs drop to the sea on two sides, so I sent frogmen." What sort of tension could make his boss speak in paragraphs?

"Sir." Why he crept out on this limb, he'd never be able to answer. Perhaps it had to do with Jane and his stepdaughter. "The woman. Is she yellow or green?" He'd phrased his question carefully, not as an argument or a request, but as a choice between two status designations, either of which would help her stay alive.

"She's his. That makes her red."

Red. A hard stop. Terminate. Never before had he disagreed with the Director, but he couldn't forget that every time he'd observed her, she'd been smiling. "Red, sir? Not yellow?"

"Red. If you like, we can debate my decision over Thai food. I hear it's your favorite."

"Sir?" He couldn't choke words past the paralyzing lump in his throat. The Director didn't issue social invitations.

"Didn't your wife mention our visit yesterday? I felt the urge to introduce myself. Best management practices."

He wasn't surprised the Director monitored his family. After all, he'd advised similar security measures relating to other key personnel. But to hear it confirmed… the world outside his phone call faded. In a fog, he listened as the Director continued.

"She resembles her photos. I have several of those too. Such an open, friendly smile your Jane has, no doubt with all her own teeth. She must take very good care of herself."

He understood the message. *I know how to find your wife. I will kill her, with intense pain that begins by pulling her teeth, if you don't toe the line.*

"Thank you, sir. I appreciate—" his voice shook, but he forced himself to carry on, "—your compliment." Jane needed to get out. He didn't know if any of his plans were good enough, but he no longer had the leisure to refine them. "I'll see that the packages are delivered as you instructed."

"Do it yourself."

"Sir?" He never exposed his identity, his first rule. When he'd audited Black and Swan field operations, certain people might have suspected who he was or what he did, but he also had CPA training and conducted a genuine financial exam. When he left the airport, he would run a real fare into the city. Truth and anonymity were his best disguises.

"You will drive them."

"Of course, sir." Once these men marked him, he was a dead man driving. Unless Wardsen dispatched all five.

In which case, the shit would roll uphill. He'd be blamed, and Jane would be dead.

THERESA MARVELED AT how candlelight smoothed the rough edges off Wulf's cliff-top fortress and transformed a late dinner in Montebelli's Great Hall into a storybook illustration. The dancing flames reflected off a half dozen silver centerpieces, gleamed on the dark mahogany banquet table and highlighted the polished swords and axes hung along the walls.

From the seat next to her, Wulf offered a spoonful of dessert. "Lorenzo left cherry-almond tortoni."

"I can't. I'll pop." She recrossed her legs, aware of how high on her thigh the black dress had risen. After two days wrapped in his attention as they toured vineyards and olive groves, she'd become comfortable showing this much skin. It always led to the chance to show more.

His gaze lingered on her bare leg until he began refilling her glass. "This wine's been made from our own grapes since—"

He dropped the dark green bottle, and it knocked over the crystal goblet, dumping ruby liquid across the table linen. Wulf sprang to his feet and yanked her out of her chair. "Move!"

"What?" Stumbling down the room's length, she registered a flashing red light over the door to the bedroom wing. "What is it?"

"Security breach." He pushed her shoulders toward the floor and shoved her under a console table. "Someone's in the castle."

A tapestry draped over the front enclosed her in a trunk-size space bounded by the stone wall at the back and X-shaped table legs barely visible in the dark. Her legs and arms tangled into a shaking knot as she twisted to face outward, and then a table leg scraped her shoulder blade through the lace dress. Surprisingly sharp, the hurt forced her to hold still and breathe deeply. The fabric covering her hiding spot twitched, and she jerked in time to avoid being bonked by the antique-looking pistol Wulf thrust at her.

"Two shots, not accurate, but it's got stopping power close-up if anyone reaches in."

Not again! Fighting the return of the terror she'd felt in the sewer, she bit into her inner lip while she tried to steady her hands enough to accept the pistol. Blood, metallic and foul after the evening's fruity wine, hit her tongue, reminding her that this wasn't a dream.

"Don't move—got that?"

Before she could reply, the cloth dropped into place, leaving her encased in darkness.

WULF DIDN'T KNOW when or where the silent alarm had triggered, but anyone who could scale the cliffs or walls was a professional who wouldn't waste time. Intruders would arrive; whether it was two minutes or two seconds, they were coming. He'd make his stand in the Great Hall with weapons that had served him for centuries. He snatched a Colt .44 pistol from a display cabinet and grabbed a custom Beretta over-under shotgun from a wall rack, then slammed into a niche next to the massive stone mantel, aware that somewhere in his castle a man—or men—hunted him.

Seconds later the bone-penetrating noise and light of a flash-bang grenade signaled the intruders' arrival, but flash-bangs didn't disorient him longer than a blink, so they were screwed if they expected him to be blinded or incapacitated.

Boom. His buckshot tore enough holes in the first man to do the job. He brought the shotgun around to a second attacker crouched behind a Louis-whatever chair.

Boom. The fool staggered to his feet with half a face, half a shoulder and a lot of Ivar's French furniture embedded in him. With three men left, shooting him again would be a waste of ammo, so Wulf lined up his Colt sights on someone else.

A minute later, after French-chair guy lurched into a sideboard filled with lit candles, Wulf knew his calculation had been wrong. He hadn't foreseen the tapers toppling onto the couch pillows, the velvet bursting into yellow flames faster than a fire log or the stupid ineffectiveness of shooting into a body already burning. Impervious to bullets, fire would outmaneuver him. And far worse, he couldn't hide Theresa from flames.

He dropped his weapon to rip a wool tapestry from

the wall. Next to the cloth, the Crusher hung from pegs. The heft and grip of his flanged mace were still as familiar in his hand as taking a piss.

Uzi *ta-ta-ta-ing*, a third man popped from the floor, but flying lead didn't matter while adrenaline flushed Wulf's body. The roar of his blood and the roar of his battle call united as, running straight at the camo-painted face, he swung the Crusher. The arm-vibrating thwack, the thud of a limp mess dropping—way more fucking satisfying than a trigger pull. Wulf's chest heaved, demanding oxygen, as he dropped the mace and beat at the flaming couch.

DURING THE SHOOTING and crashing and yelling, Theresa had obeyed Wulf's order to stay hidden. Through the first whiffs of smoke, she had cowered under the table like a puppy. But by the time the odor coated her tongue and made her scrunch her eyes, she couldn't continue hiding.

Don't think about the burns you see after explosions.

Wulf wouldn't abandon her—she believed in him to her core—but a lifetime of relying on herself didn't stop because her lover had ordered her to *stay put*. She had to judge the fire situation for herself, so she lifted the corner of the concealing cloth. On her right Wulf beat at a flaming couch. To the left a man held a candle to a dark-tinted painting of the Madonna until flames licked the Holy Child's feet. No question, she'd better move her butt.

She crawled the rest of the way out from under the table with the pistol gripped tightly in her hand, until, standing, she could cradle her right wrist with her left hand as she'd been trained.

None of the men noticed her. Her target moved to a painting of *The Last Supper* like the one hanging in her mother's dining room.

Bringing her elbows tight to her sides, she pointed both barrels of the heavy pistol at his center of mass and squeezed.

Bamm. This pistol fired at a different stage of the trigger pull than her army Beretta, the whole contraption launching from her hand like a car going seventy into a turnpike pothole.

Her shot missed. She aimed again, but only sent another wild round into a wall somewhere.

"Theresa!" Wulf shouted. "Run, dammit! Run!"

Dropping his candle, the man came at her.

The third trigger squeeze had no result. *Don't panic*, she told herself, *just pull harder.* Then she remembered Wulf's words—*two shots.*

Okay, now panic.

She threw the gun at the man and whirled away. But Wulf fought on her right, with vicious moves she didn't want to approach, and the man was on her left. The long dining table in front of her led to double doors, another way out. After springing to a chair, then to the tabletop, she scattered dishes as she ran.

The fire starter skidded and turned to parallel her, his handgun raised as he ran, but the high-back chairs interrupted his field of fire while she sped for the end of the table.

He got there first. With flames reflecting off the whites of the eyes showing in his balaclava mask, he steadied his weapon and bared his teeth like a horror-movie goaltender.

The creep didn't know how much she *liked* charging

goalies. She spotted a silver fruit bowl on the tabletop, went for the kick and connected as solidly as she had with anything she'd ever booted in college. The weapon bucked in his hand, and she heard the shot, but the bowl must have distracted him. He missed and then raised his forearms to block her missile. That left his gut unprotected. Sweeping a silver epergne out of her way, she went into a slide like she hadn't done in a decade, her right knee tucked under and her left foot leading, a spike she'd rocked dozens of times in college.

Thuukk. She connected with his soft lower stomach and the organs at tabletop height. The impact vibrated from her sole through her shin, knee and hip, all the way to her spine, while the man staggered and folded onto himself. Momentum took her off the table, into him and dropped both of them in a tangle to the floor.

He fumbled for her leg even while clutching his balls with one hand and writhing.

"No!" She twisted until her kneecap threatened to pop, but she couldn't jerk free. "Let go!" On the floor next to her hand, the tall centerpiece beckoned. She cracked it on his arm and rolled away, dragging her throbbing foot and knee, but he clawed after her.

This time she half rolled, half sat and swung the silver club with both hands. She couldn't hear the hit over Wulf's shouts, but she saw one of the pointed curlicues decorating the central column embed deep in the man's eye socket. A fist-size piece of his skull squished inward exactly like a jam-filled doughnut. His grip on her leg went slack.

Her fight finished, she slumped and closed her eyes. Her soft leather flats weren't soccer cleats, and now her foot and ankle hurt so badly that she wanted to moan. But within two breaths she realized the smoke had thickened.

Embrace the suck, her army buds always said. There was still a fire to extinguish.

NEXT TIME HE wanted Theresa to stay put, Wulf vowed to rely on rope, but first he had to save her and the castle. He pounded the tapestry on the smoldering couch as she fired a second time.

She missed.

A single round from a Lancaster .577 could take down a charging hussar, and she'd missed? The man stopper only had two shots. "Theresa! Run, dammit! Run!"

Another fighter popped over the back of a padded chair, thick-barreled handgun aimed at his chest.

He dove and rolled, but no rounds banged into him or near him. Instead a single long projectile hung quivering from a charred cushion. The orange tail stabilizer couldn't have been more visible. A tranquilizer dart. He whirled the tapestry, bullfighter style, to intercept more surprises of the syringe kind while rushing his opponent. The woolen length weighed enough that its spinning velocity knocked aside the dart gun, and they were left fighting man-to-man.

The other guy was fast and well trained. Wulf blocked a throat thrust with his forearm, but missed his follow-up kick because his opponent had spun toward a rack of spears.

Springing toward the wall to grab a broadsword, Wulf circled. His adversary's unfamiliarity with the pike showed in his grip—a mix of a high jumper's hold on a pole and infantry bayonet training. Wulf loosened his wrist with a test swing, and then the thrill of a fight like he hadn't faced in three centuries was upon him.

Seconds later, a glint crossed the corner of his vision

as his high-speed, low-drag doc kicked a silver bowl at an invader's head. He parried another pike thrust and glanced back at her in time to see her slide tackle her man in the balls. That Valkyrie was *his*, by the gods, *his*.

"No!" he heard her yell. "Let go!"

Pain exploded in his temple and knocked him to his knees. *Shouldn't have taken my eyes off my opponent.* Rolling away before his foe impaled him, Wulf popped to one knee and swung his blade upward to flip the pike out of the other man's grasp.

At the same moment, the attacker stepped forward to stab with the barbed end, his arm moving on a collision course with Wulf's sword edge.

The severed arm landed two feet away from its owner, whose momentum carried him to Wulf's feet. The answers Wulf needed spread across the floor with the man's lifeblood.

"Doc!" he yelled, and he grabbed a table runner, stuffing cloth on the arm stump as fast as blood soaked through. "Need some help here."

"Me…too." Her answer sounded like two croaks.

"Medical help." He kept pressure on the wad of cloth while he unbuckled his belt one-handed. "Got one dying."

"I…do not…care…" Her voice trailed off as she crawled into his sight line. "Damn." She scrambled to shove her hands alongside his. "Your belt—tourniquet."

As soon as he had it out of the loops, she ordered him to call an ambulance.

"Are you serious?"

"Want him to live?" Her face scrunched with concentration. "He needs blood."

"Too late." Wulf sat on his heels and stared at the

guy's fixed pupils. He'd never find out how these men had discovered Montebelli. "He's zipped in."

LEAVING RATHER THAN waiting for the mercenaries to return had been about survival, but ninety minutes after Draycott had dropped them at the trail leading to the beach below Wardsen's hideaway, his phone hadn't rung with a call for pick up. Nada, nothing, zip. Thanks to Wardsen, the South Africans weren't looking for the last name on tonight's kill list. Instead, they'd punched out. The sergeant would never know, but he'd done Draycott a big favor.

This wasn't the moment to celebrate. Jane wasn't answering, and the one person he could trust to pass the signal that she had to run hadn't called back. If Em couldn't reach her mother first, if, God forbid, Em was gone, then evading the Director was time-wasting futility, not worth even as much as the bald tires on his crappy van.

Jane and Em. Mother and daughter. Smiles so alike they could be mistaken for each other in photos.

He pushed the minibus to its tottering top speed, which had already brought him one hundred and twenty miles closer to the French-Italian border. Either he still had far to go tonight, or he had nothing at all. Except payback.

DESPITE SHOWERING AFTER he'd tucked Theresa and an ice pack for her foot into the most secure tower room, Wulf couldn't eradicate the smell of smoke from his skin. Whiffs clung as tenaciously as the cold fear in his gut. They'd stay at Montebelli until morning, when he could have more confidence that the roads were safe for them to move on. Until then, the papal tower where Ivar had once retreated from an eleven-week siege would have to shelter Theresa too.

One task remained before he joined Lorenzo to restore the Great Room: calling his brother. New York City was six hours earlier, so Ivar would be awake. Although he and his brother had spent centuries fighting back-to-back from Denmark to Samarkand, they'd drifted so far apart that Wulf had to calculate how long had passed since they'd been in the same place at the same time. Maybe three years. He liked to stop in Manhattan when his sibling was in Italy or at his island, and he visited Italy when Ivar was in New York. Keeping an ocean between them had become a habit during the Cold War, one that hadn't fallen with the Berlin Wall.

No matter how long he rubbed a towel across his chest, the phone squatted conveniently on a hall table near the bathroom door. Its taupe handset and curled cord were twenty-five years out-of-date, but change came slowly at the *fortezza*.

Ivar picked up in the middle of the second ring.

"I'm at Montebelli." No point in gilding the conversation. "The shit's hit the fire. Literally."

"How did you not understand the message I gave Lorenzo? Have you never met a woman who didn't take you for everything?"

With one question, Ivar had pissed him off. Two questions took him back a thousand years to that morning in Chang'an when he'd had to explain to his big brother why he'd lent a prostitute their Silk Road profit. Ivar never had appreciated that the girl wanted to buy her sister a respectable position as a Buddhist nun, or that their earnings were only money, something they had time to acquire again. Helping others was a connection. Ivar couldn't understand how much Wulf needed to be around normal people. His brother preferred to bond with money.

Tonight he wouldn't feel guilty about defying his big brother. He'd spit it out and not argue. "The good news is, all the men who invaded are dead and the damage to the Great Hall isn't structural. The bad news is, one of your French chairs has gone to meet its maker."

"You joke as if you don't know what you've unleashed." Deliberately precise, Ivar's voice conveyed more than disapproval. "You don't, do you? Because you've always led with your fists or your prick, not your head. Nothing changes."

No, nothing ever did, certainly not his brother's ability to send him to the flash point with a handful of sentences. "Tell me, if you're playing Odin Allfather, what *have* I unleashed?"

"You would know that answer if you'd researched Black and Swan."

"Why should I? You're dying to share." Wulf felt the hammer poised above his head.

"It's a closely held private company registered in the Caribbean."

Always, his brother had been agonizingly slow to make a point. The slower he was, the worse the point.

"Cayman records aren't easy to pry open, but after Lorenzo alerted me, I acquired the names of the three shareholders. You may recall them from a prior engagement, if you can think about something other than your libido. Francis Bannister. Uziah Gruble."

That second, uncommon name meant Wulf didn't

need to hear more to be engulfed with the enormity of his mistake. But of course his brother told him.

"And Baird Durfey."

While Ivar had guided the Continental Congress through financial negotiations with the French, Wulf's militia had chased those three and their men across the colonies, too often arriving too late to save the women and children in their path.

"You've been playing games with Unferth." Baird Durfey. The bard, Unferth. The singer-skald at Hrothgar's court had been accustomed to controlling from behind the old king's throne, and he'd resented Beowulf's success and popularity. He'd never agreed with the dictate to remain anonymous and conceal their abilities from mortals. Gradually Unferth's disputes with Ivar had shifted to a quest for power, a vendetta fought through the proxy of human wars. Using the same aliases they'd employed to rampage through the colonies to double as shareholders for Black and Swan, a company that supplied the modern American military, undoubtedly amused the cast-outs.

"You will immediately cease your activities."

"He's smuggling heroin." He was failing to make Ivar understand, failing to speak as an equal or to explain his side with clarity.

"Unferth's business interests don't matter. You understand our law. We don't risk exposure or chance injuring mortals by challenging each other." Ivar had continued the rules established by Beowulf. "Now I must resolve this crisis you've created."

By the Hammer, if an immortal had joined tonight's raiders, the fight wouldn't have ended. And Theresa was there. "I have to keep her safe." He hadn't realized he'd spoken until Ivar snorted.

"I doubt that woman needs your help. You've told her about us, but she hasn't told you who she is, has she?"

"Meaning?" On the receiver, Wulf's hand grew sticky.

"What has she shared, besides the obvious?" He didn't want to hear his brother sully what Theresa and he were building, but Ivar continued. "Did she tell you her stepfather's a capo in the Gambino family in New Jersey? Indicted three times, never convicted."

"No..." In front of his eyes, the stone wall seemed to film over.

"By chance did she mention her stepbrother's on parole for running what is termed a chop shop?" Every word flayed him until he felt like he had a hundred bleeding wounds, but Ivar had more to say. "Or that she has a cousin in the U.S. penitentiary at Hazelton?"

"Stop." Ivar didn't have to list more for Wulf to realized how mistaken he'd been, how his naive lust had led Theresa's connections to him. At least his brother shut up, giving him a moment to shred all his growing hopes without sibling assistance.

Eventually Ivar muttered, "Now you know. Move on. Lorenzo said—"

"Don't, for the glory in Valhalla, say another word." The phone handset would be lucky to survive his grip, but he wouldn't throw it across the room, because of all of them, the phone hadn't done anything regrettable. Even dumb plastic was smarter than he was.

"He said she acts as if she genuinely cares for you. Anyone could have—"

"Doesn't matter, does it? It was a setup. And now it's over." He hung up. This burning anger would get him through the cleanup, and then he'd take the five bodies far out in the Adriatic. And he wouldn't come back. Lorenzo could get rid of that woman.

Chapter Nineteen

No matter what happened in the outside world, nothing changed on a deployment. Even though Italy and Wulf had turned Theresa's life upside down, Camp Cadwalader offered the same rocks, the same schedule and the same people.

"Keep talking." Jennifer handed a water bottle to Theresa and then perched on the foot of the bunk, eyes wide and inquiring. "There's more to your story than getting robbed."

"Not really." Theresa hunched in her ratty robe, glad to be out of the cruddy clothes she'd worn for thirty-six hours on the flights from Italy. Her roommate had overcome surprise at her unexpected return better than the clerks who'd processed her at Bagram Air Field in Kabul, but barely. In the history of army deployments, she must have had the honor of being the first to show up early from leave. "Nothing happened."

"Liar." She fished in Theresa's laundry bag. "I apologize for touching your crap, and normally I would never handle your you-know-whattie's, but these—" a pair of the lacy La Bellezzas dangled off one finger, "—are not the undies I saw you pack. No *way* you bought these."

Hoping Jen would get the hint, she turned her head and shoulders toward the wall, but her roommate was as persistent as a plantar wart.

"We've shared a room for more than seven months. Spill."

"I met a guy?" Because of their ranks, Italy couldn't have ended with her and Wulf arriving at Camp Caddie hand in hand. From their first candlelit dinner, she'd acknowledged that fact, even mentally prepared for it, but the way he'd ditched her—going so far as to have his butler drive her to the airport without even a note—had sliced to the bone.

"That's a question? Like you don't know if he was a guy, or you didn't meet him, or you're trying to put one over on your best buddy?"

In a way, her roommate had hit the trifecta, because Wulf wasn't really "a guy." Surrounded by her real life, at a fundamental level she doubted the carnage in Italy had really happened, and, if it had, then there was a whole lot she couldn't tell Jen.

"What am I going to find if I dig deeper?"

"Nothing." Regardless of whether Jen meant to dig in the laundry or in her head, she wouldn't find answers. "I was robbed."

Jennifer's eyes darted around the room, confirming that their four other roommates were absent, before she continued. "Given how Chris Deavers pumped me for your hotel, and then a *certain* hottie pants left for parts unknown the same time you did, I'm putting one and one together." She rubbed her two pointer fingers against each other and waited, eyebrows raised.

The gesture was nothing but a simple joke, the type of teasing she and Jen had shared two weeks ago, before the helicopter crash, before her discovery of Wulf's immortality, before Italy. She should have grinned and tossed off a reply, maybe thrown in a line of New Jersey–style crudeness, but the muscles in her cheeks burned from the effort to contain her tears.

"I was so bored while you were gone, and I kept imagining you drinking Bellinis all day and soaking up Rome. Come on, I need to live vicariously."

Her control burst like a gallbladder, flooding her with hot pain as she wrapped her arms around her knees and curled into a ball. Even though her arms and legs felt icy and shivers drove her deeper into her robe, her face and throat felt acid etched by tears.

"I'm so sorry!" Jen's hug was solid and warm across her back. "Shhh, whatever he did, he's scum, lower than norovirus, and I'll string him up for you. What'd he do?"

"Nuhh—" she could barely speak through her heaves, "—thing."

Jennifer patted her back. "Babe, if you're crying, he did something, and it was wrong."

Time heals, Jennifer had spouted at least a dozen times over the past two days. Theresa felt like she was rooming with someone's mother. Her own mother would have tracked Wulf down and introduced him to her car bumper, but crap like *time heals* was what she imagined normal mothers like Jen's said. As she marched toward her B-hut, the laptop case she'd borrowed from her friend bounced on her left hip. She'd been so immersed in the internet at Camp Caddie's Burger King stand that she hadn't realized the midnight closing time had arrived. Now she had to skulk home without her reflective belt. The visibility aid was mandatory after dark. Ironic to worry about being hit by a vehicle in a war zone, but that was the army.

When she picked up her pace, the briefcase strap

slipped from her shoulder. She was already out of uniform without the yellow safety belt, so she gave in and slung the strap across her body, another violation of arcane regulations. She found it unusually hard to care about the petty rules when she'd decided to devote the remaining months of her service commitment to shaping her career, nothing else. She could probably get away with screwing the reflective belt, but not the sergeant.

The hassle of issuing orders to change her pay status from on leave to on duty meant she'd been forbidden to step inside her office for two days. Two full days to mope on her bed. Finally Jennifer had ordered her to get a burger and surround herself with people, as if the mere presence of twenty-two-year-olds video chatting with their nineteen-year-old girlfriends would solve all her problems.

Oddly, it *had* helped, unless that was the three orders of fries she'd scarfed while her glutes were parked in front of the computer. Jennifer would probably initiate psych eval paperwork when the boxes arrived, but before she filed Wulf in her mental cabinet and locked the drawer, she needed to understand. Presumably other women binged on chocolate, drank or got their hair cut to forget about a loser, but at Camp Caddie she had to settle for reading.

She had a lot of reading coming to her. The *Beowulf* epic had a bewildering 4,146 results at the leading internet bookstore. Some writer named Seamus Heaney had probably made it 4,147 while she'd been researching. With the royalties from her dozens of purchases, maybe Mr. Heaney could take a cruise.

Inside her hut, she hung her holster over a bedpost, aligned her boot toes pointing out with the tongue open wide enough to stuff her feet in if they had to run for the bunkers, and snagged her sleep shorts. The same routine as every other night in Afghanistan.

Tonight her fingertip poked a corner of stiff paper.

"I've been waiting two hours," Jennifer whispered. "I almost got dressed to go find you."

"What's this?" Her roommates would probably be able to hear the thump in her chest, but she managed to keep her voice low. The thing felt like an envelope.

"*He* gave it to me." The emphasis on the pronoun made clear who.

"No!" She hadn't decided how to act when Wulf inevitably reappeared, but she'd thought she'd have at least a week.

"Yes! I've been dying. Here." Jennifer clicked a keychain flashlight. "Read it!"

Theresa tried to rip the envelope quietly, but the noise sounded like a fire alarm.

"Well?" Her roommate bounced on the top mattress.

The envelope contained a sheet of paper with a single unsigned sentence: *Please join me at the track at 0530.*

"I'm still here. Waiting." Even in the dark, Theresa could see Jennifer's hurry-up hand-circles.

"He invited me to run." How would she be able to look at him, at the lips that had said so many things that had sounded like promises, and pretend he hadn't hurt her? She wasn't ready.

"That's it? Nothing else? No I'm-so-sorry-I-was-a-frigging-donkey-dick?" Jennifer's hand shot from the upper bunk to grab the note and penlight. "That's in less than six hours!"

Her friend's panic fed hers. She wanted to see him,

and she didn't. She wanted to talk to him, but she couldn't. "What should I do?"

"You should SHUT THE FUCK UP!" the transportation officer in the far bunk snapped. "An artillery battery is more fucking quiet!"

THE MORNING WAS clear and almost cool enough for dew while Wulf stretched at the dirt track around the helicopter landing zone. He hoped Theresa would accept his invitation. To outsiders this would look like a casual encounter, but he churned with his need to apologize. The day after he'd ordered Lorenzo to take her to the airport, he'd stood on his boat deck with the coast of Italy behind him, and his brain had accepted what his heart had been shouting. It wasn't possible for the woman he'd watched with her patients to be so immersed in the criminal world that she'd plan murders, or kill two men herself, to further a drug-smuggling scheme. Regardless of what his brother said, he knew Theresa. It didn't matter who her family was, he knew *her*, and she wasn't a criminal.

Wearing the black-and-gray army physical training uniform, she loped around the corner of the building. A thousand women could stand in formation wearing the same shorts and shirt and he'd find her in an instant. Images of wrapping her ponytail through his fist to pin her in place while he kissed her against the wall, then removing the elastic and spreading her hair through his fingers, surged from his imagination to his groin. To cover his reaction, he bent to tighten his shoelaces.

Without a word, she stretched a careful six feet away.

"You came." The line of her calf drew his eyes. "Thank you."

"I needed a run." Her voice was icier than the Hindu Kush. "Ready, Sergeant?"

"When you are, ma'am."

She set the pace. Within moments their steps thudded into a matching rhythm.

"I'm sorry," he started. "At Montebelli, I reacted without thinking. I wanted you out of there, but I should have spoken with you." As far as his apology went, it was one-hundred-percent truth.

"Why'd you change your mind?"

"About what?" His breath caught, but surely she'd assume it was from running. She couldn't know he'd briefly believed she and her family were involved with the heroin.

Next to him, she huffed. "When I wanted to go back to Caddie, you said it wasn't safe. Then, pfft." Her hand waved in the air, then dropped to swing loosely at her side. "You ditched me like an express delivery. Why?"

Rocks and sand crunched under their shoes. Not a good idea to admit Ivar had researched her family; women didn't like that type of thing. Instead he opted for a limited truth. "When I called my brother to tell him about the attack, he told me who runs Black and Swan. I decided you were safest away from me."

"So who…is it?" Panting, Theresa realized anger had pushed her to sprint through their first two laps, but no matter how fast she ran, he stayed next to her, damn him. "Who?"

"One of us."

"One of you?" She stumbled on a stone. "A Viking?"

"Black and Swan's controlled by an immortal named Unferth. He wasn't part of our crew." His words echoed the rhythm of their pounding feet. "He was a skald—a bard—for King Hrothgar." Beside her, he snorted. "Like today's cable talk show hosts, but with a harp."

"I don't get it."

"Unferth and my brother have a long-standing feud. Seems like I reopened it."

"Huh." As they rounded the far curve a third time, she felt better that he'd apologized, but that wasn't why she'd come. Alongside the blank wall of the hangar, she slowed to walk and linked her hands on her head to open her lungs. "I'm here because…" She had to choke out her rehearsed speech while she had the resolve. "I came to say…what happened in Italy…is over."

"Not for me." When he tugged her elbow to turn her, the slide of his hand on her sweat-slick forearm called up memories of moving against his body. This close she could see beads of sweat on his face and neck as he searched her face. "I don't think it's over for you either."

"It is. I have too much invested in the army to risk it." She stepped back and dropped her hands to her knees, bending to conceal her face in case she couldn't erase all her desire from her expression. "I'm an officer. I'm not allowed to—"

"You care about those rules?"

"We wouldn't have met if I didn't care about the rules!" She locked her eyes on the dirt and concentrated on two things: breathing and remembering the rest of her speech.

"Forget about fraternization. No one enforces that."

"Maybe not against you, Indispensable Special Forces Hotshot." That this man, who seemed to get every freaking army thing effortlessly right, would counsel her to forget about the rules—it started a fire in her stomach that pulled her up until she stood toe-to-toe with him. "Fact of life, officer or enlisted, it's the female whose career gets most screwed. But it won't be me." Her finger stopped an inch from his chest. "Do you hear? It won't be me."

"Yeah, I hear you." His chin stuck out as if daring her. "We might have something rare, something that doesn't happen to everyone, but I hear that you'll sacrifice our chance because of a *rule*."

"It's not about following rules." How could a man whose life revolved around honor not understand? "I owe the army my best. I won't give less. In seven months I'm finished, out, and I'm not willing to blow my good service for some crazy sex. Can't you see?"

"In seven months, when I fit your plans, how about dinner?" His flared nostrils and narrowed eyes challenged her to disagree.

How she wanted to say yes, to make a date and carry it in her pocket like a lucky charm, or even make reservations. Crap, if she was honest she'd admit that rehearsals of this kiss-off speech had competed with dreams about caterers and florists. But rather than admit her silly fantasies, she crossed her arms and shook her head.

"Then this isn't about fraternization, is it?" The fight left his voice.

"Not really, I guess." She saw her own anguish reflected in his eyes.

"Whatever you want—" he spoke so quietly she strained to hear, "—I'll do it. I'll get it. I'll—"

"I want a regular life." Asking for the one thing he couldn't give her started a major bleed in the cavity around her heart. "Growing up, my family was different. We had a lot of secrets." She didn't want to share the details. "I dreamed of being regular."

"I under—"

"Let me finish." The best way to inflict pain was to

do it quickly and be done. "Have you ever had a day-dream or read a book, and you know *that's* how it's supposed to be?"

"Yes. Tell me, and I promise…" His hand hovered over her arm.

If he touched her, she might not be able to continue, so she hunched her shoulder. "I want to walk a dog in Central Park. Run around the reservoir." While pushing a jogging stroller, but she wouldn't twist that knife after what he'd told her in Rome. "Live in a brownstone on the Upper East Side. One with black iron railings." She closed her eyes to dispel Afghanistan's jagged mountains and brown dust. "Go to a *nice* office four days a week. No plywood, no pistol holsters. I want to buy lunch from a street cart." She could almost smell the hot dogs and the city. "I want to be normal."

"That's an illusion."

"It isn't." She opened her eyes to see the flat line of his frown. "People really live like that. I met them at Princeton." With their run long over, her cooling sweat left her chilled, so she wrapped her arms around her chest.

"They have problems like everyone else. My brother lives in one of those brownstones."

"Look, I don't need a shrink to tell me what I'm seeking is the opposite of my own childhood. Is that so wrong?" Swallowing to hold in her jumbled emotions, she had to look away to deliver her final statement. "I'm sorry, Wulf, but you're not—" To say he wasn't *normal* sounded so awful she choked. "You're more of what I don't want." Her words sounded both cruel and completely false to her own ears, but she couldn't unsay them.

"That's not what you told me before." Anger hardened

his voice until each word hammered at her. "I distinctly recall you screaming for more. Several times."

"This is not, I repeat, not about sex." She glared back. "You're the most fascinating man I've ever known and yeah, I've never had and probably never will have such amazing sex again, but that doesn't mean I'll change my goals."

"No shit. You won't let anything change you. You have a rule book and everybody has to follow Theresa's rules." He intruded so far into her space that she squeezed her eyes shut and pressed her palms against the hangar wall. His breath warmed her cheek. Three days apart wasn't enough time for her body to forget his.

He didn't back off. His heat and scent stayed next to her like a dog on a bed. The first person who trotted around the corner would notice them and realize immediately what he wanted. Everything she'd worked for would be ruined if one of them didn't retreat, but her hopelessly weak legs wouldn't budge an inch sideways to escape.

"Hope your plan works out, Captain Chiesa." His voice vibrated on her name. "Hope you and your memories have fun screwing some *normal* man." Then he was gone.

Of course she was glad he'd left, and doubly glad he didn't turn and see her trembling and staring after him. Because if her Viking had lingered one instant longer, she might have melted into his arms. So much for her rules.

EARLY FOR THE VIP escort mission, Theresa dropped her ruck and rotated her shoulders inside her protective gear. A senator wanted to visit concrete-and-rebar evi-

dence of America's investment in Afghanistan, so she'd
been tasked to guide a tour of the new provincial hospital. She also planned to distribute the medical texts
and supplies from her backpack, which might help her
to connect with a local doctor and lay groundwork for
a program to help girls like Nazdana.

Even doctors knew that a convoy should be led by a
reinforced or armored vehicle and, at a minimum, have
a roof-mounted fifty-cal providing security. The assembled string of white SUVs seemed more like it should
belong to a half-baked relief organization than to the
United States Army. She searched the gravel lot for the
rest of the vehicles.

"Hey! Glad I'm not alone." A dark-haired woman
wearing mirrored sunglasses and camera bags trotted
over while vigorously chomping gum. "Laura Rizzotti.
Reuters. You one of our minders on this dog and pony
show?"

Theresa automatically introduced herself. Surely the
reporter's name, the same as Wulf's Italian butler's, was
a coincidence. "I'm a doctor. I'll be giving the hospital tour."

The photojournalist's jaw shifted from left to right
and back while she chewed, as if she too searched the
parking lot.

"Who or what are you looking for?"

"Got me." A dimple showed in Laura's cheek. "I'm
hoping for candid photos of our esteemed VIP."

"The senator?"

"None other. He threatened to replace Black and
Swan's cash spigot with a competitive-bid contract." She
raised her first two fingers and thumb to her mouth and
seemed almost startled to find them empty. "Mr. Chair-

man investigating corruption in person is a money shot." Her jaw never stopped ferociously chewing.

"Nicotine gum?" Theresa bit her tongue too late to stop her question.

"That obvious?" Laura's eyebrows raised above her reflective lenses while she fiddled with her camera.

Wulf rounded the corner of the motor-pool office. Theresa hadn't seen him in the week since their run. The feat should have been hard to accomplish in a camp this size, but they'd become avoidance experts.

"Put your camera away," she warned Laura as the man who *really* didn't like photos crossed the gravel.

"Why—" With her camera half raised, Laura twisted to look. "Well, that's a problem."

Wulf reached them, eyes narrowed as he stared hard at both women. "Captain Chiesa."

"Sergeant Wardsen," she retorted.

Then he glared at Laura with an intensity that confirmed the name Rizzotti *wasn't* a coincidence.

"I gather you know Ms. Rizzotti—" she didn't stunt the emphasis, "—already?"

Instead of answering, Wulf interrogated the other woman. "Did Ivar send you?"

"Not even hello? I don't do your brother's bidding, Sergeant Rude." Laura spit her gum in the dust.

"No, *that's* rude. I should make you pick it up."

"You and what army?" Laura was already scraping the foil off another piece of gum.

Theresa refrained from pointing out that one piece should last an hour. Ten minutes in Afghanistan was like an hour at home, or maybe a dog year. Even if Wulf thought she was a rule-following ice queen, she wouldn't gripe about how much gum someone chewed.

"Cut the crap, kid." Wulf crossed his arms over his chest, his brown T-shirt sleeves threatening to bust a seam. "Tell me why you're here."

"I'm an adult." Smiling without revealing teeth, she raised her camera. "With a job, remember?"

Wulf scanned the vehicle convoy. "You're not going on this sorry-ass mission." His statement sounded like a command, not a question.

"I have a photo exclusive," Laura said.

He pointed at Theresa. "I meant you."

That finger pushed her pissed-off button. Sleeping with her didn't give him a right to order her around. "I'm guiding the senator around the new provincial hospital."

"No." His voice was as gritty as the sunbaked parking lot. "You're not."

"This is my chance to help women and girls like Nazdana."

"No. It isn't."

"So." Laura cleared her throat. "Seems like you two know each other."

"Too well," he said.

"Barely," she said.

Wulf gestured at the line of SUVs. "I'll blow a goat if the guards let those out the gate."

"Buy it dinner first."

Laura snorted, but Wulf loomed so close she could've touched the vein at his temple. "I haven't busted my balls on security so you can roll out of here whenever you want to feed your adrenaline habit—"

"Security? What are you talking about?" And she was absolutely not a thrill junkie.

"Forget it," he said.

She could almost hear his teeth grind, and then understanding dawned. A helicopter pilot had started mooning after Jennifer; one of Wulf's teammates had been hanging with the transportation officer that shared their hut; and this morning the Hawaiian on Wulf's team had reported to sick call with a gastro complaint. Oh-so-friendly, he'd asked about her day. She'd mentioned this mission. "You've been spying on me!" Her nails dug into her palms as she fought to keep her fists at her sides. "You sneaky—"

"This gets better and better," Laura interrupted. "In fact, it's so good I almost want to talk to your brother, Wulf, which I generally enjoy less than reformatting my hard drive. Alas, the army waits for no woman." She tugged Theresa's elbow. "Our ride's here. Toodle-oo, Wulf old man."

Theresa followed, if only to avoid charges for kicking a subordinate. *Do not turn around*, she cautioned herself. *Keep walking. There's a hospital to visit.*

A civilian with a clipboard and earpiece motioned her to the second car and sent Laura to the convoy's rear. After wedging the rucksack of medical books by her feet, she struggled to stretch the seat belt around her Kevlar vest. Wulf's concerns were valid enough that she didn't remove her protective gear, not even the neck-compressing helmet.

"Sir." She introduced herself to the white-haired man who slid in the opposite door. In a blue button-down and khakis, the senator resembled every politician who visited the troops. They exchanged polite conversation while the convoy idled at the gate.

"Black and Swan invited me here to show why I shouldn't appoint a special prosecutor to examine their finances." The blunt change of topic, not the lurch as they passed the gate of Camp Cadwalader, left Theresa gaping. "Boots on the ground usually know more than geezers like me stuck in Washington. So tell me, Captain, what do you think of Black and Swan's services? Good value for the taxpayers?"

Gifts like the chairman of the Senate Armed Services Committee inviting her to talk about Black and Swan didn't happen often. She inhaled and started. "I—"

The boom was so close the gargantuan pressure crushed her chest. It crushed her answer, her breath, her vision, crushed the world around her until everything disappeared except one instant of understanding. In the flash one thought hung like a scalpel over her heart: she'd walked away from Wulf angry.

Now she'd never be able to tell him she loved him.

Chapter Twenty

THE SHOCK WAVE slammed Wulf's back, and he knew what he'd see when he turned. He was sprinting for the gate by the time the dirt geyser topped out, and he didn't stop running even when the guards, crouched behind blast barricades, yelled "Get down!"

Find Theresa. His heart pounded the imperative. *Get her.* She had to be okay. Snaking through the concertina wire while the debris plume changed from a brown froth of airborne dirt to black smoke, he focused on the wreckage a hundred meters down the road.

Laura. He'd almost forgotten Lorenzo's granddaughter was in that mess too. *Let both be alive.* Behind him, rescue sirens blared, but he'd reach the site first. *They're not-dead-not-dead-not-dead.* The words matched the piston beat of his legs as he closed the distance.

A dark-haired woman pulled at the side door of an SUV.

"Theresa!"

She turned, and the way his heart stuttered when he saw Laura felt traitorous.

"It's stuck!" She stumbled from the twisted door, her hand wrapped in a jacket to pull broken glass from the shattered window. "I can't open it!"

He grabbed the window frame and handle and yanked until the vehicle rocked, but the door didn't budge in its warped frame. Bracing his foot on the SUV's body above the tire, he pulled even as flames ran up the far front seat. He had seconds until fire filled the compartment. He pulled again, and this time the door popped free.

Theresa slumped sideways from her seat belt. Laura used an extinguisher to block the flames while he ripped a strap cutter off his vest and sliced the nylon restraints. Everyone else was beyond help—that was obvious—so he scooped his woman into his arms.

Her spine arched and she flailed at air as he ran toward the military ambulance. Her scream wasn't the high-pitched sound of fear. It was a gut-cry of pain.

"You're going to make it." Empty assurances sucked, but he didn't know what else to say as he sprinted with her.

"Wulf." He looked down as she moaned his name. Her lips curled back to show her teeth. "Hurts."

Slivers had cut her face, but nothing seemed to be catastrophic. "You're going to—"

He saw her leg. Her boot was gone. More than the boot. Tendons and flesh hung unconnected to anything, flapping like shredded fabric.

This nightmare couldn't be real, but gravel peppered his cheek as the ambulance skidded to a halt. Medics jumped out and the Quick Reaction Force secured a perimeter. The stretcher was a familiar flat rectangle, never more foreign than when he laid Theresa on its olive-colored canvas.

Clutching him, she howled when the medics straightened her limbs. They put on a tourniquet and stuck a needle in her, something for her pain. Each thing they poked into her bit into him too. He'd failed. He hadn't convinced her to stay inside the wire. He hadn't protected her.

She moaned as relief took hold. He couldn't be sure, but maybe she said, "Don't leave."

"I won't. I won't leave." The medics bumped him aside, but he didn't let go of her hand. "You're not alone."

"She's out now, Sarge." Someone peeled his fingers from Theresa's while someone else thrust a tube down her throat. "We're rolling."

Her blood, smeared across his knuckles and wrists, branded an oath onto his soul. As soon as he knew she was safe, he'd tear the village outside Camp Caddie apart until they pointed him to the Taliban who'd planted this bomb. The bomber would repay every drop of Theresa's blood. Tenfold or a hundredfold, from three generations or from a dozen, the guilty would suffer for hurting his woman.

TWENTY-FOUR HOURS LATER, Wulf lurked along the fringes of the intensive care wing of the Landstuhl Regional Medical Center in Germany. He wanted to sit beside Theresa and study her eyelids for flutters when he said her name, but security had already cornered him because he wasn't her next of kin or her chain of command. He couldn't risk a confrontation where a clerk might check the authority-line numbers on the travel orders Deavers had created for him. He'd bet it was paperwork, not his best friend, that had toppled Caesar too. Maybe a sympathetic nurse on the next shift would let him slip into Theresa's room. Until then, he'd wait in the hall.

It was after 7:00 p.m.—already twenty-one thirty in Afghanistan—when his smartphone flashed an encrypted message. His neck tingled as he entered codes. The only intel important enough for Deavers to send now concerned the IED. Did the team have a lead?

He read the message twice. FBI agents from Kabul had swarmed to Caddie because a senator had died, and more were en route from stateside. That made sense, but with the exception of Laura and the bodies from the wrecked SUV, the rest of the convoy had vanished. Not even paperwork remained. No record of who'd signed for fuel, no motor pool inventory of VINs—even the manifest the lead driver had given the gate guards was missing. While the guards remembered Laura and Theresa, no one could describe the drivers with more detail than "White guys." Four men and two vehicles had evaporated into the Big Fucking Empty.

Staccato taps that never came from nurse footwear interrupted his third review. The couple that turned the corner had to be Theresa's mother and stepfather. The lady, flamboyant from her open-toed heels to her unnaturally dark hair, hurried ahead of a military escort and a track-suited man who dragged a rolling suitcase.

Wulf snapped to attention.

"Where's my daughter?" The woman pinned him with dark brown eyes identical to the ones seared into his memory. Like her daughter, she wasted no time.

The breathless specialist arrived to block the door. "Ma'am, we have to wait for—"

"No, we don't." She lifted a hand and pointed. "Carl."

"Sorry, kid. Gotta listen to my wife." Theresa's stepfather lunged more quickly than Wulf expected of a man wearing crisscrossed carry-ons. With Carl's bulk crowding the startled soldier into a precarious lean, it only took a gentle shove on the shoulder to send the escort stumbling aside. Wulf whisked the door open for Theresa's mother.

With a shrug at the spluttering aide, he followed Carl. Theresa's mother circled the bed to press her cheek against her daughter's. Theresa's arms lay flat on top of sheets that were only slightly paler than her skin. Intravenous tubes, finger clamps and other equipment he didn't understand poked out of or latched on to every part of her, but it was the sight of her right leg that paralyzed him. The sheets were pulled away from what resembled a heavily wrapped log. That swaddled mess with its dangling tubes couldn't belong to the woman who'd sprinted and jumped and kicked so hard at his side.

From between stubble-darkened jowls and thick eyebrows, Carl's suspicious eyes fastened on Wulf. "You're no doctor. Who're you?"

Crowding into the room behind Wulf, the medical entourage cut off conversation.

"You again!" One of the attending surgeons ordered Wulf out.

"He can stay." Holding her daughter's hand, Theresa's mother spoke with the nasal New Jersey sound Theresa only let slip when angry.

"Mrs. Chiesa," the colonel in charge of Theresa's care began.

"Napolitano."

"Mrs. Napolitano." He started over. "Your daughter's prognosis is good. She's in the best hands for her type of injury."

"What type is that?" As she posed a question no mother wanted to ask, she looked transparent enough around the edges to float away without the anchor of Theresa's hand.

"In layman's terms, she lost her right foot above the top of her boot. We recommend a second operation to reshape the remainder of her tibia to better fit a below-the-knee prosthetic, but initial evaluation shows minimal or no brain injury." He described, without detectable irony, how the medical texts she'd straddled in the car had shielded her left leg from the blast.

While her parents volleyed questions, Wulf imagined holding Theresa's other hand. If he indulged himself and slid close enough to confirm that her skin held the warmth of the living, someone would demand he leave, so he focused on her face. The dark wings of her eyebrows were sedated into immobility, but nurses had picked shrapnel and glass from her cheeks and dabbed ointment on her scabs.

The lead physician checked his watch as the medical team filed out. "Visiting ends in fifteen minutes. Your escort's at the main desk, ready to show you to your room at Fisher House." He frowned at Wulf. "Sergeant, you go when they do. This is your final warning before we call the MPs."

In the restored quiet, Theresa's mother sank to a chair beside the bed.

The only part of Carl that looked gentle was his hand on his wife's shoulder. "You never answered me. Who are you?"

Wulf recognized the impotent rage in the other man's voice. He shared it. "Her escort." He'd used that line around the hospital. "I flew in with her."

Carl lowered his unibrow and patted his wife's back before he slipped around the end of the bed—without, Wulf noted, showing his back. His eyes fastened on the identifying patches on Wulf's uniform. "I spent 1966 with the 173rd Airborne in Cu Chi." He lowered his voice. "Don't shit me they put a guy from *your* unit on escort duty. Tell me. What're you doing here?"

When Wulf didn't answer, Carl continued. "I may

sound like a goombah from Jersey, but I read the papers and listen to NPR like the smart guys." With an Italian's regard for personal space, he crowded Wulf's chest.

Wulf stood his ground.

"I was listening to radio talk about the deceased senator when the phone rang, and then I heard my wife scream." He grabbed Wulf's arm with a grip that would have made a butcher proud. "I got that chest pain when you know, *you just know*, and I prayed I wouldn't have a heart attack right then because Jeanne was gonna need me."

Wulf let Carl steer him to the room's farthest corner.

"My girl told her ma it was no big deal that she went back to Afghanistan early." His whisper dropped so low that Wulf had to lean in to hear. "I was part of a shitty war too, and only guy I ever knew went back to 'Nam early had offed a hooker in Manila. So I'm putting that together with a guy like you standing at her door, and I want to know—" Carl was so close that Wulf could smell coffee on his breath, "—whadda-fuck is going on? You some sort of guard?"

The email he'd read meant maybe he was. But as drained as he felt, he'd be useless if needed. He realized he hadn't eaten in over a day. Damn. No wonder his vision blurred when he looked at Theresa.

"Waiting for an answer." Carl jibed him back to reality.

"Too many ears." Wulf flicked his eyes at Theresa's mother.

"Fine. Where and when?"

"Two hours." Now that he'd seen Theresa, he had to recharge. He also had to call Deavers. "I'll find you at Fisher House."

"I got one take-away for you." Not an ounce of the big man looked friendly. "Anybody messes with my girl, their gene pool gets drained, got it? I take care of my business."

"So do I." Wulf allowed his control to loosen for a moment, showing the other man how fifteen centuries of fighting could whet a man's soul to a knife-edge.

"Our ways might be pretty similar, heh." Carl half squinted. "You look like you got some *coglioni*. Maybe I could like you."

Maybe he could like Carl too, and maybe he had a new ally for whatever lay ahead. Because sure as generals expected their shit shined, if the rest of that convoy had disappeared, something sucked.

WHEN WULF SHIFTED the rental car to first gear in front of the free lodging for families of injured soldiers, a cigarette glow beside the porch marked where to stop for Carl.

"I don't usually ride with drivers who don't have references." Carl lifted the papers and small flashlight off the passenger seat before sitting. "My group life insurance has strict rules."

"Read that." He had no idea how Deavers had acquired the FBI's preliminary findings, but he owed his boss for emailing a copy. Wulf's anger choked him to the point where he knew if he tried to speak, he'd scream.

Minutes later, Carl stopped reading. "I don't get it. This says—" he licked his thumb to turn back a page, "—*blast point of origin twenty-two to twenty-four inches above road surface.*"

Wulf kept the car rolling while he fought for enough self-control to answer.

"I don't understand." But Carl's tone said he did. His voice had the slow beat of a man whose world has capsized, like when he finds out his wife had an affair with his brother or his broker stole millions. Or his country fucked with his kid.

"The bomb was fixed to the SUV's undercarriage, not buried in the road." Speaking the words made them real, meant he could no longer believe this was a Taliban bomb. "It was professional. Almost surgical. Little collateral damage." Hearing the words hammered home the message: Theresa's injury was his fault.

Carl let loose and smashed his fist on the dashboard. German engineering could handle it, so Wulf let him pound and swear until he shuddered to a halt. "Gotta keep it together. For Jeanne."

Several seconds later, his passenger's breathing was closer to normal. "She's got me doing yoga shit with her to help with my blood pressure."

"You'll need it." He squeezed the steering wheel. If he let go, he'd pound the dash too, and they'd end up in the ditch. "There's more."

"Wait a sec." Carl pulled something out of his jacket pocket. "Antacid?"

The pain of remembering Theresa and her Tic Tac box robbed him of speech. Nothing Carl offered could ease the boiling in his stomach when his soul whispered, *This was Unferth. This was your fault.*

His passenger crunched loudly. "Go on."

"A photographer at the scene recalled a Black and Swan employee directing Theresa to the senator's vehicle." He'd stood in that parking lot as well, angry and frustrated as he'd watched, but he hadn't stopped them. "Maybe that wasn't a coincidence."

"Why would an outfit like Black and Swan care about my girl? I don't do business with them. I got no defense contracts, nothing international." He floundered into silence.

"I don't believe this has to do with your business."

"She tell you what I do?" Carl's voice had a sharper edge.

"No." The moment of truth had arrived. More than once, Ivar had made his opinion about privacy clear, but Wulf no longer gave a bucket of camel shit. "My brother did."

"Who's he?"

"Beo Holdings." Revealing the connection to his brother's hedge fund was a gamble, but Carl deserved honesty.

"Shiiiit." Carl's reverence for money showed in that drawn out vowel. "And you're a noncomm dirt pounder?"

"I like it that way."

"So does my girl. Won't take nothing from us except clothes from her mother. Always has—had—has, dammit—to do it herself."

Wulf suspected his passenger's raspy voice owed more to tears than cigarettes. Like anger, grief could be contagious, and his eyes prickled. The headlights revealed the vestiges of a downsized army post, nothing to distract him from his guilt while Carl composed himself.

Finally Wulf felt able to ask another question. "You handle drugs?"

"You got more explaining to do before I answer that."

In the corner of the closed military-exchange lot, Wulf parked away from the pools of light illuminating empty spaces. Telling Carl what he'd involved Theresa in was the hardest thing he could imagine right now, but he took a deep breath and started.

"Theresa and I were in Italy together. It was…" Words couldn't capture the dinners and laughter. "Wonderful. Perfect." He didn't want to continue. "Then there was trouble." He wasn't articulate enough to describe the carnage. "My Special Forces team is investigating heroin smuggling by Black and Swan. Thought it was only an army problem, and I could handle everything. But it was about more than drugs."

"Yeah? What?"

If Carl swung at him, he'd take the hit. He deserved worse punishment for his arrogance.

"There's an old feud between my brother and the man who controls Black and Swan, but I didn't know who ran the company when we were in Italy." Maybe because he'd barely slept in two days, opening up was too easy. If he wasn't careful he'd start mentioning names. "They connected Theresa to me and my brother. Not sending her back sooner was a mistake."

For a long minute Carl breathed loud and hard in his seat, as if struggling to control his reactions, until finally he said, "No one can send her anywhere. If she don't want to go, you can't make her. If she wants to go, you can't stop her. She's like that."

Across the parking lot, a stream of happy couples exited a movie theater. At this distance, he couldn't see their ages or dress or races. They were silhouettes drifting through pools of light and voids of dark, starting cars and driving away to their lives. Normal lives. Regular people. And here he was. And Theresa wasn't.

"I had to cut her seat belt to get her out." Where had that come from? He rested his forehead on the wheel and closed his eyes to block the lucky people. "The SUV was burning."

"You saved her."

"The convoy wasn't following security procedures. No armor, no gunners. I told her not to go, but she wanted to give the hospital tour. Show how much more the Afghans need." He tasted salt on his lips. "I didn't stop her. I didn't try hard enough."

"Hell, I can't stop Jeanne from nothing even though I pay the credit card bill." He stuffed another handful of antacids in his mouth. "So's you know, fringe benefit of seniority and being a true Italian, I don't have to do everything. I limit myself to real garbage and let the young wannabes handle the other shit."

"Good. Because I will destroy the man behind this, and Black and Swan, and their drug network." A molten core of vengeance filled his emptiness, but to be free to take down Unferth, he had to know that Theresa was safe. "I can't guard her. The army won't believe she needs security. Can you protect her?"

"She's family."

He could predict Carl's next answer but still offered. "You could all disappear quietly. We'll find private doctors in Switzerland. A beach, if you prefer. Anything you want, my brother and I will pay."

Carl blew through his lips like a horse. "First, I pay for my family. Second, Jeanne can't be quiet. Third, I got a business to run. I won't hide. Anyway, Theresa wouldn't do it."

"I had to ask."

"Understood. I forgive the insult."

"Then we'll send men, across the street from your house, 24/7." Ivar would be furious at both the promise and its revelation, but he always paid blood debts.

"I'll take care of inside. My boy Raymond lives at

home and I'll set my nephew above the garage. Jeanne loves feeding him."

"You understand the risks." Wulf put the car in gear to return to Fisher House. "Black and Swan planted a bomb on a vehicle inside a secure army compound. They killed the head of the Senate Armed Services Committee. They won't think twice about some people in suburban New Jersey."

"I got security."

"So did the army."

Chapter Twenty-One

THE FIFTH ARRONDISSEMENT of Paris eddied around Draycott. The knowledge of how much Jane would have enjoyed the bistro across the Boulevard Saint-Michel made him hunch his shoulders and stare at the pavement. He knew what he looked like: a solitary *vieillard*, wearing his only suit of clothes, beat thin by living. For the first time in forty years, what he looked like mirrored the truth.

As he stepped to the curb, a chic university student, the type who might have been friends with his stepdaughter in other circumstances, swerved from his path. Her tilted head and gently curved mouth showed pity before she glanced away, embarrassed by the inadvertent eye contact.

The white business envelope contrasted with his dark glove, then momentarily with the bright-yellow postbox until it disappeared through the slot and became one of millions of letters in the French postal system. After flying over the Atlantic, it would be routed to the U.S. Armed Forces mail-processing center on Long Island, where it would mix with thousands of cards and packages returning across the ocean to Afghanistan. Once there, it would reach the hands of a soldier surely seeking vengeance identical to his own. All the information Draycott could offer Wardsen was in that letter.

The first missile had flown. Now he needed to plan the next salvo against the Director.

"Cave-in?" Wulf offered Deavers another death scenario.

"Recovery ops might fly in an excavator." His captain handed Wulf a nonalcoholic beer, the only piss allowed on deployments, then tilted on two chair legs.

In the weeks since the senator's death, the high-level attention dumped on Camp Caddie had alerted pencil necks outside Special Operations Command to Wulf's unauthorized forays into Pakistan, Italy and Germany. The memo front and center on Deavers's desk demanded copies of orders, expense vouchers, supply requisitions and flight requests pertaining to Staff Sergeant Wulf Wardsen. The list of recipients filled twelve lines.

Wulf wouldn't be going home with the team.

The near beer tasted like fizzy metal.

"Walk away. Load and go." The can in Deavers's fist crinkled. "Tonight. I don't want freaky-acronym spooks snagging you—"

"We've been over that." They'd located the mother ship of the opium processing facilities, and he refused to disappear before finishing Black and Swan. With his chest feeling like a squeezed-out meal pouch every time he thought of Theresa, he didn't really care about the details of his pending death, but he played the game. "What about an explosion?"

"You know IEDs." Deavers focused on his empty can as if it was a picture of his baby son. In the years he'd known Wulf, he hadn't broken the team's unspoken command: *Don't ask about Wulf's difference.* But lately the edges of that rule had started to fray. "They always recover some DNA."

"Can't." Other eras, other battlefields, he'd left remains to be identified, but simplicity was a casualty of modern science. No DNA left behind.

Theresa left hers. He ached to take her pain and give her his healing ability, but he couldn't. Yesterday he'd broken down and phoned Carl, who'd told him she was up on crutches and might be an outpatient by September—if she avoided infections, if she didn't develop bone spurs, if, if, if. Although the agony of fitting and learning to use a prosthetic remained and her swelling wasn't fully controlled, her progress seemed miraculous.

After six years, his friend read his mind. "She'll pull through. She's tough."

They returned to the satellite images of the heroin facility. On the surface it looked like ordinary mud-and-concrete buildings, a blip of nothing two klicks along the road to nowhere. But ground-penetrating radar scans revealed tunnels connecting several underground spaces, including one room large enough to house a basketball court. A thermal scan showed a glowing generator that pumped power to the hidden complex. This was no simple farm spread.

"Two Westerners have visited since surveillance began." Deavers pushed more photos across the desk. "Face recognition IDs this one as a Black and Swan guy, but this one's unmatched."

"CIA?" They hadn't yet linked anyone in theater to that call from the disposable phone in Italy.

"Cruz is still looking." The medic had the best computer skills on the team.

"So we hit while the contractor's there." In older photos a dry streambed marked the south edge of the compound, but in recent ones it had morphed into a churning brown mess. Wulf tapped the spot. "This can't be snow-melt."

"Tail of the Pakistan monsoon's reaching here too. Probably a lively stream through September." While Deavers talked, he hunted for his can of chew. "Maybe farmers will grow some fucking wheat next spring instead of poppies. Feed their kids instead of Russian junkies."

"Skip the explosions and shoot me. I'll fall in the water and be swept downriver."

The captain snorted around the wad in his lip. "*I* won't call you a wet pussy. Cruz will."

"You want to go in that river wearing fifty pounds of equipment, be my guest."

"Last time we practiced self-rescues with full gear, I crushed you by what, nine seconds getting out?" Wulf's boss smirked at the usual team gripe about extra pool training. The competition between Deavers and the navy officers across the post in SEAL Team 6 wasn't always friendly.

"Only a loser remembers how much he wins by, *sir*, and this water's balls colder than Gardner Pool." He had one last issue to tackle. "What about bringing an embed photographer? The pics can stand in for a body." Laura would play nice for a story like this.

"No press." Deavers spit into his empty can. "Too much can go wrong."

"With outside documentation, the Pentagon can't bury this in a secret award citation." Leaning across the desk, he prepared to convince his commander to go big as Beowulf's words from fifteen centuries ago filled him: *Better to avenge than to mourn.* "The chief, the doc, the senator—" his finger stabbed the plywood three times,

"—I don't want to destroy a shipment or a lab. They can make more opium. I want to sink Black and Swan's whole fucking boat, cancel their cushy deals, sever the world logistics contract and stop every shipment." Pens rattled when his fist hit the desk, but it didn't begin to release the anger that had built in him. "The army pays their damn mileage! I want to hack until they bleed." *Like their victims*—

"Nothing like a personal cage fight, huh?" Deavers lifted his palms to surrender to Wulf. "You vouch for this snapper?"

"Absolutely." Pulling himself back, Wulf sank into his seat. "She's an old friend."

Deavers raised his eyebrows, as if questioning Wulf's sanity. "*Another* woman?"

"I'm her *godfather*. I taught her how to ride a bike." And drive. And shoot. And mock Ivar.

"Sometimes I forget how old you…" He shook his head. "Wait a sec, another thing I keep forgetting. A Night Stalker brought this over." From a desk drawer, Deavers pulled a plastic bag containing a tangle of silver and lapis jewelry. "They found it while repairing the bird we crashed. Didn't Dostum give this to your doc?"

That casual phrase, *your doc*, flashed at Wulf's heart like a tracer round. Along the way Theresa had become his in his mind, and apparently the team thought so too. Even if that was still fantasy, when this mission was over and he'd erased Wulf Wardsen, maybe he could reinvent himself as a man Theresa would welcome into her life. Maybe she'd become *his doc*.

Heavy in his hand, the jewelry embodied his time with Theresa. Her roommate had boxed and sent all her possessions to the States, so other than this bag, noth-

ing tangible of her remained at Camp Caddie, not even
a picture. And yet every day he was reminded of her
countless times, whether by the scent of oranges or the
sight of someone else's ponytail across the mess hall.

"And this was addressed to me, but the letter inside
is for you."

Startled, Wulf looked up from the jewelry. He never
received mail. Although he couldn't recall Theresa's
handwriting, his gut said the block printing on the envelope wasn't hers.

"Sorry I read it, but my name was on the outside.
Guess someone didn't want to be obvious you were getting a letter."

The French stamps and multiple creases showed it
had traveled hard, and the message was short and unsigned. *Tell Wardsen to begin hunting for a lab in Morocco.* The second page was a list of names—some with
military ranks, others with country code abbreviations.
He'd lay odds they were all affiliated with Black and
Swan's business.

"Not the lab we want, so I don't copy." Deavers raised
his eyebrows. "Should I?"

He remembered the crushed tranquilizer he'd sent
Ivar after the attack at Montebelli. He hadn't heard from
his brother about the analysis. Perhaps this was related,
or perhaps it was a trap. Either way, he needed to talk
to his brother.

"THOUGHT YOU SHOULD hear about the operation from
me." Wulf paced the team's deserted ready room while
he waited through the extended silence. Next time he
considered calling Ivar, he'd remind himself to sleep in
wet concrete instead. Updates about the syringe contents

and Theresa's security had been polite and factual, but the courtesy heads-up about the planned raid on Black and Swan's underground lab had provoked a beast.

"I forbid you to interfere further with Black and Swan."

"Forbid?" Startled by his brother's directness, Wulf halted. Somehow he'd imagined his brother would support him after what had happened to Theresa. "This is a military op. Last I checked you weren't in my chain of command."

Ivar didn't respond to the sarcasm. "Isn't the blood debt we owe your woman high enough? You want to add to it by involving others in this feud?"

"I want to end it. For good." If he could ever acquire a permanent tattoo on his body, he'd ink a big red slash over a phone symbol.

"Attacking Unferth won't achieve that. Perhaps you recall he's immortal." Ivar lectured without raising his voice, but each coldly dripped word sent Wulf's blood pounding in his ears. "If I can't stabilize the conflict you've incited, more people may be hurt. Or worse."

His big brother, the man who had to control everything. Every damn thing. "We're not moving tonight. You can chill. We'll hit when the situation presents, so don't get twisted."

"Our disputes cannot harm mortals. That's been our touchstone since Lord Beowulf." Ivar continued as if Wulf hadn't spoken. "He may demand to meet you for *hólmgang.*"

Wulf would relish the chance to enter the ring alone with the skald, but he doubted the bastard would choose the honorable method to settle a feud. It was becoming harder to keep his voice even, but he had to try to change his brother's mind one more time. "My team is—"

"I said no."

"I heard you." Kicking a throw pillow into the wall didn't relieve his frustration. "But the senator, Theresa, the drugs Unferth's men tried on me, it's—"

"My position means I must consider greater issues. Since the dragon killed Beowulf, we've prospered. We've stayed undiscovered. I won't change our law, so you force me to contact Unferth to restore balance. Do not undermine my negotiations by damaging his corporation."

"It's not a corporation, it's a criminal gang, and he's a murderer, so your concern's a little fucking misplaced."

"In your army, you follow your commander's orders, don't you? In this, I am your leader." Finally, Ivar's voice rose louder and faster. "I *order* you to stop."

Paradoxically, the rarity of hearing his brother vent partially defused Wulf's anger, and he regretted the rift he knew was coming. "You're my brother, Ivar son of Wonred, but if you interfere, you're not my leader."

"If you act against Unferth, I have no choice. I must banish you from our brethren—" maybe his voice cracked, but Wulf couldn't be sure over a satellite-phone connection, "—as I would any other."

"So be it. Goodbye, brother." He disconnected without waiting for a response. The thirteen immortals were a shattered group, only Jurik and Bjorn worth their weight in beer. He couldn't waste time regretting banishment from the company of Beowulf's Vikings when he had a mission with his teammates, his true clan, the men who mattered to him.

"Yo, Theresa, car's out front!" Downstairs, her stepbrother bellowed loudly enough to be heard in the cul-de-sac. Three days a week, he drove her to physical therapy at the Veterans Affairs hospital in East Orange. Her mother rode shotgun. The trip felt like a middle-school car pool, except Raymond hid a Glock in the glove box.

Zipping her army-logoed windbreaker, she settled onto her crutches. Her doctors had promised to fit her prosthetic today, presenting a new skill to master. She was supposed to be excited about having an advanced obstacle course to conquer and a fresh opportunity to exhibit leadership, but the goal felt as small and lonely as the childhood bed at the end of the hall.

Below her, Jeanne held Theresa's Army Proud water bottle and dipped her head each time Theresa thumped down a stair. "Would it kill you to wear a new outfit instead of all that black and gray? Once, just once, what would it hurt?"

"Ma, I told you, this is my fitness uniform. Until they kick me out, I wear it."

"At least let me make an appointment with Gina."

Gina ran the salon her mother had patronized for twenty years. "I don't need a haircut."

"What about a little waxing?" Her eyes flitted from Theresa's forehead to the hem of her nylon PT shorts. "That you could use."

A little waxing, my ass. Her skin care was an often-mentioned affront to her mother, who wanted her daughter slathered, ripped and stripped from eyebrows to remaining ankle, as if smooth skin would balance what was missing. "Do you think I care if I look like a rottweiler?"

"Nah, your fur's like a Portuguese water dog." Behind Jeanne, Ray drew a thick middle finger across his eyebrows and grinned.

"Bite me." She pulled her lips back at her stepbrother, showing teeth.

"Whaaat? I watch the Westminster dogs with Jeanne, so sue me."

Easy for him to mock, since he wasn't the recipient of an improvement plan this week, or even this month. The honor was all Theresa's.

"Don't you want to look your best for the other doctors?" Nothing diverted her mother.

"It's PT, not a job interview." *And not a date.*

"Job, schmob." She rolled her heavily outlined eyes. "That Major Brady—"

Her parent kept talking. If she hadn't had to use both hands on her crutches, she might have made the same talk-to-the-hand signal that her stepbrother mimed from the doorway. Didn't her mother understand how uncomfortable her injury left other doctors? They chatted with Jeanne instead of her precisely because she'd morphed from doctor to patient. None of them wanted a reminder that hot metal could dice up professionals as easily as lieutenants and grunts.

"He has such deep eyes, and he told me his mother was a Ricci from Bayonne—"

Even if her mother spiked the cannoli, Major Brady wouldn't ask her out. If he did, she'd crutch the other direction faster than Ray could pop a clutch, because the truth was she was so pissed at every man she knew— Raymond was a smart aleck, Carl smothered her and Wulf hadn't bothered to send one measly email, the bastard—that she couldn't endure her mother's schemes for another second. "Mom, I have things on my mind other than dating. I'm trying not to spend my life as a fucking cripple."

Her mother shook the water bottle at Theresa. "I don't care how old you are, or how miserable living here with the people who love you most in the world makes you, you may not use that word unless you want me to wash your mouth out with soap."

"Even Jeanne can catch you now," Ray muttered.

By the time her mother turned to glare, the picture of brotherly innocence was holding the front door, looking exactly how he had whenever he was caught with cigarettes in junior high.

Following them past mounds of burgundy asters to her mother's silver Cadillac sedan she realized that when she had a prosthetic instead of crutches, people would finally walk next to her. At the end of the driveway she blew her breath out hard enough to disturb loose strands of hair on her forehead. "I'm sorry, Mom."

Raymond held the car door open with one hand while he read phone messages.

"Thanks." Theresa slipped sideways on the seat, yanking her crutches in before he slammed the door. Thirty more seconds and she'd have been situated to close it for herself, but nobody ever let her try. *I still have opposable thumbs. I can work a handle.*

Her mother's silence as Ray started the car clearly meant she'd have to go further to make up for her f-bomb. Last week her mental-health therapist had reminded the group that their injuries changed expectations for their families too. Meeting loved ones halfway, that's what they'd promised to try this week. She'd always been good at homework. "I didn't mean to be rude, but I want to focus on my therapy. Maybe later I'll want to date more."

"What about that young man at the hospital in Germany?"

"What are you talking about?" She strained into her shoulder belt to stare at her mother, who had half turned in the front passenger seat. "Who was in Germany?"

"I don't remember his name—he wasn't Italian—but he was blond and looked like he needed a good meal." The penciled-in eyebrows went higher, daring Theresa to ask for details. "Carl talked to him. More than once."

Was it true? Was her dream, the one where Wulf knelt at her bed and pressed his face against her arm and whispered that he'd come for her, but she had to fight to get better, real? "Why didn't you tell me?"

"It didn't come up." Her mother gazed past Theresa's head before she dropped her perfectly timed reply. "After all, you've been busy focusing on your therapy."

Chapter Twenty-Two

THE AFGHAN FIGHTERS asleep in this shed had foolishly reached for assault rifles instead of the sky when Wulf's squad burst in, so he rolled a body away to lift the tunnel's trapdoor. The team had waited six weeks for a dark moon to coincide with a Black and Swan contractor's presence at the target. During those long weeks, they'd rescued a kidnapped high-value Afghan, cleared Taliban out of two villages, visited Dostum and his boys, and trained a parade of Afghan National Army units. Through it all, they'd watched this compound.

The men had talked about after the mission, but they knew that tonight Staff Sergeant Wulf Wardsen would die. All day small gifts had appeared on his bunk or in his boots: his favorite beef jerky and energy bars, a wooden box with the unit crest hand-carved into the lid, waterproof topographic maps. Men who were superstitious about goodbye found ways to speak without words.

Tonight would be the last chance to put himself out front for them. He saw Kahananui and Cruz plug their ears a second before he dropped a flash-bang grenade in the tunnel's hole. Skipping the rungs, Wulf slid down the ladder's outside supports. "Clear," he said into his mike. Weapon up and ready, he advanced, scanning with his night vision gear. Evenly spaced grooves showed where machines had carved this route, and overhead beams supported the ceiling rock. Rounding the first corner, he had less than a second to identify the greenish shape of a man rushing at him as hostile——raised weapon and Afghan dress—and not the contractor they wanted alive. He depressed the trigger.

Bang-Bang-Bang. The guy fell backward.

Shit. He didn't feel rattled or distracted, but the two rounds he'd wasted wouldn't pass unnoticed. If the Big Kahuna had already activated the communication relay unit, even the guys stuck aboveground would've heard.

Thirty feet away, another human shape flickered across the tunnel's mouth and threw something.

"Grenade!" Wulf scooped a Russian-style potato masher and lobbed it into an open storage room, then hit the dirt. His heart thumped like mortar fire even though he knew his team had dropped—

Booom. Only a fraction of the explosive force rushed out the door, but the tunnel amplified sound. Expecting rock slabs to crush his back, he almost felt let down by the small chunks that pelted him, although they were a damn good advertisement for the quality of Black and Swan's construction services.

The fight in the main cavern was similarly anticlimactic. Kahananui took out an Afghan whose weapon jammed, and Cruz dropped the American contractor with a shot to the leg. Hands up and blubbering, that rat wasn't going down with his corporate ship.

"Alpha team up," Wulf reported to Deavers. "Target secure, receiving first aid. Over." Watching the guy moan as Cruz dressed his leg, he heard Bravo team call in similar results in its part of the compound. Start to finish, under eleven minutes.

"Work up more sweat in a drive-through at lunch, dude," Kahananui said.

"Don't order the mega-triple-fat-attack, amigo." Cruz yanked a knit hat over their captive's eyes.

He'd miss these guys. Bad.

"Fucking A-plus for speed." Deavers's congratulations crackled over the commo link. "Although I hear Howling Wolf owes two bucks to the tip jar. Remember, gentlemen, our taxpayer overlords own each and every bullet. In tough budget times, we operate on the one-shot one-kill principle."

"Take it out of my paycheck, sir. Okay to send Rizzotti down." Laura planned to photograph documents and upload them by satellite to multiple news organizations. After the clusterfuck of the disappearing car-bomb evidence, no one was taking chances. She'd have a big story, they'd have rough justice and Black and Swan would have a steaming mess.

"Power's up," Bravo team reported.

In the fluorescent yellow, Wulf counted three rows of six pallets loaded with heroin bags, a half dozen stainless-steel cooking vats, a small conveyor belt and one shrink-wrap machine.

"Look at this shit," Kahananui called from a corner rigged like a comic-strip cubicle hell, with sand-colored partitions, wood-veneer desks, computers, printers and steel file cabinets. "Every piece of crap here has a Property of the United States Government tag. Fuckers have a nicer printer than we do."

"This is weirder." Cruz had his hands on the lid of a chest freezer. "Want to bet there's a stinking body?" Lifting it revealed bundles of hundred-dollar bills stacked next to euro notes, all the way to the top. The air went out of the room.

"A briefcase is roughly three-quarters of a mill. That

must be…" Kahananui paused, probably calculating the freezer's volume like Wulf. "Twenty-five? Thirty?"

"In a freezer?" Cruz couldn't look away from his find.

"Rat proof," Wulf offered. "Remember the cash in Saddam's warehouse?"

"Sent a bag of shreds home to my girls. World's most expensive gerbil bedding." Kahananui hooted. "Good fun, but Jewel was pissed because it stank like money."

Wulf and Cruz joined his laughter, the shared memories consuming what they knew—but wouldn't acknowledge—was their last hour together.

"Wait—an idea—" Wulf had to catch his breath before continuing. Tomorrow was time enough to anticipate reuniting with Theresa. Tonight was about the team, and laughing sure as hell beat going out bawling. "Take off your shirt, Cruz. Show your flaming skull tat and that haul, and you'll hit the front pages and the internet."

"Special-Ops studly man with the big cash money." Kahananui doubled over, clutching his stomach as he howled. "Honeys will throw their panties at you in bars."

"I'm off panty bars." Cruz almost managed to look affronted. "Smart women, they're like, *hot*."

The shock on Kahananui's face kept Wulf laughing even after Cruz's elbow pad connected with his side solidly enough to stagger him.

"How you planning to ace one of those?" the Hawaiian asked. "You're no Wulfie, all sad kitty eyes and foreign-language-poetry bullshit."

"Sitting in a fancy espresso shop reading a book and drinking overpriced coffee." Cruz flexed. "Like fishing with dynamite."

"This load is amazing." Laura trotted out from the

tunnel and stared between the three of them. "What'd I miss?"

Cruz's grin widened. "Or maybe I'll read a newspaper."

Wulf rapped his buddy's helmet with a flashlight. "Not that one," he growled. "Back to work." He itched to open cabinets and search computers, but first he had questions for their prisoner. Questions about a car bomb.

By LATE SEPTEMBER, maples had reddened outside Theresa's bedroom windows, as good a sign of passing time as her new-old life offered. Without VA physical-therapy appointments, she might not have remembered the day of the week.

She ignored the ringing house phones. The callers were always her mother's friends.

"Theresa!" Her mother shouted from downstairs. "Are you upstairs? It's for you."

Who the hell called her? "I'm in my room." That wasn't loud enough for her mother to hear, so she yelled, "Up here!"

Trotting into Theresa's room with a portable handset, Jeanne announced, "It's one of your friends. From…" She floundered over the word, so Theresa knew it must be Afghanistan as she grabbed for the handset.

"Hello? Hello?" She couldn't catch her breath. After two months, he'd called.

"Theresa? It's Jennifer."

Not Wulf. She slumped into her mound of pillows.

"I called as soon as I thought you'd be awake. You haven't heard, have you?" Her friend's voice sounded rushed and worried, not like Jen's usual blend of peppiness and irony.

"Heard what?" Names and faces from the hospital

flashed almost strobelike in her mind, and her throat closed. "Who is it? What happened?"

"I'm fine. Everybody at the hospital's fine. It's..."

Theresa's stomach heaved with relief so intense, she wondered if she'd lose the container of yogurt she'd eaten with her morning pain pill.

"The Special Forces sergeant you knew. Wardsen."

"What about him?" Had he asked for her number or address? Please let Jennifer say she'd given it to him.

"He—" Listening to her former roommate's indrawn breath, Theresa pictured her pacing in the gravel outside their old B-hut. "Last night on an op, he was shot. He fell in a river wearing heavy gear and they couldn't grab him. They think—" her friend's voice broke "—he drowned."

"Oh." Although she knew he wasn't dead, Theresa also knew Jen expected her to respond with shock and sorrow. "Oh, no, I can't—" *Breathe harder and faster, through your mouth,* she reminded herself, *as if you're about to cry—* "Oh, no." *Oh, yes.* Her fist thumped the mattress. He'd promised to come as soon as he could, and now he'd left the army. Now he'd come to her.

The rest of the conversation was an awkward dance of sympathy that Theresa suspected Jennifer escaped with gratitude after she said she needed to think.

Thinking inadequately described the whirling plans that engulfed her as she scooted to the edge of her mattress and snapped her prosthetic on to the pin sticking out of her silicone stump sleeve. Lottery winners might feel like this, too restless to remain in one spot for more than a few seconds, unable to face other people for fear they'd blurt out their unimaginable fortune, yet too pumped for solitude. When she stood, her hard-won stability on her prosthetic felt almost like flying.

The mirror on the closet door reflected a jittery woman, elbows clenched to her sides, skin pale from lack of sun, with red blotches of excitement on her cheeks and uncontrolled frizzles. Maybe a visit to her mother's hairdresser wasn't such a bad idea, but right now her reflection was too wild to consider, so she walked across the room to the door.

Each step worked like her therapists had promised, and she no longer had to juggle backward on crutches when she opened the closet. An unexpected bonus of getting her leg back had been the full freedom to use both hands simultaneously, to open her own doors and even to slam them when she wanted.

In the closet, the corners of three bookstore boxes showed the rigors of their journey roundtrip to and from Afghanistan, then to her old quarters in Texas, then the new Walter Reed Medical Center in Maryland before they'd caught up to her in New Jersey. She didn't remember what she'd ordered, only that it had been an absurdly expensive assortment about Beowulf. Beyond telling Ray to shove them somewhere, she hadn't cared. Until today.

Her ankle adjustment screwdriver slit the packing tape as neatly as Wulf's knife had once done. Inside, glossy black covers decorated with Iron Age relics competed with manga and academic texts. The books were a connection to Wulf, his history, his people. The smooth paper under her fingers wasn't a substitute for him, but he was coming, and she could be ready. She'd start with children's picture books for basic familiarity with the

epic and work through young adult en route to the Seamus Heaney translation and the stack of life sciences.

Twenty minutes ago her future could have been summarized as go-to-therapy-rinse-repeat. Now she had a
goal. Even if her research wasn't the same as a real job,
she had a plan.

She liked her plan more than going down to lunch.
The fight scenes with Grendel and his mother were
freaking suspenseful, so she ignored her mother until
the door opened.

"What are you doing?" Jeanne assessed the books
in a glance. "Beowulf? Isn't that some English monster
or whatever?" She said it with the tones someone might
use about a really hairy tarantula. "And starfish? Squid?
What are you reading about those for?"

"Self-improvement?" Theresa finished highlighting
a passage about Grendel's bog.

"A haircut is self-improvement. This—" she gestured
at the room, "—this is a library!"

"I tend to like those."

"I know, I know. But did you have to start one here?"

"You could buy me a new bookshelf. I've heard New-
port Centre mall sells them."

Her mother's eyebrows arched with glee before they
lowered at her again. "Ha. You thought you could trick
me into leaving. Not unless you come down to eat."

"Later." She flipped pages to reach a description of
Grendel's mother.

"Now. I made lasagna."

"IVAR?" WULF CALLED his brother's name from the stairs
to the underground garage. His brother hadn't deleted
his biometric data from the Manhattan house's security

system. So either Ivar was becoming lazy or he didn't want to completely cut off Wulf. "Ivar?"

If he didn't have to face those judgmental gray eyes to retrieve his spare identity documents, so much the better. Across the river in New Jersey, close enough that if he stretched, he could almost hold her, Theresa waited. As soon as he showered off the grime he'd picked up in the five airports between Tajikistan and New York City, he'd blow out of here. By dinner, he'd be with Theresa. Or at least trying to convince her to talk to him, given that the last words they'd exchanged before the explosion hadn't been fond adieus.

He shouted a third time before stepping into the kitchen. "Ivar?"

With his brother out doing whatever international money managers did, he had time to grab a snack. As soon as he opened the fridge, a stench worse than Kahananui's socks rolled out from a gallon of yellowish milk, sludgy as yogurt. Shoving the back of his hand over his nose, he read the purple-inked date: August 4. Seven weeks ago, right after he and Ivar had argued on the phone. While the team had been waiting for the right opportunity to raid the opium facility, Ivar's milk had been fermenting.

Burying his mouth and nose deeper in the bend of his elbow, he used one finger of his other hand to pull out the meat drawer. Its contents were an unidentifiable slick of putrefied protein, and the nauseating reek engulfed him like a tsunami. Gagging, he slammed the door. He took the stairs two at a time to the second and third floors, yelling his brother's name, but the pit in his stomach told him he wouldn't hear an answer. Echoes chased him until finally, heaving for breath in his brother's study, where dust had settled thickly enough that his palms left sweat prints on the desk, he accepted the truth.

Ivar was gone.

Ivar hadn't been here for weeks.

Centered in front of his brother's chair, a padded postal mailer seemed to be waiting for someone to sit and open it. The exterior was completely blank, without postage or a cancelation mark, as if it had been hand-delivered. His brother never left clutter, or anything except a writing blotter and one antique fountain pen, on his desk. The foreboding that swept Wulf as he picked up the envelope was completely inverse to its almost weightlessness.

The sound of pull tape ripping across the flap raised his neck hairs. Whatever this envelope contained, the twisting in his gut told him it too would be his fault.

Inside were two photos and a scrap of cloth, simple items that spun the room under him until he had to cling to the desktop. The first picture showed a man's back, arms manacled overhead to a stone wall. Among the oozing round sores that covered his skin, randomly placed unmarked areas made his body resemble a half-played checkerboard.

Buzzing filled Wulf's head as he absorbed the second image. On a reflective stainless-steel background, a triquetra tattoo marked a chunk of skin that lay between a man's wrist and the hand that had been removed from it. A glossy, wet-looking triangle on the inner forearm showed where the piece of flesh had been excised. Wulf knew that tattoo. Fifteen hundred years ago, when those three dark-blue interlocking circles had been inked on his still-mortal brother, Wulf had stood next to him and sung with drunken enthusiasm.

The photo of Ivar's amputated hand—he suddenly understood how Unferth had bypassed the house security to leave this package—was revolting, but even it was surpassed by the depravity of the third item. Decorated with the triquetra's infinitely looping lines, the scrap in Wulf's hand was as flexible as suede.

It was his brother's skin.

Struggling against a need to vomit, to purge himself in the most visceral way, he swept the skin and photos to the floor and pounded the desk. The wood held as he pounded again and again. It wouldn't break. His fist wouldn't break either.

It should have been him.

A drawer front cracked from his kicks, then the chair toppled, but the destruction didn't stop his fury.

It should have been his arm. Not Ivar's. His fault.

Somehow he found a thread of control, grabbed the edge of the desk and forced himself to be still. His knuckles looked more like a goat carcass after a buzkashi tournament than like human anatomy, but the pain didn't change the facts. Theresa was in New Jersey, but his brother was in hell, and he'd caused it, so he'd have to fix it.

On the far wall, a flat television screen showed his dark reflection, chest heaving as he rubbed his face. The streaks of blood his hands left on his cheekbones resembled the war markings of the Papuan tribe. Staring at his own ghostly image, he recalled the anonymous letter sent to Deavers. *Tell Wardsen to begin hunting for a lab in Morocco.*

He had a destination.

Theresa would have to wait.

Chapter Twenty-Three

WULF DIDN'T STOP scanning out the taxi's rear window even when the X-shaped concrete terminals of Marrakesh's international airport came into view through the windshield. After four months of solo vigilance, he'd need serious distance from Morocco before he stopped looking over his shoulder. Too much could still go wrong, and all the responsibility fell to him.

Ivar was useless. His head bounced off Wulf's shoulder and rolled across the seat back as the car jarred through another pothole. What had Unferth's scientists pumped into his brother? It was stronger and longer-lasting than the ketamine used in Rome. Even stuffing Ivar with squares of chocolate roused him only temporarily before he reverted to the near-vegetable Wulf had found in the hidden facility.

"Quel terminal, m'sieur?" Entering the airport zone, the taxi driver slowed from the pace Wulf had urged for the ride from the cloth-dying district.

He'd searched Rabat and Casablanca, until finally in Marrakesh's walled center he'd noticed a half dozen Asian and Caucasian men who came every morning and left every night, as if they had jobs among the tourist traps and cloth dyers. They didn't look like they sold beaten brass bowls, so he'd tracked their patterns. They'd tried to use different routes, but they were too conspicuous, and they'd led him to an underground lab that stretched under blocks of the old souk.

"Quel terminal?" the driver repeated.

"Cargo," he answered in French. No rushing SUVs or darkened sedans behind them, and he doubted Unferth would give chase with a rickety Moroccan cab, so maybe he'd have time to load his brother onto the jet without a problem. The scientists and guards were probably still busy repairing generators to pump out the flood from the underground cistern Wulf had breached into their facility. They might not even realize he'd used the diversion to snatch Ivar.

"I am sorry, sir, but that area is off-limits. Security—"

Wulf stuffed a handful of euros and dirhams over the seat. "Get us through."

Fear and greed warred in the driver's expression. Thankfully, economic need won and he took the exit labeled Cargo Only and bumped through several more potholes.

"Sit up." Wulf shoved another piece of candy in his brother's mouth and straightened the black leather jacket every Moroccan male seemed to wear in winter months. If security peered at the backseat, Ivar needed to seem as normal as possible despite blond hair, sun-deprived skin and a wrist that ended with a raw wound covered by odoriferous gauze and surgical tape. It wasn't easy to keep the concealing glove from falling out of his brother's jacket sleeve.

His confrontation with Unferth had caused this as surely as it had caused Theresa's injury, and he had no idea how to square accounts with either of them. It might require a thousand years before the image of his brother's wrecked and naked body faded to a hazy nightmare, like the girl burned by dragon fire had become, but he would have time to atone.

The wad of money created its own green lights as they drove to the Embraer 650 jet. A red-haired man, larger than Wulf by six inches and fifty pounds, trotted out of the hangar before the taxi driver had cut his engine. He'd been Beowulf's navigator, and he could sail, fly or drive everything that moved.

"Bjorn's here to fly us out." The other immortal had dropped his boat-recovery service when Wulf called him to bring Ivar's private jet for their escape. "You're safe, brother."

"Ba—ba—" Ivar's tongue was missing, and his humiliation at being unable to speak was obvious from his squinted eyes and dipped head. Wulf didn't want to think about how long it had been since someone had carved it out. Ivar's healing process was really and truly fucked.

The stairs to the cabin were too narrow to haul Ivar in tandem, so he transferred his brother's arm to Bjorn's shoulder. The other Viking hefted Ivar around the waist until only his toes touched the steps. As Wulf followed, the clank of boots on the metal treads beat like a countdown, but until the jet left the Atlas Mountains in its exhaust stream, he wouldn't calculate the number of days—*months*—that had passed since he'd seen Theresa. Too many soldiers screwed up by thinking about home when they needed to have their minds in the game, so he'd never allowed the sight of a dark-haired tourist wandering the old city to conjure memories of her. The complete annihilation of distraction had been a brutal price to pay, but a man on a solitary op didn't have downtime.

Soon he'd have infinite time for Theresa.

THERESA PREFERRED STARING out her bedroom window at piles of brown street snow to loafing in the media room with her stepbrother and his cousin, whose jobs for Carl apparently involved dating the couch or being official food tasters. Although they claimed to be incognito game testers for Resident Criminal version whatever, the closest she saw them come to real work was washing road salt off the Caddie after driving her to physical therapy.

The emotion journal on her lap reminded her it was time to create insights for tomorrow's VA counseling group. She hadn't touched the notebook in two weeks. With her pen poised on the first page, she tried to remember her psych rotation. What she needed was an opening sentence that found the small space between crazy and fake.

"Theresa!"

Her mother's surprise appearance in the doorway startled her into bumping into her headboard, and she shoved the journal under her pillow to hide the ink-edged hole she'd driven through the paper.

"What do you do up here all day?" Her mother sank to the bed next to her and hugged her as if she was a kid. "You should come downstairs."

Theresa's heart plummeted. Not because she wanted to stay shut in her room, but because she had no idea what else to do. Four months ago she'd expected Wulf to arrive, but he hadn't. She'd spent weeks notating books that explained his origins and developing models of starfish replication without anyone to answer her questions. Now she didn't want to see him, but without confronting him she had no idea how to achieve closure and progress forward, a phrase her counselor liked to use at group sessions.

As if anyone wanted to progress backward.

Her mother was staring, waiting for her to answer or do something. She opened her mouth.

"I made so many mistakes." Where had that come from?

"Shhh, don't say that." Squeezing tighter, Theresa's mother propped her chin on top of Theresa's head. "I'm proud of everything you've done, my little girl. You're strong." The movement of her mother's chin against her hair, talking, always talking, was one of Theresa's earliest memories. "You never let Carl's business take you down the easy path. You always have such clear goals." Her mother stopped, and Theresa heard her swallow before she continued in a thicker voice. "Did something bad happen? Before your leg? Something else?"

Please don't let my mother cry. She couldn't possibly bear that.

"When you phoned me and said you left Italy early, you sounded terrible, but I thought you had enough to worry about so I didn't push…"

"I'm okay, Mom." She'd used the line so often, sometimes she believed it.

"No, you're not. You barely leave this room. You don't see any of the girls from Holy Names or college—"

"Ma, they all have kids—"

"And you haven't laughed in six months."

"You're exaggerating." She'd had to relearn how to walk, run, even how to stand up from a toilet without tipping, and her mother expected a sense of humor?

"I don't count rolling your eyes at me or making fun of Raymond as laughing." Cupping Theresa's shoulders in her hands, her mother leaned away to look in her daughter's eyes. "The man I met in your hospital room—was he someone special?"

So special, her last words to him had called him sneaky for spying on her.

"Was he hurt?" Her mother stumbled over the question but pushed on. "Or something?"

"He's not hurt."

"Dead?"

"No." She couldn't tell her mother that he was in fact the opposite.

"Married?" Her mother sounded unable to believe that any living, single man in his right mind wouldn't be courting her daughter.

She shook her head.

"Then we'll forget about him. He didn't look Italian anyway. You'll meet someone new."

If that was as easy to do as it was for her mother to say, stand up and grab a hairbrush, she would've been at the movies every night. Instead she was scooting toward the middle of the bed and trying to dodge a pink-handled implement of pain.

"I made stuffed flank roll."

That was special company food. "Which old boyfriend did you invite this time?" Since Christmas, enduring her mother's fix-ups had become a Jersey City survival show. She didn't want to spend another dinner next to some guido with gelled hair who smelled like the last decade's leftover body spray.

"Nobody. Family." Her shrug was utterly unconvincing.

Theresa tipped her head and shoulders almost to the far side of the bed, but she couldn't escape the brush of the woman who thought nothing stood between her daughter and a wedding Mass except a bad hair day. "I take it your expected guest doesn't wear a ring?"

"How did I raise such a cynical daughter?"

The bristles caught a tangle. "Ouch, Mom!"

That caused a frown, but not a cease-fire. "You have to put your best foot forward."

"Not much choice there."

Her mother shook the brush. "You know what I meant."

"Give me that already." She reached up and finished her hair herself.

"Why don't you try on that new sweater I bought last week? The pink angora one." She opened drawers. "And some earrings and lipstick so you feel festive."

"I'll feel itchy." At her mother's next tag sale, she'd probably list one daughter, as is, price: full carat or best offer. "Please say you didn't invite one of your bunko partners' sons."

"You are so suspicious." Her mother didn't turn around. "Nobody's coming to dinner."

The doorbell rang.

Chapter Twenty-Four

AS WULF WAITED on the porch for someone—Carl, Jeanne, Theresa, a chihuahua—to answer the bell, he knew that Ivar's guards were filming his arrival. He hoped his brother was watching the video link as he balanced a pink pastry box and two motorcycle helmets. Anything that connected Ivar with the world beyond his dark, dead-bolted town house was a plus.

"Wulf! My boy, welcome, welcome."

Without crushing the cake box, he fielded Carl's massive hug. At least one member of Theresa's family was rooting for him. Apparently a New Jersey real estate company owned by Beo Holdings had tipped Carl a generous recycling contract.

"Let me take these for you." The helmets dangled from Carl's meaty fingers as he led Wulf into the foyer. "I haven't told Jeanne or Theresa who was coming tonight."

When Wulf saw Theresa's mother bustling down the stairs, he prepared to drop the pastry box if necessary to catch her, but her spiky heels didn't snag the thick carpet and she arrived without tripping. Her zip-tie grip hauled him into the wedding-cake-white living room. "Don't I recognize you?"

"The hospital in Landstuhl, Germany, ma'am." He stood very still, suspecting that if his boots smudged the carpet, he'd be ejected. "But I'm out of the army now. Plain Wulf Wilson these days." His new surname didn't feel natural yet, and he hoped they wouldn't recall his old one.

"After that, where did you go?" Based on the way her tight cheeks pretended to smile, she was considering tossing him out. Perhaps he should offer to vacuum.

"Jeanne," Carl warned, "that's his business."

Her lips thinned to a single line, as sharp as concertina wire.

"I brought this, ma'am, hoping to share better circumstances at this meeting." He garbled his planned speech, but the cake box seemed to have survived the trip strapped to the rear of his bike. He tried to present the gift, but Jeanne didn't drop his arm. "May I set this—"

"You!" Theresa's voice sounded exactly like it had at Caddie when she went toe-to-toe with him. Maybe when he turned around everything would be the same. *Please.*

He turned.

She stood in the doorway, wearing a pink sweater that begged to be stroked. Some dark strands of her hair caught in the nubby fabric across her shoulders, and others crackled loosely around her face. Her eyes wanted to incinerate him in the middle of her mother's living room, but she was on her feet, hands on her hips, and damn if she didn't lick her lips.

He took a step, ready to sweep her against his chest and seize the greeting he'd dreamed of, the welcome he *needed* after everything he'd seen and done in Morocco, but Jeanne tightened her grip and muttered, "She's very angry."

"We should go." Carl yanked on Jeanne's other arm.

They made a human chain, Carl pulling Jeanne, who held Wulf, as if they could prevent him scooping his woman in his arms. He'd missed her for seven months. Seven months without touching her warmth or seeing her smile, and now she was this close.

"Let's go to the kitchen, Jeanne." Carl tugged again.

"But—"

"Strolling in here like nothing happened!" The sparks shooting from Theresa's eyes weren't the welcome he'd imagined, but they were totally part of the woman he wanted.

"I smell food burning *in the kitchen*." Carl dragged his wife through the other doors.

Theresa crossed the room as if unaware that she was moving, as if they were magnets, north and south, drawn toward each other. If he hadn't relived the moment when she'd stormed away from him and climbed into that SUV every day for seven months, he might not have seen the difference, but her gait carried less authority, less confidence. His mistakes had stolen her stomp.

"Then you waltz in after six—or is it seven? I forget—months." Gold hoops emphasized her soft earlobes as she grabbed a motorcycle helmet from the chair where Carl had dumped them. The red helmet, the pink sweater— she infused this white room with colorful, buzzing life.

He saw the windup start and held the cake box above harm's way.

"Not a call." The helmet glanced off his ribs and thankfully didn't rebound into her chin.

He remembered her lethal kicks at Montebelli, but really, she had the worst girl arm. "Guessing you didn't play as much softball as soccer." *Skíta, that was a mistake.*

She yanked the bakery box from his hands. "Not a word." The best chocolate-blackout cake in Manhattan, a bid to win her mother's approval, was about to become part of this fiasco. "Not even a fricking postcard."

"Theresa, I'm sorry." He'd anticipated groveling, but he had no idea how to defuse this level of anger. "Please—"

"Don't take that fake soothing tone with me." Five layers of chocolate came out of the box at an angle that resembled the last moments of the Titanic.

"Uh, I don't think that's a good idea." He balanced on the balls of his feet, hands out, ready to dive to catch the cake. "Please, please—" he'd be trounced before he began if that chocolate-custard-frosted missile launched, "—think of your mother's carpet."

She looked at the cake as if weighing the consequences of gooey chocolate, white wool pile and Jeanne. The calculations must have clicked because she carefully set the cardboard circle and its listing cargo on the glass-topped table.

"Thank you." He told his body to stand down, relax, because he still had a chance. Perhaps no greater than Lord Cardigan's Light Brigade, but he'd worked with less.

Then she hefted a cut crystal vase from a table and tossed its white silk lilies next to a bowl of decorative seashells.

Oh no. "That's probably your mother's—"

"If she knew you like I know you—" she gripped the vase with both hands and lifted it over her shoulder as if preparing to chop wood, "—she'd totally approve." The weight pulled her shoulders past her spine until she teetered. "Underneath the mascara, she's that kind of lady."

"She seems very gracious." He reached forward, ready to haul her into his arms if she tipped further. "I'm sure she doesn't condone violence." Actually, he suspected Jeanne would spike his balls with her pointy heels if he hurt Theresa, but he knew enough not to say that to her daughter. Theresa didn't need suggestions.

"Seven months might be nothing to you. What's that compared to fifteen hundred years? One three-thousandth of your life?" Her elbows dropped to her waist and the vase rested on her shoulder. She sounded choked as she turned away. "It's a bit more of mine."

"I'm here now." He didn't think his breathing would steady until she set the crystal down completely and he could hold her. "I'm staying."

"It's too late!" The couch pillows muffled the slam of the vase as she threw it onto the cushions. "Go away. Just. Go. Away." She sounded close to tears.

"I won't. Not again." If he could connect with her, stroke her cheek or her hair, maybe they could heal together. "Not if I can help it."

"Well, that's a convenient qualifier, isn't it? Then I'll leave." She turned to the door.

He couldn't let her walk away this time, not without taking action.

"Hey! Put me down!" Theresa hadn't expected to see the floor from this angle.

"You wanted to leave."

"I meant alone!" As Wulf climbed the stairs, the jostling made her grab for any anchor within reach. His butt was as firm as she remembered, and the surprising desire to keep squeezing caused her to let go. Then she realized how far away the hall had receded.

Below them, her mother popped into the foyer. "Ca-a-a-rl, Ra-a-ay-mond," she yelled over her shoulder. "You won't believe this."

As Wulf passed the first landing, Theresa stuck her tongue out at the woman who would trade her soul for a son-in-law. "Aren't you going to stop him? Or rescue your only daughter?"

"Mr. Wilson, would you like coffee?"

A simper. Her mother had *simpered* at the barbarian.

"No, thank you, ma'am. I suspect your daughter would dump it on me and I don't want to cause a mess." Politeness would secure his spot at the top of her mother's list. Not that many others remained on the list, but still. His manners made her grind her teeth with anger.

"Stop sucking up!" She smacked the only thing she could reach—that very nice butt—while he chuckled, dammit. "Pillaging and carrying off maidens comes naturally to you, brute."

"Maidens?" His laughter vibrated her thighs as he climbed the top steps. "Haven't met one in years, but yeah, it's like biking." When his hand curved over her bottom, she tried to kick him, but he clamped an arm across her knees. "You never forget how to grab a wench." He paused in the hall. "Which door?"

"I'm not telling." That was a new low in maturity, and totally his fault. Totally.

He shouldered open the correct one. "Were you *ever* this frilly?"

She made the rudest sound she could manage while

hanging upside down, but all he did was laugh again. Half expecting him to thump her on the bed and fall on her—half wanting him to, if she was honest—she refused to be disappointed when he lowered her gently and hovered. The individual amber-and-brown flecks that gave depth to his blue eyes drew her hand closer, and she touched his freshly shaved cheek. It felt as smooth as the silk embroidery he'd once given her, a scrap stuffed away with the rest of her dreams.

"Theresa." The whisper in her palm conjured memories of nights and days side by side in Italy. When he lowered himself to the bed, mere inches separated them, not oceans or ranks.

"Why didn't you call?" She bit her tongue for asking and stuck her hand under her pillow. "Forget it."

His cheeks and mouth sagged into something softer than anger, perhaps sorrow or resignation or…she'd never be a pity fuck. Never.

"Don't. Don't you dare feel sorry for me."

"I don't." He'd moved so close that it forced her to move to the far edge of her pillow, but she couldn't evade the hand that fell onto her arm like a weight. "I feel guilty."

"The IED wasn't your fault."

"You don't know?" His expression grew tenser, and the lines on his forehead and around his mouth deepened. "No one told you about the bomb?"

"Told me what?" Cold leached into her bones at his use of the word *bomb* instead of *IED*. He wasn't the type of man who would be imprecise about munitions. Somehow her flesh knew before the rest of her that something was about to break very bad.

"It wasn't the Taliban."

Oh, Mother of God. Fear and memories of the carnage at Montebelli choked her.

"Black and Swan planted a bomb on the SUV's frame. Inside the wire."

The minutes that passed might have been hours as her arms hugged her chest. A detached part of her knew the onset of chills resulted from deep shock, and she needed to be warmer. Wulf's body anchored the quilt to the bed, leaving her no choice but to shift close enough to steal his heat. Thigh to thigh with him, she burrowed her forehead against his chest while he ran one of his hands from her shoulder to her elbow and back, but even that contact didn't stop her shivers. The ticking part of her brain recognized she should have been upset or demanded answers, but a surreal clarity prompted her to wonder why it mattered. Taliban or Black and Swan, the result was identical. Her leg was gone. So was her job and her independence. The who and why felt irrelevant.

"It's my fault." His voice was so low that even meshed this close, she barely heard.

"Because your team was fighting the heroin smuggling?" At the VA, the Senate hearings on Black and Swan's drug corruption had been a constant on television.

"More than that." He paused for a long time. "I told you about the other immortal, the head of Black and Swan. With the personal vendetta against my brother."

His collar button would leave a dent in her cheek, but she didn't want to move.

"He must have known it was only a matter of time until the money was cut off. Apparently because I refused to give up, Ivar intended to negotiate compensation, but Unferth drugged him."

While he talked, his arms squeezed her until she could barely inflate her chest enough to breathe the air that had been warmed by his skin.

"He tortured Ivar. Badly. If you hadn't saved me in the sewer…"

Her, save him? Was that how he remembered their time in Rome?

"Unferth sent pictures of what he'd done to my brother." His voice cracked, and he paused to gulp air.

Pressed this close, she couldn't see his face, but she recognized his need to absorb the comfort of another person's hold. She'd felt that need for months, with nothing but her pillow on hand, but now she had him. Breathing the outdoor scent of his soap and another she thought of as Wulf himself, she clutched him tightly.

"I was Ivar's only chance and I couldn't risk breaking cover, not even a phone call to you. I'm sorry. Will you give me—us—another shot?"

Instead of disturbing her, his revelations seemed to slip the missing pieces into place, mirroring how their legs and torsos fit naturally together. "Yes."

The moment stretched until her eyes drifted closed and her heart steadied to match the beat under her ear.

"Will you do something completely normal with me?" His voice sounded slow and thick with lethargy to match hers.

"No sewers, castles or firebug ninjas?"

"Afraid my plans aren't that exciting. Just your mother's cooking and whatever vino Carl serves." He loosened his hold and tucked her hair behind her ear to look into her face. "What do you say to a hot date downstairs while I let your family grill me?"

"As long as you don't ask me to treat your burns."

"They can't hurt me." He trailed a finger from her ear to her lips. "Only you can do that."

"I DON'T WANT help with the dishes." Theresa's mother flipped a towel at Wulf to chase him from the sink. "I want you two to vanish, vamoose, scoot outta here."

"No, you and Carl should go." Theresa dodged the towel coming for her and scraped a plate into the garbage. Knowing Wulf shared the same kitchen, feeling his eyes on her, made even this mundane task exhilarating. Each move they made around the space felt like a dance performance, a dance she'd never thought to do again, and the bubbling in her veins signaled the finale. "You know, most mothers don't encourage their daughters to ride motorcycles down dark, icy roads."

"It's clear and dry, dear." Her mother's innocent blink had fooled the savviest Catholic-school admissions officers. "Your young man brought a spare helmet. He's very thoughtful."

"But—" How would she ever be alone with Wulf if her family didn't leave?

"Besides, you've already lost a leg like that Heather person who divorced Paul McCartney." She waved her arm, and its half dozen gold bangles, in the air. "Tell me, what else should I worry about? That you're going to do something like run off and join the army?" She slammed the palm of her hand into her forehead. "Wait, you did that too, despite my objections." A second arm joined the waving as she warmed to her favorite controversy, her daughter's life. "If I'm really lucky you'll get drunk and wake up in Atlantic City! Married!"

"Mom!"

Behind Theresa someone choked and then coughed. Undoubtedly Wulf, because decades of marriage had inoculated Carl.

"Will you *please* leave us alone? Go, already!" She winced at how much she sounded like a teenager, but Jeanne had been so *involved* all through dinner.

"Fine." Drawing out the word, she made a faux hurt face. "We'll go to the mall and find another bookshelf." Jeanne hugged her and pressed her cheek to Theresa's. "The boys are here, so you should go out. Stay out late. Maybe until Wednesday." She had never learned to whisper.

"Too much advice rivals too much information." Theresa hugged back and hoped her mother knew how much her matchmaking, annoying as it was, meant to her. Even when the odds were against her, someone—okay, weird that it was her mother—had thought she might have a date and sex again someday. "When will you become a normal mom?"

"Never, baby doll." Jeanne waved as Carl pulled her from the kitchen.

While she counted to twenty to help her flush disappear, Theresa scraped the next plate so hard her butter knife clanked on the china.

"Your mother gave me marching orders." Wulf's arms stole around her and removed the utensil to place it on the counter. "I'm supposed to ensure you get fresh air."

His lips feathered her ear, making it a fight to set the plate gently on the counter.

"The house must be stuffy. Your cheeks are pink." His lips warmed the skin up and down the side of her neck.

As she tilted her head, exposing more skin to his

heated kisses, the need to kiss him back unfurled. She had nothing to conceal because fraternization rules no longer applied. He knew about Carl's business, but at dinner he'd demonstrated respect for her stepfather. With Wulf she could be truly honest, as he had been when he'd shared his history with her. She turned in his arms, and his face was so close to hers, their breath combined. The hands on her back were gentler than she expected based on the flare in his eyes, but then her Viking burst out of the polite facade and his lips crushed hers. As soon as she opened her mouth, his tongue took advantage of the invitation while she grabbed his shoulders, his neck, his head, anywhere she could reach. The contrast of his soft hair and his bunched muscles reminded her of all his contrasts, gentleness and strength and lethality and even vulnerability.

His hands clasped her waist and hips as he pinned her against the counter, reminding her that they were still in the kitchen. Then his kisses incinerated every other thought. Thrusting his leg between her thighs, he lifted her to her toes while she pressed the part of her body that never listened to her brain against the hard desire he wasn't trying to conceal.

Bunching her sweater, his fingers left heat trails across the bare skin of her stomach, and she suddenly understood the blinding ecstasy of a moth's final dash at the light. She pressed closer, as if she could show him the depth of her need with her touch and the way she whispered his name between kisses. She didn't know if they'd make it upstairs.

But he pulled away, swallowing and adjusting his collar as if it squeezed his neck. "If we don't leave now, we'll shock your stepbrother when he wants a refill."

She panted until she could speak. "When did you become modest?"

"I'm trying to make a good impression. Fit in."

Two could play games, so she gave him a tiny smile and a chest-inflating breath with a catchy little noise. "Try *harder*. I think you'll fit. In."

Groaning, he reached for her again, but this time she sidestepped and put the garbage can between them.

"We're going out, right? Isn't that what you want to do?" She flipped her hair. His kiss must have given her mall-girl superpowers, because she didn't recall ever succeeding at a flip without eating a mouthful of stray ends, but tonight it worked. "Or are those helmets meant to impress Carl and Ray?"

Grinning like a devil collecting souls, he followed her to the foyer for coats. "I don't need to impress them, only you, Miss High Speed."

In the driveway, she mounted behind him and wrapped her arms around his waist to become part of his perfect body. The bike's vibrations lured her into a fantasy. With her eyes closed, she pushed on both footrests, as if she still had two feet, two ankles and ten toes to flex. February cold snapped at the exposed skin between her helmet and her collar and filled her with life. With a transformer leg, a Mafia family and now an immortal lover, she'd never be normal, but moments like this one were damn good.

"What's next?" He'd brought another set of helmets with transmitters, and she didn't have to yell. "You swing by my mother's house on Fridays to take me to a movie?"

"If that's what you want."

She wouldn't allow him to drop into polite crip speak. "What do *you* want?"

"Atlantic City has merits."

"Whaaat?" He couldn't be proposing. That would be insane. And it would be totally nuts to say yes, but her heart thumped like motorcycle wheels on pavement.

"Lots of hotels." He sounded like he'd decided. "With beds."

He meant what her stepbrother called the bimbo mambo, not marriage, thank goodness. Because she had zero interest in marrying him, none, nada. He wouldn't be a responsible choice. *He's just funny, absurdly gorgeous, sexy, able to handle my family and crazy about me.*

"Biiig beds."

Her bed was small, pink and creaky, not to mention Ray and his cousin downstairs with the game consoles, so a room was paramount.

"And a hot tub. Remember our bath in Rome?"

The air whipping against her wasn't enough to cool her skin when the seam of her jeans pressed at her core, a less than satisfying echo of straddling him on the underwater bench.

"You have stuff we should pick up?" The urgency in his voice tightened every muscle in her body. "Or can we go straight there and buy what we need?"

Underwear she could buy in Atlantic City, if she even needed it, but not her meds or her ankle's battery charger. Then it hit her. A room with the works—bed, mirror and hot tub—meant he'd see her stump. The end of her leg reminded her of an overripe grapefruit, shiny pink and pocked where the scars weren't smooth. Sane men didn't want sex with fruit. She knew he wanted her because she'd felt proof, but his references to Rome made it clear he meant the old Theresa. That woman didn't exist. "Home."

The return ride passed in a blur as she fought to control tears.

When Wulf slowed to a lower gear and turned onto her cul-de-sac, she registered an unusual darkness. He put his foot down and skidded into a one-eighty.

"What?" She clutched his waist as he rocketed away. "What is it?"

"The streetlight."

"It was out. So?" Over his shoulder she watched the needle fly past fifty. Alongside the climbing RPMs, her stomach rose to choke her.

"Wasn't when we left." The lover's voice was gone, replaced by the hard tone of the warrior as he charged a yellow light.

"You think something happened?" She recognized the feeling drenching her as fear.

"The guards across the street rigged a dead man's switch. If they don't hit a button every fifteen minutes, the light blinks off."

"Guards?" She'd thought the men living in the Giardinos' house had been FBI agents, and that Ray was pulling a joke sending them pizza, but they were guards? Then she processed the rest of his explanation, and her center fell away to the pavement under their wheels. She understood why the guards hadn't hit the button. He meant the guards *couldn't* hit the button.

"My family!" She thumped his shoulder blade with one hand. "Turn around!"

"I put you somewhere safe, then call Carl. What's his number?"

"I don't know. I don't have my phone!"

"Fuck." His shoulders jerked as he spat the word. "Where's his work?"

"Take me back!" The bike roared like the pounding blood in her ears.

"Where are his guys this time of night?"

"Why?"

"Thor's shield, woman! I forgot how you ask questions!"

"All you do is issue orders!" Oncoming headlights blinded her, but she recognized the huge black vehicle that swept past. "That's them! That car!"

Wulf turned and chased Carl's SUV, while she held his waist and prayed that Carl would notice them and stop, stop before they got any closer to whatever Wulf thought was waiting at the house.

Her stepfather must have spotted them within seconds, because he signaled a right turn into a self-storage parking lot.

"What you got?" Carl stepped out of the vehicle to face them, and he wasn't the man she saw around the house. He stood straighter, eyes slit in a harder face, lips pushed forward.

"Streetlight's out," Wulf said.

Carl had his phone in his hand before he finished saying *fucker*.

"Wulf!" Her mother unsnapped her shoulder belt and leaned toward the open door, smiling. The red lipstick, the perfectly lined dark eyes and the cheery finger flutter devastated Theresa into speechlessness. She'd put her mother through so much since last summer. To know her mother was about to learn what Carl had already realized made Theresa want to throw up.

"Ray's not answering."

"Take her." Wulf's grip on her waist left her no choice but to dismount from the bike. "While I go in."

"I got things in the back." As he staggered the length of his car, Carl's shoulder bumped the metal panels as if he was impaired.

Her doubts about whether either man realized she'd followed and her mother had exited the passenger side were dispelled by Carl. "Not your business, Jeanne."

"If my daughter's here, it's my business."

"Mom—"

"I'm taking youse both to Cookie's." Hearing that Carl wanted to park her with her mother made her feel as useful as the junk abandoned behind the line of storage unit doors, but she didn't blame him.

Confusion and the beginnings of concern put lines on Jeanne's forehead as she stepped out of the liftgate's trajectory. "I thought we were going home."

"Ray didn't answer the phone." The floor mat trembled in Carl's hands.

"Maybe he went out for chips or—"

"Mom—"

"Maybe he went to see a girl." Her mother's voice rose. "What's the—" She stopped when she registered the automatic weapons, handguns, magazines and bulletproof vests neatly organized in the bottom of the cargo storage space.

"He liked those video games too much for girls." Carl turned his back to her mother and faced Wulf, who stood next to her. His eyes watered at the rims. "I know he was at the house."

SLIPPING INTO THE kitchen he'd left less than an hour before, Wulf scanned the room with Carl's Heckler and

Koch MP5 automatic, ready to pay the devil's toll, but nothing moved. Like he had on a hundred other ops, tonight he had to clear a hostile building, but this time he wasn't connected to his team by an earbud and lip mike. Tonight there'd be no high fives with the Big Kahuna, no one breaking right when he zigged left and no one covering his back.

And no one to impose modern rules on ancient justice. The men who defiled this home would find their hell very hot and very soon. He couldn't afford to wait, not with Carl on his way as soon as he'd secured Theresa and Jeanne. Nothing excused his failures, and he wouldn't compound them by risking another person Theresa loved.

Silently, he opened the swinging door to the dining room—nothing stuck or squeaked in Jeanne's house— and swept the space with his rifle set on three round burst. All clear.

The white living room was next. Men skilled enough to take out the guards across the street would know when a fly landed, so they'd know he was there. He pictured the house layout. They'd be crouched behind the L-shaped couch, an effective barrier as they covered both sets of doors. They'd try to pin him while someone circled through the hall and attacked from the rear. If he didn't want to be shredded by cross fire, he'd have to jump into their nest and go hand-to-hand.

Staying low, he reached for the pocket door. Wood panels quivered at his fingertips, as if aware of their coming demise. One slide, then puffs of white marked a fusillade of bullets as they punctured drywall and sent Jeanne's oversized copy of *The Last Supper* crashing to the floor. A normal man, one like Theresa deserved, wouldn't hear the rhythm of automatic weapons. But he knew that, in the same way two runners subconsciously synchronize breathing, most shooters converge their trigger squeezes by the third burst. At the fractional pause that preceded the fourth barrage, he charged across the living room, emptying his magazine at the men behind the couch.

The tug on his right arm meant a hit, but adrenaline masked his pain as he vaulted the cushions and slammed hard to the far side. His boots connected with a chest and drove that man to the floor. He smashed his rifle butt into the other's face, crushing a set of night vision gear deep into the guy's pulpy nose and forehead. The one under his feet evened the score by shooting a point-blank through and through into his exposed armpit.

Right arm rendered useless, he dropped the MP5 and collapsed to his knees. The right side of his head felt branded where the round had continued its trajectory, and the sounds of fighting had been cut in half. His functioning left hand gouged downward for the man's eyes, but this opponent was too fast. Wulf rammed a protective vest instead of a face, but managed to grip a strap. While they rolled, he located the round shape of the man's kneecap. Popped it as easily as Bubble Wrap.

Screams filled his working ear, so he didn't hear the third guy until an arm locked around his neck and jerked his spine into a bow. The confines behind the couch hampered the move. Half his body spasmed, as if the new man's fingers were probing his nervous system from the hole where his ear should have been, and he knocked into the coffee table. Involuntarily, his one functioning hand clenched around something pointy and sharp as the guy whose knee he'd destroyed rolled toward him with a pistol—or two or three. Why couldn't he see? The man's four hands were raising two guns and two small things that looked like pens, so Wulf picked an eye in the middle and plunged whatever he held.

It was one of Jeanne's fake carved starfish. The spike sank in until his knuckles jammed up to the man's skull bone. Another one done.

The guy behind him tightened his choke hold. Blackness on the left of Wulf's vision flowed closer to the darkness on the right, but he overruled his primitive need to grab the attacker's arm. Instead he pulled the Benchmade knife from his thigh sheath, hunched his shoulders to shift the man closer and plunged the blade backward. It connected with muscle. The grip around his neck loosened enough to allow blood back to his brain.

Cleansing breath, sweet as paying his penance, and the spots disappeared from his vision. He stabbed again, but the other man had stumbled away to pick up one of the dropped pens. Wulf made it to his feet even though movement shot pain from the right side of his head. Despite the dark, his attacker contrasted enough with the remains of Jeanne's white decor that he could see the man was his height, built like a Doberman and holding knives in both hands. So why hadn't the guy sliced his throat in the first place?

They circled while Wulf's vision cleared enough to give him an answer. The thing in his opponent's left hand wasn't a second blade or a pen. It was a syringe.

He stumbled back two steps, but the other man followed.

He tried to avoid the remains of Jeanne's furniture and chunks of ceiling. *No retreat.*

If he backed away again, his defeat would be certain. This time when his opponent stepped forward, Wulf pivoted and sprang. It took his last strength, but he rammed the bulk of his useless right shoulder to impale and immobilize the other's knife while he thrust his own blade diagonally up under the edge of the man's Kevlar vest. Then he twisted the steel tip. Blood, pints of it, darkened the other man's pants and empty hands as he grabbed his gut and fell.

Where was the syringe?

Braced against the wall, Wulf slapped his functioning hand around his neck and shoulder. He found and removed the knife, but where was the drug? Panic clawed him until he stretched his arm around to the back of his right shoulder. There it was, snagged where the needle must've caught in the tiny hooks of his protective vest. He crushed it under his boot as the familiar itch started in his shoulder and ear. Injuries he hadn't noticed during the fight squirreled to be scratched, but he had to sweep the rest of the house.

A shattered television screen presided over the media room. Carl's son, nephew and an attacker lay on the floor, all dead. The invader sported a bronze fireplace tool through his gut like a harpoon. For all their slacker ways, Carl's boys had managed better than Wulf would have expected.

Noise erupted in the hall—doors, boots, shouting men—then stopped, the abrupt silence of shock. Carl paused in the doorway.

"My boy." Walking hunched like a much older man, he crouched by his son's body. Four or five gunshot wounds had made Ray's death fast, but ugly. Carl's over-sized fingers closed his son's eyelids. "My son."

The others spread through the house, cursing and searching. They left Carl and Wulf alone. Carl out of respect for his loss, but Wulf had seen the crew's expressions when they glimpsed him. Respect didn't cause the blood to drain from their faces and the whites of their eyes to show as they backed up, some with hands over their mouths. No, it wasn't respect that kept them from Wulf's presence. It was horror.

"We can't stay." With the men loose in the house, there were too many variables. Someone would call a buddy. News would spread; law enforcement would converge. They had to clear out, fast.

"He needs a priest." Carl spoke without looking away from his son.

"If we call one…" Spreading his hands to indicate the room and the other bodies, he left Theresa's stepfather to draw his own conclusions. Faith was faith, but this was a giant mess.

"I know." The old man sank to the floor next to his son. "He won't get a priest then, either. Just the feds."

"Your son fought well." Wulf didn't have to exaggerate. "But we need to protect the living. Jeanne. Theresa." With no idea what Carl would wish, he forged ahead. "My family has a custom. I would be honored to send your son to the next life with the respect due a warrior." Maybe building a pyre would cleanse him too.

Carl seemed to nod, so Wulf tried to keep him focused on the future. He could mourn after the women were safe. "You prepared to disappear?"

"I got a backup plan." His eyes had returned to Raymond.

"Use it now. These guys—" Wulf nudged the impaled body with his boot. "Their boss doesn't give up.
Your family has to disappear, deeper and further than
you can imagine."

Carl tried to brush aside his son's hair, but blood
gummed it to his forehead.

"Get the things your son loved." After helping Carl
stand, Wulf guided him into the hall. "I'll move the boys
to the dining room."

By the time Wulf and one of the others had arranged
Carl's nephew alongside Raymond on the oak table, Carl
had returned with a video game console, its plastic casing shattered by bullets, and a blue-and-white football
jersey.

"We had season tickets to the Giants, me and Ray.
Since he was nine and his mom and I divorced. Eighteen years." Carl's grief was the largest presence in the
room, dwarfing even the bulkiest of his crew. "We never
missed—never—" His shoulders shook too violently to
continue.

Standing alone holding a wet dish towel, Wulf felt a
startling amount of envy fill his chest. Grief like Carl's
came from love, a father's love for his child, accumulated moment by moment over shared time. Even if it
brought this kind of pain—and it always would because
those he loved always aged and died—the yearning to
feel what Carl had known devoured him. He'd tried.
There'd been children he'd cared for when he had a place
to stop, others like a boy from Mogadishu whom he'd
helped because they needed it, but too many times he'd
been forced to leave. Fate never allowed him to share
anyone's life for long. Fifteen centuries, but his life had
nothing worth wanting nearly so much as Carl's did.

He handed the father the towel to clean his son's face, then left.

In the garage, the lawn mower's grass-and-oil smells were like a sea wind after the house's blood stench. He located a gasoline container, then stacked magazines, broken chairs and picture frames under the table to build a tribute for the warriors Ray and his cousin had been. Keeping busy was better than thinking.

The creak of the front door hit his good ear, and Wulf erupted into the entry with his knife low and ready. His blood pounded a snare beat in his head. *Not again*, it said. *Not Carl too.*

"Wulf?" Theresa and her mother stood frozen in the brightly lit foyer, Jeanne's hand at the light switch, as they stared into the destroyed living room. "Carl?"

A second before body-slamming the women, Wulf checked his rush by hitting the wall. The crash jerked Theresa and Jeanne from their trances, and they turned, mouths open in identical horrified circles. The shattered hall mirror reflected eight, ten, twelve versions of him, all with his stubby ear like a chunk of baitfish and fresh red muscle glistening through his shredded shirt like basted ham.

"Carl?" Jeanne covered her mouth and sagged onto her daughter. "Where's Carl?"

Theresa turned her mother's face to her shoulder.

"He's fine." Wulf jabbed off the lights. They had to leave before they saw more, but he couldn't touch them with his bloody hands and he couldn't send them into the darkness alone. So he deliberately stalked them, using his otherness to back them toward the door.

"What are you doing here?" Even with one ear, he knew his question was too loud.

"We waited, but I figured whatever happened was over. I told my mother you'd—" the hesitation in her whisper made him angrier, "—win."

"Assumptions will get you killed." If he didn't unclench his fists, he'd scare them worse than he intended. "These men could have been like me."

Theresa covered her mouth and nose, as if to block the odor of bodies, gunpowder and fear. That was the smell of his livelihood. His life stunk. He knew she'd never want any part of it, or him, again, but he'd die over and over to keep her safe. "Take your mother to the car."

Outside, she helped Jeanne into the second row of the sport utility vehicle and then closed the door. Bracing herself on the dark metal, she turned to him. "Ray?" she whispered.

"Carl's with him and your cousin now." Her face lifted for a moment, a moth of hope that he regretted crushing with his next words. "They're dead."

She rested her forehead on the tinted window.

The arm's length between them loomed wider than the Atlantic he'd flown over the night before, but comforting her would have to take a backseat to ensuring her safety. "What do you need to get out of here?" He didn't expect an answer. She'd gone somewhere he couldn't follow with his bloody hands and filthy deeds, so he said, "I'll figure it out," and hurried inside.

"You—" He pointed at a man carrying a propane canister into the dining room. "Guard the women outside in the car."

In the pink bedroom he added a handful of clothes from each drawer to a gym bag and yanked what looked like a charger off the bedside table. Everywhere he saw books, lots of books, and he remembered Jeanne teasing her daughter about them at dinner. A lifetime ago.

He shoved a stack of science and nature volumes in the bag. The top cover on the second stack showed an iron dagger like he hadn't seen in fifteen hundred years. Paper tabs stuck out from its pages. *Beowulf.* The title leaped at him. He threw it in, and an empty-eyed, gold death mask stared from the next. There was an engraving of a dragon's hoard on the third, a mail-clad warrior on the fourth. *Beowulf,* all of them, as if Theresa had thought to understand his story.

Fear nipped his hamstrings like the hellhound Garmr as he swept the trove into the bag and fled down the stairs with its unzippable weight banging his thigh. Monsters were out tonight, not least him, and no one could stay here.

In the dining room, the men had finished stacking flammables under Ray and his cousin and propped the shattered *Last Supper* at the head of the table. As a group, they filed out of the house, Carl in the rear so he could leave the pungent trail of gasoline. It was his home to burn, after all.

"Wait." Wulf's command stopped Carl's hand on the matches while he finished spray-painting words on the front sidewalk.

"Empty house," Carl read aloud. "Good. I don't need no dead firemen added to my balance sheet."

Wulf saluted as the burning gasoline raced from the front door down the hall. Then it was time. Time for Theresa and the remnants of her family to leave, and time for him to abandon his idea of playing house. When everything he touched or wanted became as charred and ruined as the shell in the rearview mirror soon would be, he had to stop wanting.

WULF DROVE. MAYBE it was Theresa's books that invoked the old language, but the words matched the rhythm of the tires. *Úre aéghwylc sceal ende gebídan worolde lífes. Each of us must wait for the end of our life in this world.* If only that was true.

While they circled highways, while Carl boosted a replacement ride and even while they ditched the unlocked SUV in Newark, Wulf couldn't stop phrases from surging like the bloodshot water of Grendel's bog. *Hé þá fág gewát morþre gemearcod.* He'd started life as a man, but now he too was a branded monster, marked by murder.

By the time Carl directed him to a twenty-four-hour mail shop, Jeanne had dropped into the fog that passes for sleep after shock. *Sorh is geníwod.* Theresa's eyes were closed, but he suspected her awareness lingered as Carl retrieved a stored duffel bag. *Sorrow comes again.*

He needed something new to think about.

"Here." Carl slipped a folder onto the cracked dashboard. "Passport and license for my little girl. They're clean." His voice hadn't risen from a monotone since they'd left the house. "Drop me and Jeanne near Port Authority."

"You set for money?" Wulf followed signs for the Lincoln Tunnel to Manhattan.

"Yeah." Carl pulled a marker out of his bag and humped around in his seat. "You got a number? So Jeanne can call to Theresa?"

After a sideways glance, Wulf glued his eyes to the

red taillights in front of their car and recited a secure number.

"Nobody likes to check a fat man's cojones." Carl coughed, and Wulf heard the rustle of slick-fabric pants being readjusted. "I could write Federal Reserve codes down there."

"You're sure about leaving Theresa with me?" He kept his voice low.

"I don't know how you're still walking, after what I saw at the house." Carl stared at the side of Wulf's head. "And I'm not asking."

Wulf gripped the steering wheel to prevent himself from touching his ear. His shoulder and face itched like a fire ant parade, so he knew he must have been nearly healed.

"I gotta keep my wife safe." The engine rattle almost drowned Carl's tired voice. "I can't do that with Theresa riding shotgun. She's..."

"Beautiful." Wulf supplied.

"True, but I was thinking easy to make."

Grimy tile flashed past in the tunnel's blurred lights. A mother and daughter as vivid as Jeanne and Theresa drew attention. When one had a prosthetic leg, they drew more.

"If we'd gone to Switzerland like you offered—"

"Don't. You can't change your choices." After fifteen hundred years of grappling with consequences, he still struggled with his own advice. "Don't waste energy on what-ifs."

"You neither, son."

Perhaps due to the impossibility of following that guidance, the occupants of the car were silent until they emerged in Manhattan, where Carl directed Wulf to an alley between anonymous motels and Thai takeouts west of Broadway. "By the stack of cardboard. This city has too damn many street cameras, but last I checked, wasn't no surveillance here." Carl got out of the idling car, then went to Jeanne's door.

In the rearview mirror, Wulf saw Theresa's head loll to the side. During the drive she'd fallen into real sleep, the type the mind embraced to heal or escape.

"Watch your back," he told Carl.

"You too." Carl slung his bag over his shoulder and maneuvered his groggy wife down the alley.

Wulf hoped they'd meet again.

Driving uptown, weariness crushed him until he was too drained to plan beyond the next stoplight. He'd rest at Ivar's. His brother would help protect Theresa.

A retina scan and shifting numeric codes had replaced the failed thumbprint security system. When the first row of car barricades lowered, Wulf eased twenty feet forward into the hot box and read randomly generated words out loud until the voice scan reconfirmed his identity. Finally admitted, he let his shoulders slump as the car rolled down the ramp to where his brother waited.

Food and sleep had restored Ivar's speech and mental faculties, but his hand remained stunted, and no well-tailored suit could hide the way he hunched when he saw Wulf's ripped clothing and blood-crusted hair. Awkwardly clippered blond hair stubbled his scalp, reminding Wulf that his fastidious brother had endured lice as well in Unferth's prison. "I gather the reunion did not go as planned."

"No." Wulf paused with his hand on the car's rear door. He and his brother had used to be near mirrors of each other, only Ivar's eye color a truer blue and Wulf's smile wider, but now Ivar seemed slighter. "Jeanne and Carl are alive. Theresa's stepbrother and several others aren't."

"The security team?"

"They lost the coin toss." Wulf hadn't met them. Hadn't dined with them and listened to bad jokes like he had with Raymond, but someone had known each of those men. Either he or Ivar would have to tell someone, several someones, that those men weren't coming back.

He carried Theresa upstairs, her face pressed into his shoulder. She slept so deeply, he assumed she'd taken a pill from one of the bottles he'd shoved in her bag. On his bed, her dark hair spread across the white pillow, reminding him that a few hours ago he'd done nearly the same thing. The comforter had been pink, and he'd been filled with hope and laughter. Gone now, those dreams—as gone as the future he'd dared to imagine.

After he showered, he found his brother in the study. The replacement desk was a jarringly modern hunk of dark steel and walnut that slashed through the traditionally decorated room like a double-headed axe.

"Drink." Ivar gestured to a tray of brown bottles.

By the time Wulf had finished the beer and wiped his upper lip with the back of his hand, the hops and malted grain had revived him enough to speak. "One of the men I killed had this." He tossed the barrel of the crushed syringe on the desk. Too misshapen to roll, it slid several inches on the polished surface.

His brother stumbled into a stand holding a small Rodin bronze.

Regret soured the beer in Wulf's mouth. The old Ivar wouldn't have twitched for a guillotine, let alone backed away from a simple plastic tube. But the man Wulf had released from the torture chamber in Marrakesh wasn't the old Ivar, so he brushed the drug container into the garbage and changed the subject. "We burned one house, but left the other and all the victims." He started on his second bottle of brewed health. "It could get complicated."

"Various government agencies will lie for some time to conceal the dead men's identities." Ivar stood behind his desk, not touching the chair, and didn't rest his gaze on any single spot. "We should warn the others. They may be at risk."

That possibility stopped Wulf's beer halfway to his mouth. "You think Unferth's after more than you and me?"

"I doubt his desire for research subjects—" Ivar's good hand touched the fingertips protruding from his sling, "—has ended."

"Can you find them? Bjorn went back to his boats, and Dunstan's probably teaching somewhere, but Stig? Jurik?" Centuries hadn't forged the misfits of Beowulf's crew into a reliable team, only exacerbated their differences. He wouldn't underestimate the effort it would take to reach the others, let alone try to assemble a force to oppose Unferth.

"My list." With a jerk of his chin, Ivar indicated a paper with twelve names. Nine in one column, Unferth and his sycophants in the other. "We shall take this fight to Unferth. This time, we shall go on to the end."

"No shit." Wulf opened his third beer, the replenishing calories reestablishing whatever he might call normal about his relationship with Ivar. "Going to recite the 'we shall fight on the beaches and never surrender' part too? Been done, you know."

"Your eloquence increases with each year you spend as a common grunt."

"And your ego expands with the membership of the United Nations, but I'm too polite to comment." Like old times, he toasted with his fresh bottle.

Ivar's cheek spasmed, as if one muscle wanted to smile and the others agonized at the close call. Before he could reply, a woman screamed.

Chapter Twenty-Five

"MOM?" THERESA'S FAKE FOOT, unexpectedly attached in bed, caught in the sheets, and she flopped, half wrapped in covers, to the floor. *"Mom!"* Where was she? Had she sleepwalked after her medication?

Then memories flooded her—Wulf's injuries, Carl's devastation and Ray.

Ray. She bit her fist to contain the hot acid feeling in her throat.

Across the room, a gray rectangle signaled access to a lighter space, perhaps a hall. Two dark shapes charged low through the door and split to opposite walls.

In the corner between the bed and wall, Theresa touched a metal wastebasket. Silently, she raised it to her chest, prepared to defend herself.

One man rounded the foot of the bed, close enough he must have seen her outline, so she threw the can with both hands, like she was passing a basketball. It clunked into his body.

"Skíta!"

"Should've warned you. She has good reactions." *That* voice was familiar.

"Wulf?" The fear left her, but she still felt fuzzy and thick. "Where's my mother? And Carl?" She wasn't sure what parts of the night she'd dreamed and what had really happened.

"Theresa—" Wulf's heavy tone sat on her chest like a radiologist's lead apron.

"They're dead, aren't they?" No matter how hard she tried to breathe, the dark pressed the air out of her until she could barely squeak. "They're all dead."

A lamp flickered, but the light didn't change the facts, didn't change reality, didn't bring her family back.

"Your mother's fine." Wulf crouched at her feet, as smoothly modulated as her VA psych. "Carl took her away until it's safer."

"She wouldn't leave me!" Her mother wouldn't let her move into her own condo; no way she'd disappear. Theresa squeezed deeper into the corner. "You're lying!"

"Dr. Chiesa." Arms crossed, a man in a gray suit stood like a steel girder behind Wulf. Illuminated from below by lamplight, his face had eerie shadows and crags. "I apologize—"

"Who are you?"

"Ivar, son of Wonred."

"My big brother."

"Your mother and Carl are hiding, not dead. Your stepbrother and cousin are indeed deceased. Wulf brought you here because your condition precludes easy concealment."

Instead of using euphemisms like *condition*, he might as well have called her useless to her face. They all knew what she'd become, and it wasn't strong or tough or heroic. In plain English, she was a burden.

Ivar must've mistaken her silence for doubt. "I do not lie."

Curled with her knees to her chest and her face buried in her arms, she heard Ivar's footsteps leave the room, but she sensed Wulf waiting. Waiting, like her, until finally the pins and needles shooting through her good leg demanded that she shift positions. *Damn my legs, both of them.* She didn't want to eat the carpet, which might happen if she stood too quickly, so she paused like a dancer doing a weird stretch. *Damn you and your brother, and damn crazy immortals.* And damn everything that had led her to be stuck clinging to an end table.

Silently, Wulf scooped her in his arms and laid her on the bed. Like everyone else, he acted as if she was a doll, as if her ability to take care of herself had been lost with her leg.

Her clenched teeth blocked the profanities she wanted to yell. She knew she had to make her point slowly and clearly. "I don't want help. Don't baby me, don't coddle me, don't touch me. Not ever again."

"As you wish." His flat tone conveyed hurt, but her own pain filled her too much to care.

When the door closed behind him, the flimsy box she'd constructed around her fears finally split. The room filled with a ragged tearing noise that sounded like packing tape pulling off cardboard. Despair stung her eyes and tasted salty on her lips. Covering her mouth with her fist wasn't enough to stop the sounds, so she buried her face in a pillow and tried not to listen to her own sobs.

In contrast to the darkness swirling inside Theresa, the next morning was one of those glittering winter days with a blue sky and no clouds. No one could stay in bed with that much sunshine, no matter how much she wanted to hide, so she gave up and dragged a desk chair to the bathtub. Maneuvering in and out had become less challenging after months of therapy. Afterward she found black yoga pants stretchy enough to slide over her stump sock, a T-shirt, and a man's periwinkle cashmere cardigan piled inside the bedroom door. A gym bag she recognized as her own held underwear and her ankle charger. Wulf must have gathered them before they left the house.

As she haltingly descended to the main floor, the art collection in the stairwell temporarily diverted her from seeking a telephone. Was it Ivar or Wulf who liked sketches of dancers? She recognized the work of several Impressionists and Cubists, and suspected the others were also by artists she should have known. The money hanging on this wall alone was more than three years of medical school tuition. What had Wulf flung at her during their argument at Camp Caddy—the people in these brownstones have problems like everyone else? Right.

It had been months since she'd walked through a house unaccosted by someone trying to make her eat or drink or talk or *do* something. Her mother definitely wasn't there, which made her stop and close her eyes to hold back tears. *She's fine. Ivar said so, and he presumably doesn't care enough to lie. It has to be true.*

A swinging door led to the kitchen, where a dark-haired woman turned from the counter. "Good morning!" The greeting and grin belonged to the reporter from Afghanistan, the one who'd known Wulf. "Dr. Chiesa, right? Can I call you Theresa?"

"Um, sure. You're…" She searched for a name. "Laura?"

"You remembered! Wasn't sure since we met so quickly." The other woman fiddled with a chrome espresso machine. "Coffee?"

"Please." The kitchen's dark wood cabinets and

shiny appliances were as sleek as the coffeemaker. Mica flecks in the countertops and a row of white dish towels contrasted with the rest of the dark palette. It was the complete opposite of her mother's terra-cotta-and-fruit-themed kitchen. It was cold.

"Glad to see the stretch pants work. Wulf asked for a skirt, but I didn't have one."

Learning that Wulf had asked to borrow Laura's clothes for her felt odd. Unsettling. "You live here too?"

"I'm not in town enough to get a place of my own, and my grandfather works for Ivar." She pulled half-and-half and strawberries out of the refrigerator. They looked lost on the long counter. "Hopefully I'll be gone next week."

"You're returning to Afghanistan?" Watching Laura dart around the kitchen stirred a cauldron of emotions, but she didn't want to dig too deeply to figure out whether she was more jealous of the darting, the job or the familiarity with Wulf's home.

"Afraid not. I'm persona non grata at the military embedded media program." Laura found bowls, a chopping board and a knife without having to search. "Feels like I've been stuck with lawyers for months, but it's bogus to charge me with revealing classified information for exposing a crime, so I imagine I'll be cleared soon."

"What'll you do? If you can't go back?" How could Laura be so casual about losing her career?

"There's a dozen other conflicts to cover besides Afghanistan and plenty of soldiers who aren't Americans. Maybe I'll head to Africa." After rinsing the last strawberry, she set bread and butter on the counter. "What would you like for breakfast?"

"You don't have to wait on me."

When Laura froze, hand partially inserted in the

bread bag, to stare at her, Theresa realized her words had emerged louder and more defensive than she'd intended.

"I'm sorry. That was—" She didn't have a chance to finish before Laura waved her off.

"No offense. I know I tend to roll over people." She gestured at the fixings. "Please."

They settled on opposite sides of the kitchen island. Sharing the newspaper with Laura, who refolded each section as she finished, was pleasant enough that her shoulders relaxed. She drained her coffee and turned a page. The photo of a large colonial-style house surrounded by emergency vehicles was typical inside-page fare.

Second Tragedy Strikes Senator's Family. This was the home of the senator who'd died next to her in Afghanistan. She dropped the paper and pressed against the stool's backrest, almost tipping, while the black letters grew and swam on the page. Three dead. One daughter missing. *Not more death. Not another family.*

Wulf hadn't known this family, and he hadn't drawn Unferth to them.

"Oh." Looking from the paper to her, Laura asked, "You okay?"

Without words to describe how or why a crushing weight had lifted from her chest, she nodded. This black-and-white picture forced her to be honest. Wulf wasn't responsible for what had happened to the senator in Afghanistan, or to his family, or even to Ray. The blame belonged to Unferth.

"I got the short version from Wulf." The reporter patted her jeans pockets and then squinted and shook her head. "That sucks. I'm sorry."

"Thanks." Right now she'd welcome a new subject. "How's quitting?"

Laura snorted. "This is my third try. Maybe fourth."

"Ouch." A rumble from the kitchen alerted Theresa to another door past the refrigerator.

"Car in the garage. Wulf went shopping." Laura's eyebrows rose suggestively. "I suggest you prepare to be inundated."

Seconds later, he shouldered through the door with a computer-store tote in one hand and department-store bags in the other. "Good morning. You found the clothes."

Intellectually she understood that he wouldn't be wounded, and she'd seen him recover other times, but his perfect smile was such an unsettling contrast with last night's gruesome wounds that she didn't know where to look or how to reply.

"I bought a few things that might fit better."

"Thank you." His presence heated the kitchen until she almost felt like she was back in the sandbox.

Laura tidied her mug and bowl into the dishwasher and headed for the door. "Sorry to miss this, but I have legal bills to go incur."

Her departure didn't make speaking easier. After rejecting him last night, Theresa wasn't sure how to cross this distance. Her arms ached to wrap around him, but she hugged the blue sweater closer instead. It smelled faintly of evergreen.

"So." Outwardly he looked and sounded calm, but his tight-fisted grip on the shopping bag handles hinted that, like her, he was nervous this morning. "Maybe you'll prefer these."

The new clothes wouldn't hold his essence.

"Did Laura show you this?" He opened a third door she'd assumed led to a pantry or a powder room and revealed a blue-and-white-wallpapered nook. Sun streamed through a window to an enclosed courtyard, highlighting a toile-patterned chair and ottoman. "We eat at the kitchen bar or in the dining room, so I thought you might like to use this space." As he unpacked a laptop, she recognized her *Beowulf* books and biology texts already on the table.

Had he truly given her a room of her own? A mug filled with pens and highlighters, a printer with paper, even fresh flowers—he'd thought of everything.

He stood up from the floor where he'd plugged in the computer and rubbed his hands on denim-covered thighs.

A braver woman would have told him that last night she'd been too afraid, too devastated, to be kind. She'd been cruel when he didn't deserve it, and she owed him an apology. She let him turn toward the door.

A phone rang, and she jumped.

Even before Wulf gave her the handset, the familiar piercing request for *The-reeee-sa* filled the room.

"Mom?" She held her breath until the answer confirmed her hopes.

"Sweetie? Thank God, you're fine. You're fine, right?"

"What about you? Where are—"

Wulf sketched a half bow and silently left. He could take the clothes and the computer and office; she wouldn't miss them, because he'd provided what she wanted most.

"Carl—no, wait, I can't say that. Can you imagine now I have to remember to call him Lou, just like if he'd gone to the feds? He says I can't tell you anything. Nothing."

"It's okay, Mom. I'm so glad to hear your voice. I'm glad you're b-both—" Thinking of the two of them, alone somewhere, blocked her voice in her throat.

A public address system in the background garbled whatever her mother said next.

"Mom?" The phone she clutched wasn't warm or strong, wasn't her mother's hand.

"*Lou's* telling me to keep it short."

She wanted to yell that she wasn't ready. Two sentences wasn't enough.

The background noise grew muffled, as if she'd cupped a hand over the mouthpiece, and her mother's Jersey accent strengthened the faster she spoke. "It hit him this morning, that Ray's gone. I have to keep pushing, or he slumps over and I doan' know what to doooo." Her voice rose, panicked.

"You can hold him together, Mom, like you did for me." Since she'd come home hurt, her mother hadn't faltered. Not once. "You can. You will."

"He says we'll be moving a lot, and I can't call for a couple weeks. Take care of yourself and don't worry about us, you promise?"

"I promise." As if that were possible. "I love you, Mom." Her words came out fierce and strong, filled with the need to make her mother understand how much she loved her. "Stay safe. You're the best mother in the world. The best." She'd never let it go unsaid again. "I love you."

Her mother's *I love you, too, sweetheart* rang in her ears long after they'd both hung up.

As exhausted as if a whole day had passed, she

couldn't believe her watch indicated barely ten in the morning. Wulf and Laura, and presumably Ivar, were very quiet or else this house was very big. The rustling as she opened shopping bags seemed unnecessarily loud, but she needed to fill time. What she didn't need to do was replay last night until she paralyzed herself.

The heavy bag didn't contain clothing. Wulf had bought more versions of the legend.

He wanted her to pursue the threads she'd started to unravel.

At Camp Caddie's running track, Wulf had told her people who lived in multimillion-dollar brownstones had problems like everyone else. Studying Ivar's art collection, she'd disagreed, but after three and a half days sharing the house, she knew the brothers had problems completely different from regular people's worries over debts, love or jobs. Ivar flinched at noises, so the others living with him strove to be extremely quiet. He also consumed collegiate levels of beer and whiskey, which Wulf explained as an efficient source of calories, but which seemed to her to fulfill a more traditional desire for oblivion.

For his part, Wulf apparently suffered from an epic case of insomnia. Every morning she found a warm dent in an easy chair by her bed, and the cushion smelled vaguely woodsy like his soap, but she never caught him. When she left her office by the kitchen, he materialized with whatever she sought, whether it was towels or her water bottle. In short, he hovered, but other than one accidental brush of her arm, he hadn't touched her since the first night.

She hadn't summoned the nerve to touch him either.

Tonight, like on other evenings, she joined Ivar and Wulf for an eight o'clock dinner in the dining room. Unlike on other evenings, Laura had plans with a group of photographers. Without a partner in small talk, she spent the soup course studying Ivar. His pressed suit contrasted with his hunched shoulders and determined drinking. His hand was out of sight, but she'd noticed earlier that his fingers resembled bleached, shriveled beans.

A question had nagged her for three days. "Have you always had your arm injury?"

Both immortals froze, spoons in air, until Ivar slowly replaced his on the charger under his bowl. "No."

"So it's from your imprisonment?"

"Yes."

She'd immersed herself in academic abstracts on the internet, taken notes on DNA replication, read about starfish and salamander regeneration and studied retroviral drug treatments. Anomalies led to breakthroughs. "What's different this time?"

Ivar squeezed his eyelids shut, and his good hand pinched the bridge of his nose. Wulf neither spoke nor moved. The silence stretched.

"I'm sorry." Of all people, she knew how uncomfortable others' curiosity could be. "I shouldn't pry. I—"

He made a cutting-off gesture. "A valid question. I should answer."

Theresa felt Wulf's gaze. Turning, she received an almost imperceptible nod, as if he too wanted his brother to open up.

"Unferth's scientists removed my forearm. I've lost limbs in battle. Bone regrowth aches for an hour at most." Ivar's monotone betrayed nothing. "However, they applied an ointment to the stub and the bandages. My healing radically slowed." His words scraped along her nerves, like a metal pick on ice. "Every time my arm and hand regrew, they cut them off."

Phantom pain had been common for her first months of rehab. Sometimes charley horses in the missing calf had been so strong she'd woken in the night, but lately they'd decreased. The sympathetic pain that Ivar's words caused surprised a gasp from her.

"Each time, it took longer. And less of the hand grew."

She covered her mouth to keep from making another sound that would interrupt him. His emotions were so raw, his anger so palpable and yet so contained, that she wondered how he could sit at the table without destroying every dish and glass set in front of him.

"I lost count after the sixth amputation."

NEXT TO HER, Wulf made a sound between a moan and gasp, and she gripped his thigh below the table. It was the first touch they'd shared in several days.

He laid his palm, warm and firm like an anchor, over hers and squeezed. Out of nowhere she thought of cookies, *Cinderella* and the first time they'd held hands. Her own leg pain, or not-leg pain, lessened.

Lifting from his shoulder, Ivar raised his sling above the edge of the table. The bloodless fingertips resembled a cadaver's, only smaller and flaccid. His other hand was hard and fit where it lay alongside. "This took nearly a week to regrow, and I still do not have muscle control."

"A growth retardant?" she asked, more to herself than to the men. "Something that affects nerve regeneration?"

Released from his retelling, Ivar shrugged and reached for his whiskey.

"I've been reading that echinoderms—starfish—re-grow to complete size from one arm and a portion of the central disk." That had been one of her more interesting discoveries.

"I'd rather not picture six more big brothers."

"Don't be facetious." She glared at Wulf as Ivar drained another glass. "I'm thinking about how to *fix* his arm." Ideas welled up like lava, the hot excitement of untangling a research puzzle filling her the way it always had when she'd walked into her thesis advisor's lab. "There's a study that shows that an injection of a single-strand type of RNA molecules can enable live chicks to regenerate a wing."

"Not a language I speak, Doc." Wulf grinned. "Can you translate to plain English? Could that counteract what Unferth did to my brother?"

"I don't know. Honestly, it could make it worse." This part had scared her yesterday. "Something similar resulted in a flatworm regrowing a tail where it should've had a head."

"I am not interested in having an appendage other than a hand at the end of my arm."

"He's already a big enough dick," Wulf muttered. "Doesn't need a spare."

"Beg your pardon?" His brother stared back with one raised eyebrow.

"I was saying that near the prison in Marrakesh, I saw a five-legged dog."

"Are you certain that wasn't your brain between its rear legs?" The insult seemed to revive Ivar enough that he ate a bite of steak. "No one removed my ears."

Concealing her laughter by coughing into her napkin, Theresa felt a bubbling desire to share more of her research. "I've been reading a lot." She'd spent days immersed in the office Wulf had created for her. Interesting and intriguing days, fascinating days, but lonely days. Maybe since her theories were about their condition, they'd want to know. "Symbiotic microbes can enhance their hosts, like a glowing bacteria that helps squid improve their camouflage. I know you think you have a virus, but I'm more inclined to believe you have a parasite or bacterial infection, because their genomes are so much bigger and they're more likely to need an intermediate host like Grendel before they can become infectious. Like malaria needs mosquitoes."

From the corner of her eye she saw Wulf's grin, the one that meant she was babbling. For the first time in days, instead of grooves leading down from his mouth, he had tiny crinkles around his eyes, as if he wanted to laugh, so she took a deep breath and offered her latest, craziest idea. "If we started our own research lab, we could isolate and perhaps treat the immortality." She couldn't read Ivar's expression, but Wulf's was dubious.

"With Unferth hunting us, being mortal again doesn't sound as good as it once did," he said. "And that's the point of a cure, right?"

"You've missed the point, brother." Ivar's voice scratched over the table. "What if Unferth were mortal?" His good hand made a fist next to his dinner plate as he leaned toward her, the most engaged she'd seen him since meeting him. "I will give you anything you need to achieve that. Money, a lab, assistants—they're yours. What will it take?"

"I don't know." Her heart pounded as she realized how far beyond her expertise pursuing this idea would lead. "For starters, I'll need to compare your DNA to a sample of Grendel's. The commonality should be the infectious organism."

Both men stared at her without comprehension.

"I need DNA from Grendel's bones or blood."

Whatever language they used had the unmistakable rhythm of profanity.

"It only requires a tiny amount of bone or tissue. Like what would be in the hilt of a sword." Every version of the epic referred to Beowulf bringing the damaged sword hilt back from his journey to the deep where he'd confronted Grendel's mother.

"After fifteen hundred years?" Wulf asked.

"A research institute in Germany sequenced a mastodon's mitochondrial DNA from a fifty-thousand-year-old tooth." She cocked her head to one side. "Surely those giant beasts had finished walking the planet when you all began your fateful trip?"

Wulf began to hum a familiar television theme until his brother glared him into silence.

"Or I could use Grendel's arm or skull." She'd flagged those references in the story as well, because if the bones could be located, they might be helpful to the puzzle. "They could have extractable genetic material."

"The skull was lost in 1945 between the Nazis and the Soviet Red Army. The arm is too secure." Ivar ticked off his objections. "It will have to be the hilt."

"Stig could steal the arm." Wulf mentioned someone she assumed was another immortal.

"I'll inquire when I reach him. You realize Unferth may already have the skull? He commanded a Nazi *Kunstschutz* unit to loot on the Eastern front."

How long would it take before references to their past didn't make the hair on her arms stand up?

"Reason to secure the other artifacts quickly." Underneath Wulf's measured and rational speech, she detected a hint of excitement, as if he'd been assigned a new mission.

"I have much to think about." Ivar stood, as if dismissing them from dinner. "Good evening."

As he left the room, Theresa noticed he'd left his whiskey next to his plate.

Wulf lifted her hand from his thigh. She'd forgotten it was still there. Instead of letting go like she'd expected, he lifted it to his lips. Pressed a kiss to her palm. His strength, so long held away from her, flooded her from that connection. They'd get better, all of them, together. She'd taken the first steps down that road, and she planned to take another. Tonight Wulf wasn't going to sleep in the chair across the room. He'd spend the night where he belonged: beside her.

ALTHOUGH FORT CAMPBELL, Kentucky, was an hour behind Eastern time, Wulf doubted calling at 10:00 p.m. would interrupt dinner. The team would've redeployed home in late November, the same time he was searching Rabat and Marrakesh for Ivar, and Deavers and Kahananui and the others would've shared the holidays with their families. Last year he'd eaten turkey with Deavers and Kristin. She'd been pregnant with a second child. This year's Christmas would've included the new baby.

He had at least an hour before he could slip upstairs without finding Theresa awake, so he'd started to pack. The air was stuffy in Ivar's basement storage room, but the shelves were so well organized that Wulf could lay his hands immediately on what he needed for his trip. That left him free to stare at the phone. If redeployment went true to form, by this point the team would be restless. He could picture Kahananui working in his yard, cursing the cold, and Cruz closing down one too many bunny bars despite his claims to be reformed, because over the years he'd helped both with their preferred pastimes. Deavers would be throwing himself into All-American fatherhood as hard as he tackled mission planning, but since his wife didn't need a movement order, a rally point or an extraction plan, he'd feel a little unappreciated about now. That's the way two and a half months home usually panned out, with loose ends and lots of trying to build a routine. After three months, they usually hit their stride and found a rhythm preparing for the next deployment.

He missed the team. Ivar had shut him out, and even though she hadn't rejected his touch at the dinner table, Theresa couldn't possibly want more from him. The team would want him. And, because he didn't trust himself to succeed without someone guarding his back, a job Ivar wasn't ready to undertake, he punched a number in from memory.

"Deavers here." His friend's voice was brusque and quiet, the way he always answered a nighttime call in a house with sleeping kids.

"Chris." Wulf greeted him back with his own name, that word enough to identify himself.

"Man, oh man," He could hear his former commander's grin in the way he stretched his words, almost laughing. "I hoped you'd call someday…"

"Yeah, me too." His throat felt tight.

"How's it going? Wait, let me go in my office."

Wulf closed his eyes to picture the space Deavers called an office in his one-story rambler near the post.

Kid-size plastic three-wheelers, a washer and dryer and in the corner, two leather rolling chairs mended with duct tape set around his father's old footlocker for a table. It was the only place in the house his wife allowed him to chew.

"Kristin gave me an office upgrade for Christmas, by the way." As Deavers settled in, a chair creaked loudly enough to be heard over their connection. "You'll wish you were here."

"Not a new chair? You're not a good enough husband to deserve that."

"Hoo-ah, this bad boy's better than a chair. A top-of-the-line mini-fridge."

Wulf heard the suction of an opening door.

"She thinks I don't know it's her way of snagging more space by exiling my beer. Got one handy? I recall a promise to share a drink when we hit civilization."

"I'm ahead of you." Wulf looked at the empty bottles sitting on the shelf next to a box of European cellular phone SIM cards.

His friend's noncommittal *ah* conveyed a world of understanding. "So, the doc. How's that's going? How is she?"

At the question, the tiny screwdriver he was using to open the back of a burner cell phone jumped out of its groove. Going upstairs after dinner, Theresa had looked over her shoulder and half smiled with her eyes lowered and her head tilted *just so*. It might have been an invitation, but what if he was wrong?

"If you give me some self-sacrificing bullshit, the team will hunt you down and kick your ass until we make it hurt, no matter how long that takes. Copy?"

"Roger that." The problem with having friends who knew you this well was that they knew you this well.

"Did you go after her? That's what you were supposed to do."

"I did, but—" He'd have to hide the extra SIM cards in the phone later, when Deavers wasn't throwing him curveballs. After a deep breath, he took the plunge. "Some Class 1-A problems followed me to Jersey City."

"Wait—New Jersey? Not the torched house with the six—"

"Yeah. That was her family's place. Different last name." He didn't know how Deavers had missed making the connection. Being home with two kids must have been rougher than Paktia Province, because wall-to-wall coverage had blanketed the media for three days. Cable and internet couldn't trumpet loudly enough that both the senator's house and the house of the soldier who'd been in the car with him had burned down on the same day. The FBI wasn't talking, but reporters had dug up the organized-crime connection, and now the least sensational headlines began Ivy League-Mafia Princess-War Heroine.

"Doc and her parents are fine." With Deavers he slipped back into his nickname for Theresa. "But her stepbrother and cousin were two of the six."

Chris breathed a word that summed up the situation in four letters.

Wulf's hands hovered over a row of airtight containers before he acknowledged that he didn't have enough focus to pack a belt buckle with explosives. He'd have to leave that for tomorrow. "Six more casualties across the street, guards, but that's not public. They were all ex-FBI or Special Ops."

"Guess you're not calling to ask me to be your best man, then?"

Maybe if Theresa's idea worked, he'd have the opportunity to become a regular guy who made normal plans like that, but tonight he had a different request. "I need help."

"We can be wheels up in four hours. Tell us where and what to bring."

"SAS Flight 926 day after tomorrow, IAD to Copenhagen." After seeing Ivar's motivation, he wasn't going to delay getting started with the antiviral research. Having a goal might help his brother recover. "I need someone to watch my back while I find a Viking relic."

"We'll leave a few homebodies to cover the fort, but who do you want?"

"Cruz and Bama Boy. Nobody else." This was the part he'd known would be hardest.

"Negative on that request. Bama busted his knee waterskiing—"

"In February?"

"Went to Mexico with his sister's nanny. At least that's what he says, so you get me."

"Sir, you're not invited to this party. Nobody with kids."

Deavers continued as if Wulf hadn't spoken. "And if the Big Kahuna finds out you called and I didn't tell him, he'll cut off my nuts. Your panty knots aren't worth impairing my love life, so Kahananui's in too."

"Don't you understand six guys with our training were taken out like factory chickens across the street from Doc's? This is a bachelor party. Not you, not Big K, no one with—"

"No, you need to understand." Deavers went into his

rarely used pit bull growl. Rarely used because the team generally worked as an egalitarian unit, so he didn't emphasize rank. "Do the math. I wouldn't have kids without you, brother, just the dirt bed. Kristin got pregnant after our Fallujah vacation, where you saved my ass at least three times. If you need me, I'm in."

"Talk about a fucking martyr complex!" Wulf stopped short of pounding the wall, but he couldn't staunch his regrets over reaching out to his friend. "The people I need backup to watch out for aren't Scandinavian nannies or piece-of-shit terrorists, or even other Special Ops. There could be three of them just like me. Get that? Like me."

"Oh. Wow." On the other end of the line, Chris took a deep breath. His chair creaked back and forth while Wulf hung on to his side of the call. "Well. That'll make it harder to cover the spread, but it also leaves me with a sling load of unanswered questions."

Wulf couldn't, wouldn't, satisfy his former commander's curiosity over the telephone, but he had to persuade him to stay in Kentucky. "It's not a game. It should fucking scare you."

"Hell yes. It's a ball shrinker, but you know me. I puke before HALO jumps, and I've never missed one yet."

Deavers wasn't the only one who found parachuting from above 25,000 feet and free falling at over a hundred miles per hour to be stressful. Wulf had never wanted to test whether his condition could overcome a big splatter. "If you're trying to distract me, no dice. You're not invited. Your regular work's hard enough on Kristin. Don't go off-roading."

"All right, already." Deavers made a disgusted sound.

"Promise you're not coming, or I won't be on the flight. I'm not under your command anymore."

"Promise," Deavers agreed.

Without looking in his friend's eyes, Wulf couldn't tell if he was lying. "Tell Cruz to bring a black work passport. It's that kind of trip."

"His favorite kind."

After the call ended, Wulf assessed his packing. He was close enough to being finished with stowing the cash and gear he planned to smuggle into Denmark that he could go upstairs. At the least, he'd be able to watch Theresa for one more night. But maybe—he remembered that half smile from above him on the stairs—he wouldn't have to spend it in the chair.

OTHER EVENINGS, THERESA had folded her clothes and put them away, but if she wanted to entice Wulf to the bed, she probably had to leave obvious hints. She dropped the pink turtleneck sweater she'd worn to dinner inside the doorway, where it couldn't be overlooked, and left her long black skirt puddled two steps farther into the room. She aligned the cups and straps of her bra until she'd made an arrow pointing to the bed, but that looked weird, so she nudged it into a pile. She chickened out before removing her panties and instead donned a pair of Wulf's soft flannel pajamas. The bottom hung low around her waist, and the top button of the matching shirt fell between her breasts.

As ready as she could make herself, she concealed her stump among the blankets and waited. Anticipation, not fear, made her hold her breath when the door opened.

"Hello." Pitching her voice low was easy with the nerves inside her chest threatening to block her ability to speak. She rose on one elbow and made sure her top gaped.

"Are you sure?" He bent toward her, providing a whiff of yeasty residue.

"You smell." She pressed her hand against his shirt, as much to hold him away as to feel his body heat through the cotton. "Like beer sweat."

"That I do." His voice was slower, with a throaty sound, as if the alcohol had pulled him to another era or place where people spoke more slowly. "Shall I wash?"

"That would be nice." This wasn't how tonight was supposed to work. And she didn't have a backup plan.

"Come with me." Taking the duvet in his hands, he looked to her for permission.

In her imagination, he was supposed to climb into bed beside her in the dark, not smelling like beer, and he wouldn't need to see any part of her lower torso without clothes. Reality, as usual, was totally different, but she knew this was their chance to find each other again and she had to work with what he offered, so she nodded. "My leg's next to the bed." Not as hard to say as she'd expected.

"I'll carry you." When he scooped her in his arms, static made the empty pajama leg cling to his elbow. He couldn't see her stump, not with the long flannel flopping over it.

"But I want—" Before she'd finished her request, he popped the leg and the liner sleeve sitting next to it into her arms, like he knew how much security they gave her. She clung to him as he dipped to reach the doorknob. "Where are we going?"

"Wait and see."

At the end of the hall a set of stairs continued up to

what was probably the roof. Tucking her stump closer to Wulf to avoid bumps as they ascended, she anticipated the cold February night. Instead they entered a warm and earthy-smelling room.

"Ivar's conservatory." The exertion of climbing had erased the blurriness of beer from Wulf's speech, although he wasn't panting as he carried her past shelves of plants with multi-fingered leaves, some smooth, others with edges like bread knives. Flowers ranging from pale green to purplish-black nodded as they brushed past. "He propagates hellebores."

She forgot what Wulf had said as soon as they emerged through a heavy plastic curtain. Simultaneously inside and outside, the glass-ceilinged room around her bloomed with azaleas and tightly budded tulips. His breathing remained as even as it had been when he'd first lifted her, until she slipped two fingers between his shirt buttons and touched the hot skin of his chest. *That* made his breath catch and hold.

"Welcome to my sauna." He ducked through the door of a wooden building the size of a large closet and settled her on a wide bench.

In the cedar-scented dimness, she saw a shower as well as a stove with rocks piled around it and stacks of fluffy towels, but as soon as Wulf began to strip, she couldn't look at the sauna. "Um, don't you have to light a fire or something?"

"Gas power. It heats quickly." He touched controls by the door. Every move he made highlighted the sculpting of his arms and shoulders. Even the mundane act of bending to shove his shirt in a basket showed the muscles of his abs and torso playing together. "The steam will be ready by the time I finish my shower."

So will I. She realized she was cradling her leg to her chest unnecessarily since she was secure on the bench. No curtains or walls blocked her view of Wulf as she stowed her prosthetic under the wooden seat. She could happily lounge in this spot all night.

The sound of his zipper was louder than the heartbeat in her ears, but not faster. When his jeans came down, it was obvious he'd noticed her interest too. Heat from the stove stuck her pajamas to her skin, and her underwear felt damp as she watched him slide his boxers down his legs. Knowing she shouldn't stare so blatantly, she tore her gaze away from his thighs and groin, but not before *that part* bobbed a wave at her.

"You don't have to look away. I liked it." He definitely had.

"I—" Thankfully, he turned on the water and she didn't have to form an answer. While she watched his buttocks flex, she recalled their firmness under her hands and how she'd clutched those muscles when he pumped over her. Steam saturated the air until she plucked at the flannel clinging to her thighs. Still, she stared.

Eyes closed, he faced her and raised his arms. The motion pushed his chest toward her and delineated his abs, a work of art to admire, while his eucalyptus-scented shampoo mixed with the mist to wrap her in fragrance. When she followed the path of dissolving bubbles down his chest to his abdomen and the solid evidence of his desire, she wanted to be that water. She wanted to flow across his body.

Opening his eyes after a final rinse, he stepped out of the shower stream. "Want to join me?"

"Yes." The heat had increased. Sweat trickled between her breasts. Remembering the glide of his skin on hers, she wanted to be wet next to him, even though she didn't know how she'd stand.

He solved her dilemma by kneeling, naked, in front of the bench and raising her shirt hem while she lifted her arms. Bared to him, her nipples beaded as he cupped her breasts, one in each hand. When he bent to suck, the scrape of his stubble was a drug worth craving. Arching to push herself closer to his mouth, she felt as shaky as an addict seeking her fix. His pulls reached through her body and, she would've sworn, into her soul.

"I missed you," he murmured, his face buried between her breasts and his fingers rolling her nipples with the hypnotic rhythm of his words. "Memories were nothing compared to this. You're beautiful." He reached for her drawstring.

Beautiful. Maybe she had been, once, but certainly not now. Her thighs squeezed around his torso hard enough that he couldn't remove the last pieces of her clothing. "Turn off the lights," she ordered.

Crouched between her knees, he looked up. "I want to see—"

"No!" Humiliation trumped desire, and she jerked back as his fingers undid the knot at her waist. "Turn off the lights. Now."

"Let me take these off." His hand slipped beneath the loosened waistband.

In Italy they'd made love in sunlight and among candles, but she wasn't that woman anymore, so she crossed her arms over her chest.

"All bodies are equal in the sauna. It's an old Finnish saying."

"Well, I'm Italian, and I want the lights off!"

He finally complied, turning off the stove as well and plunging the room into darkness so complete she couldn't see her lifted hand. This time when his fingers brushed from the bare skin of her stomach to her waistband, she knew he couldn't see her damage.

"Someday you'll be comfortable with the lights." His mouth followed his fingers, trailing sensations that encouraged her to drop her knees farther apart. "I promise."

"Don't hold your breath." Her warning ended with a moan, weakening her threat, as he slid the pajama pants and underwear off her hips.

"Don't hold yours." His mouth moved lower, following his hands to the places that waited, begging, for him. "Wouldn't want you to faint."

"Modest much?" Her head lolled on the wall behind her as she flexed her buttocks and raised herself. Hard to think, harder to speak. But feeling came easier as he opened her legs and a hand slipped under her hips to tilt her off the bench. Flutters began deep inside. They matched the pounding in her blood, the rhythm of his tongue and the satisfaction from his fingers moving harder between her legs. First her stomach muscles, then her chest and arms and shoulders and neck, everything, every part of her body, felt pulled taut and stretched to breaking, until they all snapped into a kaleidoscope of sensation. She couldn't hold back from yelling his name.

As they lay entangled, she gradually floated back to herself enough to become aware of his erection against her hip. He was still hard, still wanting, while she was one of the steam clouds, shapeless and drifting.

His hands tenderly arranged her on top. He took his time kissing her. She sank into his lips, met his tongue and danced with him, and then she felt more of him than his tongue slide into her when the head of his cock breached where his fingers and mouth had already graced. He pushed into her slick readiness, pushed her back to the precipice, but flat on top of him her body didn't angle enough for what she wanted. To feel him deeper, to connect harder, required her to abandon the pleasure of his kisses, but there would be more if she pushed herself up.

The loss of his lips under hers was instantly compensated by the depth of his penetration when their bodies finally fully merged. Up and down, her thighs pushed her those inches that drove her pleasure. Under her hands, his chest shuddered. He gripped her hips tighter and bucked in a lover's rhythm of thrusts and pulls, punctuated by the slapping sounds of their sweat-slicked bodies. At the moment she quivered, ready to collapse onto his chest, he lifted her nearly off the bench as he drove deeply and shouted her name.

For a long time, neither of them spoke or moved. She breathed against his shoulder. He stroked her hair. They had no strength to do more.

"I'll miss you." His voice sounded thick and sleepy.

"Hmm?" It took a moment for his words to penetrate her lethargy. "What'd you say?"

"I'm flying to Copenhagen tomorrow. To find the sword hilt."

Her stepfather had given her a passport, but she didn't know if her ankle charger would work with European voltage and outlets. She might need an adapter.

"You'll be safe here with Ivar."

"What?" No way was she waiting in New York while he shot off to Copenhagen. She pushed away from his damp chest, but in the absolute dark, she couldn't see his expression. "Finding the sword hilt was my idea. You're not going without me."

"But—" He stopped.

"But what?" Had he learned nothing about her?

"Ahh, I like your butt?" His voice rose while his hand stroked until he found the ticklish crease above the back of her thigh, making her giggle while he stalled. "A lot."

"You can't wiggle out of this." The conviction she managed to put in her voice was completely undermined by the reflexive way her lower body rubbed against his.

"It's much better when *you* wiggle—" he gripped her waist and shifted her to where she could rub on his erect cock, "—*on* this."

"I'm going with you to Copennnn—"

His teeth found her nipple in the dark and tugged with exactly the right pressure, sending her head back and her whole body arching into the pull, but she wouldn't give up.

"—haaaahh—"

He guided himself to her entrance and pushed in again, gliding past an ultrasensitive spot as he filled her.

"—gen." His smooth withdrawal and slow return were so pleasurable on her twice-primed body that she wondered if she'd survive a third.

No way she'd let him disappear without her, not after *this*.

Chapter Twenty-Six

WHEN WULF SPOTTED Cruz, earbuds in and eyes half-closed as if napping in the airport waiting area, he whispered to Theresa, "If you recognize anyone, don't acknowledge."

"*Should* I recognize someone?" she whispered back. Even his arguments about other immortals had failed to talk her out of joining him on the trip to Denmark. When Ivar supported her position by saying she added balance, he'd given in to her insistence, but he'd need his team more than ever to keep her safe. Maybe he should have invited Deavers and Kahananui.

"Forgot to tell you." The first-class boarding announcement for their flight momentarily interrupted him. "I called in the team."

Her mouth made a little O of surprise, but she recovered while he grabbed both carry-ons. He was prepared to steady her if she stumbled on the inclined jet bridge, but she stepped smoothly over the gap from the gangway and moved briskly to their spacious leather seats. It was a good beginning, one that kindled hope that, with her research and his friends at their backs, they'd pull this off.

Near the end of boarding, a man dressed in anonymous khakis and an unzipped ski parka eased sideways up the aisle behind a Hindi-speaking family. Wulf didn't need to see his face to know his former commander. He coughed hard into his hand, intentionally making a sound that resembled a profanity, but he didn't care who he offended. Deavers deserved to be called a bastard for this stunt, and if Deavers was here, no doubt Wulf would also catch a mountain wearing a flowered shirt squeezing past all the people stuffing duty-free bags in the bins.

As Deavers shuffled past, he also sneezed. It sounded remarkably like he'd said, *You too.*

Confirmation that they hadn't listened to his warnings didn't anger him as much as he'd vowed. Since he'd erased himself in that Afghan river, every day had felt like he was missing a lung that never grew back. He'd sweated through Morocco alone, although he needed a pack as much as his namesake. So he was a selfish man, and he felt guilty too, but in his gut he'd known how this would roll even before he'd dialed. A truthful man would also admit that he wanted friends at his back because he was scared of winding up like Ivar.

Two hours into the eight-hour flight, dessert had been cleared from their tray tables and the lights dimmed. He lifted Theresa's hand to his lips. "You know the seats recline almost flat in first class? And there's a privacy partition."

With her chin tucked to her chest and her eyebrows raised, she glanced left and right and then shot him a dubious look. "You can't be serious."

He adopted a puppy face. "We could just cuddle?"

Her lips twitched and her nose flared, as if she was fighting to hold in laughter. "Right."

Just cuddle. At least Cruz was too far in the back to hear how low he'd sunk.

She focused on her paperback, but all he could process was the word *Licking* written in glowing type on the cover. It reminded him of their sojourn in the sauna, and he let his eyes settle on the rise and fall of her breasts under her pink sweater. The sweater looked soft, and her skin underneath would be smooth and warm. Perhaps if he put his hand on her thigh—

"Quit staring," she muttered without removing her eyes from the page. "Do you need something to read?"

"No, thanks." He retrieved *The Face of Battle*. If anything could compete with the scent of oranges surrounding the woman next to him, it would be John Keegan's three hundred fifty pages.

"How much longer?"

Theresa's question pulled him away from the screaming horses at Waterloo and the stinking mud of the Somme. Surprised by how long they'd been reading, he double-checked his answer. "Less than two hours. With the time difference, we land in Copenhagen about 0730."

She was concentrating so hard on massaging her leg, all ten of her fingers digging into the meat of her quad, he couldn't be sure she'd heard.

"Charley horse?"

"Uh-huh."

"Here, I can help." Starting at the top of her thigh, he pressed his thumbs until he found the rock-hard muscle, then traced it along her leg. Her response was a combination groan of pain and moan of agreement. Back to the top of her leg and down again, he kneaded as hard as he thought she could take, over and over, until her neck finally slumped forward and the lines on her forehead smoothed. He lightened the pressure to a gentle massage. "Good book?"

"Guilty pleasure." She spoke slowly, as if she'd sunk into relaxation—exactly what he wanted. "Barbecue, donuts and New Jersey."

"Sounds delicious." Maybe she was tired and loose enough to open up about her injury. "You have many spasms like that one?"

"Not often these days." She shifted in the seat, as if to withdraw, but there wasn't anywhere for her to go because he blocked the aisle. "I shouldn't have sat for so long."

His hands maintained their soothing rhythm on her thigh. "How's the leg now?"

The pause stretched so long he wondered if she'd fallen asleep. That would be ironic—him trying to get her to unwind and talk about her injury, but instead succeeding in rendering her comatose.

"The stump's probably swollen, like people's ankles get on long flights." If he hadn't been completely focused on her, he wouldn't have heard her barely audible reply over the engine noise. "And I have an increased risk for deep vein thrombosis. No big deal."

Her *no big deal* bent him like a two-hundred-pound ruck on his shoulders.

THE GLITTER OF late morning sun on the foot of snow that had stalled Copenhagen heightened the postcard view of the inner harbor from Wulf and Theresa's suite, but not Wulf's pleasure. He didn't enjoy feeling exposed, and the light might interfere with Theresa's nap, so he closed the room-darkening blinds. Then he removed the back of his phone to swap in a clean disposable SIM card. Time to locate their less legitimate supplies.

Reaching Guleed by phone was easy, because they'd talked many times over the last forty years, and rehashing how they'd met in Mogadishu brought back memories that had improved with time. Only eight years old,

Guleed had chased Wulf through a slum to demand he pay the bar bill after the messy death of a mercenary Wulf had considered to be a friend. The ambitious boy wouldn't let his mother lose a day's profit, because those pennies bought school uniforms and books.

"Anything, anything you name, I do it for you," Guleed promised when Wulf asked for a favor of the kind best kept strictly between friends who'd shared bad times in worse places. "You have saved my family a thousand times by finding for me a visa to this country." As Guleed described his chain of grocery stores dotted throughout the Copenhagen suburbs, he sounded so much like the eight-year-old with grand plans that without being able to see confirmation of his gray hair, Wulf found it hard to believe the boy he'd helped now had grandchildren.

In Somali, Wulf described his needs: winter gear, night vision equipment and weapons.

Guleed didn't hesitate. "I know a man or two, they probably have certain objects. Most are undoubtedly old and worthless, only for museums or collectors, nothing else, of course."

"Of course, of course." This type of business with this type of man necessitated a lot of chat. "But there are friends in Somalia who collect such items sometimes, no?" He hoped Guleed didn't pop up with an antitank weapon. That would be more than Cruz could resist.

"Sometimes, yes, but now there are many rules about exportation of private collections. Those who are law-abiding like you and me, my friend, find it hard to manage equal support against the militias."

"This is a shame." Wulf had to agree.

"Shame indeed. My son and I call it a paradox of

democracy. Luckily, we also practice many benefits of capitalism. Did I not tell you I bought a house in Mykonos, near the beach?"

Befriending him hadn't ruined Guleed. The boy had built a life to be envied, with a big family, good health, properties. Not all those Wulf cared about were doomed.

"It reminds me of Mogadishu as it was years ago, only the plumbing is much better." Guleed was still talking about his beach house. "The views, and the Greek women. You are my most honored guest, at any time."

Theresa might like the sunshine compared to February in New York…if he could avoid face time with Guleed, who wouldn't understand why his oldest friend still looked twenty-eight.

Once he'd navigated the complicated arrangements and farewells, he stood in the connecting door watching Theresa. Asleep, she'd lost the exhausted look from the plane, and her flawless skin glowed against the white pillows and duvet. Much as he itched to be moving, he'd made the right choice to tell everyone to rest.

He studied the room service menu. Although it was after breakfast and before lunch, finding Beowulf's sword hilt might seem more manageable after a platter of meatballs. His finger had already started to dial when he heard a knock in the team's signature pattern.

Seconds later he had Deavers locked in the buddy hug he'd been storing for seven months. "Where're the others?"

"Big Kahuna's getting a car—the legit way, no less— and Cruz is checking out a hooker hotel near the main station." Deavers took in the white leather couch, the streamlined furniture and the shiny red entertainment console. "Less pricey than these digs. And more anonymous."

"Good. I located more op gear. Should be ready tonight." Pacing to the closed window blinds, Wulf shared the unease that had been growing since the flight. "I keep feeling this trip has been too easy."

"Roger that. It's why I sent Cruz scouting." Deavers flopped into one of the cube chairs and stretched his legs across the geometrically patterned carpet while eyeing the basket of rye crackers and bottled water. "Got something better than gerbil bedding to eat? Or is the minibar here more expensive than a plane ticket?"

"I was about to order meatballs. We have a couple hours until I wake up Doc."

"Double down. I'm too married for Scandinavian models, but a man's never too married to step out on Kristin's meatloaf."

WULF MASKED HIS edginess with a joke as Kahananui maneuvered the rented taxi van through nearly empty streets. The sun set early this far north, and daylight was fading fast. "Where did a Hawaiian learn to drive in snow?"

"First post was Fort Drum, New York, bro." Acing a corner at the perfect speed and angle, no fishtailing, the big guy guided the van to a stop at the Danish National Museum. "Here you are."

"You're not coming in with us?" Theresa asked. Her excitement distracted him from thoughts of what might be inside. Part of him wanted to find the hilt and see if this curse he'd lived with for fifteen hundred years could be undone, but hope always seemed to beat a path to disappointment. Better to focus on the woman next to him and the here and now than on another what-if.

"Ma'am, this country is so *mucho* haole, guys like Cruz and me blend best by driving a taxi."

A fresh-shoveled path led through the courtyard of the former palace. The worker at the admissions desk seemed to be startled that visitors had arrived through the snow, and more so that they wished to speak to the head of the prehistory department. But she couldn't have been as unprepared to see them as he was to come face-to-face with a life-size poster celebrating a statue of Jurik. The Saint was perpetually killing the last dragon. On its back, the beast still had the fight to grasp the broken lance.

If he could do anything to shape his destiny, today would end better than that day.

"Dr. Haukssen?" Theresa advanced to greet the white-haired gentleman who came to meet them in the museum's Great Hall. "We're pleased you could see us on short notice. We're researching *Beowulf* for a documentary on the truth behind the myth."

"An appointment would permit me to prepare." His English had the clipped accent typical of some Northern Europeans as he stared over his reading glasses. "The snow discouraged my staff. Today I am left alone."

"We sincerely apologize." Theresa explained their cover story. "But our funding came through only thirty-six hours ago. The donor offered us frequent flier miles for the trip, and we had to arrange our flights and photography equipment quickly."

"Airline miles." Still unsmiling, the director of Danish Prehistory nodded his complete understanding of donor peccadilloes before turning to Wulf. "Are you a photographer?"

"No, he's stuck in Reykjavík." Wulf strove to look envious of an imaginary assistant stranded on a frozen volcanic rock. "He said he was going to try *hákarl*. I almost gave up my ticket to stay with him. Have you tasted it?"

"*Ja*, I have."

Wulf widened his eyes and faked enthusiasm for the fish dish he'd avoided for the last thousand years. "What's fermented shark meat like? Sushi? Or kimchi?"

Dr. Haukssen's mouth twisted. "I do not know kimchi, but I would say *hákarl* is like chicken left in the waste can for three months."

"Ahh." Wulf sighed deeply and raised his gaze to the ceiling. "An authentic cultural experience. I wish—"

Theresa stepped between them. "Let's focus on our assignment, *Millard*."

Ouch. That name hurt. Next time he'd choose his own alias.

"We're interested in sword hilts from approximately 500 A.D." Behind her back, she waved one hand at the floor in a patting motion.

Tone it down? Not a chance, babe. I want to see you laugh.

"Today is a slow day because of snow, so I have time to show you a few to consider. You may follow me."

As the director led them through the three-story atrium and then in and out of a series of rooms filled with car-size rune stones, ships pulled whole from the peat and gold treasures, Wulf's head spun with memories. Not all were good, so he cut ahead of Theresa and focused on Dr. Haukssen instead of the helmets suspended lifelessly in cases. "You must hold excellent dinners here." He lifted his hands to create a mock frame around a case of golden horns. "I see a bar for small-batch herb-infused aquavit in this corner. You must have a wood-fired oven for whole-grain rye bread in the courtyard. And butter churning! Women love butter churns!" *If Cruz and Kahananui could see this act.*

"There is no eating or drinking in the museum." Dr. Haukssen raised his voice as if speaking to a group of children.

"Of course not." Wulf jerked his chin back like a turtle. "I'm talking about a fundraiser, not children snacking on mass-produced crackers." From the corner of his eye, he spotted Theresa's twitching lips and flaring nostrils. He knew she'd never acknowledge wanting him to misbehave, but how could he resist teasing her when she was this easy? "Have you considered rooftop beehives? Single-source artisanal honey is the food world's next gold mine."

Theresa dropped two steps behind and almost completely muffled her snort.

Objective number one achieved.

"Beehives. No, I do not believe I have considered beehives." The director tilted his head and blinked several times at Wulf. "I thought you want to know about Beowulf?"

"Of course she does, I mean, we do."

"We are here." Their escort's shoulders sagged with relief as he ushered them into a white-painted space. "The storage units contain several swords you may view." He opened a drawer whose gliders were as silent as the room.

Disappointment crashed through Wulf as strong as the North Sea. All three swords arrayed on the plain white linen had blades, the iron black with rust and flaking with age. He hadn't thought their quest would be easy, so why did he suddenly feel like he was wearing someone's extra-extra-small body armor?

"These are wonderful, and we can use them to represent the sword Hrunting." Theresa extracted Heaney's *Beowulf* translation from her shoulder bag and waved it at the director. "But, sir, you know we're looking for a hilt alone. No blade."

She pointed to a passage. "Line 1614. 'And the inlaid hilt embossed with jewels; its blade had melted and the scrollwork on it burnt, so scalding was the blood of the poisonous fiend.'"

"I beg your forgiveness." The gentleman bowed slightly. "You, madam, have done your research." He shut away the swords and moved to another stack of drawers.

A museum with holdings this vast would have dozens, maybe hundreds, of swords and hilts. If he had to ride this roller coaster every time a drawer opened, he might start to actually age.

"The description continues." She flipped pages. Those fingers that could work miracles on patients or on him traced to the next blue highlights. "At line 1694, 'In pure gold inlay on the sword-guards there were rune markings,' blah blah, 'scrollworked hilt,' et cetera."

He hadn't realized she'd mastered so many of the books in her breakfast-room office. She'd either charm the hilt out of the old man or badger him until he gave up, but one way or another, if it was here, Wulf didn't doubt Theresa would find the remainder of the sword.

"You are quite literal, yes?" Dr. Haukssen curled his fists around the drawer pulls.

"Our documentary emphasizes facts. Since Heorot's been located near Gammel Lejre—"

He cut her off with a raised finger. "Potentially located, madam."

She waved aside his caution. "There are marshes to the west, as described in the story. Or should I say history? What if it was all true?"

None of the relics in the next drawer were the one they sought. The two hilts with lobed pommels weren't the barbed work of the giants, the third had runes that told the wrong story and while the fourth sported a bejeweled pommel of small stones set in gold scrollwork, it didn't have the dragon-eye-size ruby. Fifteen hundred years hadn't erased his memory of the jewel that had glowed like enchanted fire in the swamp while they carried Grendel's head.

"We intend to show the evidence for, and against, the truth," Theresa continued.

"Very American, your approach."

The four hunks of metal could have been forged at the same hearth where he and his brother had volunteered for the voyage. These might have been used, held, even treasured, by men he'd known. Men whose bones were dust and their names erased from the earth. But these hilts could connect him across the chasm of time. "May I hold one?"

Theresa gasped, and he looked from her to Dr. Haukssen and then he realized his mistake. These relics had drawn out his original language, a tongue he hadn't spoken, not even with Ivar, for more than a thousand years.

"You speak…not Danish." The man's watery blue eyes, bulging with surprise or, oddly, fear, consumed his lined face. "You speak the language of the Geats, do you not?"

"A teensy bit." Pinching his first finger and thumb together, Wulf switched to English and tried to salvage their cover. "We practice authenticity for our research."

"Do not lie." Like a man fifty years younger, the curator ran across the room to a red-handled alarm and rested his hand on it. "Scholars come every season. Only twice have I heard that language. Who are you? What is your true purpose?"

"Why should I answer?" This close to their goal, he'd blown it. He looked at the rows of closed drawers as frustration piled higher. One old man couldn't stop him if he wanted to search.

"From 1931, my father was director here. In 1943, two Nazi officers came and my father heard their boots." As his words picked up speed, the man pounded sharply on the wall. "Bang, bang, bang, down the hall like so, *ja?*"

Theresa's hand, small and warm, slipped into Wulf's.

"My father told me to hide in a chest, so I did not see the men who killed him, but I will never forget their language. It has been my life's study."

Theresa squeezed his hand hard enough to be his anchor as the hair on his arms rose with apprehension. He knew, even without more description, that Unferth had been one of the Nazis who'd killed Haukssen's father. From the beginning of Hitler's domination, Unferth had looted Viking artifacts for his dream of recreating Heorot.

"You were not one of those men. Your voice is different." He pointed at Wulf. "So tell me. How do you speak this language? And *why* are you here?" His pointing hand turned, changed into a plea. "Who killed my father?"

"If you can tell us about Beowulf's hilt—" Theresa jumped in to answer without releasing Wulf's hand. "I promise, he'll explain. It will save lives."

The museum director's gaze dropped to where their hands linked. As if Wulf's connection with Theresa conveyed a message, Dr. Haukssen nodded and crossed to pull a binder from a shelf. "This is a photo inventory of St. Ansgar near Gammel Lejre." After flipping past pictures of architecture and pew carvings, he stopped at a black-and-white glossy of a crucifix. "Approximately 1100, the monks and the Church repurposed pagan items by adding Christian symbols."

Mentally peeling away the decorations on the cross as Dr. Haukssen continued, Wulf struggled to wait through the description. *This one*, his blood thundered, *this is the right one.*

"The crown is formed from the original pommel decoration, an unusual barbed style. Not Germanic like most finds in Zealand." The historian's finger hovered to avoid smudging the photo, and Theresa bent so close her dark hair brushed the old man's sleeve. "The horizontal piece where Christ's arms are nailed was a sword cross guard. I have assumed it was part of a decorative or ceremonial weapon due to its large size."

For fifteen hundred years, Wulf had succeeded as a soldier and a mercenary by trusting his instincts. Now they told him to share his knowledge. "The pommel we seek would have a large red stone in the center. It looks black in some lights." He pointed to the photo. "I don't see it."

"How know you this?" Dr. Haukssen spoke in halting Geatish, the way people read aloud in French or Spanish if they have never heard the rhythms but know the letters.

"I was there." Wulf showed his respect by replying in the old language.

"At St. Ansgar?" The other man's gaze pinned him, as if searching for a lie.

"No, at the start. At Heorot." He stood unmoving before the curator's scrutiny.

"You...you can't be true." The historian stumbled over the idea as much as he did speaking the ancient tongue. "That is fifteen hundred—"

"Many ideas challenge scientific belief. God. Love." He switched to English so that Theresa could understand. "A man like me. That doesn't mean they don't exist."

"You do not look like a—"

"Ancient warrior?" Spreading his hands, he continued. "Two hands, two arms, two legs. Modern tools don't change the man. I pulled the oars with Beowulf. I fought Grendel." He touched the scar on his temple.

"A legend—" He shook his head as if his intellect balked, and yet at another level he must have believed, because he asked, "The man who killed my father? Who was he?"

"Unferth. Hrothgar's skald. He always wanted prestige and never understood it came from courage, not from violence. Now we must stop him."

"I once saw the moon shine on this cross through a window," Dr. Haukssen whispered. "A red glow came from the Christ head. The jewel is under the painted face. This—" he slid the photo from the book and handed it to Wulf, "—is the hilt you seek."

Wulf braced one hand on a cabinet as the proximity to his objective momentarily weakened his knees. Maybe with the DNA they could destroy Unferth, and then maybe—until Theresa's wild proposal he hadn't thought of the possibility in a thousand years—he could become a normal man. For Theresa. For himself.

"But the crucifix is no longer at St. Ansgar."

Theresa stared at the curator, mouth open, her obvious worry reflecting his. Had Unferth beaten them?

"The church needs a new roof and wiring. Its contents are in storage at Sagnlandet Lejre." At their blank looks, he continued. "The historical center at Lejre. It is an outdoor village museum two hours away." His bushy white eyebrows rose. "It is now closed for the winter."

Wulf assessed Theresa's coat. This would require a gear upgrade.

The museum director pulled a ring of keys from a drawer. "I believe tomorrow I shall inventory the warehouse at Lejre. Shall you meet me here at nine?"

The longest part of fifteen hundred years might be the next eighteen hours.

KAHANANUI NAVIGATED THE snow ruts to what he claimed was the seedy section of Copenhagen, but even in the northern dusk the area looked to Theresa to be less sketchy than The Mall at Short Hills. Wulf conversed with Deavers, leaving her to stare silently out the window and wonder about tonight's sleeping arrangements. She'd assumed that they'd continue sharing a bed, but maybe she shouldn't have. Perhaps Wulf had other plans, like retrieving the weapons he and Deavers had been discussing.

"Where are we?" she asked as they slid to the curb.

The yellow-and-white five-story building sported the first graffiti tag she'd seen since arriving. It was a re-cycling symbol.

"Remember Rome?" Wulf said. "New lodgings, in case we were followed."

Shivering, she imagined how cold the sewers were here in February. From the way Kahananui had been driving, with unsignaled turns and frequent mirror checks, she knew none of them expected securing the hilt to be a gimme, but at least Wulf had three of the world's toughest soldiers backing him instead of one measly doctor.

An olive-skinned woman in a skirt far too short for this much snow stopped to stare at the taxi, then shifted a hand to her hip to open her coat.

"It's a hooker hotel." Deavers stated the obvious. "Desk clerk has amnesia."

"I need my suitcase." Her leg charger was still in the previous room, and she'd be immobilized—dead-weight—without it.

"Packed everything when I sanitized the room. It's in the back," Deavers said.

She hadn't realized that's what he'd been doing when she and Wulf went to the museum. She didn't have time to wonder what else she'd missed because Wulf was al-ready offering his hand to help her out of the taxi.

Inside the lobby, an old man sat behind a counter. Without looking up from his sports magazine, he pointed Wulf to a wall of post-office-type boxes. Hundred-krone notes inserted into a door revealed a key card, two con-doms and two toothbrushes, in an admirably Scandina-vian combination of efficiency and hygiene.

"I'd be happy to carry you." Sweeping his arm to

indicate the staircase, Wulf raised his eyebrows, as if that changed his offer of aid into flirtation. "I enjoyed it last time."

He undoubtedly meant to refer to carrying her to the sauna, but she couldn't help picturing her mother and Carl standing in the foyer as he hauled her to her room in New Jersey. Wrong night to remember. Dropping her head, she focused on the carpet and tried to block out memories of her mother's laughter—a little too loud and high, but always Jeanne's signature. Her throat clogged, and she had to squeeze her eyelids tight.

"Don't think about it." He must've guessed the direction of her thoughts, because he hoisted her in his arms and took the stairs two at a time, still talking. "One thing I've learned is when you fall in a pile of shit, dig up, not down. Don't think about what's past."

"Honestly?" This close, she could see the stubble on his cheeks and the tension in his jaw. "That's not helpful. Even my VA therapist wouldn't give you a job." Contradictorily, of course, her spirits lifted. Perhaps being carried as if she weighed nothing was more efficacious than antidepressants.

"I don't have any better material to offer." Setting her on her feet next to door 318, he inserted the key card. "Except sex."

"Why, yes, I think that would qualify as better." The green blinking light, the click of the door, his hand on the small of her back—all of it gave her an almost dizzying sense of déjà vu.

Instead of leaving as he had in Rome, Wulf came in and searched the bathroom, behind the curtains and under the bed. There was no closet, or she knew he would have searched it too.

The room could've been a surgical suite, its walls were so white and the furniture so clean. "Are you sure this is a pay-by-the-hour place?" Even the oversized black-and-white photos resembled high-end waiting room decor, except for their subject matter: extremely large, extremely naked breasts and buttocks. "Maybe Danes really like modern *art*."

Wulf snorted. "Cruz is never mistaken about these things. Stay here while I recon the exits. I'll be back in four minutes."

Chapter Twenty-Seven

THERESA RAISED HER knee and shook her C-Leg to ease the pressure on her stump while she waited. Wulf had ordered her to stay in the room, but it would only take a second to check whether one of the hall vending machines sold baby powder for her sweaty socket liner. The silicone had become uncomfortably sticky from her damp stump sock.

Dismissing the snacks and ice, she fixated on the bright pink *Tabooboo* machine. Line-drawn characters illustrated the display of plain brown boxes. They reminded her of Men Working signs, except these had naked boobs. The box that showed dramatically misapplied jumper cables even had a helpful English label: Nipple Clamps.

Oooo-kay. If she didn't read the rest, she'd burst. Given the picture of a large-breasted figure holding a thick black stick, Pocket Rocket was obvious, but did the box labeled Secret Lippy Vibrator contain Halloween candy lips with batteries, or something entirely different?

Fuzzy handcuffs were seventy-five kroner. She rubbed her fingers over the bills in her pocket.

By the time Wulf came through the door, she'd returned to leaning on the wall in the room, but the two boxes tucked in her coat gave her a secret reason to smile.

"One flight up to the roof, or three down to an alley."

He drew her closer, as if to confirm she was still in one piece. "Cruz is immediately below in 218, and after they pick up the weapons and gear, Deavers and the Big Kahuna will take turns next to the exit stairs. Got that?"

While this safety brief appeared to be Wulf's way of managing risk and its associated messy emotions, she wanted the comfort of his arms. "Got it," she muttered as she slipped her hands inside his jacket. Heat from his dash up and down the stairs radiated from his body.

"Roof door isn't blocked, but with the snow and the roof pitch it's too slippery. Going up is our last resort." Disengaging from her hug, he turned to the door locks and chain. "The alley leads to well-lit streets in either direction."

Her hand hovered where his coat seams stretched across his shoulders, which weren't as squared as usual. "What's wrong?"

"Nothing." He shuddered and planted his fists on the door. "I keep thinking I've forgotten something, and my gut's telling me I've brought you into more danger."

"You didn't *bring* me. I brought myself." She wasn't a super-duper Special Forces hulk, and half the weapons talk in the taxi had been one step away from gibberish to her, but if he didn't recognize that she had a pony in this race too, if he didn't understand how much she wanted to destroy the people who'd killed her stepbrother and cousin, then he could hang his ass out a window, frostbite or no. "Beating Unferth matters to me as much as it does to you."

"That's why I let you come."

"*Let* me?" The ceiling's automatic fire sprinklers showered neither patience nor understanding on her head, no matter how hard she stared up asking for both.

"Who replaced my annoying locavore food-dork with a Neanderthal?" Instead of waiting for him to answer with a reply that would further tick her off, she left him in the entry.

"Sorry," he said, following her to the middle of the room. "Carl told me you're impossible to stop."

"In which of your foreign languages does that count as an apology?" Hands on hips, she watched him approach.

"I didn't tell you how much you helped me today. I doubt Dr. Haukssen would've opened up without you, so thank you."

The sweet words and rueful grin melted her, and his embrace was the mea culpa she needed. "Your inner epicure was doing fine," she told his collar.

"That was all for you, you know. I wanted to make you laugh."

"I gathered." Inhaling against his neck, she caught the scent of snow, if that had a smell, and a hint of his evergreen soap and the hot essence of him.

He ran his hands down her sides, pulling her so close that his coat partially enfolded her and he crushed the stiff corner of one of her purchases into her thigh. "What's that?"

"Umm." Her face started to heat to match his body. Buying the Tabooboo items had been a hell of a lot easier than sharing them would be. "Something I found in the hall."

The man in her arms alerted like a drug-sniffing dog.

"Relax." Wrapping her hand around the back of his neck, she stretched to kiss his ear. "It's nothing to worry about." With her voice pitched low, she hoped he'd understand without her having to spell it out. "Something distinctly *not* to worry about."

The muscles behind his jaw felt as taut as cables under her palms. He didn't know what she meant, so she tugged him to the king-size bed. The less said, the better. "The other guys are on watch, right?" When he nodded, she tossed both boxes onto the crisp white blanket.

He crouched, as if ready to leap and disarm them, until he interpreted their logos. "What—" he grabbed one of her purchases and wiggled it, "—is a Finger Bunny?"

As she circled behind a chair, she giggled at the absurdity of Wulf holding the ridiculous package and knew she'd be totally red-faced. If he opened it, she'd probably code out over the contents, but anticipation bubbled in her chest anyway.

"You've been busy." He shrugged his jacket onto the floor and stalked closer. "Isn't it time to take off your coat?"

The simple task of shaking her arms from the sleeves and hanging her coat on the back of the chair while he watched through half-lowered eyelids felt like stripping, despite the fact that she still wore wide-leg pants and a long sweater.

"You bought *these*—" he plucked the other box, the fuzzy handcuffs, off the bed, "—in the hall too?" He didn't wait for her answer. "This has just become a five-star hotel. No, ten."

She had no idea what to do next. The room seemed to be getting warmer.

"You want to use them?" Sounding like a man talking through a glass of water, Wulf pulled at his collar. "On me?"

He looked willing, not shocked, so she managed to

bob her head. But she wasn't sure she meant it. The toys were only supposed to be a joke.

"Goood night su-*weet* prince, there's *nothing* rotten in Denmark." With dumbfounding speed, he shucked his shoes, socks and everything else until, in what felt like less time than it took her to blink, he was naked and re-clining. One of his muscular thighs was flat on the bed, the other knee was raised and both hands rested under his head. "Flights of angels may sing me to my rest, but they'll have to wait."

Staring at the sprinkling of chest hair that arrowed to his growing cock, she watched that part move, quite literally *jump* in size, against his thigh, while she held her breath.

"Doc, this is Wulf. Wulf calling Doc. Over." He wiggled his fingers by the headboard.

"You got naked so fast!" In theory she had the ad-vantage over him, with her responses covered by cloth-ing and his fully visible, but she knew her control was illusive. If he chose, her warrior could take charge in a second. That certainty made her chest rise and fall faster.

"In the future, around you I intend to wear nothing but pelts. And handcuffs."

His complete comfort exposing his arousal sent her reeling for the safety and predictability of details as she fastened the fabric tabs of the fur-lined cuffs around his wrists. "Technically, these are called restraints, not handcuffs."

"Technically, these are called Santa's-making-up-for-my-crappy-Christmas. And now I also believe in the Easter Bunny, since he's in the other box."

She couldn't speak while she tied the attached cords in bowline knots to the headboard posts and tugged.

She knew she was a babbler, especially when nervous, but the outlines of his triceps where his arms extended on either side of his head had robbed her of words. His body was chiseled, hard, perfect. He hadn't changed since they'd explored each other in the light in Italy, and he never would. Only she had changed.

"I want to see you too." His voice sounded clogged and thick, as if he struggled to speak.

That wasn't possible. Shrapnel had left dots on the skin of her thigh and hip, like pepper on a roast chicken. She couldn't show him, not when he would remember as clearly as she did the way she'd looked before, so instead she traced a path from the edge of the cuff, down his forearm and along the meaty part of his upper arm to his collarbone. Her fingers spread to cover as much of his heated skin as they could. She'd love to watch him like this all night.

"Kiss me." His demand made her raise her eyebrows. Even tied to a bed, he wanted to stay in charge.

When he licked his lips and swallowed, the interplay of the tiny muscles focused her gaze. "Be patient." Her hand caressed his chest, then circled and flicked his nipple.

"No." His stare locked with hers as if trying to bend her will. "Kiss me."

"Stop ordering me around." She pinched his nipple a little harder than she meant to, but since he inhaled and closed his eyes as if he liked it, she rolled the light brown nub between her fingers and pulled. This time he moaned.

Under her clothes, her own nipples quickened as her chest rose faster and higher. She wanted to rub every part of herself, most especially her aching breasts, against him while she watched his responses, but to see his body, she needed light, and light wasn't her friend.

Unless... "Wait." She scrambled from the bed and found a hand towel in the bathroom without pausing to wonder whether he'd agree to being both tied and blindfolded.

"What are you—oh." He saw the towel. "Only if you take all your clothes off."

His commanding tone restored her nerve, which was undoubtedly what the tricky man had intended. "You're tied up. Not the best negotiating position, is it?" Admittedly, the headboard might fall apart if he applied his full strength, but she wanted to pretend as she wrapped the folded cloth around his forehead.

"I have no doubts about how excellent my position is, believe me." He gripped the ties above where the restraints circled his wrists and flexed. The move highlighted every upper-body muscle in perfect, Michelangelo-sculpted display. "But now I can't see, and the internet says that men need visuals, so you should describe everything you do. Out loud. If you want me to, you know, be fully happy."

She glanced the length of his body. "You don't seem to need help with fully happy."

"Please?" His request was what she wanted.

"That will get you somewhere." She dropped her cardigan, then the stretchy shirt she wore underneath. Her mouth had become so dry she had to swallow before speaking. "I took off my sweater." Simple actions she could handle describing made a good start. "And my bra."

Sitting on the edge of the bed, she told him about removing her shoes—she wore two, so both legs were the same height and she looked normal to other people—and socks—also two. Then it was time to lift her pants leg and press the release pin on her prosthetic, but she froze.

"Theresa?" He waited. "I hear you breathing and rustling so I know you're there."

She cringed and held her breath.

"I'm guessing you're doing something that embarrasses you, like taking off your leg."

Either he could read her mind or she hadn't tied his blindfold well enough.

"We had a deal," he reminded her softly. "You'd talk if I wore the blindfold."

"Not about this." As she removed it, the C-Leg felt heavier than usual. She propped it next to the bedside table.

"Why not?" He sounded gentle, not challenging or teasing as he had been earlier.

"Because." While she peeled the gel liner down her stump, the words churning in her chest sorted themselves into a burst of explanation that became more than she'd meant to share. "It's ugly, it's so ugly, and no one talks about it and nobody wants a woman who looks like this."

"My key body parts beg to differ. Your leg isn't ugly to me."

"That's not possible." Not unless he had a freak fetish. There were plenty of those on the internet, but no normal guy could want to see this pink knob where she ought to have had the long, smooth line of a well-toned calf. "You haven't seen what's left."

"Look at me. What do you see?" When he raised his hips from the bed, she couldn't tear her eyes from the proof straining up his abdomen, proof that he wanted her as much as he had when she was whole. "I could be crude and say that spending a day watching your tits jiggle drove your leg so far out of my mind, you could have six or none, I have no idea. All I want is to bone you. Right now. Or should I remind you that I'll act like an idiot to hear you laugh, so why would your leg change how I feel about you?"

Tears pricked at the back of her eyes as she conceded. His evidence was still getting longer and thicker. A man who'd allow himself to be tied and blindfolded deserved her courage in return, so she continued undressing. The grind of metal zipper teeth and the shoosh of fabric against the bedcovers filled the room. "I took off my pants."

He turned his head toward her, and fleetingly she wondered again whether he could see under the towel, but then he asked, "Are you still wearing anything?"

"Panties." His responses made it easy to say.

He groaned. "What color?" Desire lowered his voice.

To hear, she had to lean closer and brace a hand on the mattress next to him. Her hip bumped his scorching, naked skin, and she fought the urge to press her breasts against him.

"What color are they?" he repeated.

Flustered, she had to check. "Black."

"Are they wet yet?"

Touching a shaking finger between her legs, she whispered, "Yes."

"Let me feel." The words brushed her skin with heat. "Sit on me and let me feel them."

The reward for straddling his waist was the pressure of his cock pushing against the fabric, pushing and rubbing on her core each time she rocked over him. Her breasts ached too, so she leaned forward until her nipples pressed his chest, but the friction she could generate herself wasn't enough. Like every other part of her body, her sensitive points ached for more. She stretched to thrust her breast to his lips at the same time she pushed on his probing cock.

He took her offering, and his tongue twirled and lapped while she melted into him. Between nerve-tingling sucks that drove sensation all the way to toes she didn't even have, he whispered into her skin. "If I could, I'd rip your panties off and lick until you came in my mouth." Because he couldn't, his teeth pulled at her nipple. "I'd watch you this time. I'd watch how big and dark your eyes get."

Grinding harder against his steel cock, she imagined him inside her, but she didn't have to settle for fantasy. Tonight everything was in her control. It was a trick to balance on one knee and work her panties off while keeping as much of her skin pressed against him as she could—a good trick, made better by looking only at his body, not her own. The black fabric already smelled like sex from being rubbed between them. She trailed the lace over the hair at his groin and wrapped her panties around his shaft, then slipped the smooth silk up and down between his throbbing cock and her palm until he pumped his hips.

"Ride me now," he protested when she removed her hand to brush the fabric up his sternum and swirl it around his nipples. "Come on."

"Fifteen hundred years and you haven't mastered patience?"

"Nope." After she moved the fabric under his chin, he

inhaled as if seeking her scent. "Will you punish me?" He sounded eager.

She froze, uncertain how to respond.

Sensing her immobility, he also stilled. "You must be angry." So quietly his chest barely lifted, he continued. "Really angry. About the explosion and—"

"No!" Her denial came out too harshly, so she lowered her voice. But she wouldn't let him bring the outside world into their cocoon. "I'm not angry. Not anymore." She'd worked through anger months ago, reached whatever stage this was—probably acceptance.

"It's safe to let your feelings out with me. Nothing hurts me."

That was a load of crap. "I think a lot of things hurt you."

"Not physically," he said.

"I know that." Even without fulfillment, the passion of moments ago had shifted into an intimacy deeper than she'd expected.

"Sometimes I've come close to nothingness, where all I could do was fight, because nothing else touched me." Unable to read his eyes, she concentrated on his lips, which drew downward as he searched for words. "But you—you touch inside where I have missing pieces. It's why I need you. Without you, I'm…" His voice trailed away.

"Empty?" That was a feeling she knew too well.

He nodded.

"Me too." Right now she could tell him all her corrosive secrets, maybe because he couldn't see her. "A lot of the time I feel hollow, like I'm missing more than a leg."

"A shell casing." His voice was quiet. "Sometimes I pick up dead brass on the range and recognize myself."

"No." She pressed a kiss to his chest, then the base of his throat. The salt on his skin tasted like a necessity of life. "You're not empty."

"Neither are you." He paused, as if weighing a decision. "Ray, your leg, your home. I want to give you a chance to get something back, but I need to know you'll forgive me."

She pushed back against the flare his list had lit in her stomach and spoke the rational answer she knew she should give. "You didn't set the bomb."

"Promise you'll forgive me when I'm done."

"I don't understand." The last five minutes had veered out of her control, and she had no idea how, or even whether, to return to what they'd been doing. "What are you going to do?"

Instead of answering, he asked a question. "You're medically discharged, but you're still a licensed doctor, aren't you?"

The reminder of the career she'd left hurt her like he'd thumbed down on a bruise.

"You can still practice medicine, right?" This time he was louder. "Your brain's fine?"

Suddenly chilled, her flesh shrunk from his. "I don't have a traumatic brain injury."

"So you've been too busy feeling sorry for yourself to work? When did letting other people wait on you become your style?" The sneer in his tone came out of nowhere and whacked her with accusation bordering on condemnation.

"I don't let anyone wait on me." As the words popped out, she knew what he would say next and *dammit*, he was telling the truth.

"You're telling me your mother *didn't* cook your dinners and do your laundry? I thought you were a go-getter who didn't give up, but one setback and poof, you quit."

"This isn't a setback." Her nails dug into her palms, and she tried to understand how they'd gone from kisses to insults. What had gone wrong? "This is forever. I lost my leg."

"Whoop-de-do." His mouth twisted. "You have a great mind and eyes and hands. That's more than a lot of other vets."

"You don't know what it's like!" With her fist, she dammed a sob from escaping her mouth. "You're never injured for more than five minutes!"

"You're right, I don't know what it's like to sit on my ass and whine."

"So I'll get a job if you shut up! Shut the fuck up!" Like it didn't belong to her, wasn't connected to her arm or her brain, when her fist bounced off his shoulder she couldn't believe what she'd done. Ohmigod, that wasn't her. She couldn't possibly have hit him.

"See—your hands work. Why haven't you been using them to help people?" One corner of his mouth turned up. "Think losing a leg is your ticket?"

"You don't know what I've lost!" This time she knew the instant *before* she did it, and she listened for the *thwack* of her open palm on the meat of his arm. It even hurt her hand a little, but she felt a shocking stir of satisfaction, as if she'd snatched back a piece of her own strength, until the tide of self-disgust raged through her. "That was wrong! I'm sorry, I—"

"It's fine, Theresa. I'm consenting. In fact, I'm pushing you. Let all the poison out. Use me to—what's the medical term?—lance your wound. I want you to."

His voice kept her eyes focused on his lips as she

covered her mouth with both palms, afraid to free the hands which had become so unpredictable.

"The convoy." He threw out the two words guaranteed to blow up the emotions she tried so hard to lock away. "Tell me about the convoy."

It felt like he'd pulled her stomach inside out through her throat. "Why? Why'd I go?" She didn't recognize the sound that burst from her chest, a sound like crows fighting, but it was the sound of the feelings she was finished hiding from herself, from her group therapy sessions, from the whole damn world. If he wanted her to share, then she would. And she had rage enough to spare. Rage at the army that had tossed her out as easily as a pair of latex gloves, rage at the fucking Afghans and their fucking opium, rage at the whole fucking war, and somehow she smacked his shoulder again and it was louder this time. "Why'd I do it? I knew. I knew it wasn't safe. I knew it before you told me." Each repetition called up her fury at everyone who still had their same old lives, and that fury mixed with the sobs that were shaking her because she had nothing but her shitty new one in her fucking pink bedroom and even that wasn't hers anymore, it had burned along with Ray and her whole fucking life. "You were right and I knew it, but I went anyway. Because I'm stupid." Arms wrapped around herself, she rolled away from his warmth and sobbed out the full truth. "It's my own fault I lost my leg. All my fault."

"No! It's Unferth's. *You* told me that." Next to her, he struggled with his bonds. "And you're not stupid. You got in that vehicle because you cared."

"Everyone says I'm a hero, but I'm just stupid, stupid. And now Ray's dead." She collapsed onto the pillow, drained but still heaving. "Ray's dead and Mom and Carl are—are—"

"They're safe. You'll see them soon."

His voice sounded strong and reassuring, as if she could invest hope in him, but nothing he promised could change how empty and crushed her chest felt. "I've lost everything."

"Not me," he said. "You won't lose me. Not ever."

He couldn't mean that, not after what she'd done. She'd become the type of person she'd been required to report when she found bruises in an exam, a nut job who ought to be in jail.

"I love you."

Despite her violence and tears, instead of telling her off like she deserved, he'd said...*he loved her.* Her next breath wasn't so loud in the quiet room, not so hot and achy, so she took another while his words ricocheted and expanded in her soul. *He loved her.* What he'd said a little while ago about digging up, not down, when life turned into a pile, wasn't as useless as she'd thought. If she chose to start over with him, wherever they lived, whatever she decided to do, maybe they could build a future. *Because he loved her.*

She wanted to share her discovery, and she knew how to begin. Stretching, she shifted closer and looked into his face. The blindfold was askew enough that he could probably see under the edge as she bent to his lips. This kiss was slow, not rushed. Felt in her soul, not merely in her body, it linked two people who shared everything, and she didn't think it would ever stop.

"I love you." His words wrapped her in security. "Untie me so I can hold you."

"I love you too." The words felt right, but they

sounded too quiet and tiny to mark the decision she'd made. She could turn off the lamp next to the bed, or she could take her chances that his love was strong enough to see everything. "I love you." This time she said it louder, louder than the tearing sound of the restraint straps as she pulled them apart, louder than her heart pounding in her chest as she ignored the light switch.

Freed, his arms crushed her into his embrace.

She slid two fingers under the towel and lifted. Nothing on her outside could be worse than the inside she'd showed him, and he loved her. "Look at me."

THE SHOP AROUND the corner was a type Theresa recognized as universal, one that displayed today's pastries in front of yesterday's plastic-wrapped sandwiches and cigarettes. While Wulf ordered breakfast in tourist English, she glanced at a stack of newspapers. A photo above the fold featured the stone facade of the National Museum disrupted by an ambulance and three police cars.

"Buy the paper." Her stomach churned as if she'd slammed five espressos, even though she hadn't yet had her first. From the front page an official portrait of Direktøren Olaf Haukssen, 1935–2014, stared at her. His aristocratic white eyebrows were lost in the gray newsprint.

"Here." She pulled Wulf away from the register, but the shopkeeper and the glass windows made her shoulders creep with anxiety, so she stepped outside and put her back to the stone wall before she pointed at the article. "What's it say?"

He traded her for the bag of pastries. "I don't read Danish."

"What?" She had to remember to close her mouth. "You freaking speak forty languages."

"Not modern Danish." With his eyebrows bunched toward his nose, he studied the paper. "Guys in my profession like hot spots, not cold, stable ones."

"I thought you were pretending with the cashier!" Reaching over his arm, she jabbed at the image of the museum. Snowflakes melted on its surface, leaving splotches like pockmarks. "Police can't be a good thing. And two dates by Dr. Haukssen."

"Død." His finger paused under one word. "I'm sure that means dead."

When a dark, forgotten thought flooded out of her stomach, she had to grab his arm to steady herself. The contact didn't halt her spreading fear. "We overlooked something yesterday."

"I think *stikke* means stab."

"Dr. Haukssen said he'd heard Geatish twice before. Once when his father was killed."

"Uh-huh." He frowned at the page.

"The second time."

Wulf raised his eyes from the paper, and she saw comprehension. A passing cross-country skier who had to step sideways said something rude to them, but she didn't care.

She spoke the thought they must have shared. "We forgot to ask when he heard it again."

Chapter Twenty-Eight

THERESA'S HEAD BOBBED as the taxi van, its defroster
maxed to counter the body heat produced by four men
and her, slogged west from Copenhagen. After she and
Wulf had explained the news of Dr. Haukssen's murder,
the interior had fallen into silence. Jammed between
Wulf and Chris Deavers, she fought to remain alert despite the hypnotic effects of continuous white-on-white
swirling snow.

"Rest." Settling his arm around her shoulders, Wulf
tucked her as near as their lap belts allowed. "It's probably another half hour." On the map the Lejre exit was
twenty-five miles from the outskirts of Copenhagen, but
blizzard conditions tripled the driving time.

If she didn't talk, she'd fall asleep, likely with her
mouth open, which wasn't her ideal pose. "So how'd you
know the guy who gave you the weapons?"

Cruz half turned from the front passenger seat.
"Yeah, before I go *loco* from all this damn snow, what's
the story with your friend Guleed?"

Wulf shrugged. "It was a long time ago."

"Dude, this van is not in a hurry." Even Kahananui
sounded tense. He'd kept both hands on the steering
wheel for the last hour, counter to his normal laid-back
attitude.

As if to delay, Wulf lifted a paper coffee cup that she
knew was already empty.

"Well?" Theresa prodded.

"Fine. Guleed impressed me when he was a kid, and I felt like doing a good deed, so I helped him get an education. After the shit hit the fan in Somalia, I put him in touch with someone who arranged a refugee visa." His shrug brushed her shoulder. "That's all."

"Last night he made it sound like more." Cruz kept pushing.

"Gave him some money to buy his first grocery. Wasn't much."

"Well, now he has four," Cruz said.

"And apparently a crate of guns under his bed," Theresa added. Judging from what she'd seen the team load in the back, Guleed had probably handed over all the assault rifles in Denmark.

When Cruz snickered, Wulf knuckled the back of his head.

"What?" Reaching past Wulf, she cracked the window to blast away her fogginess, but she couldn't endure the wind for longer than five seconds. "What'd I say that was funny?"

"He's laughing at your word choice," Deavers said from her left.

"Guns? Oh, *that*." She rolled her eyes, replaying the ditty sergeants liked to drill into lieutenants who misspoke. *This is my weapon, this is my gun, this one's for shooting, this one's for fun.* "Glad you enjoy twelve-year-old humor."

"Too sophisticated. He's more like eight. Isn't that the age when kids love fart jokes?" Wulf looked across her to Deavers.

"Don't look at me. My oldest's still perfecting knock-knock-banana."

"Yo, backseat comedians, here's your banana." Cruz flipped them the bird.

"I'm still curious. What'd Guleed do that impressed you?" She pictured a scrawny boy rescuing Wulf from a crashed helicopter or breaking him out of jail.

"Bill me for a drink."

"That's all?" Three pairs of eyes—only Kahananui managed to keep looking forward—stared at the man to her right.

"It was a messy drink." He crushed the paper cup, then stuffed it in a bag. "The tab included a coffin. Took nerve for a slum kid to chase me."

While the earlier silence had seemed to result from confirmation of the dangers they faced, this time Theresa imagined they were considering how the former child had aged into a prosperous middle-aged man and Wulf hadn't.

Finally Cruz cleared his throat. "Well, he turned out well. Nice daughter too."

"You met his family?" she asked, intrigued by a link to Wulf's past.

"Oldest girl's an accountant. She was checking the books when we arrived." Kahananui didn't pull his eyes off the road as he answered. "I thought Cruz was MIA when he got a look at the Somali-Swede combo platter."

"Guleed married a Swedish biology professor," Wulf muttered next to her ear. "His wife's tall and rather, ah, impressive."

"As in brilliant researcher?"

"Uhh—"

"Refined my lady plan." She recognized Cruz's tone as the one he used to provoke his teammates. "Not just brainy. Number-cruncher chicks appreciate a man of action, and I could use some investment advice, so I thought—"

"No thinking." This time Wulf rapped twice on the back of Cruz's skull. "Not about any woman I've ever introduced you to, got that? I spent too many nights listening to you bitch and moan in bars on six of the seven fucking continents to want you near—"

Theresa didn't know enough Spanish to understand Cruz's interruption, but she could guess at its content from Wulf's scowl and the other men's laughter.

"Here we are." Kahananui turned right, but half the vehicle wanted to make a U back to Copenhagen. He steered into the skid, and they straightened out pointing the correct direction, if the lower strip of snow between high drifts indicated a road.

As the van inched forward, an entirely different quiet descended. Each man went somewhere in his head. She could sense them planning with an almost physical quality, as if mental readiness was actual gear they donned before a mission. Their focus rubbed off on her, because she absorbed much more than plain white hills from the scene outside. There were shapes under the snow, and it seemed like she could identify them. Fences. Shrubs. Depressions that had to be ditches. Then they stopped.

"End of the line, chimichangas." Cruz zipped his one-piece snowsuit to his neck and jumped out of the front, rifle up as he scanned the hills. Within seconds he'd put on snowshoes, goggles and a pack. "Talkie channel six, right-o? Scout out." And like that, he was gone.

After reaching behind the bench seat, Wulf dumped snow pants and a parka into her lap. "Dress." All intimacy had disappeared as quickly as Cruz.

"I'm not a dog. You don't need to bark." She strug-

gled to disentangle fabric and suspenders while feverishly hoping that the ankle zippers opened wide enough
for the pants to slip over her C-Leg. No getting around
that she was slower and weaker, but she didn't want to
end up floundering from the beginning.

"I'm in charge of keeping you alive."

Thankfully the pants fit over her prosthetic. But she
had to hump up and down on the seat to pull them over
her thighs and butt. Deavers had left the side door open
for air, a godsend because she was already panting and
sweating.

Wulf must've thought she was ignoring him. "For this
op, do as I say, immediately, *no arguments*, or I swear on
a burning longboat, I'll flex-cuff you inside the van, got
it?" His face hardened, as if the word cuff didn't bring
back memories of the night before.

She stared at her trembling hands. How much help
could she offer?

"Hang ten, Wulfie." Kahananui slapped him on the
back, but he didn't relax.

"Remember how to use one of these?" Stepping between her and Wulf, Deavers handed her a nine-milli-
meter Beretta pistol.

Automatically her wrist rotated and her thumb slipped
over the cold metal so she could both feel and observe
the safety lever. On. She must have performed that check
twenty times a day in Afghanistan, every time she put
her weapon on, took it off or cleared it at a barrel outside
a building. For months that movement had been as natural as signing a prescription, and doing it again switched
something inside her to the ready position. The pistol
was a hunk of metal, inert and black, but in her hand it
became so much more.

"Cruz!" Deavers spoke into one of the walkie-talkies Guleed had provided. "Ready to report, or you too busy jacking off? Over."

"All clear. No movement, no lights. Should I recon the targets? Over."

"Negative. Stay hidden. K and I will do close recon after we prep for departure. Over."

"Got it, Great Leader. Out."

Prepping for departure turned out to mean turning the van. She shifted gears and steered while the men pushed until the vehicle pointed toward the highway.

Flushed with cold and exertion, Wulf rested his arms on the window frame and lowered his face to be level with hers. "Ma'am, do you know how fast you were driving?"

"That depends." Looking into his eyes crystallized the urge to kiss him, as if they could sneak one of those you're-here-and-so-am-I-so-let's-kiss moments, even in the middle of robbing a historic site. "Are you the good cop or the bad one?"

"I'm the very bad—" A massive ball of white hit him in the back of the head, knocking his shoulders through the opening and making her giggle.

"Think that's funny?" He mock-growled before he kissed her, cool lips and mint candy and man, but the moment she softened, he pulled away. "Sorry I was hard on you earlier. I'm not used to…" He trailed off with a shrug.

"I promise I'll listen to you and the others. I'll leave if you say it. No arguments." He didn't have to say that she was a distraction or not up to speed. She knew. "Believe me, all I want to do is find the cross and go."

The next snowball thunked into the windshield so

hard she jerked and slammed her elbow into the steering wheel. Luckily she missed the horn.

"Got the message!" Wulf called over his shoulder. "Unless you want to stay in the van, time to get out and join us."

How she didn't fumble the door handle, she didn't know, but somehow she climbed out of the van and stood and her knees didn't shake, at least not visibly.

Within ten minutes of starting the uphill trek, her thighs were shaking and she'd revised any initial enthusiasm for getting intimate with the crunch of snow. Ardently, vigorously, adamantly and vehemently revised. Even with her smart C-Leg auto-adjusted for uneven terrain, snowshoes sucked. The metal teeth on the bottoms of these traylike contraptions didn't prevent her from sliding backward on the incline, so she walked ducklike with the fronts of the shoes pointed out. Unlike the men, she used two lightweight poles as outriggers to keep from tilting left or right, but her thighs still burned worse than a bad bikini wax, worse than a shot of cheap tequila, worse than physical therapy exercises. Chicks from New Jersey did not do shit like this. If they were jocks, they played soccer or skied in the Poconos or even joined the army, but they did not snowshoe. This was hell. That freaking cold day had indeed arrived.

Deavers and Kahananui vanished into the immense grayness where snow clouds merged with snow-covered hills, but she couldn't waste cells wondering where they'd gone. All she did was trudge behind Wulf, lifting each foot in rhythm with a silent litany of profanity that marched two-by-two like ants in a chant in her head, until finally she reached the crest.

The haphazard cluster of a half dozen structures, their

windowless walls topped with white roof humps, disoriented her. She caught up to Wulf on the porch of a barn-size building as he stuck wires into goop he'd pressed along the door frame.

"Stand back," he said.

An instant later low clouds absorbed the echoes from the mini-explosion. Where the door had once had hinges, now it was attached to its frame only by a dead bolt. A noisy break-in should have started an alarm or alerted a guard, but nothing moved. She'd grown up too close to Newark Airport to be comfortable in this blanketing silence.

Inside, Wulf flicked on his flashlight and illuminated rows of display cases and random furniture, all of which probably spent the summer months spread throughout the site.

She stared around the echoing warehouse while she fumbled with her snowshoe buckles. Her relief over finishing the hike was surpassed by the creepy sensation of being watched, and the second set of straps tangled under her heel.

Wulf made a sound, probably disgust, and reached for her hand. "Here." One slice to the palm of her right mitten let her fingers escape. "Get out your weapon. I'll take the second row."

"Guess I'll take the first then," she muttered.

Pistol in her right hand, flashlight in the left, she searched each display case for a large gold cross and checked the contents of each box for references to St. Ansgar or a *krusifiks*. The room was cold enough that her lungs hurt if she didn't remember to breathe through her neck gaiter. Somewhere to her left, Wulf searched a parallel path.

"Anything?"

Asked in a normal voice, his question startled her into a small yelp. Thank goodness the pistol required a double-action pull on the first shot. "Not yet."

She played her light beam over the mannequin at the end of her row, trying to determine why the chain mail-wearing figure made her neck shrink into her shoulders. *It's just an oversized doll, a helmet plopped on a—*

"*Aiiiiy!*" Her scream shattered the icy quiet. The helmet's eye sockets weren't blank. It wasn't an empty suit of armor. It moved, and then so did she. She raised her weapon to firing position, an automatic motion that she'd drilled for years, but she'd dropped the flashlight and it rolled under her foot. Before she could squeeze the trigger to the end of the pull, she went down. Hard. On her butt.

"Theresa!" Wulf burst around the cabinets as the thing stepped off its plinth.

"It's alive!" She scooted into a gap between boxes.

"Get out!" Wulf's submachine gun exploded with sound.

The armored warrior dove behind a stack of crates.

"Go!"

He didn't have to tell her a third time. As she crawled through a gap toward the next aisle, her hood caught on the underside of a table, but it released after a hard tug. She kept moving.

Then a howl erupted up and down the sound spectrum, a howl so otherworldly that even encased in fleece and goose down, she froze. She wanted to curl up and cover her head, hide, but that motion was more than she could force from her muscles.

"Unferth!" Wulf's shout told her the last thing she wanted to know. Another immortal was here.

The floor of a museum warehouse was shitty place to die.

Chapter Twenty-Nine

DESPITE TWO CENTURIES, Wulf recognized the skald's battle cry and emptied his magazine at the other immortal's hiding place. "Scared of a real fight?" Taunting his opponent in the old tongue felt like it carried a greater sting. "Come out and face me, you teat-sucking bag of pig shit." He tossed aside his useless weapon and slammed his shoulder against the stacked crates, relishing the chance to directly confront the traitor even while fearing the threat of another immortal to Theresa and his teammates. The best way to give them a head start was to offer himself as a target. He rammed the crates again.

The Viking leaped out. Gleams reflected from his sword helped Wulf maintain his distance as he lured his opponent farther from Theresa. Deavers and Kahananui would've heard the gunfire. They'd be here—already were, he was sure—and they'd whisk her to safety. All he had to do was occupy Unferth. "Nice costume, fish belly. Almost makes you a warrior."

Crack. A round winged his upper arm, but the problem wasn't the shot. The problem was the shooter, who had to be a left-hander because he'd screwed himself with the Chinese assault rifle's righties-only configuration and decided to rush Wulf.

Wrong choice.

He grabbed the cheap-ass Chinese rifle, shoved it skyward and went hand over hand down the barrel to

the stock while wild shots crisscrossed the ceiling. With
the magazine emptied, he couldn't waste time struggling
for a worthless metal stick. He shoved the rifle butt at
the man's chest and spotted an emergency fire axe on
the wall, then smashed the glass panel and grabbed the
force multiplier. The alarm and flashing strobe kicked
on, momentarily freezing his opponent, but not him.
Axe, meet neck.

Start to finish, the fight didn't take enough time to
tie a shoe. But it was long enough for Unferth to abandon his sword and disappear.

ING-NG-NG-NG. UNDER THE table, Theresa had heard Wulf
yell Unferth's name, then a close barrage of shots. Then
the shrieking alarm had surpassed all other noise. Her
mission to find the cross was replaced by a need to stay
sane. Holy Mary, the siren and lights spiked her brain
and limited coherent thought to the bursts of silence,
which were too short to form a new plan. *Get out*, Wulf
had ordered. So she'd go.

Before she ditched her concealment, she checked the
aisle. To her left, two men crouched, one pointing an ef-
fective-looking automatic rifle her way, the other behind.
Deavers and Kahananui. The surge of relief raised her
to her elbows and almost drew her from under the table.

Her mistake. Deavers pointed his weapon, and she
smushed herself to the floor as more gunfire doubled the
chaos. In the strobe, she spotted two figures to her right.
Unferth, still armored, had replaced his sword with a
rifle. The other man crouched behind a two-wheel cart
replica. Muzzle flashes provided the only color in the
alarm light's on-and-off flicker. She was stuck between
the shooting groups.

If she was reinvented as one of her stepbrother's game characters, she would have known how to save everyone in the room, but she was no action star. She was a crippled nobody, scared to emerge from her hole.

Time slowed enough for her to understand that Deavers and Kahananui didn't have a shot at the second attacker. She had the only clear field of fire to the guy concealed by the cart.

Wulf's order had been unambiguous: get out of danger. In the van she'd promised to obey him, but her reflexes didn't seem to care what the rest of her had agreed to. They listened to the single word that carried the argument. *Raymond.*

Her stepbrother wouldn't have hidden under a table if she'd been murdered, not even if he had the world's hottest game console. Deliberately, she shifted her elbows into a sturdy support triangle. Raymond would've charged out and whacked anyone in his reach. He'd been a regular North Jersey guy that way. His memory deserved no less honor from her. While her left hand cradled her shooting hand, her trigger finger found the hard metal curve. Strobe flashes confused her sense of timing, but the slight recoil in her grip was real enough, until the pistol stopped moving when she squeezed the trigger.

Empty.

The man behind the cart had fallen to the ground in a lifeless sprawl, but Unferth stood boldly in the aisle returning fire to Deavers and Kahananui. This battle wouldn't end as easily as the fights in Italy.

The armored monster turned in her direction.

She should've run.

WULF REACHED THE AISLE, where Unferth stood near a sprawled body. Besides the immortal, there had been only the two others, as if without Black and Swan, Unferth was reduced to his last man. Thirty feet away Theresa was on the floor in a credible prone firing position. Past her, Kahananui crouched over Deavers, who had the dark mark of blood on his light gray pants. His best friend's grimace corroded Wulf's soul. He'd invited them to this fight. He'd damn well better get them out.

He leaped and slammed the fire axe between Unferth's shoulders, but the tool rebounded off the layered metal rings. The armor was too strong. He dropped the weapon and hooked his arm around the immortal's neck as the other man turned. They toppled into a display, and quills of glass and wood punctured Wulf's parka. The chain mail loops were a slippery alloy, woven too tightly to penetrate but too thick to bunch in his fist. He kneed his writhing opponent's back but couldn't pin him.

Kahananui rushed toward Theresa's hiding spot.

"Get out!" Wulf yelled.

As soon as the big guy lifted Theresa and thrust her at Deavers, he turned to Wulf.

"No! Go!" In case his friend couldn't hear, he chanced making the Ranger hand signal to disperse. "Save them!" He'd be fine, but they had to go, and go now.

Thank Thor, Kahananui obeyed orders.

Unferth jabbed a hunk of splintered wood at his face, and he jerked to the side, the addictive adrenaline of a dirty fight revving him like the big Detroit engine in Cruz's classic car. As Wulf plunged a glass shard from his sleeve through the helmet's eye hole, he had no time to think about how clipped Deavers must have been if they were willing to leave. While Unferth's scream

blended with the alarm, Wulf dug through debris until
his hand closed around a metal chunk with a heft similar to a claw hammer. He raised it like a club.

At the top of his swing, a gem above his fist caught
the light, and like a dog blessed with color vision he saw
red in the next flash. He had the hilt.

The surge of mission accomplishment propelled Wulf
to head butt the other Viking deeper into the stack of
furniture. As he scrambled out of the wreckage clutching the crucifix, pain erupted from the back of one calf
and he fell. The bastard bard had cut his Achilles ten-
don. From the floor he could see Theresa's face—nothing more than a circle of mouth and giant fearful eyes
as she stretched one hand toward him, the other to Kahananui, who had Deavers slung over his shoulders. He
wouldn't make it to them.

"Take it!" Wulf flung the gold cross along the floor.

She dropped to her knee and made a perfect save,
catching the relic a moment before Kahananui's fist
hauled on the back of her coat.

"Go, dammit!" Wulf's arm extended toward the door,
pointing palm down, willing them to follow his command and move out even as he struggled to raise his
body.

Thumbs-up, Kahananui acknowledged, and then he
hauled the other two away.

Wulf rolled, the fastest way to move without using his
leg. Behind him, Unferth had the fire axe in one hand
and the bloody glass shard in the other. Until his ten-
don healed, Wulf would have to keep the other Viking
busy. The nearest missile was a piece of pottery, which
the other immortal didn't bother to dodge. Nor did he
flinch at the horseshoe that bounced off his chain mail.

Wulf would have traded both nuts to find a loaded assault rifle in this mess, but the longer they played cat and mouse, him throwing and rolling, Unferth batting almost blindly, the farther the others could escape.

As he slithered toward a broken oar, a hard object in his pocket dug into his pelvis, reminding him that he did have a bigger bang. Along with the rifles, Guleed had supplied a Soviet grenade. It was probably forty years old and useless as wet toilet paper, but what the fuck.

ONE OR THE other of Theresa's legs sunk in snow with every step, up to her calf if she floundered into one of Kahananui's footprints, or all the way to her knee when she broke her own craters. She'd fled without the snowshoes, and already she'd tumbled to all fours half a dozen times crossing a hundred feet. Guaranteed the only way she could have been forced to appreciate snowshoes was to try maneuvering without them, which made her previous hike seem like cruising the mall.

"Cruz, you up?" Carrying the added weight of his commander, Kahananui sank twice as deeply as she did, but he maintained calm into his walkie-talkie. "Boss is leg shot. Exit time."

Chris was muttering—maybe orders, maybe profanity—as he hovered at the edge of consciousness. A tourniquet had worked enough magic that the splotches in the snow fell farther apart, but the clock was ticking on the golden hour. Even without knowing his vitals, she assumed that he required a transfusion.

She didn't hear Cruz's response to Kahananui, but it must have been good, because he whooped and shouted something that sounded like, *I love your mama.* "Come on, Doc," he yelled as he slogged around the next building.

Icy air sliced her lungs and stung worse than the stitch burning low on her left side, but she pistoned through the drifts to catch up. No quitting, not now.

Around the corner, Kahananui had halted at an open-sided shed.

She braced on the log wall, gasping. Three snowmobiles, a dusting of white on their seats and wind guards, sat under the shed. Unferth and his fighters must have arrived on them.

"My lawn mower's bigger." Kahananui kicked the side of the machine on which he'd propped Deavers, whose skin was almost the color of the fresh powder at their feet. "No fucking way this Euro scooter will carry the boss and me."

The captain looked down at his injured leg and moaned. His eyes rolled up to pure white at the same time his head and shoulders started a slow tumble to the side. "Catch him!"

Despite his size, Kahananui was quick to grab the other man. "You'll have to drive with him."

"Tell me how it works." She stuffed her hands in her armpits, regretting her lost gloves, and hoped her frozen fingers could grip the handlebars. Thankfully Raymond had familiarized her with motorcycles.

"Starter is the red button." Kahananui talked while he boosted her in front of Chris's slumped form. "Right lever's the throttle."

"Brakes?" The seat was wider than a motorcycle, and as cold between her thighs as a morgue cart. The metal cups would be foot stirrups. She easily inserted her left boot, but stuffing her prosthetic into the other cup was like threading a needle with rubber tubing.

"Left lever." Kahananui's massive glove shoved her

foot into place. "But go easy. Better to stop by letting up on the throttle." Judging by the way he looked over his shoulder at their footprints while he cinched the captain to her body, he didn't think they had time to waste. The two-sentence tutorial would have to suffice. He ordered the man behind her to wake up.

"Owww, thasss my ha-ir." Slurred words. Another sign he was fading.

"Hold on, or else I'll pull out more, haole boy."

The snowmobile's engine turned over, caught, steadied into a rumble. She exhaled a breath she hadn't known she was holding. At least she wasn't doomed to be one of those women stuck sputtering while the bad guys closed in. She jammed the gas lever—

Boom. Her duck reflex took her and Deavers forward, but mercifully they didn't tip.

Behind her, Kahananui ignored the explosion and fired up his snowmobile. "Go!"

She obeyed, even though each bump of the snowmobile warred with her instinct to turn the machine around and find Wulf, the way he'd found her in that burning vehicle months ago. But she'd promised to leave him, and the man behind her needed more help than they could provide during a firefight.

Following Wulf's last order was the hardest commitment she'd ever made.

EXIT. WULF'S LIFE shrank to one word as the floor scorched his bare palms and the treasures around him ignited. Dragging himself forward was the only route to salvation. Behind him planks popped into flame as fire fingers chased his useless leg. He hadn't unleashed an ordinary fragmentation grenade. Guleed's treasure had been thermite, molten droplets guaranteed to sear. Rolling under a displayed boat had spared him from instant incineration, but escape meant crawling through hell one handhold at a time.

Burning roof timbers collapsed, feeding the fire with fresh oxygen. Accumulated snow dropped through the roof hole and vaporized in the inferno, and for a fraction of a second it seemed as if Loki's chilled hand brushed Wulf's cheek and tantalized him with the outside cold.

The green running-man sign beckoned, and he heaved and scrabbled onto the porch. A second later he rolled down the steps into snow—blissfully, brilliantly, killingly cold snow. The seared soft places of his lips and tongue needed moisture. He struggled to lift a handful to his mouth, but the white fluff melted on his black glove.

Glove?

He'd removed his gloves with his snowshoes. The black coating, dark and glistening like a wet suit, was layers of his skin. Where the snow sizzled on his hands, sheets of blackened tissue shed to show red muscle and white bone beneath. Decades ago, he and Jurik had speculated about how much fire it would take to end their type of life. Burning at the stake wasn't enough—Jurik had experienced it—but they'd assumed charcoal and ash couldn't heal without living cells.

Today was not the day he would discover an answer for Jurik.

As he buried his open mouth in the snow, the heel on his damaged leg finally swiveled and pushed him an inch. He'd walk soon, even if his hands were stubs.

Unferth staggered off the porch, armor glowing. Snow hissed in his steps.

"Not so tough without an army behind you." His opponent yanked at a porch plank.

"Tough enough to destroy you and your company." Pushing to his elbows and knees, Wulf prepared to test whether his leg could hold weight.

"Black and Swan was mine." Board in hand, Unferth lurched toward the edge of the hill.

"Took your secret lab too." Wulf stood, but his hands couldn't handle a weapon, and he wasn't steady enough to kick.

"Did your brother enjoy the accommodations? I'll offer a better view next time." Unferth spun a circle with the board, laughing. "Thank him for his contribution to science. He won't be so quick to treat the rest of us like thrall in the future." Unferth's humor hinted at dark knowledge beyond Wulf's and chilled him more than the snow. "He will show me respect!"

"Why should he? You're a coward and a sneak." Every minute he kept Unferth talking was a minute he grew stronger. "You styled yourself Hrothgar's bard, but it's not even your story people still read, is it? It's Galan's version of the tale." After fifteen hundred years, the Vikings knew which wounds to jab when they met.

Unferth kicked his board to the edge.

"Running away like always?"

"No honor in fighting you."

"What do you know about honor? You're fleeing like a bantling!" Wulf floundered forward, struggling to balance. "You've never had honor, not since you tried to trick Beowulf with your useless sword. Like you, it gave up on the first blow."

"But I haven't given up." He was still laughing as he dropped to his makeshift sled. "Ask your brother if he's found everyone."

Don't wrap around a tree. Theresa repeated directions in her head because her lips had iced shut, but she failed to follow the biggest one: *don't think about Wulf.* The wind blew tears out of her eyes and froze them on her lashes, but it also cleared her brain to focus on driving the snowmobile. She'd fooled around with a motorcycle less than a handful of times, but she thought she might have a knack for this machine. Survival skills weren't taught in the classes she'd taken at Princeton, but maybe she'd absorbed more from Carl than she'd realized.

Or maybe Wulf had been right when he accused her of being an adrenaline junkie.

The van materialized in front of her, its white paint nearly invisible against the snow. Kahananui pulled up behind and untied Deavers. The absence of her passenger's weight released her tension, and she slumped.

Kahananui crouched beside her, rifle up, and that was when she discerned a speck on their trail, closing quickly. Her chest rose, hope that it was Wulf warring with fear of another attack, but she didn't have time to settle on a reaction before Kahananui said, "Cruz," and lowered his rifle.

Not Wulf. He was still on the hilltop, where the museum burned like a reenactment of Beowulf's pyre. A phrase from Seamus Heaney's translation came to her: *And flames wrought havoc in the hot bone-house.*

"Wulf and a movie-character crazy headed for the woods." Cruz didn't dismount from the third snowmobile. "I want to ride after them."

"Negative. He ordered us out."

Cruz opened his mouth to argue, but Kahananui cut him off. "I don't like it either." He jerked his head at the back of the van, where he'd set Deavers's limp form. "But the boss is sucking fumes."

Theresa twitched a silver space blanket from the bench seat and tucked it around Chris's shoulders. He groaned and rolled his head, as if approaching consciousness. "We need to warm up the van."

Cruz still didn't look like he agreed, so the Hawaiian uncrossed his arms and pointed at the hilltop. "That flare is going to draw mega-attention. No way we can be here eating soup when the Five-Os arrive with sirens and lights."

Cruz stayed on his snowmobile. "Guess I missed your promotion to chief dick in—"

"Knock it off!" Theresa forced them to look at her instead of each other. Without a word being spoken, the dynamic shifted. Maybe because she was a doctor or an officer, or maybe because she was Wulf's woman—she didn't know why exactly, but she knew it was her call.

"Chris needs more medical attention than he can get here, so we go. All of us." She wanted to stay, wanted to find Wulf as much as Cruz did, but that wasn't what he'd wanted. And she knew the last thing he'd accept was another one of them getting hurt trying to help. "Get in, both of you, and start driving."

WULF WATCHED AS Unferth's board slid several hundred feet and stopped on a flat. He could leave, follow Theresa and the others. As if he floated over his own body, he saw himself collapsing into her arms and burying his face in her hair. The need to join her almost tripped him before he jerked himself back to reality.

Unferth wasn't conceding. In a day or two he'd recover. More innocents like Dr. Haukssen would cross his path. And whoever he'd stashed in another lab would still be a prisoner if Wulf didn't find out more. This fight had to end, as permanently as he could manage, even though the pain in his hands had worsened. Burns did that. Dead flesh left craters of agony that defied healing longer than a simple cut. Without his hands, he didn't have a chance of making or carrying a sled.

A rain barrel stood under an eave. He bucked it with his hip and torso until it tipped, then pushed with his thighs and elbows, aiming for the spot where Unferth's ride had started.

Below, the other man stood. "Give up yet, Wulf? You're slower than a three-day shit." At this distance the shout sounded thin and weak. "Hear your brother's calling a meeting of the Thing to remind everyone that he's in charge. Can't imagine what they'll think of his hand."

"Imagine away." Freezing air sliced deep in his lungs with each panting breath. He'd have to remember to tell Ivar one of the supposedly loyal immortals was double-dealing, although thankfully none had fought alongside Unferth today. "Where are your usual toads? Dumped you too?"

He ducked into the barrel and pushed with his stronger leg until gravity took charge of the roll. His head snapped from his chest and banged against the wood as he thumped down the slope, braced with his knees and elbows while the world churned and he rode his idea to the end.

Krrrakk. The barrel slammed into an immoveable ob-

ject and disintegrated. Blood filled his mouth, so much
that he had to spit into the snow. As he came to his knees
using the strength in his abdomen and legs, his eyes
tracked footprints from Unferth's abandoned board to
the edge of the woods. Using his elbows and chest, he
maneuvered a broken barrel stave into the pocket between his armpit and his triceps. The primitive weapon
and the wind-borne ashes fluttering around him combined to strip him of the soft lures of modern life and
drive him to his feet. Warriors went to their destinies
upright, not crawling like a worm or kneeling like a
supplicant.

The barrel had crashed into a stand of marsh alders,
ice rivulets twining between their roots like snares. He
hadn't entered this bog in fifteen hundred years, not
since they'd followed the gore trail from Heorot. Logi-
cally, he knew they hadn't walked over this exact spot.
That trail would be gone or farther south or drained by
generations of farmers, but his gut roiled with fear staring into the wasteland of his nightmares. Armed only
with a piece of shattered wood, no sword, no shield, no
brother in the lead, he had to proceed. Tonight the fight
was his alone.

THE VAN WAS too dark inside to see Deavers's injuries
without night vision gear. Why she was surprised when
Cruz pulled a set of NVG out of his bag, she didn't know.
He also provided a complete medical pack, so she set to
snipping her patient's pants in order to clean and assess
his wounds. His vitals were already improving.

Before she finished, Chris opened his eyes and muttered, "What happened?"

"Don't move, okay?" She raised one surgically gloved

hand to reassure him, but he groaned and his eyes again rolled back and out he went. She looked at her glove. Saw blood.

"How's the boss?" Cruz knelt beside her while Kahananui drove. He had to raise his voice over the grind of the van's gears, but he didn't take his gaze or his rifle scope off the road behind them. "How bad?"

She knew every Special Forces soldier had medical training exceeding that of most EMTs, so Cruz would know in a glance that the nickel-size hole inches below Chris's buttock was more annoying than dangerous. Hand on the floor, she balanced herself through another fishtailing swerve. "See for yourself."

"That's it? Did you check for an exit wound?"

"That is the exit wound." The entrance wound was an even cleaner circle on his quadriceps. "He stuck his leg out too far."

"Then what's wrong—"

"I suspect your fearless leader is having an episode of vasovagal syncope. He'll recover."

"Huh?" Cruz looked between them again, then back at the road, but the grooves around his eyes and nose had deepened. "That's one I don't know. What do you do for it?"

"Kahananui had the right idea when he pulled his hair. Does your kit have sal volatile?"

"Wulf's not here to translate that, ma'am."

No, he wasn't, and that cut into her, so she kept talking. "Smelling salts. In vasovagal syncope, the patient's heart rate and blood pressure drop after a trigger, such as anxiety caused by the sight of one's own blood. All those guys who hit the floor when they see the needle pull out after immunizations? Vasovagal syncope."

"You're saying he fainted? That's all?" As she nodded, Cruz began to grin. "From seeing his own blood?" The last word stretched with disbelief.

"He did lose a fair amount." Her caveat didn't stop the other soldier's laughter. Poor Chris. "But yeah, he's basically—"

"A pussy." It must have taken years of training to learn to steady a weapon while laughing that hard, but Cruz managed.

"That's not quite how I would've put it."

"'Course not, Doc, you're too polite. But you've got more balls than Miss Christy here."

TREE TRUNKS CLOSED behind Wulf. He stumbled over a bottle and saw a plastic bag pinned by brambles, but deeper in the woods, signs of modern life disappeared. The crunch of crusted snow, the rattle when he snagged underbrush and the squelch where patches of sulfuric mud hadn't frozen returned him to his Nordic origins.

He heard a metallic clink behind him and spun with the barrel stave clutched as lancelike as he could manage without useable hands. It slapped Unferth's chest and knocked him to his knees. Gouging with the splintered plank would've been effective, but the other Viking ducked.

When Wulf tried to readjust the angle of his wooden weapon, it fell from his armpit, so instead he kicked the side of the immortal's helmet.

Unferth's scream stretched longer than the startled flights of crows from the far trees. He rolled on the ground, clutching the helmet, and jerked it from his head.

Wulf's first look at the other man's exposed face repulsed him into backing away from the next kick. In the forge of the burning warehouse, the protective cover had melded with Unferth's scalp, jaw and cheeks. Charred skin and muscle filled the helmet, and its removal revealed Unferth's skull. A rectangular patch of skin remained around his eye sockets, where scorching metal hadn't flayed his face, but the rest of the Viking had become a death's-head.

"We're where we started," he rasped from Wulf's feet. "Aren't we?"

Horror bred pity for the man below him, and with it the need to understand. He couldn't reconcile the swathe of destruction with the broken shell at his feet. "In the name of Balder's son, why?"

The immortal tried to roll toward a rock, but the bubbling mud at the edge of the dark pond sucked at his chain mail, and Wulf remembered Unferth's earlier taunt.

"Who else did you capture?" If one of the men he'd known for centuries, someone he'd shared bread and battles with, was being tortured like Ivar had been, he'd kick the information out of Unferth. "Who?"

"Expecting a deathbed confession?" Unferth's fingers stretched toward the stone. "Find someone who dies."

Wulf no longer controlled even a stick, but with hands, the most deadly weapon, Unferth could still threaten.

Beowulf had killed Grendel with his hands.

If Wulf waited for Unferth's answers, he'd have another fight. Rotted logs dotted the waterline, and Wulf slammed his burnt arm stubs deep into a soft chunk of wood. He shrieked with the agony the impact shot through him, but the log stuck on his forearms as he raised it.

If he closed his eyes while he crushed Unferth, he could miss. So he had to witness each blow. Witness the skull, eyes now glazed, break off the neck.

And then he threw up.

But he couldn't leave the body. That would be too temporary.

On his knees at the edge of the mere, he watched until no bubbles broke the black surface of the water. Maybe the chain mail would keep the torso down, and maybe kicking the skull into a tree had doomed the other Viking. Maybe without a companion to put his head back, as Ivar had done for Wulf on the plains of Mongolia, the immortal couldn't forge himself into a man again. Maybe there was an end.

Cold gelled the blood in Wulf's veins. Slowed him, now that he didn't have to fight. Theresa and his friends and his brother would be safe. He could lay in the leaf mold, rest.

His fight had finished.

Chapter Thirty

THERESA'S NEEDLE WENT smoothly through Deavers's thigh, bringing the skin together as neatly as stitches performed in a clinic. Guleed's dining room table was a fine substitute, so long as she didn't let the sweaty, armed bodies stalking from door to window and back to table distract her.

"What can I do?" Cruz loomed at her elbow like an expectant father.

"Don't block my light." She tied off the thread. A steady saline drip had brought Chris back to grumpy coherence. Besides stitching, her task was to keep him from seeing his own blood. "If you can't cough up an X-ray, I'd settle for a shot of lidocaine."

"Vodka?"

"I was referring to him, not me." She pushed on her patient's side, indicating he should roll to his stomach so she could tackle the exit wound.

"So was I, ma'am."

"You wouldn't." She looked up. "Alcohol depresses breathing function."

Chris's throat vibrated with the sound of a man trying to transfer a load of pain. No way around it—stitches without anesthetic hurt. "Vodka. With hot sauce."

"Not a chance." She slipped the curved needle through his skin. "Only a few more."

Cruz looked at his captain. "Reindeer?"

Focused on her handiwork, she hadn't noticed the captain's goofy underwear until now.

"Married dudes go extreme for attention, don't you?"

Chris unfisted an appropriate middle finger in response, but before Cruz could reply, a double ding drove the men into ready stances. As his men bounded across the room, Chris automatically tried to roll off the table, but she braced him with both hands. Eyes and weapons swiveled to the door, which Kahananui pantomimed opening.

Guleed reached for the knob with the speed of VA paperwork.

No one breathed as the door swung a foot into the room.

Theresa recognized Ivar in the apartment hall and stretched a hand toward Cruz, who stood behind the door holding a business-size blade. "It's okay! It's Wulf's brother!"

The Americans froze. Guleed was the first to grasp that the man in the hall was a friend, and partly responsible for his successful life in Denmark, so he extended both arms in welcome.

"What's on your gl—uhhh." Chris's eyes weren't seeing her messy surgical gloves anymore, dammit, and after she'd been so careful to keep them out of his sight.

Unsurprisingly, introductions were curt, given the personalities and weapons stuffing the room. As she whipped through her final stitches with Deavers enjoying his eyelids, she filled the silence. "Glad to see you, Ivar." She was. He was out in public, moving among strangers, a good sign of recovery. "How'd you know where to find us?"

"I left New York within the hour upon learning of

Dr. Haukssen's murder," he answered. "We have a long association with Mr. Abdirahman, so I began here at his home."

"Must be how a chick feels when her boyfriend's married," Cruz muttered. "Lone Wolf forgot to mention his freaking pack."

"My brother and I are not, and never have been, furry." Ivar stared at Cruz.

Theresa wasn't certain whether he'd intended to be funny or issue a clarification, but the stink of unused adrenaline rolled through the room. "Guys, we're all on the same side."

"Where is my brother?"

Her face must have conveyed the *not here* part of the answer, because his good hand wrapped around the black-gloved fingers protruding from his sling.

"He ordered us to leave him at Lejre." Her voice was low, but carried through the silent room. "It was Unferth, by himself against Wulf, and he made us promise to get out."

"I see." He swallowed, and stared at each person in the room.

She was too exhausted to decipher his expression. Maybe it was worry, maybe disgust or anger, or maybe nothing and she was extrapolating her own feelings.

"My jet is being refueled. By the time we reach Kastrup, it will be cleared to depart." He pivoted to the door. She couldn't see his face, but his shoulders hunched enough to shift his coat.

He wasn't going to do anything? Although his inaction was nominally for their protection and part of Wulf's wishes, Ivar was abandoning his brother. She'd do well to remember that he could walk away that easily.

No one else moved or spoke, so a response, like the explanation, fell to her. Sour as her words were, she knew what Wulf expected. "After I tape this gauze, we can go."

"WE LAND AT Teterboro in forty-five minutes." Ivar placed a mug of tea in front of her. He wasn't the warmest guy, but he'd decisively removed them from Denmark before they could be connected to the chaos at Lejre. When the jet refueled in Burlington, Vermont, Kahananui's Fort Drum friends had had a truck waiting. They were the type of buddies who didn't ask questions, and by now Wulf's teammates were in the shelter of the army. Deavers would be running laps in a week, although she imagined it would be far longer before the team stopped rolling their eyes and swooning in front of him.

"We didn't clear immigration in Burlington, merely refueled. Here's your passport." He handed her a dark blue pamphlet that miraculously held her photo and several stamps, as if the person inside was well traveled.

"Where'd you get this? It looks real."

"You are my assistant." He ignored her question. "We've been in Venice for a long weekend and we had a fuel stop in Copenhagen, then Vermont, that's all."

"I've never been to Venice."

"If the immigration officer asks, blush. Imply you didn't leave the hotel."

"Oh." She squinted at him, but she couldn't imagine Ivar in the clutch of passion.

"Think of my brother if it helps." The iceman raised one eyebrow.

"Oh." Warmth crept from her neck to her ears.

Personal immigration service for executive-jet passengers was as customer-oriented as ordering at a café. To Wulf, she would have whispered, *May I have a regular skinny with my suitcase, please,* and he would have snorted and bought her one at the first coffee drive-through. His brother would have pinned her to the spot with a glare if she'd opened her mouth during the process.

Of course Ivar had a limo waiting. They were on the road to Manhattan within fifteen minutes of landing. "Where are we going?"

He ignored her to thumb through data on his phone. "He has not contacted me."

"Would he?" The glow from his small screen illuminated Ivar's frozen face, and she wondered whether he worried more or less than she did. She loved Wulf, but Ivar was the one who'd been imprisoned. "Normally?"

"I regret this waste of resources," Ivar said.

"What?" They hadn't hit traffic into the city, so she didn't understand what had been wasted.

"The additional losses without gain." His voice sounded as dark and faraway as the water below the bridge.

He didn't know. Neither she nor the others had told him, not at Guleed's, and not on the long flight when they'd all slept. "But we found the hilt." She fumbled in the overnight bag Ivar had handed her. "Here." She held out the crucifix.

He held it like a new baby, with both hands, and stared, but the plastic bag she'd wrapped around the relic obscured the red gem.

Her fingers hovered over his shoulder, but she wasn't sure he'd like to be touched.

"I have leased laboratory space. Equipment is ordered. And I've sent for someone who can acquire the arm bone for you." Headlights reflected on the sheen of his eyes. "Wait for Wulf at my home. He will come there for you."

She refused to consider other endings.

Through the windshield, the bright lights and right angles of Manhattan posed a direct contrast to the snowy hills of Lejre. The city was where she wanted to hide, where she felt safest, and where she had ideas to test and promises to fulfill. Ivar might believe Wulf would appear soon, but she couldn't forget the inferno they'd left in Denmark. And she knew from experience that immortal Vikings had a very different sense of time.

A CLIPBOARD AND questions helped Theresa control her anxiety. If she focused on the patient in the opposite chair, she might forget for a moment that Wulf hadn't returned or phoned for over a week. The woman, a refugee from Africa, had a yellow pocket of pus on the back of her hand that would have to be lanced and drained by a doctor at this women's clinic fifty blocks north of Ivar's town house.

"Dr. Chiesa, she doesn't speak Amharic or Arabic." The college student who helped as an interpreter flipped through a phone roster. "Maybe it's Tigrinya, from the north of Ethiopia or Eritrea? Our interpreter list doesn't include an Eritrean." Her wide brown eyes sought guidance.

"Try a calendar. Maybe she'll point to the day she was injured." Until New York verified her board certification and issued her a license to practice, her volunteer work was limited to patient-intake interviews.

"There's one in the next cube." The student jumped to her feet. She hoped to attend medical school.

Theresa acknowledged a different goal. She hoped helping the flow of women, twenty an hour through five exam rooms, would fulfill the promise she'd made to Meena and herself back in Afghanistan. She wanted to make a difference, and she had to balance the isolated world of Ivar's research lab and mansion with the hum of human contact.

While she waited, Theresa stared at the women's health posters covering the tan walls of the cubicle she used. *Hope is not a method.* Please let Wulf be free, not locked under stone like Ivar had been. *Are you pregnant? ¿Estás embarazada?* She'd trade the chance to look like that big-bellied woman to hold Wulf in her arms. *Chlamydia is not a flower.* That one was mind-blowingly awful, and not the calendar she needed.

The door jingled. Unseen women in the waiting area burst into giggles. *Must be a baby.*

Her interpreter returned to the cubicle, smiling. "Here's the calendar."

"Thanks." She turned to the patient in the dark skirt. "This is today." She pointed to the date. Ten days since she and Ivar had returned. Ten days without a word from Wulf. "Your sore?" She pointed to the patient's arm and ran her pencil over the week before. "What day?" While the woman answered with a burst of language and pointed to three different squares on the calendar, the waiting room giggles grew. *This should be easier, but how?*

"Last Tuesday I was cooking injera when the hot clay plate slipped from the stove burner and hit my hand." The voice she heard in her dreams washed over her from the other side of the cubicle partition. An interpreter had arrived, one called by her heart. Wulf was here.

She started to rise from her chair but couldn't depend on her knees, couldn't even breathe.

"The next day a neighbor gave me a paste to cover the burn." The thunder of her heart almost eclipsed his smooth cadences. "By Friday my hand was much worse, so now I am here to see the doctor." Wulf paused. "I was stuck in an air-cargo crate for a week."

Clearly the last sentence had nothing to do with the patient. "You could have phoned." She rested her clipboard on her knee so neither the patient nor the volunteer saw her hands shake. "Please tell my patient that coming to the clinic was very wise. We can't risk a staph infection." Remembering Wulf's instructions from Afghanistan, she addressed the woman directly. "Can you tell me what was in the paste your neighbor gave you?"

While Wulf and the patient exchanged words, she concentrated on breathing in and out.

"Avocado and boiled plantain leaves and honey. Also butter." Wulf recited the ingredients in the home remedy as fast as she could copy them to the intake form. "Sorry, but my freight pallet didn't have cell service and I didn't think I should show my face at an airport."

Realizing the man she loved was a few feet away and they were on the verge of arguing instead of kissing, she stood and smoothed her hands down her new cargo pants. If she'd known he was coming, she would have dressed…but no, these were clothes she'd bought for herself. They represented the real her. She touched her hair, but didn't have a mirror.

"My Puerto Rican neighbor says honey and plantain heal anything." Wulf's voice vibrated, as if he too was unsteady. "But I'm not so sure now. Maybe the doctor has something better." The space dividers were thin enough that she heard him clear his throat. "Maybe the doctor will marry me?"

Ohmigod. She reached for the wall. Could she stagger around it without falling?

The openmouthed student nodded like a bobblehead, and even her patient understood something larger was happening.

Theresa realized that she had her other palm over her mouth and the waiting room had dropped into complete silence. Ohmigod again. She wobbled out the door and met him in the narrow space between intake rooms.

The gray carpet and beige walls disappeared at her first sight of him in two weeks. When he smiled, it was different from the cocky grin he'd first given her in the mess hall, different from the smolder when he zipped the boots on her feet or the sexy flirting grin in her mother's kitchen. This smile made her hands damp. It made her want to cry and hug him and laugh all at the same time. He lifted her to her toes, and his kiss traveled from her lips to her heart. She flew, or felt as if she did, and opened in flight for him. Arms wrapped around her, he spun her through the hall. Every cell sang to touch him. His hair was as soft and dense as she remembered, his shoulders as strong, his mouth made for hers.

Most important, he was here, with her, and he was safe.

He set her on her feet and withdrew to look at her face. "You haven't answered my question."

The collectively indrawn breath from all the women in the waiting room must have taken the oxygen away, because she felt dizzy, but she knew what to say. "Yes, of course, yes." She threw her arms back around him, because any distance was too far. "I love you."

Her prosthetic, a stray folding chair, a miscalculation and they staggered. Wulf's legs tangled with hers, but his arms didn't let go to find balance, and his lips never released hers. She heard the thunk as he hit the wall and they stopped moving.

Then he was kissing her ear and her neck and her cheek and repeating her words. "I love you." No interpreter needed.

The women in the room jumped and cheered. He grinned, and this time he shouted, "I love you!" to the drop-tile ceiling while the patients clapped.

Life with Wulf would never be normal, but who cared? She'd have a Viking to love her for eternity.

* * * * *

Fiction Meets the Real World

I think reality is what gives fiction emotional weight. Many characters in this novel wanted to help the women of rural Afghanistan. The real world contains an organization that successfully does that, Doctors Without Borders/Médecins Sans Frontières. Every day, 22,000 doctors, nurses, midwives, logisticians, water experts and other professionals working for Doctors Without Borders/MSF provide emergency medical services to people caught in crises in more than sixty countries. They delivered more than 110,000 babies and performed more than 50,000 surgeries in 2009. By 2012, those numbers had risen to 185,400 babies and 78,500 surgical procedures. These medical providers are true heroes.

When my heroine was wounded in Afghanistan, her family stayed at a Fisher House in Germany. The Fisher House Foundation has built sixty houses (and growing) near military medical facilities in the United States and one in the United Kingdom. They provide free lodging for families of wounded soldiers, kitchens, space for children to play outside and a vital community of other families also supporting wounded warriors. At Dover Air Force Base, the Families of the Fallen Fisher House provides free lodging for families waiting to repatriate the remains of their loved ones. The United States's fight in Afghanistan may be winding down. It may be out of the news. But the need for long and extensive medical care doesn't go away when the logisticians pack up their last containers.

My family will be donating to both charities

from *First to Burn* proceeds. If you want to know more, I invite you to visit the charities' websites or AnnaRichland.com.